CORNERED

D0061696

Other **Running Press Teens** anthologies
include

CORNERED

14 STORIES of
BULLYING and DEFIANCE

· · ·

Edited by Rhoda Belleza
Foreword by Chris Crutcher

RP|TEENS
PHILADELPHIA · LONDON

Contents

Foreword
BY CHRIS CRUTCHER

H. L. MENKEN ONCE FAMOUSLY SAID, "There is always an easy solution to every human problem—neat, plausible, and wrong." We would do well to remember that quote when dealing with the issue of bullying.

Bullying is as old as big animals and little animals, so it's not as if we're taking on a new problem, but since the Columbine shootings in 1999 we have forced ourselves to take a closer look at the nature of bullying, particularly in schools. (Never mind that later studies of the incident, particularly David Cullen's masterful book, titled simply, *Columbine* revealed that bullying per se wasn't at the heart of the shootings at all.) We wanted simple answers.

The stories in this anthology give us reason to open up a dialogue and search for the complex answers. Bullying may or may not lead to school shootings, but it certainly leads to misery.

In looking for those simple answers we may have set our sights far too low. Schools have developed anti-bullying campaigns that include zero tolerance, programs to help students identify bullying and step in to help the bullied, anti-bullying

4k runs, anti-bullying bake sales; all of which play to a greater or lesser degree of success. But most of the programs focus on the students themselves.

But bullying starts with adults. It starts with controlling parents who will do almost anything to maintain that control, and teachers who don't tolerate kids finding their ways through natural developmental stages.

Years ago I worked in a child abuse project in which my employer, Spokane Mental Health, coupled with a local Head Start program in order to work with abused kids at a young age, rather than waiting until they were out-of-control adolescents. A five-year-old I'll call Kevin taught me something about bullies I've never forgotten. He was the biggest kid in the room and by far the toughest—little Popeye forearms and thunder thighs—he had *teachers* who were wary of him. He could have taken any kid in the class. Yet on his bad days he'd walk in, drop his coat on the floor, take in the room like a gunslinger and if you didn't intercept him, go after the weakest kid in the room; a little girl I'll call Jessica, who had been blinded in one eye by her mother's abusive boyfriend when he couldn't potty train her way before it would have been developmentally possible. My job in the project was to work with the parents, and I was painfully unaware of preschoolers' motivations and behaviors.

On one of those early days when Kevin got away, he surveyed the room to make sure no one was watching then stormed across, cocking his fist as he ran and brought it down right in the middle of Jessica's back. The play therapist saw him go and sprinted to intercept him, arriving a split second too late. She slid across the floor on her knees, scooped him up, and then wrapped his arms. Several staff members scurried to comfort the wailing Jessica and I expected the play therapist to do the same, or lay a blistering scolding on Kevin. Instead, I heard her say, "You must be really scared."

Kevin burst into tears.

It *felt* right to me, but I didn't understand why, so later during debriefing I asked her about it, and about why Kevin always went for the scared kid when he could have whipped the school janitor.

"He hates weakness," she said. "When he sees it, he wipes it out."

Wow.

"In Kevin's house," she went on, "you do *not* show weakness or there is hell to pay. If he's scared or worried or anxious, he has to hide it because it is *not* tolerated. It is met by punishment and disappointment."

Kevin had been taught to hate weakness. When he saw it, he rubbed it out.

If you want to find the bullies, a good place to look is among the bullied. Most of what we learn as little ones comes through our *pores*. Back before language we absorb through all our senses. If we grow up experiencing domestic violence, even if it isn't aimed at us, we learn the ways of violence. Nothing exists without its opposite; if it feels awful to get bullied, it feels *great* to bully. Once we're hardwired that way, it does very little good to try to send us the way of the peaceful warrior.

So maybe we should expand the terminology. It's too easy to look for bullying kids and try to stop them from being bullies. That usually results in making them more devious. Let's call it *meanness*. Let's call it *indecency*. And let's understand that it never starts with the kid.

I could make a case that we live in a bullying culture; that we're more interested in jumping on bad behavior than preventing it. We do it politically, philosophically, and personally. We like to find who's to blame and mete out the punishment, rather than *prevent*. We'd rather build prisons than therapy and trauma centers for families.

It's a systemic change we need.

The stories in this anthology have the power to get us talking about that change; the power to use our imaginations to create possibilities. My hope is that's how it will be used.

Introduction

BY RHODA BELLEZA

ONCE IN A WHILE, someone will ask what I was like in high school. "The same," I always say—which is and isn't true, but that's the easiest answer to give. Easier, at least, than pouring my heart out right then and there. That would require a scary amount of self-awareness I've never been willing to muster.

I'm not exactly sure why that time is so hard to talk about; I suppose for me it would feel disingenuous to describe all that passion and excitement without also discussing the pain and vulnerability I felt as a teenager. I often felt powerless and suffered a chronic inability to speak up for myself—or for anyone really—as I watched certain injustices unfold before me. Say for instance, when I got called a "slut" walking past the senior quad, or that time a pair of slanted eyes—drawn in Sharpie—appeared on the hood of a friend's car. Even years later, just recalling moments like these make my heart beat faster and my face flush with shame. The feeling is so immediate it's like it is happening all over again, this endless moment of guilt and embarrassment stretched out be relived with every recollection, which leads me to suppress it. Bury it somewhere deep. And if one memory even dared to poke its head out? To resurface after I'd exiled it to the far corners of my memory? I'd be there with a mallet, ready to pound it back down like it was a gopher in a carnival game.

I value stoicism (as well as my privacy), so to talk candidly about such a charged time is difficult. To even think about it is difficult. It demands I confront a whole lot of experiences and choices—scenarios where I've been victimized, and just as many where I'm the bully and I'm the conspirator by virtue of doing nothing. I'm not proud of this. Everyone has their tactics, and this was mine: to barrel straight past shame and embarrassment, onward and upward to more useful emotions, like denial and reticence. Who wants to stew in your own humiliation when you can claim cool indifference?

I only recently realized that this was a whole lot of effort for not a lot of payoff. This isn't a carnival game; it's my life. I hadn't beat anything or anyone, I'd only been carrying around the pain and merely reacting when a memory resurfaced. All the composure I'd prided myself on had been just the opposite: a testament to how little control I had over my own emotions and—by extension—my own destiny. *Screw that*, I thought. I couldn't be the only one; I wasn't alone. There are people to talk to and ways in which to work through the hurt, and until we realize that, we are divided.

This is all to say that before bullying was in the national spotlight—covered by various news outlets and compounded by social networking sites like Facebook and Twitter—we all had painful experiences that fundamentally changed us.

Everyone has been a victim and everyone has been an oppressor. It's part of our shared history as social, human beings.

Editing this anthology was a gift of perspective. When first put to the task, I asked my friends about their bullying experiences, and hearing their stories filled me with heartbreak and pride. On one hand I felt wronged on their behalf, and on the other hand impressed as to how they'd grown into such capable, caring individuals despite the adversity they faced. Learning these details seems instrumental to my understanding of who they are now—and it inspired me to turn the mirror on myself. It gave me the opportunity to remember a past transgression and infuse this otherwise dark memory with hope—seeing each experience as a marker from which I could measure not only how far I had come, but how much further I wanted to go.

Naturally, I reached out to my favorite authors who had a stake in the content—those who wrote books about the marginalized, the bullied, the other. Not only did I believe in their voices, but in the themes they wrote about, because each and every one captured that universal feeling of disempowerment so honestly and beautifully.

I envisioned the collection of stories would be a balance of both humor and seriousness, as well as despair and hope. This, I think, was achieved—though along the way I was surprised by a variance even I hadn't expected. Stories deeply grounded in gritty realism were placed next to supernatural tales of ghosts and afterworlds, yet all the themes seemed to converge harmoniously: vengeance, redemption, shame, and empathy. Essentially, no matter how each story is delivered they all serve as guides to overcoming adversity.

My hope for the reader is that you find a piece of yourself in this collection of stories. Perhaps it will help you take pride in who you are, confront the choices (both good and bad) that you've made, and inspire you to continue developing creatively, emotionally, and spiritually. Maybe you'll reach out to people you love, ask them to listen, and be their support system as you learn how their experiences have shaped them. And if none of these things, then my hope above all else is that you come away having read a damn good story. Or fourteen damn good stories.

NEMESIS

BY KIRSTEN MILLER

STEP ONE IS surveillance. You make a lot of enemies in a job like this, and every week I get an e-mail from some jerk trying to settle a score. The phony requests are pretty easy to weed out, but you can't be too careful. That's why I investigate my new clients before I get started—even the ones who've sent the most heart-rending pleas.

The fifteen-year-old who's just exited St. Agnes on the other side of the street told me her name is Clea. I received an e-mail from her last night around ten. The picture she attached showed a younger Clea in an identical plaid uniform. She greeted the camera with a crooked, gap-tooth grin that made me want to reach through the computer screen and squeeze her. That girl is gone for good. No matter what happens in the next few days, she won't be coming back. Now Clea watches the ground as she walks. Her shoulders are hunched and her spine bent, as if she's anticipating an ambush. You can't fake true terror. This client is the real deal.

She's rushing away from her school toward the bus stop on the corner. I can tell she wants to run, but I understand why she won't. Running would draw unwanted attention. The hunted quickly learn that it's better to blend in whenever possible. For a moment I'm confident that Clea's going to make her escape, but a pack of girls bursts through the front doors of St. Agnes. They stop on the sidewalk and scan the street. They're searching for Clea. One of the girls spots their quarry, and the chase begins.

I snap a few photos as they barrel past. Clea's descriptions have proven remarkably accurate. The girl called Kayla must be the one at the head of the pack. Mariah, Jordan, and Natalie are the kids at Kayla's heels. In the last two years, my clients have come in all shapes, sizes, and sorts. I've rescued geniuses, dunces, beauty queens, ugly ducklings, athletes, and geeks. But the bullies are always the same. They follow a leader—usually a kid with an average brain, above-average looks, sadistic tendencies, and an undeniable charisma. The leaders' lackeys tend to be depressingly ordinary. They're the sort who do their homework, mind their parents, and go to church every Sunday. Few adults would ever peg them as the kind of kids who'd torture their classmates for sport.

A bus pulls up to the corner of Ninety-Ninth Street and Lexington Avenue, and I watch Clea scamper on board. I imagine her sigh of relief when the doors close. And I know just how fast her heart sinks when the bus doesn't move. The driver has spotted the four high school girls sprinting in his direction. Now there's a fifth. When he opens the doors to let the girls in, I make sure I'm right behind them.

Clea's sitting on one of the benches near the driver. She has her face buried in a geometry textbook. It's a useless shield. I've studied the same book, and I'm pretty sure it has killed far more people than it's saved. Two girls drop into the seats on either side of Clea. Kayla and the fourth crony stand with their shins pressed against their captive's knees. I brush past them and choose a spot in the middle of the bus. I know just how far away I'll need to be to fit all five girls in my camera's frame. As soon as the bus makes its first lurch forward, I pull out my phone and hit record.

I pretend to be texting, but the ruse is unnecessary. Since the day NEMESIS went live, no one has ever suspected that I might be the one who's behind it. Vigilantes aren't cute. They're angry bitches in black leather pants who curse, chain-smoke, and design their own dragon tattoos. Imagine the opposite, and you'll have a pretty clear picture of me. My mother says I'm dainty. My father still calls me Princess. I like my hair to look glossy and my nails to be polished. My clothes are expensive, and they're always perfectly pressed. I don't look like a vigilante, but I wouldn't pass for a victim, either. Not anymore.

I prefer to watch the camera screen instead of the action. It helps me keep an emotional distance. But it doesn't always prevent me from feeling ill. The first time I filmed a confrontation, I finally understood why everyone else looked away. It's hard to see a fellow human be destroyed. You find yourself needing to believe the victim earned her punishment. You want to think that an innocent girl would never be tortured, and that the world couldn't possibly be so cruel. When I started my site, I used to ask my clients what made them targets. Most of the kids were a lot like Clea—they just didn't know.

Kayla has a filthy mouth and an impressive imagination. She's called Clea a pervert, a stalker, and a spy. Those are only the slurs I'm willing to repeat. She's accused Clea of watching her friends undress before gym class. This poor kid who's afraid to take her eyes off her textbook has been branded a peeping tom. It's so ridiculous—such an obvious lie—that I don't know whether to laugh or vomit. Then one of the lackeys slaps Clea's book to the ground, and the girl stares at the empty space left behind. Harassing a mute must not be much fun, so Kayla reaches over and yanks Clea's braid hard enough to uproot a few strands of hair. The girl yelps with pain, and her cry feeds the frenzy. The insults grow louder, until Kayla is shouting obscenities three inches from Clea's face. I've got it all on tape. It's among the most disturbing footage I've ever recorded.

...

STEP TWO is the calling card. Ordinarily I'd wait a few days and try to get a bit more on tape. But I'm not sure Clea can hold out that long. She said in the e-mail she's scared for her safety, and everything I've witnessed tells me she should be. When bullies begin to get physical, the situation will often escalate quickly. It's up to me to put an end to it. No one else will. The bus driver has been watching the whole scene in his rearview mirror. He could have stopped the bus and forced Kayla and her friends to get off and walk. But he won't get involved. They never do. I'm sure this guy has a perfectly good reason for staying on the sidelines. I wish I could tell him where to shove his perfectly good reason.

Clea lives on One Hundred and Twenty-Seventh. We must be nearing her stop. I have enough footage to work with, so I slip my phone into my backpack and pull out my cards. I purchase blank business cards from Staples and stamp them with the NEMESIS logo—a single, unblinking eye. I used to add the name of my website as well. But I've been doing this for two years now, and every kid in New York knows the URL. Most people want their businesses to succeed, but I find it frustrating that mine has lasted so long. I used to hope that the more videos I posted, the fewer cases I'd have. In the beginning, I'd get six e-mails a month. Now I get twice that every day.

I head to the front of the bus and grab a pole just across the aisle from Kayla. I slip one card into her handbag and another into a backpack that belongs to the girl standing beside her. The bus stops and Clea pushes past her captors and hurls herself toward the exit. As the last two bullies brush against me on their way out the door, I deliver a card to each of them. Then I watch from the window as the four beasts stalk their victim. I silently pray for Clea's safety, but I won't intervene. My work demands anonymity. I can't risk blowing my cover for one kid when there are thousands more to be saved.

The next time the bus stops, I jump off and take the subway

downtown. I live on the opposite end of the island, and I'm anxious to get home and get started on Step Three. Now that NEMESIS is the talk of the town, my calling cards scare off the bullies in about half of my cases. But I'm not sure a piece of paper's going to cut it this time.

. . .

"Hello! I'm home!" I shout as I enter my dark apartment. It's a little joke I share with myself. No one is ever here. Sometimes I don't hear my parents arrive until after I'm already tucked into bed. They both work seventy-hour weeks in order to give me a beautiful home, a first-class education, fancy clothes, and all the computer equipment a girl could desire. It's a huge sacrifice, I've been told.

I had a nanny until the end of eighth grade. She was a stout Swedish woman named Emelie who made my dinner, taught me French, and loved me like her very own daughter. Before she left each evening, she'd pack my lunch for the following day. On Thursday nights she and I always baked cupcakes. The next afternoon, one would be waiting for me in my lunchbox. Emelie decorated each Friday cupcake with sprinkles before writing "E ♥ G" in red icing on top. It was a bit silly, but by eighth grade it had become a time-honored tradition. I never imagined that a pink frosted cupcake would mark the beginning of the worst year of my life.

I was wearing one of my baggiest blouses that Friday. It was the first week of eighth grade, and I was still recovering from the embarrassment I'd endured the day school began. I'd made the mistake of wearing a form-fitting T-shirt, and the chest I'd learned to live with at summer camp had taken everyone else by surprise. By third period, I'd covered up with my jacket, but I was still drawing eyes. Including those of a boy named Eli.

Back then, I spent most of my time with three girls I'd known since our preschool days. Josie was my best friend. Morgan and Olivia were more Josie's friends than mine. And I'd always been a bit wary of Olivia. When she was in a good mood she sparkled like a pixie, but when she got mad, that magic felt malevolent. Olivia had spent the entire seventh grade swooning over Eli, but he had always been blind to her charms. Unfortunately, his eyesight improved dramatically whenever my new boobs were around. The second Olivia caught her beloved ogling my chest, I became her mortal enemy.

Of course, I was still convinced we were friends. For four days, I remained blissfully unaware of the rage that was building inside her. Then I sat next to her at lunch and pulled out my Friday cupcake. Olivia took one look at "E ♥ G," and the anger finally erupted. She knew that *E* was for Emelie. Over the years, she'd spent more time with my nanny than she had with most members of her very own family. So I was confused when Olivia grabbed the cupcake and held it up for the whole lunch room to see.

"Look who Gaby loves!" she shouted.

It was the first time an entire room ever shared a laugh at

my expense. My face must have been as red as the icing when I exclaimed, "It stands for Emelie!"

The second round of laughter was worse.

Within a week, I was the school pariah. An eighth grade slut engaged in a torrid lesbian affair with a Swedish servant. I tried to argue, but they wouldn't listen to reason. I tried to fight back with words, but my tongue always betrayed me. I tried to ignore them, but the insults only got uglier. I tried to hide, but Olivia always managed to find me.

I didn't cry until the day Josie called me a "carpet-muncher." I didn't even know what it meant. Or how stupid and offensive the word was. I just saw the hatred on my best friend's face, and I crumbled. Over the following months, Josie did her best to destroy what little was left of me. But through it all, I refused to ask Emelie to stop making those cupcakes. Every Friday afternoon, I'd sit all alone in the cafeteria and make a show of swallowing every last bite.

I never uttered a word to my parents. But they must have gotten wind of something, because one day in March, my mother announced that I was too old for a nanny. I cried for three weeks after Emelie was fired. I didn't think I'd survive. I could have made it with one person behind me. When Emelie left, I had no one.

After we graduated from eighth grade, my classmates all enrolled in Manhattan high schools. I chose a school in Brooklyn and started my freshman year expecting my reputation to follow me. Thankfully the rumors never made it across the East

River. Now that I'm a junior, my classmates would probably say that I'm popular. When I'm not working, I do all the things people my age tend to do. But I'm not like them. I watched the whole world desert me. And once you know you're alone, you can never, ever forget.

Still, in a strange way, I'm almost grateful. I spent a year stumbling through the darkness at the bottom of a hole. When I emerged, I discovered I'd been granted special powers in exchange for my suffering. Now I can see things others won't. I can withstand pain that would break most people. I possess a determination that's practically superhuman and the wrath of a fearsome goddess. I am the avenger. The punisher. The dispenser of dues. I'm the seventeen-year-old girl known throughout New York City as NEMESIS.

• • •

STEP THREE is really just a formality. I post new video footage on a private page of my website. I hunt down any e-mail addresses that my clients weren't able to provide. Then I send links to the bullies, their parents, and their principals. When I first started, I never intended to go any further. But Step Three rarely changes anything. Depending on which part of the city they hail from, the parents either threaten to beat me or sue my pretty little pants off. The principals never respond. They probably think that what happens off school grounds is none of their business. I've heard that the bullies like to share the footage with their friends.

I upload my new video and send out my e-mails. I make it clear that should anything happen to Clea, we'll go straight to Step Four.

. . .

STEP FOUR is payback. That's when I move the footage to the public part of my website. I make sure to provide the bullies' full names, schools, and addresses. NEMESIS gets more traffic than the *New York Post*. And my videos almost always go viral. Sometimes it takes a while for the full impact to be felt. Eventually my dimmest "stars" realize what's happened. My video will follow them for the rest of their lives. Their families, their friends' families, their teachers—even their priests, pastors, and rabbis will see it. Every potential employer, boyfriend, and in-law will watch it. It will be discovered by admission committees when they apply to colleges. It will still be around when their own children are born.

It won't be long before they find out just how many of us have suffered at a bully's hands.

We'll ruin their careers, friendships, and love lives. We'll have our revenge. And we'll teach them all that payback is hell.

. . .

I'm waiting across the street from Clea's school. My phone keeps vibrating in my pocket. New cases never stop coming in. But I won't accept a new one while an old one is still pending. I need to be sure that Clea is safe. I hear bells ring, then just like yesterday, she's the first one out of the building. Nothing appears to have changed. She still seems harried and miserable. That doesn't mean much. She'll wear that look for a while. But this time she makes it to the bus. It pulls away just as the school's doors are thrown open again.

I spot Clea's tormentors among the crowd that spills out. They're looking around, only this time they're searching for someone holding a camera. Their eyes pass right over me. If Clea says the day went well, tonight Kayla and her cronies will all get an e-mail. I'll commend them on the wise decision they've made, and warn them that I'll always be watching. The threat is essential. These girls aren't going to change. They'll never see the error of their ways. But they'll realize that their actions have consequences. And I'll make sure they know just how bad those consequences can be.

I hit the subway. As soon as I'm home, I check my e-mail. There are five new pleas. Another two or three will probably arrive before bedtime. I scan through the first four. They're all more of the same. But it's the fifth that really gets my blood rushing. The letter is signed Olivia. I try to keep my hopes in check while I click on the photo that the girl has enclosed. You can't spit in Manhattan without hitting a kid my age named Olivia. But when the picture finally flashes up on my screen, I know the heavens have answered my prayers.

I've dreamed of this moment. I've spent two years fantasizing about it. But I never imagined my day would come.

I laugh all the way through Olivia's note.

Olivia's school is the one my parents always hoped I'd attend. They were mortified when I informed them that I'd deposited the application (and several more like it) in a trash can instead of a mail box. A high school in Brooklyn was the only institution in town that received the paperwork my father's secretary had kindly prepared. Some people might call me a coward for giving my enemies Manhattan island, but I've never regretted that decision and I certainly don't regret it now. The girls filing into Olivia's school look like they're strutting down an invisible runway. Their clothes are designer, their diamonds are real—and most of their noses are not. Olivia should consider herself lucky. Violence is rare at ritzy schools, and the principals are terrified of bad publicity. Whenever I take a case on the Upper East Side, it's usually the clients who end up posing the problems. They don't understand that I can stop the bullying—but I'll never make their snooty classmates accept them.

I skipped school so I could be here this morning when Olivia arrives. I have my hair pulled back, and dark sunglasses hide half my face. I doubt the disguise will be necessary, though. I've grown up a lot since Olivia and I last crossed paths. When I see her coming down the block, I realize that she hasn't grown at all. Back in the eighth grade, Olivia was the same height as the rest of us. That must have been the end of her growth spurt. She's still five foot one, flat chested, and scrawny. She doesn't look like a pixie anymore. She looks like a little girl.

No one so much as glances in Olivia's direction as she heads toward the building. Too many parents on the street, I suppose, most delivering their precious spawn to the grade schools nearby. According to Olivia's e-mail, a group of older girls ambushes her during lunch hour, when juniors and seniors are allowed to leave campus. Olivia claims the abuse has gotten so bad that she now eats her PB&Js while hiding in one of the school's less-frequented girls' rooms. I wonder if she got the idea from me. I guess her bullies don't waste their time ransacking the whole building. The way Olivia used to.

I snap a picture right before Olivia disappears into her school. It keeps me smiling for the next four hours.

At noon, I'm sitting in a café on the Upper East Side. Olivia said she'd be here just after the hour, and she's certain the bullies will follow. As soon as I see them, I'll hide in the narrow hall that leads to the ladies' room. Once Olivia and her companions have settled, I'll make my grand appearance and grab a good seat for the show. I won't be wearing a disguise. I want to watch everything that goes down today, and I want Olivia to know that I've seen it. And before I leave, I'll make sure she knows that no one is ever going to come to her rescue.

When I spot Olivia crossing the avenue, I let the waitress know I'm heading to the ladies'. I don't want her to think I've skipped out on the bill. Then I slink around the corner to wait. Olivia chooses a table close to mine. I hear the waitress inquire if she'll be dining alone. The voice that answers doesn't belong to Olivia.

"We need three more menus. The four of us are together."

I hear the waitress's footsteps fade away. "Hello, hobbit," the same girl sneers. "Who said you could crawl out from under your rock?" I have to clap a hand over my mouth to muffle my giggle.

I peek around the corner and see three girls have joined Olivia at her table. She seems so tiny sitting next to them. She stays silent and still. Like a porcelain doll taking part in a make-believe tea party.

"They shouldn't let you eat in restaurants. No one will be able to keep their food down if they're forced to look at you," a second adds.

The third girl just snickers. There's always one dunce in the bunch.

"Please. I just want to have lunch," Olivia pleads. She sounds so numb and exhausted. I'm enjoying this far less than I should.

"It doesn't matter how much you eat. You'll always be a short, hairy little hobbit."

"I heard your mother has to buy your clothes from Children's Place. Is it true?"

"Her parents are too cheap for Children's Place. I bet they go to secondhand shops. That sweater looks just like something my nine-year-old sister wore last year."

The second girl gasps. "Oh my God, do you think they've been going through your trash?!"

I'm not taping this. My phone hasn't left my bag. I'm not watching a screen. The faces I see are all life-size, and their expressions are easy to read. The snarl on the leader's lips. The glee in her lackeys' eyes. The pain twisting Olivia's features, and the effort she's making to hold back her tears.

She deserves this. She deserves an entire year of it. I want Olivia to suffer, but I no longer have any desire to watch. I step back around the corner and stare at the wall of the corridor. I wish there was a rear exit, some way to escape. Then I hear a commotion in the café. A glass shatters, and Olivia squeals. Someone has knocked over her water. I don't need to look to know that Olivia must be soaked.

I can't wait any longer. I pull a twenty out of my pocket. I'll pass it to the waitress on my way out the door. If I move fast enough, I might go unnoticed.

But Olivia instantly sees me. Her spine straightens and her eyes light up. She's looking at me like I'm her long lost best friend. A smile starts to form on her lips, then it freezes. I can tell she's remembering everything she did to me. And I can see the horror on her face when she realizes that I must be NEMESIS—the last person left that she could turn to for help. I was Olivia's only hope. And now that hope is gone.

This is far too painful to watch. If it were one of my videos, I'd hit fast-forward. But I don't think I've ever captured a moment like this before—the instant a victim decides to give up. I can almost see Olivia's life leaving her body.

That's when I do something I've never done before. I drag a chair from another table and take a seat next to Olivia. It's three against two now. Us against them. I'll help Olivia fight this battle. Together, we might even win her war. But she and I will never be friends. I'd still love to kick her ass someday. That sort of punishment might fit her crimes. But no one—not even Olivia—deserves to be left all alone.

On Your Own Level

BY SHEBA KARIM

IT ALL STARTS when I'm waiting for the bathroom at a house party. Of course, I'm not wearing my glasses. Contact lenses irritate me, so it's either see 20/20 and look like a dork or accept a little blindness for the sake of beauty. Plus, my eyes are my best feature: large and deep brown, framed by thick, long eyelashes. The rest of me I hate, especially my curls, which—no matter what expensive pomade or gel I try— refuse to behave. And my body, forget it. I have short legs and wide hips, and I hate dancing to bhangra at Pakistani weddings because my tricep flab starts jiggling ten times faster than the music.

I haven't had any alcohol tonight but walking around without glasses is a little like drinking, because sometimes I bump into things. Or, like now, I can't tell who's coming toward me until they're pretty close—though I can tell it's a guy, and that he's drunk from the way he's pressing against the wall as he walks.

The drunk guy enters my field of vision. Broad shoulders, cerulean eyes, light brown hair streaked blond by sun and salt. Oliver Jamison. The leaves have turned orange and red, but

Oliver is still tan from his summer of sailing. Oliver smiles at me. He does this at school too. Some of the popular kids act like you're not even there, but Oliver smiles at everyone.

He tilts his head toward the bathroom door. "You waiting?"

"Yeah."

He sways forward a little, then steadies himself and looks at me. I hope he's looking at my eyes and not my mustache, which is growing back from the last time I got it waxed. "You were in my history class last year," he says. "You sat underneath Ulysses."

What he means is I sat underneath the big photo of Ulysses S. Grant on the Civil War timeline poster. "Yes."

"Yeah. I remember. You always seemed kind of worried."

Worried? I'd understand dorky, or attentive maybe, but worried? Is that what I seem like?

"What's your name again?" he asks.

"Shabnam," I say. "*Shab* like rub, *nam* like numb."

"What's it mean?"

"Morning dew."

"Morning dew," he repeats. "That's really cool. Morning is my favorite time of day. Best time to be on the water."

"I hate mornings," I tell him. "Because I have to wake up . . . not because mornings are bad or anything. I mean, mornings are great." *Well done, Shabnam. Way to sound like a complete idiot.*

"Shabnam." He's still pronouncing my name wrong but I don't care because at least he's saying it. "What language is that?"

"Urdu. And Persian."

"My cat is Persian," he says.

"I've never had a cat. My mom's allergic."

This time, Oliver doesn't respond—and why would he when I'm so clearly failing at conversation? I'm searching in vain for something to say that might engage him when I realize that he's smiling at me, so wide that not one but two small dimples appear on his cheek.

"Morning dew," he says again. "Nice."

And that's when Oliver moves forward, one hand braced against the bathroom door, and kisses me. *Kisses* me! I've only ever kissed two guys, and I don't know what to do. But Oliver makes it easy. He starts out soft, and I get up the courage to part my lips, and his tongue is touching mine, softly, gently. He tastes like beer and peppermint. He puts his hand on my shoulder, and I'm worried he can sense how crazy fast my heart is beating. Then Oliver starts kissing me harder, and I stop thinking about anything except how good it feels.

The bathroom door opens and Oliver almost loses his balance. He moves away from me, his fingers still gripping my shoulder. Natasha is standing before us, hair swept up in a ponytail, high cheekbones shimmering with blush. The whole hallway smells like perfume, strong and sweet.

"Oli. What are you doing?" Natasha asks. She glares at me, and I remember how my best friend, Maggie, recently overheard her saying something about how Oliver was the last guy left on her list.

Oliver takes his hand off me and blinks a few times. "Hey,

32

Natasha," he says slowly, as if he's not sure he got it right.

The fat diamond studs in Natasha's ears catch the light as she shakes her head, sighing. "Let's go, Oli," she says, linking her elbow through his. He doesn't protest or even say bye when she starts to lead him away, toward the music and the keg and the kind of people Oliver is supposed to be seen with. When they're halfway down the hall, she turns around and looks back at me, and I'm glad I'm too blind to see her face.

• • •

The next morning, there's a strange man at our kitchen table. I'm about to go inform my parents when I realize it must be the uncle my father calls *Chacha jaan*, who they picked up from the airport last night. Chacha jaan is staring out at our leaf-covered backyard, his hands cupped around one of the fancy glasses my mother only brings out when we have guests.

Chacha jaan is completely bald, but he has a big beard—a thick, black, menacing arc of a beard—extending from ear to ear. He's wearing a *shalwar kameez* and polished leather sandals. He reminds me of the mullah who hosts a religious advice show on one of the satellite Pakistani channels my parents subscribe to. The mullah sits at a desk and answers the callers' questions, which range from "If you change your clothes do you have to perform your ablutions again?" to "What happens on the Day of Judgment?" to "Can men wear gold?"

I'm contemplating skipping breakfast altogether when Chacha jaan notices me and jumps a little, some of the water spilling from his glass. Then the surprise on his face changes to something else, sadness maybe, and he sets his glass down and smiles at me. "You are Shabnam?" he asks in Urdu.

"Yes. *As-salaam alaikum.*"

Wrapped around his neck is a red scarf decorated with green Christmas trees, and he uses one end of it to wipe the water from his *kameez*. *"Wa alaikim as-salaam. Kaisee ho?"*

"I'm fine," I tell him, in English.

My mother joins us. She's also wearing a *shalwar kameez*, which she often wears at home, except today she's draped her *dupatta* over her head in a gesture of modesty. *"As-salaam alaikum!* You'll drink chai?" This is a rhetorical question because of course he'll drink chai. All Pakistanis do. Then my mother says in chirpy Urdu, "Your coming here has made us very happy," and she means it—the only relative my mother's ever been unhappy to see was Daadi, my father's mother, and even then she hid it well.

Before I can leave with my bowl of cereal, my mother grabs my arm. "Did you say *salaam?*" she whispers.

"Yes. I have to go do some work. I have a big paper due tomorrow I haven't finished."

"You shouldn't leave things until the end," my mother says, but she doesn't argue.

As I'm heading to my room, my father opens the front door and steps into the foyer, the Sunday *New York Times* tucked in his armpit. He's wearing plaid pajamas and a white under-shirt. He has a basketball-sized gut and the dark tufts of hair sprouting from his shoulders are starting to turn gray. I hate it when he goes outside without a shirt on.

"Did you say *salaam* to Chacha jaan?" he asks. With my father, it's never *hi, how are you,* but *did you do this, why don't you do that. Be respectful, say* salaam, *get into a college that will impress everyone and secure your career. Don't go around in the company of boys, because, even though we know you are a chaste girl, someone from the community could see you and get the wrong idea.*

"No, Abba, I didn't say *salaam,*" I tell my father. "I told him to get lost."

My father frowns. "No, you didn't. Why do you think that's funny? What's wrong with you? Can't you be normal?"

I respond by continuing up the stairs.

. . .

Natasha finds me at my locker. She's dressed like a school girl, with a short pleated skirt and a white button-down blouse that shows off her a-little-more-than-two-handfuls cleavage. There's an expensive silk scarf tied around her neck, like those air hostesses who wear the small, round hats. Standing next to her makes me acutely aware of each excess hair and inch of blubber on my body. I was hoping she might forget about the weekend, but she's glaring at me so hard I'm too nervous to look back at her. I'm also too nervous to look away.

"I saw that shirt at Target," she says.

I'm wearing a black cotton long-sleeve v-neck. I wore it because it has tiny eyelets so it's a bit see-through but you can only tell if you're really close. And I thought I might run into Oliver today. "So?"

"So Target is for socks. And period underwear," she says.

"Oh." I wonder what she'd say if she knew that pretty much all my underwear is period underwear. I don't own sexy underwear; no one sees it anyway, plus my mother would freak if she found out I'd bought some because why would you own sexy underwear unless you were planning on showing it to someone?

"What you did Saturday night is pretty messed up," Natasha says. Her expression is still mean but her voice is totally calm, which somehow makes it even worse. "Oli doesn't even remember what happened, you know," she continues. "I can't believe you took advantage of him because he was drunk."

I'm too stunned to defend myself. Could it be true? Was the best kiss of my life with someone who doesn't remember?

"You're not so unattractive," she says. "I'm sure there's someone out there who'll kiss you when he's sober. So go find that guy, and stay away from mine. Understand?"

She waits for me to nod—say *yes, I understand*—but I'm still reeling from her comment about Oliver not remembering, about me taking advantage of him. The bell rings. Her eyes narrow as she crosses her arms. "Unbelievable," she says, and before I can correct her, she tosses her head and walks away.

. . .

Oliver is leaning against his car, talking on the phone. I don't know whether to walk right by him, which would mean a potential encounter, or avoid him completely. Ultimately my body decides by moving in his direction. I'm so nervous my heart is drumming inside my chest and my ears are filled with air. I watch my feet step on the asphalt, too nervous to look at him, but then he says hi, and now he's all I can see.

"Hi."

He tucks his phone into the pocket of his perfectly faded jeans. "We should meet properly. I'm Oliver," he says, extending his arm, muscular and tan and brushed with dark golden hair.

"Shabnam." Considering the last time I met him his tongue was in my mouth, this formal introduction seems a little weird, but I'm grateful that he's acting cool. It's helping me maintain mine. But then I accept his hand and our fingers intertwine and my entire body starts tingling with heat.

He lets go. "About this past weekend. I drank way too much. I wasn't exactly thinking straight. I'm not usually like that. Had a rough day. Not that that's an excuse. So, I'm sorry if I offended you. I hope you don't think I'm a jerk."

A jerk for what? Being drunk or kissing me? Does he remember kissing me? Does he remember how good it felt like I did? Or was Natasha telling the truth? But I'm too shy to ask this, so I nod and tell him, "It's okay. Don't worry about it."

He grins. "Awesome," he says, and opens his car door. "I'll see you around."

"See you around."

One thing is painfully clear—he didn't kiss me because he secretly liked me. That little fantasy of mine has been completely crushed. I keep walking to my car, and with every step it's like I'm sinking. I tell myself not to be so stupid; of course my kiss with Oliver would be just that, a kiss, because high school is like a snow globe: sometimes it gets shaken and strange and wonderful things can happen, but soon enough, everything settles back down to where it was. In the end, gravity always wins.

. . .

I'm lying in bed mourning my existence when someone tries the door. I know it's my mother because my father always knocks first. "Go away!" I yell, but she doesn't, so I stomp to the door.

"What were you doing?" she asks in Urdu after I let her in. My mother doesn't understand locked doors. When my father goes to conferences, I sleep next to her because she doesn't like being alone.

"Nothing," I say.

"We're taking Chacha jaan to the Afghani restaurant," she says.

"Have fun."

"What, have fun? You're coming with us." My mother places her hand on her hip. We have the same hands, square palms and short fingers. But that's about the only thing we have in common. I wished I had inherited more from her: her long face, her thin frame, her fine, straight hair. When I was little, she had no idea what to do with my curls, so she kept my hair really short. There isn't a single picture of me as a kid that isn't utterly embarrassing.

The last thing I want to do is go to the Afghani restaurant with my parents and Chacha jaan. I only stopped crying an hour ago. "I don't feel like it. Please, Amma, don't make me go."

"Why?"

Any chance I might have of convincing her is ruined by the arrival of my father.

"Rukhsana, something's wrong with this zipper," he says. My mother starts fiddling with his sweater, and he frowns at me. "Why are you not ready? Chacha jaan is waiting downstairs."

"She doesn't want to go," my mother says.

"Nonsense. Of course she's going."

"But I don't feel like going," I protest.

"Life is not about what you feel like doing. You think your mother and I feel like going to work every day?" he replies. "And what will Chacha jaan think if you stay in your room only? It's abnormal."

"I don't care what Chacha jaan thinks. He looks like a mullah anyway."

"Chacha jaan is no mullah. He is an educated man. He was the vice president of a pharmaceutical company."

"Maybe he was, but he still looks like a mullah."

My mother is still trying to fix my father's zipper but he

steps away so he can focus fully on reprimanding me. "And what would you like? Would you like me to go downstairs and tell Chacha jaan, who was so good to me when I was young, that my daughter will not go to dinner with him because of the way he looks?"

"Yes."

My father turns to my mother. "Rukhsana!" he says, which is his way of asking her to please do something before he loses his temper.

My mother sighs. "He didn't used to have a beard, but he's become quite religious since his wife died. He's a very nice man and he's lonely, Shabnam. He loved his wife very much. And he is our guest. So get ready. Now."

And I hate both of them, for giving my uncle's loneliness precedence over my pain, for making this day even more difficult, for making everything about my life difficult. "Jesus," I mutter as I walk to my closet.

"Jesus!" my father cries after me. "Why does she always say this? She's a Muslim! What kind of Muslim goes around saying Jesus, Jesus?"

"*Bus*, Sohail, *bus*. Enough." My mother places her palms against his back and gently pushes him toward the door. "Let her get ready."

• • •

After we get in the car and I think life can't get any worse, my mother mentions that we're stopping at the mall first because

Chacha jaan wants to buy his granddaughter an iPod. I know better than to complain in front of Chacha jaan, so instead I fume silently in the backseat listening to my father say, "Over there is the town hall. And there is Dunkin' Donuts—they make America's best coffee. Have you tried it? And that is a diner—New Jersey is famous for its diners, they are open all night. And down that road is Shabnam's school. She is one of their top students, *masha'allah*." I wish he wouldn't make me part of his stupid tour. I wish I wasn't here.

Chacha jaan is wearing a crisply ironed black vest over a long white *kameez* and a wide, white *shalwar* stiffened with starch and those same ugly polished leather sandals. He must have put something in his beard because it's a little shinier than before. I watch him stare out the window and wonder if he's even listening to what my father is saying. In his right hand, he's holding a *tasbih*, a Muslim version of a rosary. The beads are made of stone, deep orange in color. He hasn't let go of it the entire car ride, moving through it bead by bead. The beads might make a nice bracelet, but it's too feminine to be used by someone like him.

My father takes an exit, and I realize he's heading toward the most upscale mall in our area, with marble floors, expensive stores, and organic options in the food court. We almost never come here. "Why are we going to this mall?" I say quietly to my mother, but she ignores me.

When we arrive, I debate refusing to get out of the car, but I know my parents won't stand for it. Thankfully it's Monday, so not many people are around. I walk a safe distance from my parents and Chacha jaan, who still has that stupid *tasbih* in his hand. I'm more than half an escalator behind them when I see who else but Natasha on the landing above. She's leaning against the railing, a little Louis Vuitton purse on one shoulder and a brown Bloomingdale's shopping bag on the other, wearing cowboy boots and a denim skirt that barely covers her ass. My family steps onto the landing, but instead of continuing on they stop to wait for me. That's when Natasha notices Chacha jaan.

I want to run backward down the escalator, but I'm frozen and moving closer. Natasha hasn't noticed me yet, but my father exclaims, "*Jaldi karo*, Shabnam!" and Natasha turns to see who he's talking to.

I don't make eye contact with her as I step off and am forced to acknowledge my parents and Chacha jaan as my own, but I can still feel the revulsion on her face all the way to the electronics store. There, my parents instruct me to help Chacha jaan, and I'm relieved when he directs his questions, in fluent English, to a sales clerk. After a little while he walks over to me, holding two iPods, one lime green and the other hot pink.

"Which one do you like?" he asks.

I point at the pink one.

"Are you all right?" he says. If you can get past the beard, which is hard to do, his face isn't actually that bad—there are some pockmarks on his cheeks, but he has a nice nose and light hazel eyes. If he was clean-shaven and a lot younger, he might even be handsome.

"I'm fine."

"My wife's hair was just like yours. You remind me of her. Especially when you smile," he says, and I wonder when Chacha jaan has ever seen me smile, because I certainly haven't done so tonight.

We make it to dinner without any more mishaps. The Afghani restaurant used to be a diner and has a neon sign that says HALAL in the window, booths of ripped red vinyl, and a menu with everything from Afghani meat stews and kabobs to hamburgers and chicken wings. We sit down in one of the booths and my father orders too much, as usual.

Before he begins eating, Chacha jaan says, "*Bismillah ar-rahman ar-rahim.*" In the name of Allah, the most merciful, the most benevolent. Yeah right. If Allah really was so merciful and benevolent, He wouldn't have made me a Pakistani American girl with frizzy hair. I stare at the two chicken wings on my plate. Natasha wouldn't eat chicken wings. Natasha would never set foot in this restaurant.

My father stops decimating his food to ask me, "Why aren't you eating?"

"I'm not hungry."

He pushes the plate of rice with meat, raisins, almonds, and slivers of carrot toward me. "Try the *pilau*. It's good."

"I don't want any." I say this nicely, because I know my parents don't want Chacha jaan to think I'm some American teenage brat who is disrespectful to my elders and disconnected from my heritage.

"Chacha jaan," my mother says, taking a chicken wing from my plate. "They say that the Pakistani restaurants in Houston are very tasty. Was the food good?"

"It was okay," Chacha jaan replies.

My father drinks his water in one gulp. "Why don't you give Houston another try? It's a very nice city."

"I did try," Chacha jaan replies. "But my heart could not become attached to that place."

"But there are so many problems in Pakistan, Chacha jaan," my mother objects. "In Houston, you have two sons, and such excellent health care in case, Allah forbid, you become ill."

Chacha jaan sighs a little. I notice he hasn't eaten very much either, which is really annoying because he's the reason we're at this restaurant instead of at home, where there are walls and doors and curtains and no one can see us. "My barber in Pakistan has been telling the same old jokes since the first Bhutto," he says. "I thought I was tired of them, but I went to a barber in Houston and it didn't feel right. I miss the old jokes, my old barber."

Everyone's quiet, then my dad holds up the plate of rice and says, "More *pilau*?" and my mother asks for the check. Of course it's sad that my father's uncle is an old widower who misses his wife and his corny barber, but he said it himself—he belongs over there, in Pakistan, not here, next to me.

• • •

I'm late for English because I get my period and have to hunt for a tampon since the dispenser is out. It's first period on Tuesday morning and most of the students usually act like zombies on muscle relaxers, but when I walk in a bunch of them suddenly wake up. Elliot stops his doodling to stare; Ryan is looking at me like I have horns on my head; and I swear Jenna is smirking at me. I'm worried that maybe there's a blood stain on my pants, but I can't see anything.

"Have a seat, Shabnam," Ms. Haverford says, and returns to her dramatic reading of Keats. "'Oh what can ail thee, knight-at-arms, alone and palely loitering? The sedge has wither'd from the lake, and no birds sing,'"

When I get to my desk, Maggie, who sits across from me, starts mouthing something.

What are you saying? I mouth back.

She scribbles in her notebook and tilts it toward me. *Have you seen the e-mail?* she writes.

What e-mail? I write back.

Maggie winces and starts playing with her phone under her desk. She slips her phone inside a library book and hands the book to me. I open it and there's Chacha jaan and me, right there on Maggie's phone. It's a photo of us at the electronics store. Chacha jaan is holding up two iPods and I'm pointing at the pink one. I look annoyed and my hair is taking up a third of the frame. Chacha jaan's eyes are squinting in concentration at the iPods, his beard and Pakistani clothing in full view. At least you can't see his *tasbih*.

The subject line of the e-mail is: LINCOLN HIGH SCHOOL

SENIOR HELPS AL-QAEDA BUY AN IPOD!

I scroll up. The e-mail's been forwarded a few times, but the address it originates from is a bunch of jumbled letters and numbers. Of course Natasha's too smart to use her own e-mail address. What I didn't realize is that she'd be this mean.

"Shabnam."

Ms. Haverford has to say it again before I hear her.

"Yes?" My throat feels dry. On the board, Ms. Haverford has written "the spontaneous overflow of powerful feelings."

"Can you tell us—" She stops. "Are you okay?"

Is it that obvious?

I swallow the little saliva I have. "I'm fine."

The whole class is staring at me now to figure out whether I'm fine or not. How many of them have seen the photo? Did any of them believe it?

"Is that guy your uncle you said was coming to visit?" Maggie demands after class. "Shabs—do you have any idea who did this? And what happened? I go away for one weekend and there's an e-mail going around about you?"

I haven't told Maggie yet about the kiss or what happened at the mall, and I'm not about to now. Maggie's way more confident than me, the kind of confident that lets her rock thrift store bell bottoms at school when everyone else is wearing skinny jeans. If I tell Maggie, she'll get upset and immediately confront Natasha, and that will only make everything worse.

"I don't know. Honestly," I tell her. "Someone saw me in the mall, I guess."

"It's cruel!" Maggie says. "Even if someone was out to get you, though I can't imagine why, to do it like this is so . . . low and dumb and so . . . not chivalrous."

"Jesus, Maggie, this isn't one of your Merlin fantasy books. There's no chivalry in high school!"

Danny, Maggie's sometimes boyfriend, puts his arm around her and kisses the top of her head, which means they must be on again. "Shab-a-dub-dub," he says to me. "What's up with that photo? Who is that guy?"

"He's my uncle."

"Is he some kind of cleric?"

"No."

"Nor is he al-Qaeda," Maggie says.

"You're sure, right?" Danny says, winking at me.

"Yes, I'm sure." I wish I didn't sound so defensive, but I can't help it.

The rest of the morning is torture. It's easy to tell who's received the e-mail and who hasn't; the ones who have either stare at me, or, if they know me, ask me the same things Danny did. It's my uncle, visiting from Pakistan. He's not a cleric. He was the vice president of a pharmaceutical company. He's not really that religious; he just likes the beard. Some find it funny; some feel sorry for me. "But you look so normal," Paige says to me. Ali, who I don't know very well but who's also Muslim, tells me one of his uncles in Kerala looks a lot like Chacha jaan. Jacob asks me how they even let my uncle in the country, and some sophomore I don't even know asks me if

47

I'm from Afghanistan.

By the time I get to gym, I never want to say the words "uncle" and "Pakistan" again, and thankfully Mr. Polk has set up a circuit course, so I don't have to talk to anyone. I push myself really hard, hoping the physical exertion will distract me from everything that's been going on. And it works, sort of, until I reach the squats station. I hate squats because they're hard and it's scary to watch your thighs double in size as you go down. Somewhere around squat ten, the first tear falls. *For God's sake, pull it together, Shabnam. Don't you dare cry in the middle of gym class.* Mr. Polk blows the whistle, signaling us to move to the next station, and I hope no one can tell that it's not only sweat I'm wiping off my face with my T-shirt.

After gym I'm in the bathroom, sitting on the toilet in the stall, where it's safe, trying to figure out what I should do. My biggest fear is that Natasha has more planned for me, that she has even more photos and who knows what she'll do with them—post them on the Internet maybe, and then some parent would see them and tell my parents. Or, since it's the era of "if you see something, say something," the FBI might come knocking on our front door. If my parents found out, my dad would flip and the principal would get involved. There would be an investigation and maybe my parents would find out it all started because of my kiss with Oliver and then I don't even *know* what they would do. The possibilities are terrifying.

Two girls come in laughing. They pee, flush, meet at the sinks.

"I'm going to surprise Adam by shaving it all off," one says. "Or I was thinking I could do an A."

"An A? That's so cheesy."

A phone beeps. "This is the second time I got this e-mail."

"You mean the photo of that girl with that guy who looks like a terrorist? I saw it. Why would you go around with someone like that?"

"Maybe it's her father."

"If my father looked like that, I'd move out."

"Maybe it's her boyfriend."

Laughter.

"I think I saw her at Aidan's party on Saturday."

"She was there?"

"Yeah, I remember that hair."

"Someone should tell her to straighten it."

"Seriously."

Silence. Then, more quietly, "Someone's been in that stall the whole time."

I tense, hold my breath.

"They're probably taking a dump."

More laughter. I stay perfectly still, my cheeks burning with shame and wishing that this was one of Maggie's books, where the stall would turn into a portal and I'd be transported to a better world. One with chivalry. There's the sound of the paper towels being pulled, and the squeak of the door, and finally the bathroom's empty again.

I have to end this, before it gets any worse. I can't make the photo that's out disappear, but I can talk to Natasha, ask her to forget all this and to please not take this any further. I'll get down on my knees if I have to. Except I can't do it at school; if I actually have to humiliate myself by begging, I want it to be in private.

· · ·

Illuminated waterfalls flank the entrance to Harmony Woods, the development where Natasha lives. The plots are so big it takes a minute to drive from one meticulously landscaped lawn to the next. Natasha's house is different from the others; it's modern and boxy, made of steel and a lot of glass that you can't see it at all from the road, which suits me fine.

After I ring the bell, a little girl answers. She's clutching a stuffed stegosaurus and a red bowtie hair clip is slipping out of her whitish-blond hair. "Yes?" she says.

The door opens wider. It's Natasha. She has another little girl in her arms who's an exact replica of the one who answered the door, minus the stegosaurus. Natasha puts the girl down. "Go play," she says to the twins, but neither of them move.

"I don't want to play," stegosaurus twin says.

"Eleanor has something to show you in the kitchen," Natasha says.

"Eleanor smells," the other girl says.

"She's making butterscotch cookies. You better go before all the dough is gone," Natasha tells them. They run off giggling and Natasha steps outside. "What are you doing here?" she says. "I didn't say you could come to my house."

"I . . ." *Come on. You can do this. 1, 2, 3, go.* "I wanted to talk to you."

"We've got nothing to talk about."

"I know you sent the e-mail."

Natasha folds her arms over her velour hoodie. I take comfort in the small red zit on the narrow bridge of her nose; the only thing marring an otherwise flawless complexion. "I may have seen you with that . . . that man at the mall. But I didn't send any e-mail."

She isn't going to admit it. Why would she? It doesn't matter anyway. I came here for a reprieve, not an admission. "Okay. What I wanted to talk to you about—what I wanted to tell you, I mean, is that I'm sorry."

She raises her thin eyebrows. "Sorry about what?"

"I'm sorry . . ." I hesitate. Now that I have her attention, I have to say the right thing. What should I be sorry for—no, what would she *like* me to be sorry for? Should I apologize for momentarily disturbing the high school hierarchy? And then I realize what it is she really wants.

My kiss.

So I give in. "I'm really sorry I kissed Oliver that night. It's just that he's so cute and popular and out of my league that when I saw him drunk at the party I . . . I took advantage of him without even thinking. I'm sorry. It was totally wrong of me."

There. I said it. I feel a little queasy, and I *definitely* feel like crying, but I'm fighting the tears, because what little dignity I have left does not want Natasha to see me cry.

"It was wrong of you," she says, nodding. My confession has pleased her. "Well, I really hope you learned your lesson."

"I have." This time, I'm not lying. I've learned some lessons all right. To make sure to distance myself from anyone who looks too Muslim. How easy it is to sacrifice your pride. "Anyway, I'm sorry."

"It's okay. Everyone makes mistakes. Stick to guys on your own level and I'm sure you'll find someone." Natasha's smiling at me now, the way you smile when you get a letter from a child you've sponsored for fifty cents a day. She thinks she's being magnanimous. Let her believe it. Just please let her move on.

"Yeah. I will." I take a deep breath. "But . . . I'm really embarrassed about that photo and I don't know what to do—what guy is ever going to want to date me after seeing that?"

"Oh, don't worry about it. I'm sure everyone will forget about it soon," she says. It may not be an outright promise, but it's the best I'll get.

The stegosaurus twin comes outside and announces, "She's not making cookies! She's making lima beans. I hate lima beans more than taxes."

"You don't even know what taxes are, silly." Natasha scoops the girl up in her arms. "Say bye."

The girl waves her dinosaur at me. "Bye-bye!"

"Bye."

The door shuts.

I've never felt so alone, or so worthless.

•••

The sun is starting to set by the time I walk into the kitchen. "Where were you?" my mother asks. "You didn't pick up your phone."

"Spanish club meeting ran late."

My mother doesn't question this. She's not the suspicious type. "When Chacha jaan and Abba get back from their walk Chacha jaan is taking us to Red Lobster."

"Red Lobster? Are you serious?"

"I know," my mother says. "I was going to cook, but it's Chacha jaan's last night with us and he wants to take us out. Plus your father feels like shrimp."

My father feels like shrimp. I've had the worst day of my life and all that matters in my house is that my father feels like shrimp. "And what about me? What about what I feel like? Does anyone care about what *I* feel like?" Though I'm trying hard to remain calm, I'm on the verge of exploding. I can't remember the last time I was this upset, when this world seemed this horribly unfair, and all I want to do is scream.

My mother steps forward, concerned. "Shabs? *Kya hua?* What's happened?"

"I've had the worst day of my life, that's what's happened, and it's all because of him!"

"Because of who? Chacha jaan? But what could he have done?"

"Someone at school saw me at the mall with him and now everyone in school thinks I'm related to a terrorist and they were all asking me these ridiculous questions!" Even though it's a relief to tell my mother what happened, I can't tell her the part that hurts the most, that I gave back the best kiss of my life to a girl who doesn't deserve it.

"A terrorist?" My mother's forehead creases with confusion. "I don't understand."

That's when I finally snap. "That's what Chacha jaan looks like, Amma!" I yell, and my mother recoils at the tone of my voice, but I'm way past caring. "It's embarrassing! *He's* embarrassing! He needs to go to Pakistan and stay there! I don't want to ever be seen with him again! I don't want to be seen with any of you!" I kick my backpack. Pens spill out of it, and I kick those too.

"Shabnam."

I turn around to see my father and Chacha jaan standing in front of the door to the garage, which I've of course forgotten to shut. I've never seen my father so angry, and Chacha jaan, he looks stunned, and hurt, and also sad—like he feels sorry for me—which upsets me more. I've had enough of people's sympathy. And anyway, how dare *he* feel sorry for me! He doesn't even know me.

"Apologize to Chacha jaan," my father orders.

There's no way I'm apologizing to anyone else, not today, and especially not to him. So I run away, out of the kitchen, down the hall and up the stairs, and slam my bedroom door. I know my mother is going to start knocking in two minutes but an hour goes by and nothing. Nobody. By the time my mother arrives, I've stopped bawling and my fury has been subdued by remorse and shame. Though I still don't ever want to be seen with Chacha jaan, I feel terrible that he had to hear me shouting it.

"Are you okay, Shabs?" My mother approaches the bed slowly, like she's worried I might lash out again.

I pull the covers over my head. "Go away."

She doesn't say anything, just starts pressing each of my toes, starting with my left pinky. This is how I learned to count to ten in Urdu when I was little. "Chacha jaan left. Abba's taken him to a hotel next to the airport. He'll catch his flight to Karachi straight from there tomorrow. Abba didn't want him to go, but Chacha jaan, he insisted."

So Chacha jaan was finally gone. I ought to be rejoicing, but instead I feel sick. I didn't want him to go like this. It wouldn't have mattered if he'd stayed the night, since I'm planning on never leaving my room anyway. He must really hate me. He must think I'm an awful brat.

"He left something for you." My mother reaches into the pocket of her slacks and holds up Chacha jaan's *tasbih*. I don't move, so my mother lays it down gently on top of the blanket.

"It used to be his wife's *tasbih*. You never met her, but she was a very kind woman. After I married your father, I stayed for some time at his family's house. I was very nervous being a new bride at the in-laws, but Chacha jaan's wife was so kind to me. Some of the other people in the house weren't very nice to her, but I never heard her say anything bad about anyone."

She pauses, waiting for me to respond. I don't.

"What exactly happened at school, Shabnam?"

"Not now, Amma. Please."

"Fine. I'll come back later." I must look really pathetic, because it's not like my mother to leave me alone so readily. "But then we have to talk."

"Just no Abba, please."

"All right. But you'll have to talk to him too, you know."

"I know."

My mother kisses my forehead and leaves. I stare at the *tasbih* for a while, hesitant to actually touch it. Why did he give it to me? His wife and I may look similar but she never would have behaved like I did tonight. What does he expect me to do with it? Surely he's feeling its absence, like when you wear a watch all the time and then go one day without it. I hope it isn't making him miss his wife more. But I'm sure it is.

I want to hide under the covers again and feel sorry for myself, but I can't, because I keep seeing Chacha jaan, hunched over on a bed in some ugly, lonely hotel room—his fingers instinctively moving down the prayer beads that are now lying next to me—missing his kind wife with curly hair. So I pick up the *tasbih*, close my eyes, and say a prayer for both of us, hoping that maybe, somehow, he'll be able to feel it, and understand.

The Shift Sticks

BY JOSH BERK

I WAS STANDING at a little sunglasses stand in the middle of the mall. A banner at the kiosk displayed a picture of a sun wearing sunglasses. Why does the sun need sunglasses? It shouldn't really, but neither did I. It was just something to look at while my aunt and little sister shopped. I got the distinct feeling they didn't want me around. Possibly training bras were involved. Something girly for sure. Hannah was eleven, and doing just about anything with her was weird now. So I split off and proceeded to roam the mall, killing time in every way I knew how.

Mainly that meant video games and soft pretzels, neither of which lasted long. Soon I was bored and out of money. So the sunglasses stand it was. I tried on a flashy pair of brushed silver, aviator-style, very-not-me glasses with mirrored lenses just to amuse myself. Could I buy these flashy glasses and somehow become a different sort of person? It was a fun thought, but no, that's not how it works. Plus they made my big nose look even bigger somehow. And also there was the whole out-of-money thing. Maybe I could become the type of person who steals sunglasses? I have these types of thoughts. Then, unexpectedly, I heard my name.

Actually "unexpected" doesn't even *begin* to describe it. I was visiting my aunt and uncle's lame suburban town—fifty miles east from my own lame suburban town—and it wasn't an exaggeration to say no one knew me here. Outside of Aunt Tina, Uncle Eli, and Hannah, I didn't exist. This was a rough yet young *teenage* girl sort of a voice; it was the kind of voice that clearly did not come from a member of my family.

"Bryan Forbes?" the voice said again, and before I could turn to look, I felt a hip smack into mine. I lost my balance and almost knocked over the stand, then steadied myself and looked over. Indeed, the voice did belong to a girl. The hip too. She was trying on a pair of sunglasses herself—bright neon green ones—and the price tag whipped around like a kite as she spun to greet me.

"Um, yeah?" I said, pulling off the aviators. "Do I know you?" Something in her face looked familiar, but I didn't know anyone like that. Not with the bright yellow dreadlocks and lip piercings. Not with rock star jeans. Not with the pierced nose. And the tattoos! An army of strange figures and phrases marched up and down her arms in brightly colored ink.

"Dude, it's me, Tiffany," she said. Her voice was raspy, like a smoker's. "We went to elementary school together." My brain went fuzzy for a moment. Then the words formed very slowly in the back of my mind. Tiffany. Sanz. Holy. Shit.

• • •

What I remember about Tiffany Sanz:

We weren't very clever. What we were was mean. We called Tiffany a dog. All the time. I don't know what started it, but once we decided she was a dog, that was it. Sometimes we would bark when she walked by, or maybe throw a stick and ask her to chase it. One time we found a pile of dog turds under the slide and someone said, "Oh, Tiffany, what did you *do?*" and we just about died of laughing. And always, someone sang the jingle from a popular dog food commercial when she was around. Sometimes she would just take it or sometimes she would run away. We liked it when she ran because it meant we could chase her as we sang, "Puppy chow, puppy chow! Make your lucky pup say wow!"

I never saw her cry, but she must have wanted to. Even then I knew it was cruel, and I took comfort in the fact that I wasn't the ringleader. But I was for sure a follower, and in a lot of ways that was even worse. I was right there, third or fourth in line, running around the playground after Tiffany with the wind in my hair and a smile on my face. "MAKE YOUR LUCKY PUP SAY WOW!"

. . .

"Don't tell me you're not Bryan Forbes," she said, punching me in the shoulder. "It says your name on your jacket." She still wore the neon green sunglasses, which she lowered to glower at me. I couldn't deny being me. I was wearing my North High cross-country jacket (more like a lame Windbreaker) which clearly said B. FORBES across the back in block letters.

"Tiffany Sanz?" I asked. My voice bubbled out of me like I was underwater. Like my lungs were filling with blood. It was amazing how quickly the name came to me. Like third grade was yesterday, not half a lifetime ago, back when we were all freaking out about learning Roman numerals.

"How many other Tiffany's were there in Mr. Clarke's class, Bryan Forbes? Of course it's me." Man, her voice was rough. How many cigarettes can you smoke by seventeen?

"Wow," I said, still feeling like I was in a dream. "Mr. Clarke. I haven't thought about him in years."

"He was cool. I mean, moving out of that crap school was the best thing that ever happened to me. But Mr. Clarke was cool. He taught me a lot about writing." She smiled as if something about her saying that should be clear to me. Was she a famous writer now? Seemed unlikely. What did I miss? I barely remembered anything besides Mr. Clarke giving us root beer-flavored candy if we got the right answer. That seemed like a stupid thing to bring up right now, so I said nothing.

Tiffany took off the sunglasses and grabbed another pair that were way too big for her face. They were the type of dark-orange, old person sunglasses designed to fit over your regular prescription glasses. She looked like a blind person, which is to say she looked ridiculous. I think that was the point.

She smiled and took a long sip of her drink, then pointed toward my jacket with the straw of her cup. "You go to North I see. I guess that's where I would have ended up if we didn't move out of that particular circle of hell."

"Yeah," I said without any heart. "Go Vikings."

"Soooo, at North . . . are you one of the cool kids, Bryan Forbes?"

I paused. It was weird to be asked so bluntly. I mean, people talked about who was cool all the time, but they didn't *talk* about it. It was like this unsaid thing. We all could name the cool, the uncool, the sorta cool. There was no disagreement. It was like someone sent out a mass text and we all were bound to follow its instructions, then delete it and never speak of it again. That was the thing. You never just talked about who was cool and who wasn't.

I shrugged. I knew right where I stood. Precisely in the middle. Just like back in elementary school. Just like my whole life. Neither top nor bottom, cool nor uncool. But I didn't want to be direct about it. "Kinda I guess. Um, you?"

"Ha!" she spat. "Am *I* cool? That's a no, Bryan Forbes. But I do not mind. I was bad at being normal, but good at being weird. Amazing how easy it was to switch." As if to illustrate her point, she put on a different pair of sunglasses. These were small purple circles. Could it be that easy to change who you were?

"Huh," I said.

"Aww, you turned out cute, Bryan Forbes."

"Thanks?" My voice came out like the crinkle of a brown paper bag. I felt my face get hot, and I suddenly felt thirsty.

"So what are you doing at this mall, in this town, Bryan Forbes?" she asked.

"I'm uh, visiting my aunt and uncle. They live out this way."

"Hey, is your aunt Tina *Forbes* the real estate agent?" Tiffany asked. "She has those commercials! Tina Forbes: Let ME help YOU find a home. Your new life begins TODAY."

"Haha," I said. "Yup, that's her."

"So, in town for just the day or . . . ?" Tiffany let her question trail off. She popped in a piece of gum, chewed it, and blew a huge bubble until it popped.

"Through the weekend," I said.

"Awesome. Come see my band. Tonight. I play guitar and sing. We're called The Shit Sticks. Long story. And okay, they won't let us put that on the marquee so it will say 'The *Shift* Sticks' which totally misses the point"—she moved a dreadlock that fell in front of her face—"and okay, it's not a marquee, more like a chalkboard, which is all sorts of lame, but whatever. A show is a show, you know?"

I nodded in agreement. Sure, I knew all about the world of being in bands and how *shows are shows* or whatever. She pulled a pen from a pocket, grabbed my hand, and started to write, presumably the address. It was sort of hard for her to write because my hand was really sweaty. I pulled it back and wiped it on my shirt, mumbling an apology. She tried again and kept talking. "Vortigern's Coffee Shop down on Main. We go on at nine or so. I'll dedicate a song to you."

Wait: Did I just get invited to go see Tiffany Sanz perform? Did I want to go see Tiffany Sanz perform? Did Tiffany Sanz say I was cute? It was too weird. I tried to get out of it. I'm always trying to get out of stuff.

"I don't know. I'm, uh, not much for coffee," I said.

"They also serve tea," she said sharply.

"I'm not a big tea person either."

"I should have taken you for a hot beverage discriminator. But you could probably get a cold soda. Unless you also hate sodas. But everyone needs liquid. Except robots." She narrowed her eyes. "Are you a robot, Bryan Forbes?"

"No, I'm not a robot," I said, answering in a tone far too serious. "I'm just not much for coffeehouses."

"You won't catch gay or something. And it's not whiny coffeehouse music. We rock pretty hard. Do you not like rock and roll music, Bryan Forbes?"

"Yeah, no, I mean, I like rock okay, but . . ."

"Cool, fine, I get it. Forget it then," she said. "Not your scene. You have sports games to watch and jock strap fittings to attend. It's fine."

With that she spun on her booted heel, shoved her hands into the pockets of her hooded sweatshirt, and walked away. What the hell? I stared into my hand. I was still sweating and the smudgy ink was becoming hard-to-read. I didn't care. I didn't want to go anyway. Yet for some reason there I was, repeating the address over and over in my mind, trying not to forget it.

I caught my reflection in the little mirror on the side of the kiosk. I looked like I had seen a ghost. I stared at myself for a few seconds—not something I normally love doing. But hey, some people think I turned out cute. I watched Tiffany until she disappeared into a clothing store, stuffed with people and loud music. She turned out cute too. Who would have guessed? I never thought I'd be into tattoos and piercings, but hey, maybe people do change. Maybe I could just become a different me, at least for a little while.

People always say it's a small world, but it really isn't. You can be a few towns away and, if you don't want to be found, it's like you moved to the end of the earth. You can walk from the sunglasses stand into Miss Fashions for Teens, set your Facebook to private, and it can be like you're on another planet.

Even as part of me was trying to memorize the address to the coffee shop, part of me doubted I'd ever see Tiffany Sanz ever again. I wouldn't really go. Would I? My mind wandered to those tattoos. I wanted to ask if they had hurt? If she has others, hidden ones she could show me. . . .

I realized I was just standing there, zoning out. The sunglasses guy, who was middle-aged and Indian, was looking at me like "are you going to buy some freaking sunglasses or just stand there for nine hours?" So I put the glasses back on the rack and mumbled something like "not my size." I saw an empty bench and walked over to it. I sat down to think, or to try *not* to think, about Tiffany Sanz. I failed. An unpleasant, acidic feeling kept rising up in my chest. It wasn't this new, rock-star Tiffany I was thinking about. It was the old one. The scene from elementary school played unwanted in my head over and over. "Make your lucky pup say wow!" I felt a little sick, and it probably wasn't from all the pretzels I'd been eating.

My phone beeped, making me jump. It was a text from my dad. "ARE YOU BEING GOOD?" it demanded. Somehow even his text messages had his signature stern tone of voice. I fired back a quick "yes, sir." It was good to keep it short with my dad, otherwise I'd end up saying the wrong thing like I always did. Plus I wanted to talk about the Tiffany thing, so I texted my best friend from home, Nate. I knew he was unlikely to provide much insight, but it was worth a shot.

ME: dude you'll never guess who i just saw: tiffany sanz!

NATE: you didnt give me time to guess. i was going to guess tiffany sanz

ME: u were not!

NATE: then give me time to guess next time

ME: fine shut up. isn't it crazy though?

NATE: not really. it is fairly impossible to predict the exact location of anything with certainty, sure, but it's not that odd that she would have turned up at the mall in westport the same time as you

Nate was on cross-country like me, but also in all honors classes (not like me). He was always relating everything to math and physics, and very often I had no idea what he was talking about.

ME: how do u know we were at the mall?

NATE: what else is there to do in westport?

ME: good point. it felt weird seeing her. i felt so bad.

NATE: bad about what?

ME: the way we were back then, u know

NATE: i'm sure she's over it

ME: would u be?

NATE: i doubt it, but i'm sort of a vengeful bastard that way. does she still look the same? those glasses! and remember that sweatshirt with the cats she always wore?

ME: no totally different!

NATE: hot?

ME: more like all tattoos and piercings and stuff

NATE: whoa! So . . . hot?

Nate had his own weird look these days—not at all classic nerd, but more like a hybrid hippie/heavy metal guy. He had shoulder-length hair and a thin mustache that he thought made him look tougher, but really just made him look like a perv. I imagined him hunched over his phone, waiting to hear my attractiveness rating of the new Tiffany Sanz.

ME: kinda cute i guess

NATE: dude, you gonna try to see her again while you're out there?

ME: maybe. she's in a band. invited me to go see the show

NATE: you gotta go! you need more weird in your life. go where life takes you, bry. that's my motto.

ME: i thought ur motto was "rock out with your cock out." u have it cross-stitched on a throw pillow.

NATE: that's more of an unofficial credo. going where life takes you. that's the real motto. you gotta go to that show.

ME: eh i'll think about it. gotta run. i see my aunt & sister

I slid the phone back into my pocket and waved hello to

Aunt Tina and Hannah. They waved back.

"Hey," I said, pointing to their bags. "You find anything good?" Hannah giggled, and I immediately regretted asking.

"We did okay," Aunt Tina said. "You?"

"I didn't buy anything other than soft pretzels. You know, research for my study into the quality of mall pretzels around the world."

"Someday the world will build a statue in your honor," she said with a smile. Aunt Tina didn't look like the coolest lady in the world. She had "mom hair" even though she didn't have kids and always dressed pretty much like you'd expect a real estate agent to dress, but she was cool. Yeah.

Then, spurred on by the voice of Nate in my head (the thing about going where life takes you, not the part about having your cock out) I found myself blurting: "And—weird thing—I ran into a girl I used to know in elementary school."

"Oh yeah? Small world . . ."

"I guess. She's in a band now. They're playing at some coffee shop on Main tonight. Vitamin's?" I stared into my hand. "Something like that."

"I think I know the place. You need a driver? I mean a passenger?"

"I'm not sure if I'm gonna go," I said, then muttered. "Jock strap fittings."

Aunt Tina cocked an eyebrow, but didn't ask me to clarify. Stupid Tiffany was in my head. We headed outside toward the car. It had Aunt Tina's face on the side and her tagline.

TINA FORBES: LET ME HELP YOU FIND A HOME. YOUR NEW LIFE BEGINS TODAY.

• • •

So I tried to get there on the late side, to reduce the amount of time I'd spend awkwardly sitting in Vortigern's (not Vitamin's) Coffee by myself. What? Of course I went. What did she mean, *not my scene*? I could go to see bands if I wanted. I didn't just plan to sit around watching sports with Uncle Eli my whole life. I could hang out with tattooed girls if I felt like it. I could do anything I wanted. Maybe I'd even come back from Westport with a tattoo of my own.

Okay, that was probably pushing it.

Uncle Eli let me drive me the short ride to the coffee shop.

"What time should I pick you up?" he asked.

"I have no idea how long these things go on."

"Okay, then just call the house when it's over. I'll be up. And um, if it's after twelve we just won't tell your father."

"Cool," I said. He gave me a high five. It was impossible to believe that he was my dad's brother.

I walked in to Vortigern's Coffee Shop and heard the jingle of a bell strung to the door. No music though, besides the low background of a stereo playing a quiet, old song. The show hadn't started yet. So I *would* be sitting around, waiting. I didn't see Tiffany and part of me wondered if she was just messing with me. But, no, there on the chalkboard "marquee" was the name of her band in big white letters: THE SHIFT STICKS. I noticed a few bearded heads turn and look at me as I weaved through the tables, but most everyone was locked in to their own intense conversations over steaming coffees. I really didn't like coffee. But I felt like I should have something to sip on, just to feel less awkward.

I walked up to the counter and a large, friendly girl smiled at me. She had a huge flower behind her ear and wore a T-shirt that said, IT IS FORBIDDEN TO FORBID. It appeared homemade, written in a style that made it look like the letters were dripping blood. She was confusing, but I liked her smile.

"What can I get ya?" she asked, wiping the counter with a towel like an old-fashioned waitress.

"I'm not really typically a fan of hot beverages," I said, feigning confidence. "But I'm feeling adventurous. What's the house specialty that isn't coffee?"

"That would be the Yerba maté," she said. "Tea. You'll love it."

Without giving me time to explain that I didn't like tea either, she quickly turned around and started preparing the beverage. A few moments later she set a strange contraption in front of me. My face must have belied my confusion because she explained.

"It comes in a gourd, not a cup. You drink through that metal straw-thingy. Let it cool a little first." I must have still looked confused because she added, "It's from Argentina." As if that clarified anything.

"Got it," I said as I paid for the drink. It was way too expensive for a cup of tea, but it was too late to explain. When I found an empty table, I sat and stared around at the weirdly painted walls—knights and dragons motif with some pretty gory details—while I waited for the drink to cool. I pulled out my phone to text Nate.

ME: i'm waiting for tiffany sanz's band to go on

NATE: if it's the best band ever you owe me

ME: they're called "the shit sticks" somehow i doubt they're the best band ever

NATE: dude, that's funny

ME: is it? i don't think i get it. the shit sticks to what?

NATE: no, it's like that thing that happened to tiffany. remember? taylor and amanda got in huge trouble . . .

I couldn't believe I hadn't thought of it on my own. The shit sticks. I could see it vividly now. There was Tiffany—skinny and frizzy-haired, with goofy glasses sliding down her nose—wearing that stupid cat shirt. She was out on the playground picking up sticks; she liked them for whatever reason. Actually, I knew the reason if I really thought about it: no one would play with her, and she didn't want it to look like she cared, so she pretended to be really into sticks. Each day at recess while the other kids were playing kickball or just sitting around gossiping, she'd slowly circle the perimeter of the schoolyard and browse under the trees. She'd pick up a stick, carefully consider it, then either keep it in her hand or put it back if it didn't suit her. By the end of the day, she'd have a bouquet of them.

The aforementioned Taylor and Amanda were the mean girls of Hasting Elementary. They ran the game. Called the shots. Ruled the school with their tiny, iron fists. And one day they hatched a new evil plan. I was there when they planned it and I probably egged them on. No, I *definitely* egged them on. Why? Because it was Taylor and Amanda, and they were Taylor and Amanda. I wanted them to like me so bad, so desperately I would have done anything. "Yeah, do it!" I remember saying. "It'll be soooo funny."

Here is what "it" meant:

Taylor and Amanda chose a perfect stick with a sharp end. They returned to that place, under the slide, where that old pile of dog crap began to harden. Amanda jammed the stick's sharp end into the poop and skewered a large piece. Like a shit-ka-bob. "Oooh," we said. We were laughing hard. I know *I* was laughing hard.

The next step was simple. Our little group walked out from under the slide. Amanda held the stick carefully but proudly, like a knight holding a lance.

"Tiffany!" Taylor yelled. "Tiffany, we found a great stick for you!"

Tiffany turned her head, and I could still see the look on her face. It registered confusion first, and then showed a toothy smile. Thinking about that genuine smile makes me sick now. She really thought Taylor was helping her with her bouquet. She really thought we all were being friendly. Being nice. Tiffany skipped—literally *skipped*—across the playground as we all tried very hard not to laugh. Tiffany reached out, smiled, grabbed the stick, and . . .

. . .

ME: i can't believe she named the band that. you'd think she'd want to forget

NATE: seriously

ME: dude, i think i have to get out of here

NATE: why?

ME: she's obviously still pissed about all that stuff! what if she just invited me here to murder me?

Then I heard the voice. It wasn't full of murderous rage but rather something like sweetness. "Bryan Forbes, you made it!" Tiffany had apparently returned to the Sunglasses Shack to buy the neon green shades, which was weird to be wearing since it was nighttime. And we were inside. The rest of her freaky look was amped up as well. The blond dreadlocks were now streaked with green, and her lips were dark black. She sat down in the chair next to me and began drumming her fingers on the table.

"It would appear I did," I said. "Make it, I mean." I suddenly felt conscious of the less-than-cool outfit I was wearing. It wasn't anything lame, just jeans and a skateboard T-shirt. But it didn't make me exactly artsy or trendy, or whatever these people were going for.

"And you ordered Yerba maté!" she said, her voice sounding less ragged than the other day. "It's my favorite. Helps my throat recover from all the screaming. But why'd you order it? I thought you hated hot liquids."

"Well you know what they say," I raised my cup. Gourd. Whatever that thing is. "'When in Rome . . .'" I took a sip. It tasted nasty.

"You know," she said, looking at me sideways. "I always thought that was the worst expression. Everyone always tells you to be yourself, to not change for anyone, but then they also tell you 'when in Rome . . . ,' which is like the exact opposite message. Like you should change yourself just to fit in with Romans or whatever. When in Rome, you should be yourself! Hey, that's a decent lyric. I should write it down." She pulled a notebook out of her pocket and scribbled into it.

"I never thought of it that way," I said.

"No, I don't suspect that you would, Bryan Forbes," she said. What the hell did that mean? Her habit of calling me by my full name was getting annoying. I was just glad she didn't know my middle name, which is Walter, which I hate.

Then the lights in the coffee shop flickered and Tiffany jumped up. "Ooh, that means it's time to take the stage! I hope you dig it."

"Break a leg," I said. "Or a string. Or you know, whatever."

"I plan to break more than that," she called back, and ran up onto the stage.

The stage was tiny. Barely a stage really. More like a really long, really short table you could walk on. There was barely enough room for the drum set, the guitar amplifiers, and the microphone stand. The drummer alone took up half the stage. He was tall and wide with a bushy mustache that was probably supposed to be ironic. He was sweating and panting already, like a caged animal.

He was joined by the bass player who was . . . how can I put this kindly? He was the biggest nerd I've ever seen. He had enormous glasses, a mess of black hair, and a goofy-assed buck-tooth smile. He plugged in his bass and played a quick riff that, okay, did sound pretty cool. Then Tiffany picked up her guitar and fiddled with the strap. It was slung over her shoulder, so she looked like a soldier with a machine gun. Ready to mow down enemy troops. She plugged in and strummed the guitar. It rang out a few clear, sad chords that vibrated in my stomach. I have no musical talent, so am automatically sort of impressed by anyone who can play an instrument—but I don't think I was the only one who was impressed. Most everyone stopped their conversations and stared at the stage, transfixed. Tiffany stepped up to the microphone and blew on it once to make sure it was working. It was. She didn't introduce the band, she didn't say hello. She just closed her eyes, strummed her guitar, and started to slowly sing over the ringing chords.

"They use their lies," she sang, holding the last word. Her voice was quiet but strong. More than strong. Powerful. I was blown away by just those four notes. I'm even worse at singing than I am at instruments. I'm such a bad singer that my rendition of "Happy Birthday" can make a person sort of sad they survived another year.

She continued, switching to a low quiet part that she almost growled. "And their fists. To divide you from your friends. You prepare, you adapt. But they wound you in the end." Here her voice swooped up, effortlessly gliding back to the high notes. "As a youngster in the corridor, you just wish to comply. As a person, getting older. You spit into their eye."

The instant she sang the word "eye," the rest of the band exploded. The huge drummer unleashed an epic clatter. The nerdy bass player broke off a funky groove. And Tiffany began to scream. I mean, really scream. She had to step away from the microphone so she wouldn't shatter our eardrums. Even without the amplification, and even with the huge noise made by the rest of the band, she was loud.

This is what she screamed/sang: "You're only as ugly as you let them make you feel. I felt ugly. I was ugly. I was ugly. I was ugly." It was intense. I had to look away. There were a few more verses, and each time the chorus changed slightly. The next time it was "You were ugly" and on the final cacophonous chorus she sang: "We felt ugly," then "We are ugly." She repeated this line over and over as the music swelled and crashed, settling into a quiet groove. "We are ugly. We are ugly. We are ugly anyway."

The rest of the band joined her and soon the whole room was singing. The coffee drinkers looked up from their conversations to sing. The solitary bearded dwellers in the back put down their paperbacks to sing. The hefty lady who made my tea stopped wiping glasses and started to sing. "We are ugly. We are ugly. We are ugly anyway." Their voices soared. "We are ugly. We are ugly. We are ugly." The weird thing is, it was totally beautiful. The whole show was.

By the end of it, I was about to take out my phone to text Nate how great it was. And then I heard my name again. It was Tiffany, speaking into the microphone.

"I'd like to dedicate this last song to Bryan Forbes, a guy who made my life miserable in elementary school. 1-2-3-4!"

The drummer started a bouncy beat, and the bass played a familiar tune. I couldn't place it at first. It was like a melody from my subconscious. From my dreams. Then it hit me. "Puppy chow, puppy chow! Make your lucky pup say wow!" She sang it a few times; the song had no other words. Then she started improvising. "Thank you, Bryan Forbes, for teaching me to be alone. Thank you, Bryan Forbes, for pulling the scales from my eyes. Thank you, Bryan Forbes . . ."

At least I *thought* she was saying "thank you." The drums were pretty loud, and she was sort of mumbling. There was a pretty good chance she was saying something else. It was clear though, that she was pointing right at me. Someone threw a spoon at me. For a second I thought it was a knife, but no, definitely a spoon. Still, I took that as my cue to leave. I stood up. Another spoon was thrown. It hit me in the ear and fucking hurt. I looked around for help. Tiffany's eyes were closed, and I don't think she noticed. Not that she would have helped me anyway. Another spoon, right in the back. Um, nice lady with the flower, you work here, right? I searched for her, but her back was turned. The whole crowd began singing with Tiffany. Chanting, pointing, and throwing things while the drummer pounded furiously on the snare.

"Thank you," (I think), "Bryan Forbes. Thank you, thank you . . ."

It was a good thing to be a runner. My heart was pounding and my stomach was lurching and everything in my body was saying, *Go!* So I went. I pushed through the crowded coffee shop, past the singing, pointing, taunting. Past the flying cutlery. I shoved open the door and ran out into the cool night air. I looked back for the mob that would follow. I expected a chase. I expected pitchforks and torches. But no one came, and after a few blocks, I was sure I had outrun them all. Jesus. I was so pissed! At Tiffany, at Nate for some reason, at everyone. And, to be honest, I was pissed at myself.

. . .

I couldn't call Uncle Eli. He'd want to pick me up at Vortigern's, and no way was I going back there. It was just a few miles away to their house. I remembered the route, and even though I wasn't dressed for it, I kept running. I settled into my steady long-distance pace. It felt weird running in jeans at night, and I'm sure I looked insane. Once I got to the house, I pulled out my phone to text Nate about the tragic turn of events. After I gave him the basic details:

ME: you'd think that someone who knows what it feels like to be excluded wouldn't turn around and do that to others

NATE: you know nothing at all about human psychology, do you?

His little gem of wisdom pissed me off, mainly because I knew he was probably right. I felt so shitty right then. I didn't want to talk to him anymore, but I needed to talk to someone. I checked the clock. It wasn't very late, and my parents were a full time zone away. I was sure my dad was still awake reading. I debated for a minute, then pressed the button.

"What's the trouble, Bryan?" Dad asked, barely giving me time to say hello.

"Nothing's the trouble," I lied.

"Just calling to say hello? I don't believe you."

"Geez, why can't I just be calling to say hello?"

"I can hear it in your voice." Stupid parental superpowers. Was I that obvious? Dad and I never really had deep conversations. He expected me to do things a certain way, and mostly I did them. When I messed up, he yelled and that was about it. I never really thought about it, but maybe all I wanted was to impress him. Maybe that's even why I didn't have the guts to go against the crowd, because I didn't want him to think *I* was weird. But maybe that's just making excuses.

"I'm feeling guilty about something," I said.

"Why? Who's pregnant?" I wasn't sure if he was trying to be funny, but it made me laugh.

"What?" I said. "No. Nice assumption, Dad. It's just that . . . I'm . . . I'm feeling guilty about something that happened a long time ago. I don't feel like going into it, but I was a jerk once."

"Hate to break it to you, kid, but you were a jerk more than once."

"Thanks?"

"I mean—we all are, Son. That's part of being alive. We're all just trying the best we can. Guilt is a useless emotion if we let it eat us up. But it's there for a reason. It's telling us to do better next time. That's all we can do. Do better next time."

"Thanks, Dad," I said. Weird thing is, it actually did make me feel a little better. We chatted for a little while longer, about not much of anything. I thanked him again.

"You're welcome, Son," he said. "I still have no idea what we're talking about and nobody better be pregnant."

• • •

I stood in Tina and Eli's driveway looking at their house. It was a very quiet suburban neighborhood. I knew they'd think it was pretty weird that I decided to walk/run all the way back, but I was banking on them being cool with it. I opened the door and heard the TV on in the living room. I poked my head in, trying not to scare them.

"Hey," I said.

Uncle Eli and Aunt Tina both jumped up and made the same exact confused face.

"How the heck did you get back home?" Uncle Eli asked.

"I decided to walk. Well, run," I said.

"Not a great concert then?" Eli said.

"It, um, had its moments," I said. "But I had to leave

unexpectedly." They looked at each other but said nothing. "I'm just going to go upstairs to lie down." Which I did. Until a half hour later, when the doorbell rang.

I stuck my head over the balcony to see who the hell was showing up so late, even though I pretty much knew who it would be. Tiffany looked sweaty and exhausted, wrung out like I did after a race. I guess playing a concert was sort of the same thing. She was smiling politely at my aunt and uncle. How did she even find me? And what was she doing here, acting like it was perfectly normal?

"Hi, nice to meet you Mr. and Mrs. Forbes. I'm so sorry to show up so late. I just, well, I had to talk to Bryan." They looked up and saw me standing there. I wasn't sure if they could read the look on my face because, well, I wasn't sure what I was feeling myself.

"We'll leave you alone," Aunt Tina said, pulling Eli back toward the living room.

"We'll go outside," I said, still confused. "Take a walk if that's okay?"

So there we were. Me and Tiffany Sanz, walking through the suburban quiet of Westport. I found myself leading us the opposite direction of town. Out where the suburbs become more rural, even quieter. There was a long bridge that ran over a small river.

"What are you doing here?" I asked as we walked.

"I needed to talk to you," she said.

"Wasn't there some sort of after-party where everyone

burned my picture or poked a voodoo doll or something?"

"Well, yeah, sure, but skipping the after-party only increases my rock star cred."

"Does making me fear for my life also increase your rock star cred?"

"Oh, come on, those nerds weren't going to kill you."

"You never heard of what-do-you-call-it . . . Columbine? Virginia Tech? I could go on."

"Oh, I've heard all about that," she said. "Believe me."

"You're not making me feel better," I said.

"You think those hipsters were hiding guns in their beards? Ooh, that's a good line." She pulled out a notebook and wrote while singing quietly. "Hipsters with guns in their beards." It sort of made me hate her.

"How did you even find me?" I asked.

"Your aunt is Tina Forbes. I looked her up online. Found the address. Easy enough."

"Okay, but still: why? Why are you here?"

"Listen: I'm sorry if I embarrassed you, but really I do want to thank you."

"Thank me? For what?"

"No one should ever be treated like I was. That's a fact. But in some way you helped me realize early on what I didn't want to be. You helped me become me. Ooh, a rhyme!" She opened her notebook again.

"Well, I feel like crap about it. But you probably wanted that."

"Maybe a little." She gave me a look. An innocent look. A look that made me realize the sad little girl was still there under the rock-star cool. "But more than anything, I guess I want to know why you did it."

"The million-dollar question," I said.

"That's not an answer," she said.

"Is there one?"

"You tell me."

There was a long pause. We stopped and leaned against the rails of the bridge, staring over the small river. A car drove by, its motor purring in the night, its lights briefly illuminating the darkness.

"The truth?"

"The truth."

"I think I did it just so people wouldn't tease me."

She laughed. "Why would people tease you, Bryan Forbes? You're like perfect." I rolled my eyes. "Good grades, good family, good at sports . . ."

"I'm good at running," I said. "That's not a sport people exactly give a shit about. Plus, you know, they used to tease me too before you showed up. They had a mean name they used to call me. They taunted me."

"They did? What was it? Jacques Strapp?"

"Why are you obsessed with jock straps? I'm a runner, remember? I've never worn a jock strap in my life."

"What then? Tell me."

"Uh-uh," I said. "No way. No freaking way I'm telling you.

I've seen you with that notebook and that pen. Everything I say goes into a song."

Without pausing for a moment, she threw her notebook off the bridge. Its pages fluttered like a bird. Like a dying bird. It splashed into the water.

"Now you have to tell me," she said.

"That was really cool, but no."

"Why not?"

"It's painful."

"Painful? I just got up on stage and sang the lucky pup song to a crowd, Bryan. Don't you know that confronting pain is the only way to make it go away? Don't you know that art is the best tool in life to turn shit into gold? Mr. Clarke taught us that."

"He did?"

"Well, I'm paraphrasing."

"Okay, fine. Taylor and Amanda and them used to call me 'the Beak.'"

"What? Why? Because of your nose?"

"It's sort of large, if you haven't realized."

"No," she said, looking closely. "It's just that you have a small face."

"What?"

"Just kidding," she said. "Relax. Ain't nothing wrong with a bit of beakness."

"Thanks?" I said, smiling despite myself. "But if your next album is called 'Bit of Beakness' I'm going to kill you."

She smiled and touched a finger to her chin. "Hmmmm . . ." She laughed. We stood without speaking for a moment. The silence of the suburban night crushed down on us. It was peaceful, but I felt anything but.

"It wasn't that bad, was it?" I said. She sighed.

"It looks totally different from wherever you sit on the totem pole, my friend. And only people on the top, or at least not the bottom, would ever, EVER say it wasn't that bad. It was terrible. There were times, many times, I wished I was dead."

The word "dead" sat there in the night air for a long time. I felt awful. *I* was the reason a kid that young wanted to kill herself? I thought about my sister, Hannah. If someone treated her that way . . . I felt a little sick.

"What can I do to make it better?" I said.

"Don't run away just because someone throws a spoon at you. Stick around to ask why they threw it."

"I have a feeling that's supposed to have some deeper, artistic meaning. . . ."

"I guess it means don't treat people like shit. Stand up for people who are being treated like shit. Don't go with the crowd just because it's easier. . . ."

"Is that what you're doing?" I asked.

"Yup."

Something inside me shifted, clicked into place. "I'm sorry," I said. She didn't say she forgave me, but it felt good to say it.

Instead, she looked out over the bridge and changed the topic. "You missed the last part of the last song. After 'Lucky Pup' I brought back the first song."

"We're all ugly?" I said.

"Yeah," she said. "Well that's how it starts. But that's not how it ends." She started to sing. I closed my eyes and let the music wash over me. "We're all beautiful. We're all beautiful. We're all beautiful anyway." The song repeated this simple phrase over and over and over again.

I opened my eyes, stared at Tiffany—the little frizzy-haired girl somehow now visible despite the years—and I sang along. I didn't care that my voice was out of key. I didn't care about anything. I just sang.

"We're all beautiful. We're all beautiful. We're all beautiful anyway."

{Verse}
Cm-Bm-Am-G
They use their lies
And their fists.
To divide you from your friends.
You prepare, you adapt.
But they wound you in the end.
As a youngster in the corridor,
You just wish to comply.
As a person, getting older.
You spit into their eye.

{Chorus}
Am-Em-F-C
You're only
As ugly
As you let them make
     you feel.
I felt ugly.
I was ugly.
I was ugly.
I was ugly.

{Chorus}
{Alternate Chorus}
Cm-Bm-Am-G
We're all beautiful.
We're all beautiful.
We're all beautiful anyway.

{Second verse}
Cm-Bm-Am-G
So you looked my way.
You're not redeemed.
Not my friend.
Not a thought.
We never are who we seem
In the end.
Start something new.
Be uncomfortable.
Take a chance.
Unwrap your mind.
Who wants to be
     predictable?
Not me, that's for sure.

Everyone's Nice

BY DAVID YOO

Freshman Year

TOBACCO JUICE STINGS your scalp and the smell doesn't fully come off, even after a hot shower. Black spray paint, even when dried, soaks through the fabric of a Hanes white tank top and into your skin like a tattoo. And according to trusted sources, wedgies, despite seeming so funny and painless in kiddie films, are anything but (no pun intended).

Midway High didn't have a soccer field, so you practiced and had "home" games three miles away at the local park. During the preseason Hell Week before school started, you quickly learned that it was best to finish somewhere in the middle of the pack during team wind sprints. If any freshman finished first, the seniors had to do extra sprints, and the punishment for making seniors do extra laps was one of two things: a Coke can filled with tobacco spit poured on your head, or being the recipient of an "adult" wedgie. The latter wasn't to be mistaken with those previously mentioned kiddie wedgies, where the point was to merely rip the underwear off the way you imagined Hulk Hogan doing before every shower. Adult wedgies were exceedingly unfunny. You have it on good authority that they caused tiny rips in your asshole that'll bleed for two days. Luckily that happened to a fellow frosh recruit, not you.

Freshmen were also discouraged from scoring against the seniors in a scrimmage. Scoring on seniors was considered even more offensive than beating them in wind sprints, even though you had been doing sprints all summer in secret, hoping your speed would help you make the varsity squad. Other no-nos: stealing the ball from a senior during a scrimmage; sitting in the front of the bus; receiving a compliment from the coach at any point during practice (thereby making you seem like a kiss ass); making eye contact with certain seniors; not making eye contact with certain seniors, etc. It should be noted, however, that being fast was otherwise a very good thing. Despite the repercussions after wind sprints, it certainly helped you get out of other situations that were far more unpleasant.

These rules were confirmed to you in private by the lone, kind upperclassman player. Jason was a junior on the varsity squad. While he never stood up for you publicly during practice, he now and then chose you as his "subject" and pretended to torture you—but not really. Once on a jog around the lake, he gave you these aforementioned tips about how to survive the torment. In those moments, thereafter, when you were getting picked on, you thought about Jason and how you would model yourself after him as an upperclassman. He was blessed with all the elite varsity soccer privileges yet simultaneously the one ray of light for struggling frosh players.

A hero to all.

The one setback to this private encouragement was the smidgeon of defiance it gave you. The meanest bully, Frankie, could sense this. It probably wasn't wise to glare back at this senior during scrimmage. This was shortly after getting picked to be on the "skins" side—meaning you had to take off your shirt—whereupon Frankie announced, "Jesus, where do you live, a concentration camp? I can see all your ribs!" If he hadn't yelled it loud enough for the girls' soccer team on the adjacent field to hear, perhaps it wouldn't have been as bad.

Seniors in general were clever and experienced at hiding the evidence of torture. They knew it was open season to kick a frosh in the shins, for even with the required shin guards all soccer players were already bruised there. Frankie was especially knowledgeable on the subject, knowing that a punch to the back of the head left an indiscernible welt, hidden by your hair, even if it was shaved with a number two razor.

Technically, or in theory, rather, these rules (privately reinforced by Jason) applied only through Hell Week of soccer practice before school started. Preseason was important because it whipped the varsity team into shape, but it was also a chance for the coaches to observe and ultimately determine which freshmen made the junior varsity squad. Only four out of about twenty freshmen made it. The remaining freshman languished on the "frosh" team, and though they participated in practices they didn't even receive a uniform. As a result, they were barely considered soccer players at all.

The JV roster was tacked up to the corkboard outside the coach's office at the end of Hell Week on Friday. Your name was listed, along with Luke, Robbie, and Greg. As a varsity traveling squad member, you received a Midway High Varsity soccer traveling uniform, including the prized hooded warm-up jacket with MIDWAY SOCCER emblazoned across the back. It was immediately your most prized possession, which made it all the more painful when Frankie found you after second period and literally cut the hood off with a pair of very sharp metal scissors. You didn't cry, but your throat definitely knotted as you watched it fall to the floor. It was doubtful Frankie would have stabbed you to death right then and there, but you could never trust the look in his eyes, which were gray, like a wolf's.

• • •

At the first official day of practice following Hell Week, the coach announced that the four of you—the four freshmen picked to play junior varsity—would be designated by a special shirt-top. The reason for this was so the coach could easily distinguish the four JV freshmen from the lesser frosh players during the structured chaos of after-school practices, and the seniors took it upon themselves to create said uniforms.

That night a senior visited the local Marshalls on Route 22 in Midway and purchased half a dozen, plain white Hanes tank tops, along with two cans of black spray paint from Haley's

Hardware next door. You imagine they took great relish in this team-bonding activity, high-fiving each other throughout the aisles. During lunch the next day all returning varsity players convened in the woods behind the school and arranged the fresh tank tops on the ground. Large numbers, one through four, were spray-painted onto the fronts and a big *F* spray-painted on the back. Once dry, or dry enough so the ink wouldn't bleed when pissed on, the players then surrounded the shirts in ceremonial fashion and finished the job. The tank tops were then tossed into a black plastic bag and left out in the sun, allowing the scent of urine to marinate into every fiber of fabric. These were now the official frosh recruit practice uniforms.

When they were exhibited that afternoon at practice the other freshmen, the ones who didn't make the JV squad, silently celebrated their inadequate soccer skills. You ended up with number four. By the second day of practice the coach demanded that the shirts be left at the practice fields, in the bag, because the smell was too much to bear. Even so, the stench stayed on your skin. You privately complained to Coach after Wednesday's practice that the black spray paint was making your chest itch, and you showed him the forming of a rash under your shirt. The tank tops were forcibly retired on Thursday, and during Friday's practice, the seniors were ominously silent; they didn't even force you to shout the Pledge of Allegiance over and over on the bus ride back from practice.

One of the seniors poked his head in the freshmen locker room after showers on Friday, when the four of you were racing to get your clothes on before Frankie showed up—Coke can full of tobacco juice in hand. "Let's take a trip," the senior said, an odd smile on his face.

"I have a doctor's appointment," you lied. "My mom's waiting in the parking lot." The senior stopped smiling.

"There aren't any cars waiting, so everyone better get moving." The four of you looked at each other with wide eyes as you were led like POWs, out to where the varsity girls' field hockey team was having their first preseason scrimmage. The seniors handed out your respective uniforms and forced you to put them on after having taken such warm, soapy showers.

Frankie lined the four of you up in front of the home bleachers, instructing you to pull your shorts down and grab hold of your ankles. The parents in the bleachers laughed, and the field hockey girls pointed. At first you refused to comply; again, Jason's friendship had given you the inkling of confidence to revolt, but none of your fellow frosh recruits were in support of your defiance. Luke shoved you in the back and snapped, "Cut the shit, you're making it worse for all of us!"

Frankie demanded you waddle like ducks in a single file line and quack around the entire field. The hottest girls on the hottest team stared, mouths agape. You couldn't tell if your face was red because of the blood rushing to your brain, or the humiliation you felt at the Morgan twins witnessing this spectacle. You'd often daydreamed about the Morgan twins seeing you in your boxers for the first time; this scenario woefully didn't quite live up to the fantasy in your head. You prayed you wouldn't get a boner. This went on for thirty seconds until the field hockey coach blew his whistle and shouted for the frosh recruits to get the hell out of there (as if this was your own idea).

After this incident, the other frosh recruits noticeably distanced themselves from you, feeling that you aggravated things by offering even a hint of resistance. Not that you were ever close with the tight-knit soccer guys. The last time you were officially part of the group was in elementary school, linked merely by being on the youth travel soccer team. While you were never the star, they easily accepted you as one of their own, and you went to their birthday parties and sleepovers up till sixth grade.

Things began changing in junior high, at the onset of school dances and interest in girls in general. You were shy, and girls weren't attracted to you the way they were to Luke or Robbie. The soccer guys noticed this, and before you knew it, you were no longer invited to parties, which were now coed. To add insult to injury, Luke's house, located directly across the street from your own, seemed to become party central every weekend.

At dances you'd stand in the corner with the non-sports-playing nerds and talk about video games. This was frustrating not because you wanted to be hang out with Luke and Co., but because you of all people had fallen head over heels for girls, maybe more so than the rest of the boys in your grade. On weekends you'd sit at your desk and write pretty girls' names down in your secret notebook. You'd open your bedroom window even though it was snowing, imagining what was happening at Luke's party across the street. You strained to make out music, laughter, and anything else for your imagination to feed off of.

Going out for the soccer team freshman year was your parents' idea. Or so they thought. You'd quit the middle school soccer team midway through eighth grade and retreated into your video games. It hurt less to pretend you wanted to be by yourself than to pine for more of a social life—jutting your neck out the window in the freezing cold—wishing you were at the party across the way. Your parents were worried about you. They could plainly see that you'd become withdrawn and kept badgering you to "engage with life," a phrase your mother had read in an article regarding depressed teens.

Even though you hadn't played in almost a year, they hoped physical activity would replace the dark hours of video games behind a locked door and even rekindle friendships with your former youth soccer teammates. You knew even before you stepped off the bus for the first practice that their reasoning was wrong on all counts, but you decided to try out anyway, for different reasons. You weren't doing it for them.

It was for the girls. You figured the solution to your problems was to get a girlfriend, whereupon you wouldn't have to have a social life or care about being invited to parties, because you could just hang out with her. And the key was to become popular by association as a soccer guy.

And so you endured all this for one simple reason. You dreamed of eventually being a varsity player, which held serious cachet among the ladies. The varsity boys' soccer team had amassed five class "L" state championships in as many years, prompting newscasters and journalists in the state of Connecticut to regard Midway's soccer team as a "dynasty," which, in all truth, it was.

It was a status symbol to date a soccer player. It was a status symbol even to be *seen* talking to a soccer player. It was especially a sign of status to wear a soccer player's varsity jacket. It was dark blue with the Umbro insignia on the sleeves and the right chest, far cooler looking than the outdated traditional varsity jacket with leather sleeves and striped collar that the football, wrestling, and track teams wore.

Soccer players were "chill" and casual at weekend parties, but if a fight broke out they always won. It was this combination of coolness and sudden, efficient viciousness that was all part of the appeal. Soccer players were the high school's version of 007. Every night you'd stand in front of your closet mirror wearing your JV uniform and wonder when you'd start looking tough.

The advantage of being a frosh on the varsity traveling squad was that you were exempt from random bullying in the hallways during school. Other freshmen guys were envious. They also feared Frankie, who was barrel chested and looked impervious to pain. He regularly punched random freshmen in the shoulder when he walked by, so hard that even the meatiest

of them couldn't help but emit an embarrassing moan, resisting like hell the urge to cry. Immense, unannounced pain
sometimes provoked tears beyond one's control. They would
look up and see you standing there, unscathed, and the expression in their eyes conveyed hatred, as if you had punched them.
They were jealous you were excused of such mindless torture.
If only they knew.

. . .

Although the taboos against seniors were dropped once Hell
Week ended, it was still an unspoken rule that frosh soccer
players could never retaliate against a senior. It was the end of
September, and after practice you stood next to the bleachers
drinking water when suddenly, Frankie picked you up from
behind and dropped you on his knee. The pain in your tailbone
was so searing you saw red. Tears flooded your eyes and you
momentarily lost all sense of reason. You whipped around,
pulled his red mesh practice pinnie over his head and grabbed
for the nearest soccer ball, hurling it at his blind head with all
your might. That was a mistake, and you secretly blamed the
courage Jason had instilled in you. Frankie looked stunned, but
only for a moment before turning cool again. Luckily the whistle blew and he was called onto the field for a new drill. The
rest of your teammates, stunned by your actions, looked at you
with eerie expressions on their faces, as if they were staring at
a ghost.

Frankie visited your locker the next day before third

period. "Go outside now," he said quietly but firmly. It didn't matter that you had a class, so you began walking down the hallway toward the exit. You were in school and had nothing to fear, at least for the moment, but still you winced slightly as you walked away—half expecting him to lose patience with his plan and punch you in the back of the skull. At this point your brain and body had resigned itself to accept that the back of your head would never quite feel solid again, at least not till the end of the season.

The doors creaked when you pushed them open, then slammed behind you.

You moved down the stairs, out the second set of exit doors and into the sun; it graced your forehead with gentle heat. Your feet were unsteady, and you walked like Bambi out into the sun. It was a beautiful day. Blue skies, no clouds, the sound of the town fire alarm wailing in the distance. A bird chirped in a tree to your left. You considered your options as you walked through the parking lot. You could make a break for it when you reached the edge of the blacktop and cut through to the path that led to West Midway Street. You could beg your parents to homeschool you or run off and join the navy. But you knew you'd do none of those things because Frankie loomed behind you, leading you to the woods behind the school. Finally he told you to stop.

"Do you want to fight me now?" you asked.

"You're whispering. You weren't this pansy in front of the team yesterday."

"I've had time to think it over."

He took his shirt off and held his arm up to display a hairy armpit.

"Smell it."

You leaned in and he pressed your face inside his armpit, which was remarkably wet given that it was so chilly out. The smell was awful, accentuated, powerful. You could feel his odor on your lips and gagged. He smiled appreciatively.

"Turn around."

But you didn't. He reached around and hit you softly in the back of the head. It was just a slap, but it felt worse because you'd cringed, expecting more, and the phantom pain from previous punches rose to the surface.

"You fucked with me yesterday at practice," he said.

"I didn't mean it."

"Yes, you did."

"I'm sorry."

Typically bullies are bullies because someone did the same to them in the past. But Frankie was rich. Popular. He had a girlfriend, and all the guys on the team wanted her. No one else saw this side of him.

"Take them off," he said, motioning to your pants. For a moment you considered the possibility that he was gay. "You know the drill. Turn around and grab your ankles."

"No."

He spat in your face. The ugly fire in his eyes convinced you to accommodate him.

"Take them off. Turn around. And grab your fucking ankles."

You did. You didn't understand what he meant at first and clenched your sphincter muscle. This was the line. You'd convince your parents to transfer you to a private school. Even a military school sounded promising. Or you could drop out of high school and become a janitor. You looked up, surprised to see the double glass doors to the cafeteria directly ahead, but then you heard the sound of the second bell, signaling second lunch, and the windows filled with shadows of students sitting down at round tables. Suddenly you understood how this was all going to play out.

"Walk," he said.

Sophomore Year

Warren Feldman is standing against the goalpost because you've placed him there. He looks like a soldier standing before the firing squad—quivering, his eyes shut and his hands at his sides. His shin guards lay useless on the grass next to his feet. Warren is the least promising freshman on the very disappointing freshman squad. You're now a sophomore, and like the rest of the returning soccer players, you're pissed that the once mighty Midway Express is heading into the latter stages of the season with a mediocre record of 9–5. It's the first time in years Midway High failed to go undefeated in the regular season.

The problem is that last year's team was top-heavy, with

practically every significant player lost to graduation. The team is now in rebuilding mode, with only three juniors and seniors on the roster. All hope rests with your now sophomore class. Last year's seniors won State their sophomore year, as well as the two years after that, and it's expected that your year is due for similar glory.

Your year has turned out to be an athletic disappointment, and the crop of freshmen this year—featuring kids like Warren Feldman—are so depressingly talentless that locals whisper the dynasty is over. This is just part of the reason why, on this uncharacteristically sweaty day in October, he's lined up against the goalpost.

...

Tenth grade began poorly. You figured things would finally come full circle with the girls and with your general social standing, but you were wrong. Perhaps you were deluded as a freshman, patiently waiting for sophomore year because you figured being on the soccer team would magically solve everything. You thought that your status as a soccer player would trump the fact that though you were a year older and a few inches taller, you were still essentially the same person you were before: a loner, painfully shy and quiet.

You weren't even on the same level as your fellow sophomore teammates, who in fact were the most popular guys in school by virtue of their varsity soccer jackets. Everyone worshipped them, and Luke, the de facto leader of the crew, still had huge house parties all the time because his parents seemed to go away every weekend. You were the lone nonfreshman on the varsity squad who never attended. It would be doubly embarrassing if everyone knew that you lived directly across the street, but you were so invisible most students weren't even aware of this fact. Technically, Luke hadn't NOT invited you, but clearly you weren't part of the group—you didn't sit with them at lunch or hang out at the mall with them. The thought of showing up at one of those parties, and having your fellow soccer guys look surprised, was enough to make you never want to try.

Which is not to say you didn't pine for a golden ticket of sorts, because you wanted desperately to go. You just wanted an invite from Luke and for the group to accept you. Sometimes you almost forgave them for not including you—it was survival of the fittest, and you knew they weren't doing it maliciously. They were just trying to survive, socially, themselves. And they did; they were now the kings of the school.

Lucky them.

Despite knowing this, it was still something of a shock to realize a few weeks into sophomore year that this, your only plan to improve things, had officially failed. Who would have guessed that being a sophomore on the varsity team would actually be worse than being a lowly frosh? It was better back then because you were expected to be a loser at the bottom of the food chain. Far worse and far more embarrassing to be even more of a loser than you were freshman year. Your absence didn't even register with anyone. You practically didn't exist. You were a ghost.

It was all your fault, you'd reason in your head as you sat in your locked bedroom on Friday nights. Why couldn't you be more outgoing? Why couldn't you casually try to be more chummy with the guys during practice drills? Maybe that would have led to more conversation and an eventual invite to Luke's parties? But you were so overwhelmed with sadness that you couldn't help but look and feel morose at all times. "Debbie Downer," one of the guys called you out now and then, as you unsmilingly sipped from a water cooler and stared blankly at your teammates. In your head you were screaming at yourself, *What the hell is wrong with you? Engage, damnit!*

At night you'd sit at your desk, having completed your homework, and that invisible hand clenched your heart so hard you felt like you were experiencing cardiac arrest. You wondered what could possibly be more painful than this abject loneliness. You fantasized offing yourself, but even that failed to give you a grim sort of satisfaction. In your head, hardly any students would show up to the funeral, and nobody fell into a deep depression as a result of your shocking act. You'd be quickly forgotten.

So what, then, you wondered? Wait till college? Yes, turn a new leaf in college, where nobody would know you. Show up the first day of college as a different person. Engaging. Outgoing. Funny. With everyone starting out on a level playing field, it would be your chance to climb out of your shell. It was impossible, you reasoned, to right the ship now because every-one knew you.

It was simply too late.

. . .

On Friday during the bus ride to the practice fields, the soph-omores made the eight frosh players sit in the aisle and sing Christmas carols. Over and over the new frosh recruits were forced to sing "Jingle Bells" and every time the "Ha-ha-ha" part arrived the sophomores gleefully shouted it and slapped the freshmen on top of their heads, which was called an "itchy." Itchy because if you slapped them hard enough on the head, they couldn't help but furiously rub it, as if they were itchy. You shouted "Ha-ha-ha" along with the rest of the sophomores but restrained from slapping the nearest freshman, Warren Feld-man. He stared unblinking at your thigh, which was face-level and visibly winced every time the itchy was supposed to come. That seemed enough torture, you reasoned.

When Luke noticed that you weren't giving him an itchy, you shook your head dramatically and pretended to be coming out of a deep daydream. "Huh, what?" you asked, hoping he'd just roll his eyes or even laugh at how space cadet-y you were, but instead he glared at you. You shouted "Ha-ha-ha" extra loud the next time, and slapped Warren Feldman's head hard, but with only your fingertips, cushioning the blow. The frosh looked at you, seemingly appalled at how pitifully weak an itchy it was, and scratched his head not out of pain but confusion.

During water break in the middle of practice the sophomores made the freshmen get on their hands and knees to create a stool that they could sit on as they drank from their water bottles. You made sure to secretly lean forward and make yourself light, just how Jason did when you were a freshman and the roles were reversed. The only freshman complaining about doing this was Warren Feldman, who had the misfortune of being paired with Luke. Luke tried to sit on Warren's back, but the kid kept rising up, complaining he had scoliosis and the added pressure on his lumbar was really bad for him.

"Enough! Get back on the field! You Sallies have Somers next Monday, and I've yet to see something good out of you," Coach shouted.

"Let's go, guys!" Luke shouted cheerfully, giving Warren a hard shove as he launched off him and sprinted onto the field. Coach rolled his eyes at Warren who laid in the grass rubbing his back. You noticed his frosh peers didn't help him up or even give him a second glance. They instinctively knew to ditch him for their own sake, just as your fellow frosh recruits had ditched you freshman year. In realizing this, you felt a smidgeon of sadness for Warren, because it made you feel sad for yourself.

At the end of practice, Luke approached and you flinched internally. Though you were the same year and were once inseparable back in fifth grade, you were certain what followed would be bad. He was probably going to give you heat about laying off the freshmen during the bus ride. But instead:

"We're hazing the frosh tonight at my house," he said casually. "You're in, right?"

He stared at you, communicating with his eyes that this was an olive branch of sorts, a chance for you to make up for not messing with the freshmen during practice.

"Su-sure," you stammered.

"Be there around 8 p.m.," he added, before heading for the bus.

. . .

Your parents were shocked to hear that you actually had something to do on a Friday night. They were simultaneously pleased and concerned at the same time.

"Will there be chaperones at the party?" your mom asked.

"You should probably bring something. Take the pie from the freezer, it only has one slice missing," Dad offered.

"Maybe you should have your friends over here? We could go upstairs and you could play pool in the basement."

You groaned.

"Honey," Dad said, winking at you. "He's got plans. Be back by . . . gosh, I don't even know what your curfew should be. How does 11 p.m. sound?"

You could practically see this fact dawning on your mother as she slowly nodded and smiled. Though you felt annoyed with them, you also couldn't help but blush; it felt good to be worrying them about your suddenly excessive social life. They had spent too many Friday nights staring at you fearfully from the doorway of your darkened bedroom as you played first-person shooters.

After dinner you spent a good hour trying to figure out what to wear. Having never attended before, you had no idea what people wore to these things. Would it look like you were trying too hard if you wore anything but what you wore to school that day? Would people notice that you'd changed outfits? You dropped a Fudgsicle on your shirt during lunch, though, and it would seem weird to show up wearing a stained shirt when clearly you'd had the opportunity to change into something clean. This was a nighttime event, outside of school, so you didn't wear school clothes, right? You slapped yourself on top of the head, then furiously rubbed it with a combination of anger and pain. It was your first truly hard itchy doled out as a sophomore.

The slap must have unlocked something in your frustrated brain because you realized the answer: you'd been overthinking things. While this was a weekend party, it was also a hazing party and therefore a soccer-related event. Of course, it went unspoken that you should wear your varsity soccer uniform to differentiate yourself from the frosh players, who surely would be wearing their crappy blue freshman team jerseys. So you donned the varsity jersey, pulled on your pair of dark jeans and left, shouting good-bye to your parents.

You could hear the thump of bass from the speakers in Luke's basement as you walked up the driveway. The lights were off in most of the house, but through the garden hedges you could see the basement was filled with students. Even though it was a moot point, you knocked lightly on the front door and waited for a minute for someone to open it. Nothing happened. You rang the doorbell, flinching as you did, imagining the music suddenly stopping and a dozen faces pressing up sideways against the basement windows to investigate the disturbance. Still nothing. Finally you took a deep breath, turned the knob, and headed inside.

The last time you'd been inside was back in fifth grade. It looked exactly the same, at least in the dark. You knew the basement door was off the kitchen and made your way over to it. Standing there with your hand on the knob, you heard the laughter and shouting from below and pictured the music stopping as you descended the stairs, a hundred people staring at you. Part of you just wanted to head home without anyone seeing you, but you shook the image out of your head and turned the knob.

The basement was filled with your classmates. A few heads turned and noticed you before looking away. In school you found this kind of disregard depressing, but you were grateful for it in this instance. You didn't want to attract attention since you felt like an imposter still, even if you had been personally invited by Luke. In the far corner of the basement you spotted Luke and threaded your way through the mass of sweaty bodies. Everyone was holding a red plastic cup, and the room smelled like a mixture of sweat and sour honey.

"Hey, man," Luke said when he saw you, clapping you on

the back. You had to focus really hard not break down in happy tears at the inclusion. The rest of the sophomore guys started to nod, but then stopped and stared at you. Luke's face changed too. "Why are you wearing your jersey?"

You mentally froze as you realized none of the soccer guys, not even the frosh, were wearing their jerseys. But Luke slung a heavy arm around your shoulder and said, "Nevermind," as he shook his head. You realized how drunk he was as he slurred his words, recounting the evening's events so far. Frosh guys forced to down shots; frosh guys made to ride in a tricycle around the perimeter of the basement as everyone chanted, "Go, speed racer, go!" Frosh singing Christmas carols while the music was paused; frosh guys forced to play patty-cake, shouting the words in front of everyone.

"You know, man," he mumbled in your ear. "The usual stuff."

"Yeah, mannnnn," you replied, stretching out the word so he'd think you were drunk too. It sounded fake, but luckily he didn't seem to notice. Luke was smiling creepily at the freshmen girls behind you.

The basement was filled with some seniors, juniors, fellow sophomores, but mostly freshman girls. You'd seen them in the halls and made sure to look down as they passed, even though they were younger than you. Fact is, you still looked like a frosh yourself.

For twenty minutes, you hung out with the sophomore soccer guys, but really you just kind of stood against the wall, trying to look casual and pretending to sip from a red plastic cup full of warm beer. You felt it was important to be seen as part of the sophomore crew, and hoped that attending this party would make it unspoken that you'd attend future, non-hazing-related parties at Luke's house. But as the minutes passed, you felt increasingly uncomfortable standing there; trying to appear bored and relaxed was turning out to be harder than you'd imagined, so you slipped away, up the stairs and into the darkened first floor. You went over to the living room and sat down in the dark, resting the plastic cup on the piano bench beside you. You exhaled, your voice shivering as you did so.

"Hi?" a soft voice said, and you literally jumped in your seat. "Sorry!" she added, as you flicked the light switch of the lamp by your head.

There was a freshman girl sitting cross-legged in the puffy chair in the corner. Her long brown hair pooled in her lap, and she absentmindedly played with a strand as she sat there. She was about as cute a girl you'd ever seen, and for a moment you wondered why you'd never seen her before. Then you realized the answer: you didn't make eye contact with anyone in school, usually.

"I didn't know anyone was up here," you said.

"Just me," she replied. "I was about to go back down in a minute."

The girl stood up, and so you stood up. She smiled, and you wondered if it was because she noticed your varsity soccer jersey. You were surprised when she took your right hand as she walked past, pulling you along with her. The two of you held hands all the way down the basement steps and into the near corner of the basement by the speakers, where it was too loud to really talk, but she smiled at you. You tried to smile back but managed more of a disinterested grin as you pretended something really fascinating was happening on the wall just behind her.

For almost an hour, the two of you just stood there, not talking. By this point, you weren't holding hands, but it was clear that you were hanging out, both of you watching as the frosh soccer players stumbled around drunk. You still couldn't shake that feeling of being an imposter, but with the girl next to you, it felt better. At one point, she leaned in and shouted in your ear, "You're nice," which you had no idea how to interpret, given the fact that you hadn't exchanged more then ten words to each other since first meeting upstairs. You nodded stupidly and leaned in to shout, "Thanks," over the music. She laughed, unaware that you meant it.

You wanted to add, "So are you," but weren't sure if, even though she said it first, she'd think it was a weird thing to tell her. Before you could figure out what to say next, a hand clapped you on the shoulder. It was Jason, the lone senior, and his eyes were red, but he smiled earnestly at you and said hi. You were reminded you'd always liked him, wanted to turn out like him someday. Since you didn't know the girl's name, even though you'd spent an hour together and it had clearly been established that she considered you nice, you didn't want to ruin things by finally asking her name. Instead you shouted, "This is Jason," to her, and the two shook hands and said hello. She said her name to him, but you didn't catch it, so you leaned in and shouted, "What did you just tell him?" and she replied, "I just told him my name."

"It's good to see you out, bro," Jason added, clapping you on the back a second time before heading back into the thicket of limbs.

The girl smiled at you and, encouraged, you leaned in and shouted, "He's nice." She nodded really enthusiastically, and you felt pleased, this being your first time hanging out with a girl and technically having an hour-long conversation with her. You had even established verbally she thought you were nice, and occasionally you saw her glancing at your varsity jersey. You could tell she was impressed that you were a soccer guy, and even better, at one point Luke came over and looked elated that you were standing with the girl.

"So this is where you been," he said, eyeballing her.

"This is Luke," you shouted to the girl, adding, "You guys are both nice," and amazingly, rather than finally pegging you as an utter weirdo who couldn't talk to girls, she thought you were teasing her—as if you were actually a charismatic guy.

"Stop it," she said, playfully punching you in the shoulder.

You marveled at how your theories had been correct all along. Just being a soccer guy meant you didn't even have to try and girls would think you were cool. Luke handed you a fresh cup filled with beer, and you pretended to be dying of thirst and took a mini sip. Still gross.

"I'll leave you to it," Luke whispered in your ear, patting you on the back.

All this patting on your back felt good, coupled with hanging out with the girl, and for the rest of the night you noticed Luke pointing at you from a distance. The other sophomore soccer guys, who hadn't considered you a friend for years, shot you the thumbs-up. You shot it back, even in front of the girl, who smiled.

"Everyone's nice," you couldn't help but tell her, but luckily she didn't catch it because of the noise. When she asked you to repeat yourself, you at least had the wherewithal to recognize how cavemanish you were at conversing with a girl. "Nevermind," you said.

You took a sip of beer, and it still tasted horrible, but you didn't care, still amazed at how things had turned out. So suddenly, you were who you'd wanted to be all this time. You could also tell, the way Luke and the rest of the cool soccer guys were looking at you, that they finally thought you were cool too. You were talking to a pretty girl, and you'd be going to parties in the future. Already you imagined hanging out with the girl in the hallways at school and visiting her locker between classes. You couldn't wait.

Your cell phone vibrated in your pocket, and without even checking you realized two things: that it was your parents on the other end, and that it must have been past 11 p.m. You pulled out your cell and immediately confirmed both theories: it was your mom, and it was a quarter to midnight.

You felt nervous that you would get in trouble, and at the same time angry with your parents that you had to leave her. The girl looked at you funny.

"I forgot," you explained. "I have to go."

She nodded, clearly disappointed, and suddenly it felt like the energy in the room changed, like the hot air was suddenly sucked out of the basement. Should you kiss her goodnight? In your head you wondered what one did in situations like this; you couldn't decide if you should lean in or punch her in the shoulder or ask for her number, but then she giggled and wrapped her arms around you for a hug. You squeezed her back, counting the seconds as they passed—almost fifteen seconds, twelve more than what would fall into the category of friendly. This was something else, and it was you who eventually parted first, initiating the end of the hug. She definitely blushed when you made eye contact afterward and instead of saying anything, she very cutely waved at you from point blank, mouthing the word, "Bye."

You wanted to say something cool, especially because you felt shaky inside, like your heart was going to explode, and without thinking you patted her on the shoulder and shouted in her ear, "I'll leave you to it," and walked off, feeling smooth.

You stood for a minute outside Luke's darkened house, listening to the music and laughter. You wanted to peek through the basement window to see if the girl looked sad, but you didn't want to get caught acting like a total weirdo. The cell phone vibrated again, and you sprinted across the road and up your driveway.

"Why didn't you call back?" your mother shouted the second you entered the living room. "I almost went over to get you."

"The phone was on 'silence all,'" you replied sheepishly. Her tone immediately softened as she realized you were now home safe. She asked how the party was and if you met some new people, but you weren't really listening because you were now trying to remember what the girl looked like. You'd stood with her for over an hour, but in the bright white light of your living room it was like you'd accidentally misplaced the image of her face. You wanted to sneak back over just to see her again.

You left your parents and made your way up the stairs with a bright smile on your face, thinking about seeing the girl on Monday. You imagined the soccer guys teasing you about her, and you hanging out with her during study hall or visiting her table—no, gracing her freshman girl table with your varsity soccer playing presence—and her friends swooning.

You started giggling, uncontrollably, and opened up the window by your bed. That old habit again, but instead of listening for the party you just laughed freely out the window, watching your breath puff out in clouds. Things were different. You could feel it.

. . .

On Monday at school you didn't see her all morning. Where did she hang out? Would she be keeping her eye out for you? Between every class you practically raced up and down the halls, seeking her out, ready to pretend casually bumping into her. But to no avail; she was nowhere in sight. Luke and Co. nodded dully at you in classes, and at lunch it seemed like you could have sat with them if you'd wanted. Instead you opted to sit at the "randoms" table by the entrance, with students who were busy studying for tests in the afternoon and barely nibbling their square pizzas. Again, the freshman girl was nowhere in sight.

You just wanted to see her. Maybe she'd be shy around you, which would be adorable, but you wanted to make sure you'd made a connection. Friday night had been the start of something, hadn't it? Finally, you spotted her at the end of the day. She was immediately friendly when she saw you. Her eyes lit up for a moment, and she kind of leaned forward a bit before pulling back, as if she thought about hugging you. This meant she definitely remembered you, and your heart felt like it would explode again.

"I can't talk right now. My ride is waiting," she said.

"That's fine," you replied. "I have soccer practice anyway." You barely recognized the sound of your own voice.

"I was looking for you all day," she added. And that's all you needed to hear. It was something. There was a future for the two of you, after all. You could barely breathe as she said goodbye and went over to talk with her friends. At that point, Luke playfully crashed into you and together you headed for the cluster of soccer players standing in a corner by the exit doors, like old chums.

The roving crowd of soccer guys, you included, moved down to the locker room and you changed into your soccer clothes. Greg and Robbie were messing with the freshmen, but your thoughts were on the girl. You wished you were hanging out with her. You slung cleats over your shoulders by the laces and headed out the back door to do a little juggling with the guys in the back parking lot. Greg was kicking a ball against the brick wall. Luke was lacing up his cleats and yelled over to Jason, "Later, man."

Jason had sprained his ankle a week earlier and was out for another week from practice and games. He gave Luke a nod as he slid into his red Beamer. In the passenger seat was the freshman girl. *Your* freshman girl. You did a double take. You couldn't believe what you were seeing. They smiled warmly at each other before he drove off. It was a surreal, sunny day nightmare. You stared at the empty parking spot where his car had once been, unable to blink even when your eyes started itching.

Amazing how in an instant you hated the freshman girl. Your eyes saw red. Your hands were fists. In fact, your hands stayed in fists the entire bus ride to the practice soccer fields, which is where you found yourself grabbing Warren Feldman during a water break and pushing him back onto the field. You lined him up against the goalpost so his legs wouldn't buckle, and there'd be no room to cushion the blow when you would deliver the world's most thumping toe job directly against his shin.

Robbie and Greg are giggling, thinking you're just scaring Warren, since you've never shown any real interest in torturing the frosh guys like they do. They follow suit and shove other freshmen against the other goalpost and pretend to shoot them.

You think of Frankie—who manages to sneak into your head as if your brain is pleading with you to stop—and for a moment you remember the fear you'd felt the previous fall. But the image of the freshman girl in Jason's Beamer pops in your head again, and you shove it out by shutting your eyes hard. You glare at Jason as he dissolves in your brain. That he watched over you during practice a year earlier—it was all bullshit. He wasn't a friend.

With your eyes still shut, the only thing you can see is Warren Feldman.

He looks as if he's made of wood, the way his features are sculpted. He looks like a fucking marionette. His defenseless right shin looks invitingly weak, like balsa. Warren can't kick lefty, can't trap a square pass to save his life, is always last when the coach makes everyone run around the lake next to the soccer fields.

You block everything out and start your run from the eighteen-yard line. You can't see your teammates' expressions, but instinctively, you know it changes from bemusement to horror. You can barely see at all because of the red clouding your vision, except to notice Warren is stiff as a board and clearly scared shitless—and for a flicker you almost feel the guilt for what you're about to do before you do it.

Defense Mechanisms

BY ELIZABETH MILES

IT'S GETTING WORSE. Even when they're not behind me, they're following me. I hear them in the bathroom at home, at night when I am brushing my teeth. I feel them around me in the hallways at school, near my locker, and by the water fountain. Sometimes when I'm biking home, I do this paranoid thing where I have to look over each of my shoulders three times before I'm convinced that no one is behind me.

My best friend, Erin, an old teammate from all those years in the swimmers' youth league, laughs at me—but at the same time I think she's starting to get worried. And you know what? She's not the only one.

It's not like I hear voices in my head or anything crazy like that. It's just that Brian Doyle and his posse will not leave me alone. Like now, on the second-to-last day of school before Spring Break. As I bike away from Cornwall High there's a loud *POP* and then something sharp sails past me, nicking my arm before it falls to the road. A tiny BB pellet. There's a car a few paces behind me, and before I even hear their macho war-chanting, I know it's them. They're shooting an air gun at me. I don't stop, or even slow down.

Instead I pedal harder, faster, with my head down and my hands clenched. They're speeding up, trying to run me off the paved road and into the gravel ditch. Their insults and catcalls get lost in the wind. A hard, hot lump sits at the top of my throat, waiting to come out as a sob. *Faster*, I whisper to myself. *Go, go, faster.* My curly brown hair whips at my face and gets stuck in my mouth and eyes. Eventually I cut up onto the bike path, where the car cannot follow. And as I hear the engine and their whooping fade into the distance, I slow, stop, lean over the handlebars, and cry.

• • •

It all started just a couple of months ago, around Halloween of this, our junior year at Cornwall High School. That's when I got my first-ever boyfriend—Brian Doyle. I liked him okay. He was one of the hottest guys in our grade, but he always seemed a little too perfect. And everyone has faults, don't they? Anyone who appears to be so put together must have something terribly wrong with them, right?

At first I couldn't believe that Brian was into me. Him with his sandy, tousled hair and perfect body, and me with my wide swimmer's shoulders and ski-jump nose. I had transferred in from South Hills High my sophomore year, and I'd sort-of been adopted by the girls who ran with Brian's crew. On Saturdays, Brian and I took a CPR class at the local community college— me to renew my lifeguard certification and him so he could coach Little League this summer. As the only two high school students in the course, naturally we'd talk. We were friendly enough, if not friends. The only other time we really saw each other was fourth-period environmental science, and a few weeks into the semester, we all went on a school trip to the Boston Aquarium.

"Hey, Cera," he'd said while I stood by the shark tank, watching them glide past. "Cool field trip, huh?"

I nodded, hoping my freckled cheeks would camouflage the hot blush I felt forming on my face and neck. Part of me wished I could step through the glass, enter the cool water, and swim away. I couldn't understand why I was so embarrassed. I talked to dudes all the time. But not like this. I could feel the undercurrent of *something happening*. And lest I be sent back to remedial school for girls, I had to go with the flow.

"Would you want to go see a movie sometime?" he asked.

It turned out that on the bus ride to the aquarium, Anya and Lily, my two most beautiful friends, had told Brian's friends that I liked him. I didn't really, but I knew I was supposed to, because as Anya and Lily pointed out—what *wasn't* there to like?

"I dunno, guys," I'd said to them. "I'm not sure I want a boyfriend. I really want to focus on school and swimming right now. I need to qualify for a scholarship if I want to—"

"You'd rather *swim* than hang out with Brian Doyle?" Anya asked, cutting me off.

"It's not just that," I said. "He's cute and everything, but he's not really my type." Maybe that excuse would go over better?

Not so much. "He's *everyone's* type!" Katie shrieked. "You are so adorable. Are you just, like, supershy?"

I was the girls' pet project—always encouraged to wear their clothes, try their makeup, and, most of all, *kiss a boy for chrissakes*—and I started to feel kind of obligated to play along. They would absolutely kill me if I turned down Brian Doyle. And that's how it started, how the boy who wore well-fitting J. Crew T-shirts and loved to snowboard ended up being my boyfriend. We spent the first few months talking on the phone a lot, going to parties together, and sometimes going on "dates" to the Olive Garden and a movie. I was crossing a lot of "firsts" off of my list, like first boyfriend-kiss and first meeting of boyfriend-parents. Sometimes it seemed worth it because he was popular and others expected me to be part of a couple, but other times I wondered why I did it. My fears about losing practice time were totally realized—I was barely doing Saturday morning swims anymore—and I didn't get to see Erin half as much as I usually did.

Then one afternoon after school about three months ago, when we were hanging out at his house "doing homework," Brian tried to stick his hand down my pants. (It was actually the second time he'd tried it; the first time was in Sean Talcott's laundry room around Thanksgiving.) I pushed his hand away but he moved it back, pressing his weight on to me.

"Come on, Cera," he'd whispered. It makes my skin prickle just to think about the way his breath had left a cold wetness on my earlobe. I remember picturing myself as a bullet, shooting upstairs, out of the house, and far away from him. In that moment, I realized I just wasn't attracted to him. Where were the fireworks when his bare skin brushed against mine? The goose bumps and the heart flutters? I was pretty sure you're *not* supposed to feel something like disgust when your boyfriend touches you.

Anyway, long story short, I broke up with him. Not, like, then and there, but a couple of days later, right around Christmastime.

"It's not you," I told him—and honestly, that was mostly true. "It's just that I'm not . . . ready for this."

"But we're barely doing anything," Brian said.

"I just want to spend more time with my friends," I said. "And I don't think I want a boyfriend right now."

I divulged the half-truth to my girlfriends, a group that at that point still included Anya and Katie and Lily. "He wanted to do too much." I let them infer my meaning. He wanted to go too far, too soon. Classic after-school-special type stuff. It was the only reason I thought they'd understand.

And yeah, maybe they'd think I was a prude, even if they didn't say it out loud. So I made sure to point out that I *had* let him feel my boobs, that I *had* rubbed my hand over the outside of his pants. It wasn't like I was frigid, or anything. These girls had all gone farther than me. Lily wasn't even a virgin. But they nodded like they were sympathetic, and I thought that was that.

Until.

"Brian told Matt Kimball that he thinks you're a dyke,"

Anya told me matter-of-factly over cafeteria pizza about a week after the breakup. "He said it's a swimmer's thing," she added, invoking Cornwall legend Eva Nolan, who had graduated five years ago and went on to become a championship swimmer and a lesbian activist.

"Of course," I said, keeping my tone sardonic. "If I don't want Brian's fingers in my underwear, I must not like boys. It makes perfect sense." I congratulated myself on having such a well-honed sense of sarcasm and took another bite of pizza.

It was weird how Anya just offered a half smile in return, as though she was mulling something over. Later that afternoon, I caught her whispering something to Katie. They were both looking at me like I had something on my face.

Turned out that it wasn't an isolated rumor. Within the course of a day, more started to circulate and eventually made their way back to me.

Cera Asher doesn't even like to French kiss. Cera Asher slapped Brian Doyle when he touched her bra strap. Cera Asher likes girls. Like-likes them.

"Sorry, we're saving this seat," Katie said when I tried to join my friends the next day at lunch. Brian saw it happen from his end of the table and gave me a self-satisfied smirk. My face burned and I turned away, realizing I had been officially shunned. As I scanned the cafeteria for another place to sit, I heard someone call out to me.

"Hey, Cera," Anya said loudly as she put her tray down next to Katie. Everyone turned to look. "So, I have a question. Are you, like, *scared* of kissing boys?"

That was the worst part—that it wasn't just bitter Brian Doyle who was doing the name-calling and whisper-campaigning. It was my so-called friends too. I was still too new to have any real allies, and over the next couple of weeks my reputation plummeted.

During gym class, Katie would shoot basketballs straight toward my nose. Someone stole my biology lab from my cubby in the science wing, and I got ten points deducted because I handed in the do-over late. It was reported to Principal Noyes that I had plagiarized an AP English essay. I started eating lunch on the benches outside the auditorium, just to avoid any cafeteria incidents.

At the Valentine's Day dance—which I decided to go to because I couldn't bear to tell my parents why I was skipping it—Lily and Anya purposefully bumped into me, spilling bright red punch down the front of my dress. I called Erin while crying.

"I shouldn't have gone," I sniffled. "I don't know what to do."

"You need to say something to them, Cera," Erin said firmly. "This isn't okay."

And so, the following week, I cornered Anya alone by her locker.

"Why are you doing this to me?" I asked, willing myself not to cry. "Why did you take Brian's side over mine? We used to be friends."

She stared at me. "Because you embarrassed us," she said, fiddling with her necklace. *I* embarrassed *her*? It didn't make any sense, but before I could probe further, Katie and Lily came sashaying up behind us.

"God, Cera, could you *be* more obvious?" Lily sneered. "Anya, is she bothering you again?"

They came closer and Katie's shoulder checked mine, hard. I teetered off balance and felt the left side of my body smash into a metal locker. When I glared at Katie she shrugged.

"Sorry, Cera. I thought you were the butch kind."

Well, that didn't go as planned, I texted Erin. *Not quite the reaction I was looking for.*

Maybe you should go straight to the source, Erin suggested. *Confront Brian.*

So I tried to approach him—my asshole, rumor-spreading ex-boyfriend. Stupid, stupid idea. I caught up with him after school the next day. "Brian," I called out. He was walking in a pack with some other guys, and when he turned to face me his eyes narrowed.

"You think she's gonna beg him to take her back?" I heard one of the boys say under his breath.

"Nah—she's not into guys," another responded. My face burned.

"Can I talk to you for a second? Alone?" I jerked my head toward a doorway.

"Why don't you look for a *chick* to harass," Brian said. "You said you wanted to spend more time with girls, right?"

Bewildered and humiliated, I stood rooted to the spot as he high-fived his friends and moved down the hallway.

And so now I've reached a point where the only time I feel really safe is when I'm curled up with my cat, Zero, listening to scratchy vinyl on a secondhand record player. Or when I'm with Erin, watching TV marathons and eating Combos. When my mom and dad get home I pray they'll ignore me, because at least that means I don't have to answer any embarrassing questions about what happened to all my other friends.

* * *

That's how I got here, with one school day left before Spring Break. I couldn't wait; it would be a welcome reprieve from my hellish new life. After that, I could begin the countdown to summer, senior year, and getting the hell out of here.

I was sitting in front of my computer, listless and unable to concentrate, with a bruise on my arm because some asshole shot a goddamn BB gun at me on my way home from school. What a bunch of hicks. My attentions flickered between the flash cards on my desk and Zero, who had decided the corner of my biology textbook was his second dinner. Mostly I was just rubbing my arm and thinking about whether I could convince my parents to let me move to Canada for my last year of high school.

I was about to force myself to go back to vocab drills—

I had a Spanish exam in the morning—when a pop-up ad zoomed onto the open laptop screen on my desk. I clicked the X at the top of the window, but it refused to close.

"DEFEND YOURSELF," the advertisement blared in bright red letters. Then, in slightly smaller ones: "Do you want to feel in control? Women's self-defense classes. Five sessions. Taught by professional law enforcement officials at the Hillsdale Community Center." The price was listed in tiny font at the bottom of the ad. Eighty bucks. Was the ability to *defend myself*—I pictured myself in a Rosie the Riveter stance—worth two shifts at the video store, where I earn my pocket money? It might not have been. But the second line: *Do you want to feel in control?* I replayed the last couple of months, the hostility and humiliation. *Lesbo. Dyke. Loser.* The words rattled in my brain, and I knew the answer was yes. I did want to feel in control, thankyouverymuch.

Notwithstanding the pellet that had been shot at my back just hours ago, it wasn't like I really feared for my physical safety, per se. But there was no denying that I felt increasingly powerless, like I couldn't tread water much longer. And the idea of spending the rest of the semester, this summer, and my senior year avoiding run-ins with my tormenters . . . it made me feel closer to drowning. If it had taken just a few months to get this bad, what would happen next fall? Would I spend my senior year hiding from the people who I thought were my friends?

I rummaged through my bag for my "emergencies only"

credit card and signed up then and there. It was clear that this was getting to be an emergency.

...

The room in the community center was large, windowed, and carpeted with a flat, hard, blue-and-gray-flecked rug. When I arrived at 6:55, a group of women was already milling around a registration table and filling out paperwork. I tried not to make eye contact. I was second-guessing myself.

"Welcome," a tall, pony-tailed woman said to me, sticking out her hand assertively. "I'm Diane. Former detective. I run this thing."

I did my best to smile normally and shook her hand. "I'm Cera. Cera Asher. I signed up online? I paid already. Is there something I need to fill out? Do I need to be wearing sweat-pants?" I could hear myself rambling and tried to shut up. It didn't work. "Because I didn't know . . . I wasn't sure. . . ."

She probably got this a lot. This nervousness. Women and girls like me who felt somehow embarrassed for being there. "You're fine. We're just doing intro stuff today. You'll need athletic clothes for tomorrow's session."

Over the course of the next hour, with all of us sitting in plastic chairs that were arranged in a circle, I met the other twelve participants, including Gerrie, a pixie-haired college student who volunteered for the campus rape hotline; Ashley, a bleached-blond woman wearing too much foundation—"My ex is stalking me," she told us, picking anxiously at her nails;

Rose, a middle-aged social-worker who signed up to refresh her skills; and Madeline, a fit young cop who pulled out pictures of her two kids to show everyone.

I appeared to be something of an outlier, at least in the sense that these ladies all seemed to be really super gung-ho about the class and I was, well, skeptical. I mean, in the day and a half since I told her that I signed up, Erin had taken to calling me She-Ra, and I wasn't crazy about that moniker. Not to mention the fact that when Ashley started talking about her psycho ex and all the other women in the room started nodding sympathetically, it felt uncomfortably like group therapy or something.

"Hi," I said quietly when it was my turn. I didn't know what to say. I didn't want to tell the truth. I crossed and uncrossed my legs. "I'm just doing this for school credit," I lied. "My friends were all going away for Spring Break, but I'm . . . not. So I thought this would be a cool thing to do." I pasted on my fakest smile, hoping they'd get the hint and move on to the next victim.

But that was just the beginning.

The next night, with all of us dressed in sweats and T-shirts, Diana got to the good stuff. We left behind the touchy-feely *kumbaya* circle and started kicking and punching. Which felt great, actually. The only downside? Every time we exerted ourselves, whether we were hitting the air with our fists or chopping into it with our feet, we had to shout "NO!" at the top of our lungs. Seriously. And not, like, *No thank you* or even *No way.* It was "NO!" Like, *No chance you're getting any closer without me kicking you in the balls!*

We were a roomful of chicks, shouting "NO!" over, and over, and over. I wanted to die a little at first. It was so embarrassing.

Still, the kicking and punching felt damn good. I left that session sweating, and I smiled the whole way home.

But then, when I turned on my computer later that evening, my smile faded. Someone who went by Cornwall-Sweetheart had written me an e-mail: *"Hey Cera, Just wanted to let you know I have a video of you changing in the Cornwall locker rm. See you on Monday! xo."*

I actually gagged. I didn't know if it was true or not, nor did I know what this so-called Sweetheart intended to do with the supposed video. But my stomach fell to the floor all the same. The last thing I needed was half-naked images of me plastered around the school. I pressed my head into my hands and forced myself to breathe.

• • •

On the third night of class, Diana taught us more advanced holds and escapes. I took out my fear and frustration on the cushioned mannequins, shoving them furiously and slamming my sneakered feet into the rubber padding. With each blow, I tried to release some of my bitterness.

"Nice energy, Cera," Diana said.

At the end of the session, I was breathless and pumping

with adrenaline. I took longer than usual gathering up my belongings and I ended up being one of the last to leave. I heard the women's good-byes bouncing around the parking lot as I jogged down the concrete steps and bent over my bike to disengage the rusty padlock.

I was struggling with the lock, sweaty and annoyed because I was trying to make it home in time to meet Erin for our weekly nachos-and-reality-TV date, when I saw something shimmering in the corner of my eye. I straightened up fast and squinted into the street, which was awash with yellow-orange light. At first I couldn't pinpoint what caused the disco-ball effect in my side-vision. I was about to turn back to the lock, to the infuriating task of prying it open, when I saw them.

Wings. Moon-white, reflecting the light like ripples on a lake. Long, paper-thin, and translucent, with strong veins running through them. There were wings, like that of a dragonfly, extending out of Ashley. Their grayish silver pattern danced before me, glinting and undulating as they reached their full span. From where I stood, each wing looked to be four feet long from shoulder-blade to tip.

I blinked and blinked again. Turned around to see if anyone was behind me. If this was a reality show gotcha grab, it was brilliant. But I was alone. I turned back to see if a blond, winged woman was still standing by the bus stop on Sullivan Street. There was.

Remember what I said before about not being crazy? Yeah, well, at that second, I felt pretty damn insane.

My lips were dry and my heart was pounding. My feet no longer felt like they were firmly planted on the pavement. I considered simply backing away. But how do you back away from a lady with wings? Um, you don't. Then she whirled around and caught me staring.

"Cera!" She cried out, sounding less alarmed than surprised. "I didn't know you were still here."

"I, uh, sorry . . . ," I trailed off, sure that I was seeing things, sure that a trick was being played on me. I half expected someone to pop out of the bushes with a video camera, like they were filming the whole thing to post tonight online.

"I know this may seem strange, but you can come closer," Ashley said, moving toward me. I felt rooted to the spot, completely in shock. Slowly, I began to realize that this was no trick, at least not a trick of the eye. The woman standing before me was definitely Ashley—right down to the cakey foundation and bony elbows. And she had real, verifiable, non-costume-shop insect wings sprouting from the spot between her shoulders. She was saying something to me: "Don't be scared."

I looked over each shoulder three times. Licked my lips. "What's going on?" I asked. "Who are you?"

"Don't ask questions now," she said, her wings fluttering almost imperceptibly behind her. "I was scared too, at first. You'll understand soon enough."

Before, Ashley had often appeared pinched, fearful (much like I probably did, at school). But now her wings made her beautiful—and not just because they were stunning—

but because with them behind her, she appeared stronger, straighter, self-possessed. In charge of herself.

Her left wing leaned toward me slowly, and intuitively I reached out to graze my hand against it. Like a moth's, there was a hoary deposit of dust on its thin surface; when I took my fingers away, they felt velvety against each other.

"What . . . are those?" I asked, my voice coming out in a hoarse staccato.

"They're my defense," Ashley said, returning my eye contact. "When I want to, I can fly away." As if to punctuate her point, her wings whirred behind her.

. . .

I had so many questions. The night went by excruciatingly slowly, exacerbated by the fact that Erin bailed on our TV date to hang out with some of her ski-team friends. I was alone, trying desperately to stay composed, dying for the next and final self-defense class. Images of Ashley's wings flickered in my mind as I made my way to my shift at the video store. I rode my bike furiously along Hillsdale's suburban streets, as if the days would pass quicker if I pumped my legs harder.

About an hour before my shift was over, I heard a familiar screech echo through the video store aisle. This was, unmistakably, Anya's flirting mechanism. Imagine, if you will, a boy tickling her or threatening to throw her over his shoulder. Then imagine a fake, piercing, "*Noooooooooooooooooo*," that begs yes with every added syllable. That's the sound I heard.

Shit. I'd been mercifully free of asshole run-ins this week; some of my tormenters had gone away for Spring Break, and I studiously avoided the typical cool-crowd hangouts like the Riverside bowling alley, Barry's Ice Cream Pavilion, and the Portside beach—places I used to go all the time.

But now here they were, waltzing as a pack into Reel Them In. Anya, Lily, Katie, Sean, this jock named Mike, and—double shit—Brian. Brian Doyle. I wanted to sink into the floor and duck behind the counter, anything to avoid whatever they had planned. Instead, I pretended to be *very* interested in the Reel Them In computer system. *Chill out*, I told myself. *Maybe they really just want to rent a movie.*

No such luck.

"Hey, Cera," Lily said loudly, "could you point us toward the *lesbo* section?" Cue ridiculous explosions of laughter from the rest of the group. My boss, Pete, looked up quizzically from where he was shelving movies.

"Our GLBT section is over there," I said, pointing to the far-right corner of the store.

"Figured you would know," Anya said to more giggles. Brian's face was twisted into a simpering smile.

"Well, I do work here," I said curtly. "So yeah, I know the sections of the store."

"Gosh, there's no need to be rude," Anya said, loudly enough for Pete to hear. "I'm so sorry to have bothered you." As she sashayed past him, I heard her say something along the lines of "unhelpful." Terrific. Maybe I would get fired on top of everything else.

They took forever in the store, taking movies off the shelves and putting them back in the wrong places, opening a box of candy before paying for it, and generally making a scene. Of course they didn't rent anything.

"It was so great to see you," Katie said drippingly before they finally left. "You should really get outside some more, though. You look like the girl from *The Ring*. Have you seen that movie?" They started to leave, amidst an outburst of hysterics.

"You look like the girl from *Precious*. Have you seen that one?" I called after them. Katie whirled around, speechless. It wasn't like me to fight back. In fact, I kind of shocked myself. Katie glared at me, then she turned on her heel and left.

"If your friends aren't going to rent anything, they can't come in here," Pete said gruffly once they'd gone. "I don't want them aggravating the other customers."

"They're not my . . ." I gave up halfway through. "Sorry about that, Pete. Won't happen again."

• • •

"I hear our veil of secrecy has been lifted," Diane said with a knowing smile at the start of class that night. I'd gotten there early, practically been bouncing in my seat waiting for the rest of the group to arrive. I was dying to see Ashley again and find out what the hell was going on. Now, every head in the room swiveled to face me. Diana asked the group: "Should we do a demonstration for Cera?"

My palms started to sweat and I felt a little like I was on a boat, bobbing up and down over huge swells. I felt a tingling in my feet, like they were waking up from having fallen asleep. I waited. I knew I was at the edge of something big.

One by one, the women stood up. Here is what I saw:

First there was Gerrie. I watched her lift her arms like she was about to start a yoga session. "Cover your ears," she warned. Then she emitted a brief, ear-shattering scream that made the rest of us drop to the floor, grimacing. I looked around wildly. What the hell was happening? But everyone else seemed unconcerned. In fact, they looked impressed.

Then Rose stood up, squeezed her eyes shut and clenched her fists, and suddenly her skin appeared to vibrate slightly. When the vibration ceased, Rose's body was covered in armored plates, making her look like a cross between a woman and an armadillo. My mouth hung agape.

When Madeline arose from her seat, needles were already emerging from what looked like goose bumps on her arms and legs. Once they were fully in place, she lifted her leg, pointed her toes toward the far wall, and yelled, "Hah!" As she did, a fistful of needles shot out of her body, puncturing the wall and staying there, quivering. Like arrows. "Jesus hotdamn," I whispered to no one in particular.

One by one, they revealed their talents. There were feathers, gills, springs implanted into feet. Diane, her auburn hair pulled back from her face, watched with a satisfied expression. She was the last to transform. I saw her feline features become more angular and defined, and watched as pointed, curved claws sprung from her fingertips. "I can see in the dark, too," she added proudly.

"You're . . . superheroes," I said, trying to fit these women into whatever categorization I could think of.

There was a murmur of amusement.

"Kind of," Diane said, approaching me. I took a step backward, and she retracted her claws. "Let's check back in, ladies," she said, and I saw the women start to transform back into their normal—allegedly normal—selves.

"How . . . how did you do that?" I stuttered, not directing the question at anyone in particular. "Who *are* you?"

"You're here to learn how to defend yourself," Diane said, repeating the words from the advertisement. "You're here because you deserve the chance to control your own destiny."

"Only certain people can see that ad," Rose piped in. "You newbies saw it because you needed it."

I glanced around to Gerrie, Madeline, Ashley. "So this is new to you, too?" They nodded, and Madeline offered: "But it happened to us almost immediately, like after the first night. I got my quills two days ago."

"Do you *use* these powers?" I asked, incredulously. "I mean, you'd think people would know that we have a Catwoman in Hillside. . . ."

"We use them," Ruth said. "We do. Once you have a power like this, you're always using it. Just not . . . overtly."

"These skills aren't for showing off," Diana added. "In fact, it's practically impossible to flaunt them."

"So you don't wear your porcupine suit to your kids' show-and-tell day, I get that," I said, motioning to Madeline. "But how about you, Ashley—can your ex see your wings?"

She cocked her head and stared at me, weighing her response. "I think he can see that something is different," she said. "I'm not the same as I used to be."

The others nodded. There seemed to be some consensus, and I was starting to understand.

And then, the scariest and most exciting question of them all: "Am I like you?" I looked down at my arms, my legs, half expecting to see scales or fur or lightning bolts. "Do I have . . . something?"

"Of course you do," Diana said as if it was the most obvious thing in the world that yes, I had some type of nascent magical power. "You wouldn't have seen the ad if you didn't. But it'll come out on its own. We don't rush these things. Usually our strength has emerged by the final sessions, but there are exceptions. You may be one of them."

She was right. Nothing special emerged that night, or by the final class. And that concluded She-Ra's five-session self-defense course.

· · ·

On the Sunday before Spring Break ended, I agreed, uncharacteristically, to go bowling with Erin at the Riverside lanes. The alley was mercifully empty, which left me confident enough to suggest we ride our bikes to Barry's for milk shakes. Erin was taken aback, but she jumped at the chance. We had a dessert before dinner ritual, and we hadn't gotten to indulge our ice-cream cravings—or anything that involved emerging from my house—over the last couple of months.

When we rolled up to the shack, I saw Brian and Matt sitting on the hood of Brian's car. For a moment, I stiffened. But my anxiety lasted for only a second. I didn't ask Erin to leave, and as we ordered, I didn't feel the usual eyes burning into the back of my head. I just pretended the boys weren't there, even when they tried to bait me.

"Hey, Cera, is that your girlfriend?" I heard Matt call out from across the parking lot.

I gave him the finger over my shoulder.

Once sufficiently full on milk shake, we headed back to my place, where we ordered spring rolls and Pad Thai while watching old episodes of *Friends* on DVD. I was dying to tell Erin about the women and their defenses, but I knew I couldn't. At least not yet. *Oh, so guess what? I may have some sort of superpower. . . .* Yeah. Not so much. She'd be having secret meetings with the guidance counselor—if not the nearest mental institution—by noon tomorrow.

But then, out of the blue, she asked, "What's up with you?" I snapped my head in her direction. Was I being that obvious? Or worse: was I transforming right in front of her? I stole a look down at my hands and body. All clear. Just plain old Cera Asher.

"Nothing's up," I answered, moving the noodles around on

my plate. A laugh track rang in the background. "I'm fine."

"I know," Erin said. "That's kind of why I'm asking. I saw Brian and that cretin friend of his at Barry's. But you didn't even seem to care. You seem calmer. Calmer than usual."

Huh. I didn't get that one a lot. "Really? I dunno . . . I guess I do feel kind of a bit more at ease."

"I haven't seen you look over your shoulder once all day." Erin whirled a strand of auburn hair around her finger. "It's been like hanging out with someone who isn't a paranoid delusional! Quite a change of pace."

I threw a balled-up napkin at her. "Thanks, babe. What a compliment." I shrugged. "I guess I'm not that worried about tomorrow. I mean, whatever happens, happens. I really don't want Brian and Anya and the rest of those idiots ruining the rest of the year." *Or the rest of my life, for that matter.*

Erin nodded, her eyebrows raised so high that they were, like, in the middle of her forehead. "Totally," she said. "I mean, I agree completely. It's just a bit of a one eighty."

"Well, my other strategy wasn't really working for me," I said wryly. "By which I mean not at all."

"I won't argue with that," Erin said. She crawled over the couch to where I was sitting and hugged me, hard. "This is awesome, Cee. Just let it roll off your back."

• • •

Erin passed out in a food coma around ten o'clock, but I wasn't the slightest bit tired. I covered her with an afghan on the couch, turned off the light in the den, and went upstairs to take a shower.

She was right—I felt serene, like the feeling I get when I'm coasting down a hill on my bike, kind of carried by the breeze.

I lingered in the shower, letting the warm water run over me, soaping up my hair twice, shaving my legs. I was finishing up my right calf when I felt a sharp prickling in my back, like something was uncoiling between my shoulders. The razor clattered to the tile floor as I stood up, twisting and craning my neck to see behind me. My pulse quickened at what I saw.

Two tiny dark things, springing swiftly and painlessly from my back. I saw they would soon be too large for the shower enclosure. I stepped out onto the bathroom floor, still dripping, and gazed into the mirror.

Like Ashley, I had wings, but that's where the similarities ended. While hers had whirred anxiously, mine fanned out majestically. They were wide, long, and muscular—I could see the tight tissue working between the tendons, strong and flexible. They were black and shiny, like those of the diving cormorants we'd seen in the Everglades on last year's family vacation. I stood perfectly still, trying to isolate the muscles in my back that manipulated them. With great concentration, I discovered that I could fold my wings in and spread them out. The movements were jerky at first, but at least I knew I was in control. I watched myself in the mirror, in awe of my visage.

The rest of my body was covered in a soft down, and off of

that, the water from my shower was rolling. Beads formed atop the fluttery feathers, and if I shook from side to side, water sprayed from my body. *Like water off a duck's back*, I said to myself, almost laughing at the perfection of it all.

The next step was obvious. I mean, new wings beg for only one thing, right? To be flown? And so I *obviously* had to put on clothes, before I gave the neighbors the weirdest show they'd ever seen. I shimmied into a strapless dress —something loose and flowing that wouldn't crimp my feathers—and then I crept outside, being careful to skip the third stair, which creaked. What would I say if Erin or my parents woke up? *Oh, just trying out an early Halloween costume!* Thank god everyone I know sleeps like they're on sedatives.

Outside on the lawn, I allowed my wings to unfurl to their full span. I felt powerful and otherworldly. And also confused. How do you start to fly if you've never done it before? They should put that on the SAT. I tried to jump and flap my wings at the same time. No go. I tried getting a running start. Ended up falling face first onto my mom's geranium planter. Oops. Then I tried pumping my wings until I was kind of hovering above the ground, and *then* propelling myself upward. It worked. I zoomed into the dark sky, leveling off around the tree tops. Buoyed by exhilaration, wind, and my new, working parts, I flew. Down my street. Past the bike path. Along my route to school. Everything looked miniature from up there.

When I soared above Cornwall High, my mind swam with visions of Brian slobbering on my neck, my former friends pointing at me from their lunch tables, my teammates shying away from me in the locker room. I felt my body tense up; my wings came together in a narrower, more aerodynamic fashion. I started speeding downward, like I was going to dive-bomb the school. I sliced through the air, and I didn't even feel like I was falling. As I pitched toward the ground, I heard myself shouting, at the top of my lungs, "NO!" Over and over. "NO!"

And just before I smashed into the building, I made a smooth arc and began to climb back into the sky, flapping my wings, thrusting myself upward and above it all.

Sweet Sixteen

BY ZETTA ELLIOTT

"OH! OH! I have to go! I have to go!"

This bitch is gettin' on my *last—fuckin'—nerve*. I been stuck in here all day with these hyper, snot-face brats—it's like fuckin' romper room! These kids are laughin' and playin' and tearin' around like this is some kind of party. Like they're at Chuck E. Cheese and all those social workers out there are waiters about to bring in the pizza. I want to snatch them up and yell, "YOU'RE IN CUSTODY, STUPID!" But then they'd start whinin' and cryin'—and one of 'em already pissed his pants. I can smell it. Goddamn! And this white bitch— little Miss Mary Poppins—she's been playin' nanny to all the rug rats, but the social worker just took the last one away. They always take the little kids first. People show up for little kids.

Now it's just me and this whitegirl, and I can tell she ain't never been in custody before—she's freakin' out and I swear, if that bitch don't calm the fuck down, I'm a go upside her head with that stupid plastic dollhouse over there. *After* I finish my nails. They call this color "Galaxy Moon" but it looks just like regular old silver to me. When I get home I'll add a coat of glitter. That'll make it pop. Chynna says find somethin' to think about while you work. I focus on my nails.

"Oh . . . I have to go!"

Whitegirl's pacin' up and down, mumblin' to herself. Except the room's a mess so every few steps she has to stop and bend down to pick up a toy or book or stuffed animal. She must be some kind of maid 'cause she looks like she's used to cleanin' up after other folks. Her arms are full of toys and she's tryin' to pick up even more, but then she trips on a little dump truck and lands on her ass. I laugh out loud, but then this rubber ball hits the floor, bounces straight at me, and *almost* knocks the bottle of nail polish right out my hand.

I give her a look that says, "Don't fuck with me, bitch." She don't apologize, but she sure looks scared! She picks herself up and goes over to the far side of the room. I smile to myself and keep blowin' on my nails. I still got it. It's been a while, but I still get respect.

Few minutes go by and this whitegirl starts moanin' and pacin' again, talkin' 'bout how she gotta go—like I ain't got someplace to be my own damn self. Finally I get sick of hearin' her mess and say, "Chill, girl! You ain't goin' nowhere till that lady comes back and calls your name." I raise my voice a little so whoever's behind that two-way mirror can hear me. "Bitch took my phone!" At least I still got my purse.

"But I must go! I must! My baby needs me. . . ."

Baby? I stop blowing on my nails and take a good look at this whitegirl. I guess she's about my age, but she's dressed like she just stepped out of a time machine. She's wearin' this big baggy dress that's got long sleeves and buttons all the way up to the top of her neck. And it's pink—like the color of chewed-out bubble gum. She got these ugly-ass shoes on, too—clunky brown loafers that you almost can't see 'cause her dress is so damn long. She looks like Cinderella before she met her fairy godmother. "YOU got a baby?"

Whitegirl ignores me and just keeps on fussin'. "She needs me—my baby needs me. . . ."

I watch as her long braid swings back and forth while she paces. I don't know why, but I decide to talk to her. Nothin' else to do in here. "Where you from, girl? *Little House on the Prairie?* No offense, or nothin', but you don't look like *that* kinda girl."

"What kind of girl?"

"The kinda girl who gets busy AND gets pregnant. You look more like a nun or somethin' in that corny dress. You know—uptight. Goody Two-Shoes."

"I am NOT uptight! I'm upset! They took my baby!"

I take my compact out of my purse and flip it open. Ain't nobody I'm tryin' to impress up in here, but I still want to look my best. The cops hauled me outta the house in the middle of the night. Lucky for me I was in between customers and had my favorite little black dress on. Tarell bought it for Chynna just last month, but he says it looks better on me. Every time I wear it, I think of the look on that bitch's face when Tarell told her to shut up and go put on somethin' else. Chynna thinks she's Tarell's favorite. I wonder if he's bailed her out yet.

"Damn, girl—relax! You're gonna wear a hole in the carpet." I put just enough edge in my voice so she knows that's an order and not a suggestion.

The whitegirl stands still but keeps up with her sob story. "They lied—they lied to me!"

I click the compact shut and look at Laura Ingalls. "Who lied to you?"

"The social workers—the police. They tricked me! I did everything they said, but they still took my baby away. . . ."

Next thing I know, this whitegirl starts to *bawl*. She catches me smilin' and turns away so I can't see what a mess she is. I roll my eyes, then feel kinda bad for the newbie. That's what Chynna calls me, uppity bitch. She's only a coupla years older than me, but Chynna treats me like I'm a child. I look at this whitegirl and think maybe she could use a little help right about now. So I pull up my legs to make space for her on the tacky, stained sofa. I move my purse onto my lap and pat the seat loud enough for her to hear. "Come on. Sit down 'fore you fall down."

She glances at the sofa, then at me. She hesitates, then accepts the offer and sits down, still snifflin'. I dig a tissue outta my purse and hand it to her. She waits a second, then takes it and blows her nose.

"So. Is it a girl or a boy?"

She panics. "What?"

Maybe she's slow. Maybe that's why she's dressed like a reject. "Your baby!"

Whitegirl smiles softly and starts to rock back and forth. "A girl," she says in this real soft voice. "Her name's Abigail."

Abigail? I pity the kid already. My mom gave me a crappy name, too—Verline. First thing I did when I left home was change my name. I got five or six now. A girl needs a few stage names in my line of work. I look at this whitegirl and wonder if she's got a name as ugly as her baby's. "Who's the daddy?"

She hangs her head and mumbles, "My only interest right now is my child."

"In other words, you don't know who the daddy is."

"Of course, I do!"

"So what's his name?"

She clamps her mouth shut like she don't wanna say.

"Uh huh. That's what I thought. Don't sweat it—ain't no big deal. A trick's a trick, right?"

Whitegirl turns to face me then and starts to nod. "Yes—they tricked me!"

I sigh. I've definitely been there before. "Happens all the time. Trick says he got a rubber on, but 'less you wrapped his dick up yourself, you're just rollin' the dice. By the time the deal's done, you could have AIDS, gonorrhea, or even worse—a kid up inside of you!"

She sputters and stands up. "A—rubber . . . ?" she says, her mouth wide open like she's shocked.

I look up and see her face has gone from pasty to pink. Even her ears are red! "Yeah. A rubber. You know—a condom?" I roll my eyes and sigh. "You put it on a trick's dick so you don't catch nothin' nasty—and so you don't get pregnant! That's Sex Ed 101, girl. Where you been?"

Whitegirl picks up a one-eyed doll off the floor. She smoothes down what's left of its blond hair and looks up at the ceiling. "Man's seed must be spilled so the tribe may thrive and prosper. It's a sin to defy God's will."

I look at the ceiling to see what she's gawking at. Ain't nothin' there. "God? What the hell's he got to do with it?"

She leans in close to me and whispers, "What a man and a woman do in bed is . . . sacred!"

I cross my legs and fold my arms across my chest. This pushes my boobs up and that makes her look away. "Oh yeah? How 'bout what they do on the floor—or up against a wall— or in the backseat of a car? Is that sacred, too?"

She twirls her fingers in the doll's stringy hair. "Well— uh—so long as the union has been blessed by the Prophet. . . ."

"Profit? Now you're talkin' sense. 'It's all about the almighty dollar.' That's what Tarell says, anyhow."

She sits back down and holds the doll in her arms like it's a real baby. "Who's Tarell?"

"Tarell—he's like . . . well, it's kinda complicated." I wait to see how curious she really is, but this whitegirl looks like she's been raised to mind her own business, so I just spill the beans. "Okay, so Tarell's like my boss, but he also takes care of me. I mean, I live with him in this big ol' house out in the burbs, and he buys me clothes, and he takes me to get my hair and nails done . . . stuff like that. And if any punk messes with me, Tarell kicks his ass."

"So . . . Tarell's your husband."

I bust out laughing. "Hell no!"

"He's your father?"

I snort like a pig when she says that. My *father*?

Whitegirl frowns and tries again. "Your brother?"

"Girl, you somethin' else. I told you, I WORK for Tarell."

"So he's your . . . uncle?"

I stare at her. She really is slow. I glance at the two-way mirror, then hiss, "Tarell's my pimp!"

The whitegirl glances at the mirror as well, and nods. She inches closer and whispers, "What's a pimp?"

I stare at her until I realize she's for real. "Girl, where you from?"

She shifts back over to her side of the couch and starts fussing with the doll. "Upstate," she says in her mousy voice.

"Hunh. You go to school 'upstate'?"

She shakes her head. "I was homeschooled by my mama."

I just suck my teeth at that. "Seems like your mama forgot to teach you a thing or two 'bout men."

That turns her cheeks pink—don't nobody like it when you talk about their mama. "My mother taught me how to be a faithful wife."

"Wife? You're MARRIED?"

Suddenly the whitegirl panics and tries to clamp her hand over my mouth. "Sssshhhh! I wasn't supposed to say that."

I fling her hand away and check to make sure my lip gloss

ain't all messed up. "How old are you?"

She looks over her shoulder like this is top secret information. "Sixteen."

Same age as me. "And how long you been married?"

She sits up tall now like she's proud to be somebody's wife. "Our union was blessed three years ago." Whitegirl pulls a chain out of her collar and shows me a thin gold band. No diamond— just a plain ring. No wonder she keeps it hidden inside her dress. I would too if my husband bought me some tacky old ring like that! "Damn," I say, shaking my head.

She beams at me, then realizes I ain't exactly impressed. "Where I'm from," she says, "it's customary for a girl to wed once God has touched her . . . inside. You know, once she gets her . . . 'monthly friend.'"

Nothin' much surprises me, but this shit's freakin' me out. "Lemme get this straight. You're tellin' me that 'upstate,' girls get married as soon as they get their period?"

She goes back to her "it's a secret" voice. "But only if the Prophet has selected a suitable husband for them."

"'The prophet'? What, like Moses and the Ten Commandments?"

She nods excitedly. "The Prophet is the holiest of men and the leader of our tribe."

"And he tells you who to marry? That's fucked up. If I gotta get hitched, I'm a pick my own damn husband!"

Now it's her turn to look shocked. "Women aren't meant to question the will of God!"

I'm starting to feel like I'm in church or talkin' to a missionary or somethin'. "What you keep bringin' up God for? You just said your holy 'prophet' was the one callin' the shots."

"Yes, but only the Prophet knows God's will for us, His children."

I just shake my head. This whitegirl definitely has some screws loose. "So who'd 'the prophet' pick for you to marry?"

Her face turns pink again and she looks away. "A good man. An honorable man."

"Honorable, huh? So where's he at?" I smile a little as she bites her lip and keeps her eyes away from mine. I remember when I first moved in with Tarell and Chynna figured it was her job to school me on life. "Lemme break some things down for you, Homespun. Men . . . are dogs. They eat all kinds of crap, sleep half the day, piss on every pole, and shit all over the place. They're dirty, dumb, and covered with fleas. But worst of all, they'll try and fuck anythin' that moves—it don't have to look good, just smell a little funky and there they go, howlin' and humpin' and pantin'. Men are dogs. And dogs . . . are disgusting."

Her eyes get so wide they take up half of her face. "Back home, we have dogs—we keep them as pets. They're loyal, loving creatures!"

"That's 'cause you TRAINED 'em to be that way. Your dogs may not shit in the house, but deep down they're no different than all the other stray mutts. A dog may wear a collar 'round his neck—or a ring on his finger—but at the end of the day, girl, ALL dogs are WILD." I pause to let my words sink in. "Shit. Your man's probably sniffin' 'round some other bitch right now. . . ."

That strikes a nerve. Whitegirl jumps up like she's ready to fight for her man. The doll she was holding on her lap drops to the floor. "You don't know what you're talking about!"

"Really? I think I been around the block a few more times 'n you. . . ."

"That may be. But the Bible says the righteous man shall be rewarded with many wives. It's not a sin! It's not!"

"Many wives? What the hell you talkin' 'bout?"

She starts pacin' again, her fingers clawin' at her neck like she's tryin' to get at the ring hidden under her ugly dress. Finally she thinks of a comeback. I know it's gonna be weak. "If all men are dogs, what about Tarell?"

"What about him?" I say calmly. I never lose *my* cool.

"You said he takes good care of you. Is he a dog?"

I just shrug. "Like I said, Homespun. I WORK for Tarell. It's in his interest to take care of me and keep me lookin' good. He's got to protect his investment."

She don't know what to say to that. She shifts from foot to foot and asks, "What exactly do you DO for Tarell?"

I cut my eyes at her and try to figure out whether or not she can handle the truth. Sometimes folks play dumb just to get all up in your business. "He's my pimp. I'm his 'ho."

"'Hoe'?"

"Yeah, 'ho—'*ho*!" She scrunches her eyebrows together

like she's trying real hard to understand. Stupid people get on my nerves. "WHORE. Get it? Tarell's my pimp, and I'm his whore. One of 'em, anyway."

"Does Tarell have many . . . hoes?"

"Five of us are regulars. The others come and go."

"And men—pay you to . . . to . . ."

"Suck 'n fuck." I say it straight, with no shame, and watch her prissy face burn up again. "That's right. I get paid to do what you do for free. 'Cept my customers don't pay me, they pay Tarell. I get to keep my tips, though."

"But . . . if you do all the—work—why does Tarell get all the money?"

That's a question it don't pay to ask. It's like they say, "Pimps up, 'hos down." I dig in my purse for a tube of mascara and take my time thinkin' up an explanation. "Overhead, Homespun. That's the cost of doin' business on your back. Tarell breaks me off a little change now and then, but it's not like I need a whole lotta dough. I mean, I don't pay rent or nothin'. I get three meals a day, and there's always a little dust on hand if I need to clear my head." I put the mascara away and check the mirror for clumps. "Shit. 'Fore I met Tarell, I was sleepin' on the street."

"The street?! But . . . why? What about your family?"

"What about 'em?"

"Did they know where you were?"

"My mama's the one put me out! Said I was 'too fast.' Hunh. Couldn't move fast enough to keep away from her grab-ass boyfriend. Nigga thought he could get two for the price of one. . . ."

"Your own mother turned you out of the house?"

I feel my cheeks get hot but know she can't see what I'm feeling inside. Black don't crack, and it also don't advertise. "I guess shit like that don't happen 'upstate,' huh?"

"Well . . . it did happen once. Polly Jenner, she wouldn't submit to her initiation, so the Prophet made her leave."

"Initiation? What's that?"

"Once a girl has been touched by God, the Prophet takes her to the holy bed inside the temple and he—he—"

"Oh, I get it. Tarell did the same thing to me. He breaks you in, nice and easy, so you ain't too scared or too tight. So, this Polly girl—she wouldn't give it up, huh? And 'cause of that, she had to leave home?"

"Polly was driven out of the tribe. She left us with nothing more than the clothes on her back. That was five years ago, and no one has seen her since." Whitegirl stops and holds her hand over her heart. "She was my best friend."

I wanna say, *Yeah, right. If she was your best friend, she woulda taken you with her instead of leavin' you behind.* Instead I give her the once over and say, "Maybe your friend's at the mall buyin' herself some new clothes. All a y'all dress like that?"

She smoothes out her ugly dress but tries to act all righteous. "Yes. Vanity is a sin! Women ought not to tempt men with their beauty. . . ."

"I'm tellin' you, Homespun—dogs don't care how you look."

"Then why do you wear so much makeup?"

I wet my middle finger and slick my eyebrows. Be time for another waxin' 'fore too long. "I do this for ME—'cause it makes ME feel good. Shit. I'm fine as hell! Don't need no trick to tell me that." I take a good hard look at this whitegirl. I stare so long and so hard that she blushes and turns away. "You could look cute, too, if you fixed yourself up."

"Really?" She touches her drab hair and plain face, then turns to look in the two-way glass.

"Sure. You just need to ditch that dress, maybe cut your hair and add some highlights—and definitely get your eyebrows done."

She looks at me then in my slinky black dress, and I *know* she wishes she could look fine like me. I pretend not to notice, though. She comes over real casual like but I just keep on admiring the view in my compact mirror. I'm so busy tryin' not to notice her that I don't see her reachin' for the gold in my ear. I pull back and slap her hand away. "What the hell?"

She pulls back and holds her hand close to her chest so it don't reach out and touch me again. "Sorry," she says softly.

I don't know why, but I'm startin' to feel sorry for this girl. "Lemme guess—'the prophet' don't allow no jewelry neither." She shakes her head, clearly disappointed. I suck my teeth and proudly finger the gold in my ears. "You got outhouses up there? I saw on TV once how some folks don't have cars or electricity or toilets or nothin.'"

Her chin goes up when I say that, and she gets all huffy

with me. "Our compound has every modern amenity. We have indoor plumbing, cars, microwaves. . . ."

"You got any computers up there?"

She shakes her head. "Only the Prophet."

"So you never been on the Internet?" She shakes her head, not so high and mighty now. "How 'bout TV? You got cable?"

She shakes her head again. "We watch DVDs sometimes—but only those which the Prophet has approved."

"That prophet's got you locked down, girl. 'Upstate' sounds like prison to me."

"Our simple life frees us from temptation. In our tribe, we devote ourselves to serving God and loving one another."

"Uh huh. I bet there's a whole lotta lovin' goin' on up there. Folks must be bored outta their minds!"

"There's no time to get bored. Caring for children is a full-time job."

"Yeah, but you only got one kid to take care of." She frowns and puts her hand over her belly but says nothin'. "Know what I think? I think you need to break outta that 'tribe.'"

Whitegirl bites her lip and turns back to the two-way mirror. She pulls her long braid over her shoulder and starts to set her hair free. I watch her for a second, then stand up and go over to stand beside her. I don't know why, but I help her spread out her long hair, and then I show her how to arrange it so she looks sixteen and not sixty. "See? It looks good, right?"

She nods and smiles at her image in the mirror. Then she turns and smiles at me. I can't remember the last time someone smiled at me like that—someone my own age, someone who hasn't just paid me to do something nasty for them. I want to smile back, but instead I take up my purse and fish out some lip gloss. "Hold still," I say. The whitegirl stands beside me like a statue while I apply the gloss. "Now pout. Good. Now do this." I roll my lips together and make a smacking sound. She tries to mimic me, then giggles and touches her lips. We look at each other in the two-way glass. "You're a hottie, girl! All you need now is a divorce."

She stares at her reflection, but after a few seconds her smile starts to fade. "Is Tarell coming to get you?"

I flop back onto the sofa. "Naw. I gotta wait till my aunt shows up."

"Are you going to live with her now?"

"Hell, no! But CPS will only release you to a family member. Tarell slips my aunt a few bills, and she bails me out. Then I go back to work." I shrug. "Least that's what happened last time. Who's comin' for you?"

This gets her going again. She starts wringin' her hands and pacin' 'round the room, whimperin' like a lost puppy. "Aw, hell . . . here we go again. Homespun—RELAX! I bet your mama's saddlin' up her horse to head down here right now."

She freezes and bites her lip. Then she turns to face me and says, "My mama's not coming for me."

"How come?"

With shaking hands she starts rebraiding her loose hair. "No one's coming for me."

So much for tryin' to help a sister out. Soon as she wipes the lip gloss off with the back of her hand, she's back to lookin' homely again. "You mean nobody in your whole entire 'tribe' is goin' to bail you outta here?"

She shakes her head and pulls at her fingers. "They can't."

"Why the hell not?"

"Because . . . they're in custody, too." She turns away, ashamed.

I stare at her, not sure I understand what she means. "ALL of 'em?"

"There was a raid . . . someone called the police . . . they said the children were being abused. . . ."

"Oh, I know all about that. Nosy fuckin' neighbors—they need to mind their own damn business! Half the time it's some trick's dumb wife, callin' the police when she oughta be takin' notes. He wouldn't be comin' to us if she knew how to keep him happy. . . ."

I stop when I realize that the whitegirl is quietly sobbing. Her arms are wrapped around her belly, and she's doubled over as if she's in pain. "Hey—you all right?" I glance at the two-way mirror, and shift to the edge of the sofa. Suddenly she starts to wail.

"You better quit wailin' like that or they gonna come in here and give you somethin' to make you quiet. And trust me—you don't want that." She tones it down a bit but keeps on rockin' and moanin'. I glance at the mirror again, then get up and go over to her. I put a hand on her shoulder and shake her a bit. "Come on, now. Pull yourself together. You can't be cryin' and fussin' like this—think about your little girl!"

That gets her attention. "You gotta be strong—for her. Right?" The whitegirl wipes her nose with her sleeve and nods at me. She quiets down, and I lead her back over to the sofa. She clutches the doll to her chest and rocks it back and forth.

"Don't worry—they gonna give your little girl back. They got to. It's not like you was abusin' her or nothin.'" I cut my eyes at her. *"Right?"*

"No, no—I'd never hurt my baby! I wanted to save her—I had to save her from . . ."

"From what?"

She hangs her head and I have to lean in close to hear what she's sayin'. "I had to save Abigail from all the things that happened to me. The Prophet, he . . . he . . ." She stops and looks straight into my eyes.

"I hear you," I say, even though she hasn't actually said the words. "It's always the high and mighty who turn out to be the biggest freaks. Huh. You should see my customers—politicians, preachers, even cops sometimes." She's sobbin' again, so I wait a minute for her to calm down. "It was you who called the police, wasn't it?"

She's shakin' all over now but still manages to nod. "Polly said . . . Polly said it was the only way. . . ."

So maybe this Polly really is a good friend. "Well, hell. A girl's gotta do what a girl's gotta do." I push up close so that our shoulders are touching. "So. You can't go back upstate. What you gonna do?"

She sniffles, shrugs, then grows still. "You said Tarell has a big house?"

"Yeah. So what?"

"And some of the—girls—who work for Tarell. They're just . . . temporary?"

I frown and wonder where she's goin' with this. "Yeah . . ."

"You think Tarell would let me work for him?"

I look at this mousy whitegirl and think she must be playin' around. But she looks at me with those puppy dog eyes and I realize she's for real. "You?" I crack up laughin' and she turns pink again, so I try to explain myself. "It's just that—well—you don't got a lotta experience with men, bein' married 'n all. . . . plus, Tarell don't want no babies at his place. Bad for business, he says." Ask Chynna.

She grabs my arm and pleads with me. "Abigail's a good baby—she's real quiet and almost never cries! Plus, I—I know how to please a man. . . ."

I seriously doubt that, but she swears it's true.

"My husband always said I was his favorite wife! He spent more nights with me than any of my cowives."

"Well . . . I didn't know much when I was startin' out. . . . Tarell had the other girls show me what to do, and I had to watch hours and hours of porn. I guess you never seen no porn, huh?"

"What is it?"

"Oh, right—no cable or Internet upstate. Porn's like dirty pictures or movies where folks have kinky sex. Most of it ain't real. It's just actors moanin' and groanin' and fakin' it, but porn helps some folks get off."

She slowly starts to nod. "I think I did see porn—once."

"Really?"

"The Prophet . . . sometimes he had us watch movies before . . . before we were initiated."

"Damn. Sounds like your 'prophet' was more like a pervert."

She blushes but don't try to correct me. Instead she tries to make a case for workin' for Tarell. "I'm a quick learner and a hard worker, plus I already know how to run a big houschold. I can cook, and clean . . . and I can sew!"

I *had* to laugh at that. "Tarell ain't gonna want none o' us wearin' your kinda clothes!"

She looks over at my spandex dress and tries again. "I don't need a pattern—you just draw what you want, or show me a picture, and I can make it! Honest, I can!"

"Even lingerie? Skimpy, see-through stuff with lace?" She nods eagerly and for the first time I start to take this idea seriously. "Tarell could make a lotta dough off a snow bunny like you." And there might be somethin' in it for me if I bring her on board and make it work. Not even Chynna could top that! And I wouldn't be the newbie no more.

"Snow bunny?"

"Tricks'll pay more for a white girl like you." She ain't blond, but we can take care of that. Whitegirl nods like she understands, but I know this girl is clueless. It'd be up to me to train her and keep her from runnin' away. "You still got a kid, Homespun. Unless . . ."

"Yes?"

"Unless you decide to . . . give the baby up." She jumps up so fast that the doll she's been holdin' falls to the ground. She wraps her arms around her belly and makes a sad, desperate sound. I stand up and try to make her see sense. "She's probably already in foster care. You're young—you're in trouble. You don't wanna raise your kid in a whorehouse."

The whitegirl seems to disintegrate. "What am I going to do?"

We're both surprised when the door opens and a social worker enters holding a clipboard. This one's a lot older than the others and looks like she's about ready to retire. She gives us a fake smile and reads a name off her clipboard.

"Hester? We're ready for you now."

I look at the whitegirl, surprised by her name. "I guess that's you, huh?" She nods, takes a deep breath, and gets ready to leave. I glance at the social worker and then suddenly pull Hester back and whisper, "Don't tell 'em nothin.'"

"What?"

"You in the system?"

"System?"

I shake her to make her listen. "You been arrested before?"

"No!"

"Then they don't got your fingerprints on file. No fingerprints, no identity—no identity, no past. Get it? You're brand new! You can be anyone you wanna be. . . ."

I look straight at her and Hester nods but I can tell she don't really understand. She drifts toward the social worker who's sighin' and tappin' the clipboard with her pen.

"Come along, dear."

Hester tries to leave, but I pull her close again and try to give her somethin' that'll help her survive out there. "They probably gonna put you in a group home. No big deal—you be outta there in no time! When you get out, if you still lookin' for a job, come to 589 Walnut Lane—got that? 589 Walnut Lane."

"Hester—"

"She's comin', bitch, relax!"

The social worker presses her lips together and inches a bit closer to the door. I can tell by the look on her face that she's afraid of me. I look at Hester and see that she's kinda scared, too. And here I am tryin' to help her! "589 Walnut Lane," I whisper one last time. Hester nods and this time I let her go when she tries to pull away from me. The social worker opens the door and waits for Hester to join her. Just as she's about to be escorted out of the waiting room, I call her back.

"Homespun—hold up!" I hastily remove one pair of gold hoops from my ears and press them into Hester's hand. "You can do what you want now, right? You're free."

She smiles faintly but gives just a weak nod. Her lips say "thank you" but no sound comes outta her mouth. Then the social worker guides her outta the room and closes the door. I just stand there for a minute. I look around this crappy room, full of toys and pee smell and me. I head back over to the sofa, stooping to pick up the old ratty doll Hester had been clutching. I sink onto the sofa and look at the doll. Its one glassy blue eye winks at me. I ain't got time for dolls no more. I toss it on the floor with all the other broken toys and reach for my purse. I reapply my lip gloss and examine my face in the compact mirror. But right now it's showing me something I don't wanna see, so I shut the compact with a soft click. Then I reach down for the doll, wrap my arms around it, and try hard not to cry.

Like Kicking a Fence

BY KATE ELLISON

THE BLOOD SPRAYING out of Norman's nose is thick and deep red, clotting like grape jelly beneath his septum. It sprays as Jean-Carlos kicks and kicks, kicks harder because it's spraying now like an open hydrant along his new jeans—the nicest pair he owns—which fall halfway down his boxer shorts and cost him zilch because he stole them from Gadzooks. It was all on a dare, and not even a Double-Dare, but Jean-Carlos is valorous and does not shirk from dares, no matter what kind.

The blood sprays onto Norman's jeans, too. Norman's nice, clean, pressed jeans with mustard-colored stitching along the seams and cuffs. The sight of them—dirtied-up now, untidily blood-smattered—makes Jean-Carlos giddy and light-headed, like how it feels to wake up to a snow day.

Norman with his new jeans and wonderful, little lunches. His mother packs him sandwiches in fancy food-preserving bags and writes him notes that say, *Normy: have a nice day, honey, you're so smart and so good and Dad and I love you so much.* Jean-Carlos knows this because he takes Norman's lunch sometimes when he doesn't have his own. Jean-Carlos's mother used to pack him Thanksgiving-sized lunches in brown paper bags, but now she's always sleepy and forgets to do things like bring food home.

He saves every one of Norman's notes. Uncreases them if they're creased and crosses Norman's name out to write his own in its place. *Jean-Carlos: have a nice day, honey, you're so smart and so good and Dad and I love you so much.*

A snapping sound; a crunch of cartilage and bone. Norman clutches at his face, but it's all blood. Blood eyes and blood cheeks and blood tongue. He's trying to beg. "Please," he gurgles through the goop in the back of his throat, "Please stop . . . please stop." But Jean-Carlos keeps kicking him in the braces. Snow soaks the warm blood, melting it so deep a clump of dirty, frozen grass pokes through.

It feels like nothing if you close your eyes, Jean-Carlos thinks, *like kicking a fence.*

A front tooth cracks beneath its metal cage and spills from Norman's mouth on a string of red mucus, almost delicate in its descent.

"Have a nice day, Normy," Jean-Carlos says. "You're so smart. You're so good. You're so smart. So good."

. . .

Norman raises his hand at every question in Algebra and gets every answer correct. He already gets stupid notes in his lunches. He already makes people proud. Jean-Carlos knows all of the answers too, but does not raise his hand even once because it's already Norman's show. When this happens, something in him starts to crack and he can feel little shards of it piecing away from the whole, growing into a separate universe of grievances inside of him. He is afraid of what will come out if he tries to speak. So he does not try.

And today, Jean-Carlos didn't plan it but found himself following Norman after class—across Main Street and past the rows of sheet-metal shacks that line Forsythe Ave—to the elementary school where Norman goes to collect his younger sister. She must get notes every day in her freezer-pack lunch bag, too. He tracked behind Norman, bootless in the snow, the cold wetness licking up his calves that will leave white sodium rings around his stolen new jeans when they dry.

As they neared the elementary school, Jean-Carlos heard laughter from a different realm rising up around him. Children's voices that triggered a maddening memory, that released a violent urge. So as Norman walked the little shrub-lined path leading to the school, Jean-Carlos came at him from behind and tackled him—just out of sight from the teachers and crossing guards—pushing him onto his back into the snow.

And as he did, Jean-Carlos felt his now-slender body grow thick again, his belly blossoming as it had as a child when he devoured crinkly bags of oily pork rinds and half-stale blocks of fudge.

But he is better than that now. He can pick locks and throw bricks through cars windows. At thirteen, Jean-Carlos already has a mustache so thick and lustrous a junior with giant gazun-gas named Lisa-Mo Leesa once told him she thought he was sixteen—while baby-fat, one-eyed Norman has no mustache at all. It doesn't matter that Norman's mom scrawls him notes every single morning that say the same thing, over and over again, because now his face is half-broken, his glass eye stuck into a raw socket of his skull.

So. Kick. *Smart.* Kick. *So.* Kick. *Good.* Kick. *So good, Norman.* Kick. *So smart.* Kick.

"No," Norman gurgles. "Jean-Carlos, please. W-why? Stop . . . why are you—" His mouth is slung open. He cannot form words that sound like words.

How can Jean-Carlos explain as he kicks Norman's face in that you do things because you can? *Because once, I couldn't. Because, once, these things were done to me.* But Jean-Carlos does not tell him; instead he says everything with the frozen tip of his tennis shoe. Kick, kick, kick. He tries not to return to that memory—tries to kick his way out of it, but it finds him any-way—that day in the third grade at the Claude E. Williams School for the Potentially Future Gifted. It was the single day everything he used to be was burned out of him, and he got to choose what kind of boy he would become when he emerged from the ash, rebuilt.

• • •

That morning he woke from a dream which felt very, very long. An underwater dream that sometimes repeated itself and which he enjoyed because, otherwise, he had no opportunities to swim or speak with sharks. He remembers creeping into the cold bathroom, brushing his teeth and dressing, kissing his mother lightly on each of her cheeks before walking to school.

Classes at the C. E. Williams School for the P.F.G. crept gently on.

The art project that day involved silhouettes of clown-jesters. Construction paper and glue. Jean-Carlos's more closely resembled a bug-eyed monster with one large, front tooth. His teacher declared it abstract and hung it proudly on the blackboard. It started out a good day. He was praised, patted on the head like a puppy dog, and he liked the way that felt.

He was eight years old and chubby. He wore high-waisted jeans his mother dug out of the one-dollar bin at the Salvation Army. When class time transitioned into recess, he could not be concerned about the kickball game going on without him, though he would not have been invited to participate even if he were.

It always went the same way: him standing, kicking up gravel on the side of the wide field, waiting to be picked and not being picked. He'd be the only one left—walking backward, away, into the corner of the playground where he could return to his book and read in the heavy shadows of tall, lurking trees. There was a group of boys who would jeer as he retreated, who'd puff out their cheeks and wobble side-to-side like fat little penguin-boys, because this is what Jean-Carlos was to them. A fat little penguin-boy. They wanted to be sure he knew he was another species, a less-than-human one. And so he would sit there, alone in the grass, badly wishing that the words inside of his book might grow huge and swallow him up.

She worried in private, his mother. She worried about the seeds of anger that root when children are young, before they understand what is growing up inside of them, filling the open space of their bodies like weeds. Thick and impossible to cut down. It'd happened to Jean-Carlos's father when he was young—the short dark man who'd pushed himself inside of her in an alley outside of Mexico City, who'd dutifully married her two months later. He always came home late, sweaty and slurring, and died, selfishly, when Jean-Carlos was three-and-a-half. His mother had part-time work at a grocery store but nothing more.

But the young Jean-Carlos was not angry yet. He barely remembered the man, even if he looked like him, even if he'd inherited his softness around the middle and his long, feminine eyelashes. He loved his mother. He loved gummy candy. He loved episodes of *Jeopardy!* He loved doing next week's math homework as he licked candy-sugar from his stubby fingers.

...

Jean-Carlos's white shoes turn from red to brown as the blood starts to dry, caking up in the little air holes of his sneakers. Norman's good eye is shut, and his glass eye stares blankly up, like a paperweight stuffed into his face.

"Faggot," Jean-Carlos spits, "faggot-faggot-faggot." He says this without knowing if chubby, one-eyed Norman has actual sexual inclinations toward other boys, but it doesn't matter because either way he's a capital-F *Faggot*. And so he keeps saying it as he kicks, and Norman thrashes, slurring and bleeding.

Norman's fingers dig into the dirt beside him. His face does not look like a face.

Jean-Carlos bends down over him and digs change out of the pockets of his Faggot coat. Three quarters, one dime, one crusty nickel. Not even enough for a pack of gummy worms.

• • •

After recess, after kickball, after bathroom-stall-skulking, there'd been a math quiz. While his classmates grumbled and sweated, the young Jean-Carlos finished early. He sat fingering the holes near the hem of his favorite ill-fitting turtleneck, remembering the bag of gummy candy he had secreted away in the back of the pantry.

He ate tons of the shit. Hoovered it down his throat. He would run to it when the final bell rang, belly jiggling, heart thump-thumping, saliva gathering in a thick pool beneath his tongue. His mother would not be home from work for two hours, and he would gorge himself, smacking his lips and licking each finger, alone. Alone. Alone.

He had liberated his fingers from the holes of his turtleneck, thinking of how it might be to dip gummy candy in a cold glass of Cola. Would the sugar soften and fall to the bottom of the glass, or would it simply absorb the additional sweetness of the Cola, making the gummy candy even more appealing? Then: *the Thing* escaped him, out of his ass and into the world.

It began as something like a raucous howl and ended like the high-pitched scream of a small child. The fart had been surprising—a startling, bewildering thing, ripping through the near-silence of the classroom. Before that there had only been the calm of pencils scratching paper, the occasional shuffle, sniffle, sigh.

Had he been paying attention to the state of his stomach that afternoon, he may have noticed a low bubbling curving its way around his intestines, preparing to tear through the cool sweetness of classroom air and destroy it. But he had not.

And when It untrapped itself into the classroom air, the fallout was a silence so icy and still it could only be qualified as utter, dumbfounded horror. He was already the chubby outcast of his third-grade class, and they required no further reason to torment him. But this, this would go beyond torment.

The other children sat frozen for several moments in the aftermath until the lot of them became like a single cell, suddenly spliced, bumping like mad against the walls of the classroom.

• • •

Norman stops squirming, his flap-lips like two lazy donkey tongues, melded to the cold ground. Jean-Carlos is bored and leaves as the school bell rings; children pour out across the grounds. Norman's little sister sits waiting on the steps for a very long time, head rested against her prayer-folded palms. As Jean-Carlos walks back up the path he looks away when he sees her hug her princess book bag tight into her chest, her mouth starting to wobble.

. . .

Miguel, Jean-Carlos's father, is watching his son from high-up and far-away. From the Realm of the Dead. Miguel is not some heavenly creature in white; he does not know what he is, but he watches. He watched as his son's hands dug in the pockets of the boy with the bloody face, and he watches now as Jean-Carlos walks away, the boyish parts of his son's face changing to something blank of humanity.

And through the mess of blood and faces he remembers Juan, his Juan, and how they'd been together in a mucky pit behind Juan's father's farm so many years ago. The heat rushed up around their muddy clumsiness and burst through his fingers and toes as they kissed. Pigs gathered nearby, snorting their disapproval, but he could not stop. Miguel remembers this as the single best thing that ever happened to him, because in these moments he did not ever have to question that this was true. It just was.

He remembers his anticipation the next morning as he walked the rocky path to the classroom, wondering if they would eat lunch together, somewhere apart from the other boys. Miguel pictured Juan's fingers moving slowly to the dirt just beside his knee—so close he could feel the vibration of

Juan's skin beside his own—drumming the pulse of the secret they shared. But when he arrived that morning, Juan refused to look at him.

And when it was time for lunch, they did not go somewhere private.

No. Juan chased him—with every other dirty-kneed, adrenaline-wasted boy in their classroom—across the dusty field glutted with scrap metal and other discarded things. Chased him straight into the outhouse on the other end of that field where in the dark, rank box, Juan dunked Miguel's whole face into the steaming reek of other people's bowels. "You come back here, you die, *Cabroncito*," he warned him.

He never returned to school or ever saw Juan again. Instead he kissed women and did not feel the burst of heat-light through every inch of his skin, the wildness through his chest as he touched them. Felt nothing except a slow closing up of his insides, a spreading deafness, contaminating every other sense.

Miguel watches as Jean-Carlos retreats. A little fountain of blood erupts from between the boy's lips that his son has left lying on the ground, but Jean-Carlos is too far away to notice it now.

• • •

That day, that horrible day, Jean-Carlos remained glued to his too-small plastic chair. His belly was pressed hard up against the edge of the attached desk. He had been too terrified to move and the teacher did nothing to stop the children as they crumpled up their tests and slung them (with an accompanying symphony of mouth and armpit fart-noises) at Jean-Carlos— who shielded his face with his hands. His math test was still intact, and he stared at it with a devoted intensity as though it was a solar eclipse—the last very bright, perfect, dangerous thing he would ever see again before his corneas burned away to nothing.

• • •

In the griddle-heat of his memories, Jean-Carlos's father is transported. No longer a long-dead man but a boy, plugged firmly into Mexican earth and mud and other people's shit. He remembers his childhood dog—*Cabroncito*—a white and brown mutt with long, furry ears. The dog his own father had dragged from an alleyway one rainy Easter, brought home, and let him name. Miguel chose *Cabroncito* because it was the last word Juan had ever spoken to him. *Cabroncito.* That one stupid word and how it stuck to him. How one word can superglue itself to your skull and not even the strongest, ungodliest hands can rip it from the Velcro of your brain—*Cabroncito*—

• • •

The teacher must have noticed, but barely tried to intervene when the classroom devolved into a simian landscape of howling and mimed fecal-flinging. Their cruel taunts directed at the stoic but crumbling figure of chubby Jean-Carlos—

slow-limbed, farty creature—still seated, head-bowed, shielding his eyes to prevent the other children from seeing tears begin to mow their hot way down his face. She rapped at the blackboard several times with the sturdy silver ring on her pointer finger and cleared her throat twice before she yelled, "Children! Calm DOWN!" Miss was distressed, always distressed. She looked down and rubbed the drippy folds of her face with both hands and sighed heavily.

Jean-Carlos retreated back into the isolation of his own skull and listed the things he loved. As long as he repeated this list he did not have time to worry about the relentless surge of crumpled-up paper. He moved his hands to cup his ears and let the paper continue to ping his skull. *Ping ping ping ping.*

He loved his mother. He loved gummy candy. He loved licking sugar from his fingers, watching *Jeopardy!*, and wearing soft turtlenecks with holes in the hem. He loved. He loved.

He stared at his math test until the blackness of numbers became like ants, until the whiteness seemed to besiege the little insects and they simply marched off the page. Some flew, without wings, rising into space because they willed it so. And when they had all ascended or crept or spiraled from the page, he had been left with a terrible whiteness that made his eyes feel marble-hard. His brain forgot, just plain forgot, to see anything at all. Likewise, his ears had shut off, and his body sort of flattened into itself, like how tap water must feel when introduced to the ocean, swallowed into something that is itself and is not.

The other children were bleating, their eyes gibbous and red with glee. He barely realized he had been biting his tongue, hard, until with every swallow, the metallic taste of blood replaced the nothing taste of saliva. It was this taste that brought him back into his body, into the reality of his small plastic chair.

It was a reality he could no longer bear. Something was wincing in him, threatening to snap.

His father watched this day, too, watched as his son escaped his too-small plastic chair, belly jiggling prodigiously, and ran to freedom. As he beelined it for the door the other children ran to block his way, creating a sturdy wall of No-Go. The teacher rose from her desk like very slow smoke, rapped again at the blackboard with her sturdy silver ring, hoping that perhaps this time it would have some effect.

Which, of course, it did not.

The only way out now was in the other direction—the window—and Jean-Carlos pushed his way through a crowd which tried to hold him back again. But he would not, could not be contained for he was a torpedo, a whirling jet with sweat-slick hair. When he reached it, he lifted it easily with both hands and hurled himself to the snow. The other children and the teacher came to the window, watching him squirm; his arm was hurt and he struggled to his feet in the slippery ice and mushy snow.

"Are you hurt?" the teacher called down, and with no response she continued, "Well, say something, Jean-Carlos! Do you need the nurse? Jean-Carlos. Answer me! Jean-Carlos! JEAN-CARLOS!" She kept repeating his name in a frenzied kind of yelp.

But all her voice did was propel him forward, across the wide lawn of the school, the arm he'd landed on throbbing as he tried to run. Her voice echoed his name across the snow until he could hear it no longer, until he collapsed, breathless, between a row of bushes on the far edge of the school grounds. He lay there and did not move, did not wish to ever move again.

Everyone walked past him at the end of the day as he hid, still lying between the prickly, snowy bushes. He lay there so long he missed *Jeopardy!* that night, which he'd never done before. When he finally snuck home, he threw all of his turtlenecks into the trash and cut his own hair in the bathroom. Parts of it he cut too short. They looked like bald spots, which made him look sort of mean and deranged.

Which is what he wanted.

His mother did not try and stop him, but she dug his turtlenecks out of the trash later that night and tucked them into a dark corner of his closet because they could not afford to throw away perfectly good clothes like that.

...

Norman's eyes are open wide and they stare up at Jean-Carlos, who has come back for reasons he doesn't understand. He steps backward and stares into Norman's peeled-open eyes and does not know what he's done. He does not understand it, though some part of him can't help but liken it to that day, to the hours he'd spent shivering alone in the snow. Something inside him crumpled, like the paper balls his classmates once threw at his soft-haired head.

He has carried that day with him in, deep in his gut, even as he flirted with Lisa-Mo Leesa who thinks he's sixteen though he's only thirteen and in possession of the finest of mustaches. Even as he's stuffed jeans he could not afford into his bag, sprinting out of the store on a dare that wasn't even a Double-Dare.

He remembers the dizzy feeling in his skull as he ran, wildly, through the cold streets toward the grocery store where his mother had worked stacking waxy produce in pyramids all day long. He remembers when his mother had work and the dinners they'd eat, side by side at the small wooden table, and how she'd hold him near her as they watched *Jeopardy!* together. She would murmur in awe as he got every answer right.

And he's got that same dizzy feeling right now as he stares at the snow which should be white but is brown and red, clumped up in weird little fists sticking out of the dirt. Norman's hands. One is clenched and one is open wide, pressed out as though to put a stop to what has already happened. No one is around. No one has stopped this.

He thinks of his mother's gloved hands lifting the cool fruit, separating perfect from bruised, smoothing the labels flush. He thinks of the baskets of ruined fruit that used to fill their dining room table and how they would sit there, uneaten, until they melted into each other. Rotten.

He looks at Norman's mouth, flung open. At the snow, now a curtain of blood beneath his back. Jean-Carlos stoops in the snow and lets the wetness soak through to his knees as he pulls Norman's head onto his lap, not knowing what he has done because it makes no sense.

Norman's head lolls in his lap. His sister is gone, and Jean-Carlos realizes she doesn't know where Norman is. She doesn't know his face no longer looks like a face. She doesn't know that he's still breathing but barely, and she doesn't know that Jean-Carlos dials 911 on his cell phone, says what he needs to say and runs, runs like some fanatically trained action hero through the snow and back down Forsythe Ave, past the sheet-metal shacks and the high school he now attends, where he knows Norman has his lunch stolen and the shit beat out of him every single day.

When Jean-Carlos hears the yowl of the ambulance his legs stop working, and he falls again, back into the snow. A thin dog creeps from the shadowy triangles of an alleyway and sits beside him, nuzzling into his shoulder and whining softly. It's then Jean-Carlos realizes he's crying into its coat and the dog is letting him cry. He thinks that Lisa-Mo Leesa would know he was only thirteen right now if she saw him, but he doesn't even care.

In the rush of the wind through the fracture-branched

trees, there's still the sound of the ambulance. It's not far. He could go back. He could explain about the notes Norman gets in his lunches and his own mother, always in bed. He could tell them about all that fruit, rotted in bowls on their kitchen table and his father, dead so long.

But instead, he stays, and he waits. And then, when the whine of the ambulance grows too distant to hear any longer, he runs.

How Auto-Tune Saved My Life
BY BRENDAN HALPIN

YOU WOULDN'T THINK fifty minutes would be so tough. I mean, you can pretty much endure anything for less than an hour—except that I spend the whole time just waiting for Kruzeman to go off on me, which he does, every day without fail. So when I have him after lunch, I have *The Sour Stomach of Dread*, which prevents me from eating even the cafeteria's chocolate chip cookies, their only edible product.

My mom works two jobs so we can keep the house, and she's never around when I get ready for school. So I just throw on whatever and leave, which is apparently not cool at Boston Classical High School, where the West Roxbury kids—even the boys—spend like an hour getting ready and making sure their sneakers match their flat brims. They all get new clothes from Hollister or Abercrombie while I rock last year's clothes from Target. And I'm not especially good about making sure things are tucked in and straight and all that stuff, because I guess I don't really value order all that much. But I know someone who does.

So I walk into class. I take a squirt from the hand sanitizer mounted on the wall and try to scoot around the crowd at

Kruzeman's desk so I can slip quietly into my seat. No such luck, though. "Mr. Michaels!" he calls. "No word from the *What Not to Wear* crew yet, I see. Well, fear not. We've sent them photos. They're bound to call."

A few people laugh just to kiss his butt, but really, this couldn't possibly be funny anymore. He says it like every single day.

The bell rings and today—like every other day in Kruzeman's class—we're all in seats, a black ink pen in hand and a blank piece of paper in front of us. Kruzeman looks up from his desk. "Heading," he says.

We all begin to write our headings in the top right corner of the paper. His name, our name, and the date. They must be one inch from the top and a half-inch from the right side. As his ritual, he walks through class with a ruler and every once in a while, he'll slap it down on someone's desk to measure whether their heading is in the right place. "One inch from the top. Very good, Mr. Flaherty."

"Ms. DiNuzzio. One point five inches from the top?" He picks up Toni DiNuzzio's paper and rips it in two. "Fail. Better luck tomorrow." I can only see the back of Toni's head, which is mostly her long black hair, but off to the side of her ponytail I see her ears getting red.

Kendrick sneezes, and Kruzeman's head whips around. "Mr. Hazelton!" He yells. "Garbage!" Kendrick gets up and throws a tissue in the trash and starts to return to his seat.

"Sanitize!" Kruzeman says. Kendrick walks over to the

sanitizer and takes a squirt, rubbing his hands together. "Fifteen seconds, Mr. Hazelton," Kruzeman says.

Of course he reaches my desk and slaps the ruler down. He picks other people at random, but he's never missed me. "Mr. Michaels! Your heading is correct! If only you could bring that level of precision to your shoe tying." I look down. My right shoe is untied. A couple of people titter. I reach down to tie my laces as he walks away, but he flips around.

"Reaching into your shoe for answers, Mr. Michaels? I'm disappointed, though I can't say I'm surprised. Fail——" He grabs my paper from my desk and tears it up. "And demerit. Academic dishonesty is a serious offense. You will, of course, be brought up before the dean for an academic tribunal."

I grit my teeth. *Don't say anything stupid. Don't say anything stupid.*

"I was tying my shoe," I say. "Look." I take off my shoe and sock. "There's nothing in there but my foot."

Kruzeman looks down at my foot and wrinkles his nose. "Mister Michaels. You must think me an idiot. You know as well as I that you could have thrown your cheat sheet far across the room in the moments when I wasn't looking. In the meantime," he gestures down at my foot, "I believe the air quality of this room will no longer be safe for breathing if you do not encase the offending appendage."

I look around the room. Nobody says anything, laughs, or even looks at me. They're all busy being thankful it's not them, and I don't blame them.

I can't punch him in the face, as much as he deserves it. I can't cry, even though I kind of want to. So I do the only other thing that makes sense. I remove my other shoe and sock and stretch my bare feet out in the aisle between the desks.

I take out my iPod, pop the earbuds in, and start blasting the metal backing track I put together on my computer to shred over, as soon as I actually learn to shred on my guitar. It calms me down. My eyes are closed, my shoes are off, my headphones are in, and I just breathe. In. Out. In. Out.

My fists unclench after a minute or so, and then I open my eyes to see Kruzeman standing in front of me wearing a surgical mask and purple latex gloves. His face is red and his glasses are starting to fog up. Maybe he's yelling, but I can't tell. I look at him, but I don't remove my headphones.

I glance around the room. Everybody is laughing. I reach down and pause the iPod to hear this muffled-through-the-mask rant. "—cheating, and now violating the school electronic policy *as well* as endangering the health of your classmates with unsanitary behavior! Put your shoes on and get out of my classroom now! And place your iPod on my desk!"

I stand up, throw my bag over my shoulder, and grab my shoes and socks in my hand. I start walking toward the door, feeling better than I have in months. As I reach Kruzeman's desk, I pull the iPod out of my pocket, drop it in a sock, and toss it all on his desk.

For about ten seconds, I feel fantastic. I stood up to a bully, and yeah, I failed the test, but instead of me getting upset and yelling, *he* was upset and yelling. And with my sock on his desk, he's probably going to have to disinfect his whole room.

• • •

My big victory lasts only until I get to the guidance office. My guidance counselor, Ms. Williams, gives me the standard lecture about the tradition of Boston Classical High School. "As one of the oldest public high schools in America and one of the very few public schools that still follow the classical curriculum, we have high standards for our students' behavior as well as their work." It goes on and on like this. I'm not really sure I get the point, but at the end she asks, "Do you have anything you would like to say in regards to today's incident?"

"I wasn't cheating. I didn't have any answers in my shoe. He told me my shoe was untied, and I went to tie my shoe. Is it against the rules to tie your shoe?"

"I think you know it's against the rules to listen to an iPod and take your shoes off."

"Yeah, but I was already in trouble by that point!"

"Well, right now you're clearly having some anger issues. Do you think you might benefit from anger management classes?"

"I mean, when you get accused of something you didn't do, doesn't it kind of make sense to get angry?"

"Well, is anger ever an adaptive behavior in school?"

"I don't know. Maybe you should ask the guy who was yelling in my face five minutes ago. Now *there's* a guy who could benefit from some anger management classes. Have you ever recommended that to *him*?"

She sighs, closes the manila folder on her desk, and gets up. "You're using sarcasm to avoid taking responsibility for your actions. We'll talk more tomorrow at the hearing. We're clearly not going to reach each other right now."

She walks out of the room and leaves me sitting there for twenty minutes until she finally comes back with a slip of paper in her hand. "So I've spoken to your mother. You'll have your suspension hearing tomorrow at nine in the headmaster's office."

"I thought it was an academic tribunal."

She glances at her notes. "Whether that's happening depends on the outcome of the hearing."

• • •

I guess I didn't really understand what a hearing was. I thought it was the kind of thing where they would listen to what I had to say. You know, like *hear* both sides of the story. Not the case. First of all, Kruzeman isn't even here. He's sent along a hand-written note, which the headmaster, Mr. Kelly, reads aloud. "Student disrupted class by removing articles of clothing and placing headphones in ear."

"Well, this seems pretty clear," Mr. Kelly says. "Son, do you have anything to say about this? Do you agree that it's factually accurate?"

"I mean. It's not really the whole story."

"I didn't ask you that, son. I asked if the note was accurate."

And before I get a chance to answer, Mom chimes in. "I think we need to talk about the circumstances. Mr. Kruzeman mocks my son's appearance every day, and he tore up his test and accused him of cheating with absolutely no evidence at all!"

Mr. Kelly looks at my mom, writes something down on the pad of paper in front of him, then looks back up. "Mrs. Michaels. We need to understand each other. I don't know how you discipline your child at home, but here at Boston Classical, there are no circumstances under which placing one's bare feet atop a desk while listening to headphones is acceptable behavior. Is that acceptable behavior in your house?"

Mom's face turns red. I recognize the look she's shooting Mr. Kelly. It's the *I can't say what I really want to say right now, but just wait till later look.* "What happens in my home is not at issue here," she says. "You've got a teacher whose behavior is out of control, and—"

"Whereas, dear, I would say that you have a child who is out of control."

"Did you call me 'dear'? Because you don't know me well enough to call me that."

"Ah. I see. Well, in any case, the facts of Kevin's behavior are not at issue. He is suspended for three days."

I wince, waiting for the explosion, but what comes next is shocking: Mom doesn't say anything. She gathers up her bag and whispers, "Come on, Kevin." She doesn't say anything as we walk down the long hallway, our shoes clacking on the floor. And she doesn't say anything as we get in the car. We ride home in silence and I'm not gonna lie: I'm scared. Every few seconds I kind of sneak a look at her from the corner of my eye. She's doing her angry clenched teeth thing that makes her bottom jaw stick out a little bit. It always, without fail, precedes me getting yelled at. I keep waiting for it, and it keeps not coming, which makes the whole thing that much worse. We get into the house—okay, apartment—and I say, "Um. I'm sorry, Mom."

She looks at me finally. "Oh God, Sweetie. It's not you. I mean, taking off your shoes and putting the iPod in was dumb, but I know a lot of fourteen-year-olds who are doing things that are way dumber than that. I just——" She closes her eyes, runs a hand through her hair, and gives a long, slow exhale. "It makes me so angry that you get punished for standing up to him, and he gets nothing for being cruel and irrational to you. Does he treat everybody else like this?"

"Yeah. He tore up Toni DiNuzzio's paper because she didn't have her heading in the right place. . . ."

"See, that's the kind of thing I'm talking about. That's not rigorous. That's crazy. I'm sending out an e-mail right now to all the other parents in your class."

I really want to tell her *please don't do that, it's gonna be embarrassing*, but she is already attacking the keyboard like it's Mr. Kelly's head, and there is no way I'm getting in her way when she's like this.

She sends an e-mail to some ninth grade parents' group, and by the next day she has ten responses. Three are from people who say they're glad to be a part of the Boston Classical tradition, and the only problem the school needs to address is retaining too many students who should be allowed to fail out. The other seven are from people, including Toni DiNuzzio's mom, who think Kruzeman is a whack job.

In the three days I'm suspended from school, I get all my homework done, and the apartment gets a thorough cleaning. Mom is way angrier at the school than me, but she still wants me to "learn a lesson" about doing stupid things like taking my shoes off during class, so my punishment is annoying but not too severe. She takes the PS3 controllers to work with her and feels the TV to make sure it's cold as soon as she gets home. Fortunately she doesn't take the computer or my guitar away, so I spend most of the day flailing away on the seven-string Ibanez that Mom got off eBay for my birthday last year. I don't really know how to play very well, but I mix up a nice backing track on Garage Band. So that's good.

Then it's the weekend, so I have two more days to worry about what it's going to be like going back to school. On Monday, Mom drives me in because she and Mrs. DiNuzzio and two other parents are meeting with Mr. Kelly again.

It's day three on the block schedule, meaning I have Kruzeman before lunch, so at least I'll get to eat. I got his homework off his website so I'll be prepared for the quiz. All I have to do is get through him mocking me when I walk in to class. "Mr.

Michaels!" Kruzeman sings out as I walk in, ducking behind the crowd to get my mandatory squirt of hand sanitizer.

I give a wave and head to my seat, but Kruzeman isn't having any. "I'm sorry, Mr. Michaels, but I didn't hear you!"

I take a deep breath and say, "Good morning, Mr. Kruzeman."

"Well, it was until just a moment ago. We've had such a nice three days here, but I suppose all good things must come to an end."

"And bad things, like his life, just go on forever," Toni DiNuzzio whispers at me as she walks past. I smile at her and she smiles back, her big brown eyes lighting up. Maybe there's something not so terrible about this class after all.

Class starts and I clench my teeth, waiting for whatever torture Kruzeman has in store for me for a welcome back present. I put my heading in the right spot; I practiced while I was at home. My heart pounds as he stands just inches away from my desk for what feels like an hour before slapping the ruler down and seeing that my heading is right. I'm sweating, and I sit there just staring at the pen in my hand. It starts to shake, and Kruzeman moves on to somebody else's desk.

The quiz is a normal quiz, except when Eric Bos whispers, "What was the answer to number 3?" as he turns in his quiz. And Kruzeman tells him. *Out loud.* Even though there are still people who haven't turned in their quizzes.

Suddenly Kruzeman looks up at the class. "Who heard what I just said?" he asks, loudly. I look up slowly from my quiz paper and do my best to put a puzzled look on my face. I think I can probably sell it since I sit so close to the back of the room.

In the front row, though, is Julie Chen, whose hand shoots up. I feel bad for the kid—she doesn't get it. I don't know how you could get through nine years in American schools and still believe that hard work and honesty always pay off, but Julie certainly seems to. Kruzeman is about to change her mind.

"Well, Ms. Chen, you'll get number three wrong."

Now, I've been in classes with Julie Chen since the seventh grade. I don't think I have ever heard her say anything that wasn't the answer to a direct question. Until now. "What?" she says.

"I said, you'll get number three wrong. You heard the answer, so you can't get it right." Unless you're like everybody else in the class who just pretended they hadn't heard.

"But——," Julie Chen starts. "I had the answer right! Look at my paper!"

"Well of course you've got the right answer *now*," Kruzeman says.

"But that's not fair! You said the answer out loud!"

Kruzeman laughs and rolls his eyes. "Fear not, Ms. Chen. Your 102 average may dip to 101 briefly, but——"

And then Julie Chen *interrupts the teacher*. I take a quick look out the window to make sure no pigs are flying by. "That's not the point! You're being unfair! You made a mistake, and now you're punishing me for being honest!"

If this were a cartoon, I'd see the red creep up from Kruzeman's shoes all the way to the top of his head, which would then shoot steam from the ears before exploding. In real life, though, he goes from zero to crazy in like a second. "What did you say?" he says to Julie Chen.

"I said you made a mistake, and you're being unfair."

This hangs in the air while Kruzeman's face contorts into a pink mask of rage. "*I* made a mistake? I made a mistake?!" He screams as spittle flies from his lips. "Who do you think you are, Julie Chen? Do YOU think you can run my class? How dare you? How dare you!?" And Julie Chen, sobbing, runs from the classroom.

I'm not gonna lie. My first thought is not about how unfair this is, or how I feel terrible for Julie Chen—who's never even been friends with anyone who got in trouble—or how Kruzeman has really lost his mind. Nope, my first thought is just, *Thank God it wasn't me this time.*

Kruzeman looks at the rest of us. "So does anybody else have anything to say?"

Nobody does. And like someone threw a switch, Kruzeman is back to what passes for normal. For him, at least. "All right, then. Let's continue with class, shall we?" For the rest of the period, nobody laughs at a single one of his corny jokes. It's pretty weak as rebellions go, but I guess it'll have to do.

When Mom gets home from work, I ask how was the big meeting was. This is a decision I regret almost instantly because Mom is off to the races. "That Kelly guy is such a jerk," she says. "He doesn't care about students. He just yapped at us about the tradition of Boston Classical and not every student is ready for this level of rigor and blah blah. And when Mrs. DiNuzzio told him about Toni's quiz getting ripped up, do you know what he said? 'Well, teenage girls have been known to exaggerate.' Arrrgh!"

Mom immediately retreats to the computer in a huff and spends the rest of the evening banging on her computer keyboard, sending angry e-mails, I guess. I, however, spend the rest of the evening shredding my own face off with headphones hooked up to my amp. By which I mean slowly picking out one of my favorite solos at one-third speed while hitting like every third note wrong.

The next day Kruzeman opens class with the following. "You know, it's come to my attention that certain parents have made complaints about my class. Well, let me just tell you this. The staff at Boston Classical talk to each other, and we're all very unlikely to write a college recommendation for someone who makes trouble around here."

When he says this, Toni DiNuzzio looks back at me and rolls her eyes. She's not fazed, but I'm freaked out. So if I go here, I won't be able to go to college? Is that what this guy is telling me? Because my mom complained about something?

After class, Toni comes up to me in the hall. She smells good. "You know that's bullshit, right?" she asks. "My mom's friends with Ms. Dornbusch . . . you know, the AP Bio teacher?" I have no idea, but I nod like I know what she's talking about.

"They all know he's crazy. It's not like he can turn every teacher in the school against us."

"Well, that's good, I guess. But still . . ."

She smiles at me. I notice she has one crooked tooth on the bottom. It's strangely cute. "But still, only a hundred and thirteen more days of this, and then we never have to deal with him again. And at least the worst is over for the day."

That's what she thinks. I'm just heading into my study period after lunch when my guidance counselor, Ms. Williams, intercepts me.

"Can I talk to you for a few minutes?" she asks.

"Um. Well, I've got like thirty-five problems for math homework, and—"

"It'll only take a minute," she says and stares at me. So I guess I'm being told rather than asked. Got it.

I follow her to her office and sit in the chair opposite her desk. She settles into her chair and says, "So. How do you like it here?"

I look around. "I'm not crazy about the painting. Is that, like, supposed to be the Boston skyline or something? I mean, no offense. It's okay. It's just not my thing. The plants are cool, I guess. The furniture, though—"

"Stop it. I'm being serious."

So was I. This chair I'm sitting in is ridiculously uncomfortable, and the painting is hideous. But I knew what she meant.

"I mean, it's cool, I guess. I know everybody."

She smiles at me. "Having some difficulty this year, though? A little tougher than eighth grade?"

I know what she means, but I'm not going to talk about it with her. "Math, definitely. Algebra two is a big step up. I mean, it goes a lot faster. But otherwise—"

"Well, I'll tell you something. This is a rigorous school." I do not roll my eyes. They talk about the rigor here all the freaking time. The next thing that comes will be the tradition. "Boston Classical has a long tradition"—ding!—"of excellence, and, as you've discovered, this is not a place where anything less than excellence will be accepted."

So far this is the same, canned speech that we get the first day of school and at parents' night and at the open house in the spring when the new students come in to see the school. Am I really missing study for this? I've got serious homework to do.

"And in this pursuit of excellence, it's true that not every teacher is going to necessarily be as kind and gentle and nurturing as you might be used to. Our staff is a demanding bunch; they expect the best and they don't suffer fools gladly."

This pisses me off. "So I'm a fool?"

Ms. Williams smiles at me, but it's a creepy smile with no humor behind it. "Well, none of us act as wise as we should at times, now do we? But here is my point. You are, what, fifteen now?"

"Fourteen." My birthday is in the file sitting right in front of you. Why are you asking me questions you know the answer to?

"Okay. So as we grow, we're expected to mature. This means

we avoid juvenile behavior like removing our shoes in class; but more importantly it means we start to show more accountability for our actions. And it means that when we encounter difficulties, we face them head-on." *It means it means it means.*

"Um. Okay."

"Do you get what I'm saying here, Kevin?"

"Not really."

"I mean that as we grow older, we can no longer rely on our parents to solve our problems. If I have a bad day at work, I can't expect my parents to handle it for me. And it's time for you to start showing some of that maturity."

And she goes on and on, but it basically comes down to this: Don't tell your mom what goes on here. Are you a man or a snot-nosed little boy? Not that she actually says any of this, but it's pretty clear to me what she means.

The bell rings, and I've lost my entire study listening to this crap.

After dinner, I'm sitting at the kitchen table doing my homework like I always do, and Mom wants to know why it's taking me so long to finish tonight. "I missed my study," I say.

She looks up from the laptop. "Why's that?"

"Ms. Williams wanted to talk to me." I'm hoping I can just get out of the conversation and back to the math.

And now the laptop gets closed. I am seriously never going to get my math done. "What did she have to say?"

"Uh, just that, you know, I'm a big boy now and I can't be running to Mommy with my problems all the time."

"She said *what?*"

"I mean. She didn't really say that. But that was the general idea."

"Tell me *exactly* what she said." And we're off. I spend another twenty minutes telling Mom about my forty-minute conversation with Ms. Williams, and then she's clacking away at her keyboard again and calling Mrs. DiNuzzio.

By the next day, Mom and Mrs. DiNuzzio have booked a meeting with the superintendent of schools. It's scheduled for a week from now. The week goes pretty quietly, which is to say Kruzeman taunts me at the beginning of class every day but otherwise doesn't pick on me. When Friday afternoon comes, I'm so relieved I feel like I could float out of school.

So far so good, until the day before the meeting. It happens to be the same day Jimmy Flanigan comes up to me outside of Kruzeman's class and announces he's gotten Unearth tickets for an all-ages show at the House of Blues. He asks if I want to go, and I'm stoked beyond belief, so I go up for the high five. Unfortunately Jimmy turns his head at that moment to watch Suzy Simpson walk down the hall (and, I mean, who can blame him), so we miss our high five and I end up smacking Jimmy in the face. It's pretty funny, and Jimmy and I are both cracking up until Kruzeman suddenly appears. "Mr. Michaels. I'm not sure why you find assaulting a fellow student so amusing, but that is behavior that cannot be tolerated at Boston Classical. To the dean's office, sir."

I look at him for a minute waiting for him to crack a smile.

I mean, I know the guy doesn't really have a sense of humor, but I figure he's just messing with me. "Mr. Michaels. I said go to the dean's office."

And this is how I wind up getting suspended for assaulting a fellow student. Jim comes to tell them the whole thing was just a joke, but no dice. "Bullying is a serious matter," they tell him. "We know victims are often too intimidated to speak up and may even cover up for their bullies for fear of reprisals."

I am five feet four inches tall and weigh a hundred and twenty pounds. There is not a single person in this school who is intimidated by me. Seriously. The seventh graders aren't even intimidated by me.

When Mom gets home, the first thing she says is, "We have to do a quick cleanup, kiddo. Mrs. DiNuzzio is coming over so we can strategize. I think she's bringing Toni, too."

"Wait. Toni DiNuzzio is coming *here*?" I may have a girl in my bedroom. This fills me with panic and arousal, and I head to my room and go into a frenzy of cleaning. By which I mean shoving stuff under my bed and into my closet. Metal posters, guitar, amp—cool. Incredible Hulk poster—probably not that cool. Down it comes.

Finally I remember that I got suspended today and I should probably tell Mom. So I do. It all pours out in one jumble because maybe if I say it fast it'll sound less ridiculous. "Oh, yeah, by the way, Mom, I got suspended again today for missing when I gave Jimmy Flanigan a high five and I accidentally hit him in the face."

Mom looks at me, annoyed. "Kevin. Be serious. Nobody gets suspended for a high five. That didn't happen. You're just messing with me, right?"

"Mom, I swear to God. Jimmy even told them it was just a mistake, but they told him I was a bully and that he shouldn't be intimidated by me. . . ."

"Well, not much danger of that." Mom actually snorts.

"Mom!"

"Well, I mean, look . . . I love you and you are an awesome, wonderful kid. You even look like kind of a badass when you play your guitar, but nobody's ever going to accuse you of being intimidating."

"Somebody already did. Mom, do they know you're meeting with the superintendent?"

"Well, Dr. Jackson said she would be doing some investigating, and——"

"Agh, Mom. That's why! They're punishing me for this!"

If you've ever seen one of those survival shows, they tell you not to get between a mama bear and her cub, because she'll maul you without even thinking to protect her offspring. Well, Mom sets her jaw and gets this steely look in her eyes, and I realize maybe this isn't just true for bears.

"We will appeal this," Mom says. "And they will be held accountable. I promise you. They're not going to win."

I'm not going to argue with Mama Bear, but I don't really believe her. She doesn't have to go in there every day. And no matter what they tell her, when they've got me alone, they're gonna make me pay.

Well I might as well enjoy the fact that Toni DiNuzzio's coming over. When they arrive, our moms take over the kitchen table with a bottle of wine and leave us sitting in the living room. I don't really know what to say, and I wonder if I should start a conversation or turn on the TV. It's kind of awkward. No, actually painfully awkward.

"So. Sorry you got suspended," she finally says.

"Thanks. I guess it'll give me time to learn a couple of new songs on the guitar."

"Cool! You play guitar?" This big smile breaks out on her face and she raises her left eyebrow. I've rarely seen her like this at school, but then again, I'm not exactly at my happiest there either. "Can I see?"

Now, every kid with a guitar sells his parents on the idea somehow. *I love music, it'll keep me out of trouble, I need a hobby . . .* or whatever. But this is why a boy really wants a guitar. So when he tells a girl he plays, she'll smile and say, "Cool!"

We head into my room, and she takes it all in. I am SO glad I took that Hulk poster down. "Whoa. That thing is badass!" she exclaims when I pick up the guitar. I flip the amp on, turn up the distortion to a level I hope will be loud enough to drown out my inevitable mistakes, and crunch out a few chords.

"I—I mostly do metal stuff. I make, like, backing tracks on Garage Band and stuff. And then I play along. Or try to. But, you know, it always sounds better in my mind than it does in real life." Why am I telling her this? It sounds pathetic.

"Nice," she says. I examine her face for traces of sarcasm. I don't find any. "Do you ever put anything up on YouTube or anything?"

"Oh God no. It sucks way too bad for that."

"I bet it doesn't. But most stuff on YouTube is horrible. I mean if *I* can get twelve hundred hits—"

"On what?"

"It's dumb. I just mixed some horror movie footage together and put a Disney Channel song under it. Disney filed a copyright violation complaint after half a day and they took it down, but I got twelve hundred hits before that. And I . . . I have a vlog."

"What is it? I mean, what do you—"

"Just look me up. But like, not while I'm here. It's way too embarrassing. ToniDBoston."

There's a weird moment when we just kind of look at each other. Making your own terrible metal tracks and doing horror movie video mashups are not cool things to do at our school. Probably at any school. We've just exchanged information that could ruin us both. It's weirdly intimate. Which I guess makes it weirdly hot. Which I guess is what makes it awkward again.

"Anybody want ice cream?" My mom calls out, all extra loud. This kills the moment, which is kind of a relief in that it stops me from accidentally ruining it.

. . .

We can't appeal the suspension until a hearing officer from the central office is available, which means I have to serve out my suspension and then they'll have the hearing. From what my mom says it'll probably be overturned, and then officially, my three-day suspension will never have happened. Except I'll still be missing three days of notes—and I'll have a test and three quizzes to make up on my own time—which means less time in studies for at least a few days after I get back. Unlike last time, Mom concurs I did absolutely nothing wrong, so at least she doesn't punish me by taking anything away.

Not that it would matter, since I have so much homework to do. It's not like I can just kick back and watch movies or something. I spend all morning on the first day trying to stay caught up in Kruzeman's class. Actually, that's not true, because I also watch Toni's vlogs. She's really funny and caustic. Just the way I like 'em. So that's cool, but I can't forget that I eventually have to go back to school. I'm all alone in the house, and when I start thinking about returning, I start to despair. Kruzeman can't be beaten; Boston Classical can't be beaten. Mom tried to go to our city councilor about the whole thing, but he never returned her phone calls because of course, he's a Boston Classical alum.

And then the day turns around when my phone buzzes during what would be first lunch period. It's a text from Toni. *K man was priceless today. Made J Chen cry again.*

Wish you could video it. It's entertaining when you don't have to be there, I send back.

Excellent idea! I'm totes doing it tomorrow. Stay tuned!

This is how it starts. While I'm suspended, Toni starts her video project. She cuts a little hole in her bag and records him the whole time she's in class.

When I make my big return from my bullshit suspension, I take a deep breath and count to ten before walking into Kruzeman's room. As I expected, he lays into me pretty good:

"Mister Michaels! I hope you've learned a little lesson. But I'm sure you haven't. People like you never do."

I look at Toni's bag and see the light glint off the camera lens and smile.

"Do you think it's funny, Mr. Michaels? That you'll never amount to anything?"

"I do not," I say.

"Good. Sit down," he barks.

It's not funny yet, I think to myself, but it's going to be.

Toni comes over on Saturday with her camera and two SD cards full of Kruzeman video. "So I had an idea," she says. "Do you think we could make this into a song? Can we Auto-Tune him like they do with those news videos and stuff?"

The thought of making an Auto-Tuned song kind of makes me cringe. I'd much rather make a metal song. But Toni's the one with all the footage and if we do her project, I'll get to sit next to her at the computer for probably hours at a time. And she still smells good.

The first thing we do is watch hours of video and pick out Kruzeman's greatest hits. "Let me take this audio track and see what I can do," I say.

It's against all my musical instincts, but I take the audio from Kruzeman's greatest hits video and take most of Sunday assembling an Auto-Tuned dance pop song with Kruzeman on vocals. "You're a disgrace," he warbles on the chorus. I e-mail the file to Toni and don't think much about it until she comes up to me at lunch, smartphone in hand, and says, "Look at this!"

On the screen is a YouTube video entitled "Bringin' Crazy Back." And it has ten thousand hits. "It's only been uploaded since last night! We've got ten thousand views already!"

I like how she said "we."

The next day, I turn on the radio while I'm eating breakfast and the Morning Zoo guys are playing our song.

"Can you imagine if that guy was your teacher?" one says.

"I think I would have been expelled," the other guy responds.

The following day, Mom gets an e-mail from the Massachusetts Anti-Bullying task force. They want to talk to all the parents whose kids are in Kruzeman's classes as they investigate allegations of educational bullying.

Three days and one point two million views later, the news trucks show up at Boston Classical High School. Bridget Tran y Garcia from Fox 36 stops me on my way in to school. I panic for a minute. Toni told me how she created a new e-mail and a different YouTube account through anonomizing proxy servers, like I have any idea what that means, but I'm still afraid they've nailed me as a co-creator. "Excuse me, young man. We're here to get student reactions to the 'Bringin' Crazy Back' video. Have you seen it?"

"Yeah."

"And how do you think it reflects on Boston Classical High School that one of your teachers is the laughingstock of the nation?" Oh man, I am *totally* recording this. That phrase is just music to my ears.

"I guess it doesn't make Boston Classical High School look very good."

"How do you like the video?"

I can't help smiling. "I freaking love it," I say.

...

I wish I could say that Kruzeman resigns in disgrace, but no.

Here's what happens instead: an assembly for ninth grade students in which Mr. Kelly reads to us some Massachusetts law statute or whatever about how videotaping someone without their knowledge or consent is forbidden. Oh yeah, and then there's the fact that they've figured out that the footage came from our class. So every member of our class gets called in one by one.

I look at Toni when they start calling people out of our class, and she smiles at me. It's nice to know my co-conspirator won't give me up.

When it's my turn to get to Mr. Kelly's office, I sit down and he says to me, "We know it was you, Kevin."

"Funny," I say. "But apparently you've said that to everybody you've had in here today." He really doesn't think students talk to each other?

This actually seems to catch him off-guard for a second, but he quickly gets his mojo back. "This is a serious matter. Tell me everything you know about this video."

"I know it's kind of a dance-pop number. Not my favorite kind of music, but that 'you're a disgrace' hook is really catchy, I'm not gonna lie. Is it based on, like a Justin Timberlake song? Lady Gaga, maybe?"

Mr. Kelly takes a deep breath, and when he speaks again, he's very quiet. "When we find out who's responsible for this, there will be serious consequences."

"Well," I say. "Good luck with that. I don't know a thing about it."

"That's not what Julie Chen told us," he says. I look at him. It's a good try, but he just picked the wrong girl.

I reach into my backpack and pull out my agenda book, which contains the Boston Classical code of conduct.

"Honor is crucial to academic excellence," I read. "Cheating, plagiarism, and other forms of dishonesty undermine the Boston Classical learning environment and will be dealt with within the code of discipline."

I look up at Mr. Kelly and smile.

"Are you accusing me of lying?" he says.

"No, sir. I just like to recite the code of conduct. I find it comforting."

"Get out of my office," he says.

• • •

When she gets home from work that day, Mom asks how school was.

"Oh, you know, the usual. Mr. Kelly called me in to the office and asked if I made the 'Bringin' Crazy Back' video."

Mom looks at me. A hint of a smile creeps to her lips. "And what did you tell him?"

"I told him I had no idea who made the video."

"And is that true?"

I'm not sure exactly how to play this. I don't think she'd be mad, but I really don't want to risk a lecture about how you have to follow the rules and not take stupid chances, or whatever kind of thing she might say.

"Mother. I'm shocked that you think I would lie to the administration at Boston Classical High School."

Mom gives me a squinty-eyed stare. I think she knows. Or suspects. "Well," she finally says, "I bet that kid's parents are pretty proud."

"I certainly hope so," I say.

"Yeah. You can count on it," she says.

• • •

YouTube pulls the video a couple of days later after Kruzeman complains, but of course it's been posted by like twenty other people by that point. They use it on the comedy shows where they make fun of stuff on the Internet, and somebody smarter than me prints up shirts that say "You're a Disgrace." The star of some reality show is wearing one in my mom's US Weekly.

And then, a week later, somebody posts a video of their toddler falling over as a golden retriever loudly farts in his face. Babies, dogs, and farts—you can't compete with that, and "Max Takes a Tumble" dethrones us as the most popular video in America. "Bringin' Crazy Back" passes into pop culture history.

Kruzeman doesn't exactly turn nice or anything, but maybe because he's not sure when he's being recorded. At least he stops being as abusive as he has been in the past. He doesn't make fun of my clothes or tell anybody they're a disgrace anymore. It probably won't last, but if it gets me through to the end of the year, I'll be fine with that.

And the day after "Max Takes a Tumble" gets its ten millionth hit, Toni runs up to me after school. "Hey, Kevin. You have any of your metal songs lying around?"

"I mean. Yeah, but—"

"Because I could never have . . . that whole thing was . . . well I just wanted to thank you for the Kruzeman thing, and I know it's not your kind of music, but I have like tons of horror movies and stuff. So if you want I could make a video for one of your songs. You know, only if you want . . ."

I smile. "Yeah. That sounds great. You want to . . . uh, we can talk about it on the bus and stuff? On the way home?"

"Yeah," she says. We start walking toward the bus stop, and I honestly don't know if it's her or me who starts it, but we're holding hands. And even though we were supposed to talk about our next project on the bus, we don't end up saying a word.

The Ambush

BY MATTHUE ROTH

VADIM SOUNDED SURPRISED when I called him to hang out, but he didn't say no. He told me to meet him at the public park, in the baseball field where nobody played baseball. It was across from a hollowed-out swimming pool that the neighborhood kids used for roller hockey during the day and other things during the night. I didn't know what. I only knew never to come here after dark. When we came to America, Vadim and me, fresh off the plane, the American kids told us that they caught children after dark and sold them. But we were new here. We didn't know how it worked, America in general, or the way kids dealt with each other. You could tell us anything.

"Why'd you want to meet here?" I asked.

"Why did you want to meet at all?" said Vadim.

"We have not seen each other since last year." I poked his ribs like my uncle who always tries to be funny and never is. I was being clever, you know? Yesterday was Rosh Hashanah, the Jewish new year, and the dual meaning was not lost on Vadim.

"That doesn't mean we must see each other *this* year," he shot back.

I tried to ignore the uneasiness. It was good to talk to Vadim—to open up my mouth and have him understand everything. All my words and all my intentions. We spoke our own language, a combination of English and Russian and words from science fiction books. Nobody understood me like he did.

"Hey, Vadim," I said. "You know how you're supposed to ask forgiveness from everyone you know, for anything you did to them, whether it was on purpose or by accident?"

"Yes." He refused to make eye contact.

"Well . . . do you forgive me?"

"For what?"

"For you know what."

"For maybe I think you should *say* it," he said.

"For losing my accent and getting all new friends and ignoring you for the entire first whole month of school."

I held my breath. I hated saying stuff like that, stuff that was true and damaging. It made me feel like I was poking holes in my own stomach.

"A good start," he offered.

"So, do you?" I said.

"Do I forgive you?"

"Yes!"

"Not yet."

I felt stunted and impotent. I remembered from some-where—from that lone year of Hebrew school, maybe—that you had to ask someone if they forgave you three times. If they didn't, at the end of the third asking, you were absolved and you didn't have to ask again. But before then, you were still guilty. Forgiveness wasn't an on-and-off switch; it was a combination lock.

And Vadim, it seemed, for now still held the key to that combination.

I fumbled for something to say.

"Uh . . . how were your services?"

Vadim looked at me askew—but at least now he was looking at me. "Are you really asking me that question?"

"Sure. Why not?"

He looked disgusted, even less likely to answer. "How were yours?"

"Crazy. We went to that Orthodox synagogue. There was a wall separating us from all the women. The only thing you could see was the outline of their breasts. So, guess what I spent all services thinking about."

Vadim's face broke into a big toothy smile like he'd been waiting for this. No matter how he felt about me now, I was still the only person in the world he'd ever been able to candidly talk about girls with. And by *girls,* I don't mean the female species that was created on whatever day, but I mean the objects of the all-consuming lust that suddenly possessed our minds and bodies.

"What are you looking at me like that for?" I chided. "At least your parents' synagogue is Reform. You can actually *see* them."

"Is even worse, Jupiter. They sit right *there*. Right in front of you. And we're there for four hours. It's almost like you're *supposed* to stare at them. And they're *praying*, which only makes you feel worse and more guilty for checking them out. You're feeling all spiritual and *pobozny*, because you're connected to the universe and you can do anything, then you open your eyes and there *they* are, and all you wanna do is touch 'em."

"Wow." I was stunned. Riveted. "Whose?"

Vadim hesitated. "Karla Bozulich."

"But she's your cousin!" I cringed.

"I know." Vadim looked down at himself, miserable. "That should feel wrong, shouldn't it? But her breasts are nice ones."

I couldn't argue with that, and Vadim couldn't bring himself to say anything else. I sat in silence, letting him lead. After a while, he checked his watch.

"It is twelve o'clock," he said. "I have to go."

"What? Already? I just got here. . . ."

"It's twelve noon. I need to visit my cousins. Come with me?"

• • •

When we were little, the kids in the park, the Americans, used to play games with our minds. We knew they were tricking us, of course. The way they laughed. The way they'd beat us up if we didn't do what they said. Somehow we always ended up in this playground anyway.

I was small. Vadim was tiny. Together, we made a better target practice than either of the video arcades at Roosevelt Mall. A common getaway from a common enemy: this was how Vadim and I decided to be friends.

Now we were wiser. Now we knew names for the things that went on in this park: *betting* and *gangfights* and *dealing*. We knew more things, but it didn't make us safer.

Today, Vadim and his invitation—*Come with me?*—felt dangerous. Vadim was never dangerous. It was Saturday, and you only got one Saturday a week. Did I want to give it to Vadim?

I did. I came.

...

As we walked, the houses grew incrementally bigger and more well-maintained. Vadim's cousins—not the Karla Bozulich cousins, his other side—lived in Rushing Waters, a cushy development that lay between the Yards and suburbia. Rushing Waters was its own self-contained community of immigrant families.

It just so happened that the opening of Rushing Waters coincided with the collapse of the Iron Curtain and several zillion Russian families immigrating to the United States. The Jewish Federation bought the entire development, and Rushing Waters was informally renamed Russian Vodkas. Each family got a free house, and they stuffed it to the gills. Friends and cousins back in Russia would get plane tickets for New York City, plan a two-week vacation, and never go back. You'd go to someone's house and the door would be answered by any one of twenty-three identical cousins, each with the same Russian bowl-cut hairstyle. Everyone slept together, five kids to a cot, older cousins on the sofas.

The houses still smelled of fresh paint, with new sofas and refrigerators that made ice when you hit a button. There were definitely no soldering machines to wake you at 5:30 a.m. every morning. It was a lottery. Sometimes you got the jackpot, and sometimes you didn't get anything but a useless ticket and silver crap under your nails. For every family who *didn't* get placed in Russian Vodkas, they had to find somewhere else.

Vadim's family was given a freestanding house where—like most of these kids—he had his own attic bedroom. For my parents, they found a vacant factory. I lived in Secondary Processing and shared a bedroom with a conveyor belt. Sometimes I woke up with black soot on my face.

We had no say on how the Jewish Federation spent money on us; we just checked the mail and saw what new toys we had coming. That part was made even more incongruous for a family like us living in a factory. Out of nowhere they would send us brand-new water filters, or three full frozen chickens for Friday night dinner, or a really nice new Serta California King bed. The deliverymen were always confused. They weren't sure if we were really poor or really rich.

. . .

As Vadim and I descended the main drive, the one that led from the main road into the valley of Russian Vodkas, I felt a palpable change, the America evaporating from the air as the Russia started to sink in. Goose bumps peppered my bare, T-shirted arms and crept stealthily up my spine. I could have lived here, I reminded myself. If we'd been one notch higher on the list of Poor Russian Aid Victims, my family could be here. My parents would have a house. I would have friends who understood my words and forgave my accent, because they would have one too.

"*Blyad,*" Vadim muttered. "I hate this ghetto. I'm so glad we got a house on our own."

"What? Five minutes down the road can make that much difference?"

"All the difference in the world," he said at once. "Could you imagine having the kind of computer setup I have if I lived here? Thirty people would be over every night, bugging me to let them check their stupid Hotmail accounts. If no one stole it from me, I mean. And could you *imagine* what kind of a security system I'd need to protect my comics?"

Actually, I could. Vadim had once exiled me from his house for two weeks after I breathed too heavily on his *New Avengers* #32, the one where Power Man's baby might be a shape-changing alien. I could see his point.

The street names—Maple Glen Road, Fairview Lane, Buttermilk Bend—were all cruel forgeries, promises of an Americana that we would never achieve. Not only because this neighborhood was in the dead zone between city and suburbs. Not only because we were Russian. But because everyone was too stuck in their own lives to even *want* to try to get out.

We passed tons of people on the street. It seemed like everyone who lived there had chosen that moment to leave their house for the market, or to walk the dog, or just to see what was going on. It was like no one had day jobs.

They all stared at us. Not the way that people stared downtown, the normal people who fixed us with that vacant, angry *what-are-you-doing-here* stare. No, here they stared as though they knew exactly what we were doing here, even if we didn't know ourselves. In our thrift-store clothes and our dirty backpacks, they could tell we were trespassing.

"So, Vadim—uh, not to be dense, but why are we here?"

"You wanted to hang out with me? Well, this is what I have to do today. This is how we can hang out."

He had answered me in straight Russian. That was how I knew things were about to change.

We stopped in front of a perfectly white door with tiny flecks of paint peeling from the outermost corners, red and white polka-dotted curtains hanging in the windows. Loud metal music blared from inside. My friend Bates had been teaching me to work out his favorite metal bands, to recognize them from the tenor of the lead singer's yells and the first few notes of each riff: Danzig, Deicide, Morbid Angel, Godflesh. This band was none of them. Their sound was less bleak, less deathlike and more pretending-to-be-deathlike. I felt a weird, secret power over whoever was playing this music, but at the same time, I was scared.

Vadim reached up and rang the doorbell. It was a normal electric doorbell noise. I don't know what I expected.

After a considerable time and what seemed like a struggle, or a conversation, someone came to the door. It was Peter Khazarimovsky, Vadim's cousin. I'd met him a few times before, but it was always with his or Vadim's parents around. I was more comfortable with it that way.

Peter (born Piyotr) was over six feet tall. He had thick hair that was cut short and yet still treated with hair gel, and both his ears were pierced on the bottom and top. On anyone else, it would've looked gay. But Peter Piyotr had this glint in his eye—you could feel it even when he was wearing his $500 Oakley sunglasses, which was pretty much always—that seemed to suggest he might very well have a switchblade in his back pocket.

He looked us up and down. Then he looked me up and down again. Finally, he nodded coolly. He offered his right hand to Vadim, positioned in the air opposite his considerably wide shoulders. They did a kind of combination handshaking/ hug thing, and then he motioned for us to come inside.

I knew Peter Piyotr's parents lived there, but I had no idea how they managed to manifest their presence in the house. The shades were drawn, and bottles of wine and vodka lay strewn around the darkness. This wasn't even my father's kind of drinking, concentrated and private and starting at midday. This was balls-out, show-your-friends-what-you're-made-of, early-morning drinking. Two guys sat on the floor in front of the TV and another lay on the couch. So did a fourth guy, although it took me a while to notice, because he was passed out and only half an arm was visible.

"Who is this?"

"I—" My mouth wanted to protest, but the words refused to come out. Peter Piyotr had met me at least twenty times. Our moms played Pachinko together. Where did he get to be all who-is-thissing me?

"This is Jupiter," Vadim cut me off. "He's fine. He won't give us trouble."

"I won't give you *trouble*?" I asked. "Vadim, who is Piyotr pretending to—"

"Sit down, Jupiter." Vadim's voice was cold. Even and tighter than before, like a robot. I ducked into the living room. The sofa squeaked when I sat.

Vadim and Peter Piyotr spoke in whispered hisses for a minute. I heard him say that our parents were friends, and the words *from my synagogue*. Our parents?

"Fine. He can stay," Peter Piyotr said to Vadim at last. To me he smiled indulgently and said, "Shalom." I heaved a sigh.

Vadim walked over to the TV in the living room, where he high-fived two guys that I didn't recognize at all. "Vadim, what are we doing here?" I said quietly.

"Stop asking questions," he hissed.

I bit my lip and reclined into the stiff boarded leather.

"Are you angry?" I said.

"You said you wanted to come," Vadim said at a normal

volume. The TV guys looked over. Then—louder—he said, "You wanted to hang out with me, remember?"

"Because we're *friends*," I said. "I wanted everything to be cool with us."

"Which is, of course, something you and only you are able to do," said Vadim. He smiled like he was joking, but his voice didn't sound at all like it was joking. "What's wrong, my droog? Scared? Is Jupiter out of his element?"

I looked at Vadim. Had I really known this person on two continents, torn my sandwich in half for him on the first day of school, confided in him my secret fantasies about Emma Frost and Psylocke? This was a completely different Vadim.

"Since when is this *your* element?"

"How would you even *know?* You never pay attention to anybody's life except your own."

"Please. Do you even realize how much of an effort I make to pull you along with me?" I got in his face. "Other people, when they get popular, they ignore their old friends. I would never do that."

"Of course not. You're so much better than that. Instead, you drag me along so there's someone around to look even more pathetic than you do."

I pulled back, stunned. "Did you just say I look pathetic?"

"For all you think you understand people, Jupiter Glazer," said Vadim, "you're more clueless than all the rest of us put together. You wear these falling-apart clothes that are supposed to look like the ones they charge hundreds of dollars for downtown, but everyone knows they really are Salvation Army trash. You think just because you know Devin Murray, that automatically makes you rich by association—that your life will be easy and it'll take you far far away from the Yards. But that doesn't just happen, Jupiter. You need to *work* to get out of here."

Vadim didn't know how far from the truth he was. I wore the least scabby, torn, thrift-store-looking shirts and jeans I could find. I had plenty of clothes that might have looked cooler, but they were also more dangerous, easier for someone to casually tease, *Hey, where'd you get that—the Salvation Army?* And Devin Murray didn't waste any more time talking to me than I cajoled her into spending. We occasionally said hello in the halls. It was the kind of friendship that was awkward and forced, and I felt guilty just being in it. If I didn't constantly keep watering it, it would evaporate.

But I didn't say that. I said: "This is what you define as working hard enough to get you out of the Yards? Slumming around a gross living room in Russian Vodkas, dragging me to some sleazy drug deal? Are you trying to make a point?"

"Hey!" said Peter Piyotr.

"What?" I said to him. "Am I very wrong, or are Vadim and I here for a drug deal?"

Peter Piyotr started to argue, then changed his mind. "Nah, you're right," he shrugged. "It's a drug deal."

"You see?" I said to Vadim. "You're going to fry the brains of some innocent little kid and damn them to a life of prostitution. . . ."

"My mom does that, and she's not even on drugs," some guy from the kitchen called. The two in front of the TV laughed. How many people were in this house right now?

I turned to them. "Do you guys all live here?"

They ignored the question. "You know what is so great about this place?" asked one of them. "It is so quiet. Very desirable. No one ever comes here. No cops, no nobody. From inside these houses, you can hear nothing."

"Oh, Jupiter knows all about that," Peter Piyotr said, moving closer. He stood inches away from me when he spoke, almost into my ear. Under different circumstances, it might have tickled. "Our Jupiter, he lives in a warehouse. It is even bigger and more isolated. Isn't that right?"

"Yes," I ventured. With him this close, there was nothing to do but agree.

"I bet he has room to store shit there. Lots of shit. And at good cool temperatures, too. I'll bet Jupiter would do that for us for free. I bet he would do anything we say."

"I bet he would." Vadim smiled wickedly. *Wickedly.* Is this why he'd brought me here?

"Are—are you serious?" I asked. Usually I only spoke Russian to my parents and having to use it now made me feel violated on every level of my brain.

They started laughing. For real, now. Peter Piyotr, the guys on the floor, even Vadim. Vadim laughed hardest of all— toothily, scarily. His laugh filled the room. It was like a stench of a million farts at once. You couldn't tune it out. It pressed against me on all sides.

"*Blyad*, Jupiter, I don't even know why I brought you," Vadim said after he caught his breath. He sounded more whiny than angry. "Just please grow up a little?"

"Fine," I said. "Just stop talking to me. I'm out of here. I'm out of your whole life. Just say the word."

"You want a word? Here is the word: *sick*. I'm sick of you. I'm sick of your little social games. You can't keep getting off the phone with me to talk to Devin Murray just because she has boobs and I don't. Or Crash Goldberg. Or Bates, who God knows what his appeal is, but he is for sure not cooler than me—not with all those spikes and chains. Or maybe you're into that now?"

"Fine Vadim. Just stop insulting me."

"What? Did I hurt your pretty little ego? What could some unpopular nobody like me say to bother someone like you?" Vadim's eyes danced wildly. He was playing with me.

"Okay, that's it," I said, moving toward the door. "I'm leaving."

"No, don't," says Peter Piyotr. "Really, keep fighting. This shit is great."

Of all the things that piss me off about Peter Piyotr Khazarimovsky, this is the biggest: he isn't even Jewish.

Not to sound prejudiced. Most of my friends aren't Jewish either. To be honest, there isn't much that actually makes me Jewish, except that people would tease me about it back in Zvrackova, and the government kept records on us along with the rest of the Jews. But Peter was such an asshat about it. When he borrowed ten dollars from Vadim and never gave it back, he'd say, "Oh, I'm sorry . . . it must be my Jewish side." His parents, Vadim's stepuncle and his wife, had lied to the Jewish Federation and told them their family was Jewish, filled out all the necessary forms and got a free ride all the way to America. It wasn't that simple, but it basically was. Peter was always bragging about it, how easy it was to rip off the rich American Jews.

It was wrong of me to think, but his house, his parents' jobs, even his respected (if dubious) social status—all of this could have been mine. If we'd gotten here a little earlier. If I'd gotten to live in Russian Vodkas instead of some run-down factory. If this really was the land of equal rights, instead of the country of take-what-you-can-get.

A cell rang. Russian disco. A bleeping, tinny, cheesy melody that nobody in the rest of the world would think was cool after 1977. *Please*, I thought, *shoot me now*.

Peter Piyotr reached into his pocket and picked up.

"Da. Da? Da."

Three quick staccato sounds. Then he hung up.

"Joe is here now. You," he said motioning to one of the guys in front of the TV. "Go outside and help him bring the goods inside."

• • •

Joe was the archetype of the rock star, if by "rock star" you think of someone from the '80s. A number of fat gold chains hung around his neck, and his eyes were shielded by a pair of sunglasses that looked like they had their own backup generator. Over his shoulders was draped a studded leather jacket. He moved fast, brisk, and dangerously, as though any movement of his hand could land at the base of my throat.

"Here is loot," Joe said. He and other guy held bulging brown paper bags and overturned them, spilling its contents all over the table.

Out fell hundreds, literally hundreds of tubes of Wint-O-Green Life Savers.

The cascade ran dry eventually, and Joe and Peter Piyotr stared at Vadim with an air of expectation. "Is good?" asked Joe.

"This is perfect," said Vadim, running his fingers through the stash. "I'll take them up to the lab I set up and pulverize them for you, right?"

He watched Joe when he spoke. So did everyone else. It was painfully clear to the entire room that Joe was the one in control. Now, Joe nodded with approval. "Is good," he proclaimed once again, this time a statement.

Everyone was nonchalant. I was the only mental slowpoke in the room. "Uh . . . ," I stumbled. "What are you going to do with them?"

"Grind them into powder," Vadim replied. "And probably remove those stupid-as-hell sparkles. They make it look like impure product."

"Impure . . . ?" I said. "But what are you going to do with

that? What do you use it for?"

"We sell," said Peter Piyotr. "The kids, they like to snort. Also use when going down on the girlies—it turn into fire sparks."

His upper lip curled into a jurassic smile. Clearly, he was amused by my ignorance.

"We go upstairs," said Joe. "Follow."

In a spare bedroom, Vadim had set up a virtual manufacturing plant. Glass beakers, metal boxes with dials attached to their sides, aluminum rods suspended at weird angles.

Immediately, Joe and Peter Piyotr got to work peeling open packages of the Life Savers. So did the other guys. Vadim was busy on the controls. I took advantage of my outsider status and stood next to him, observing quietly, hoping my inaction would be mistaken for actively helping.

The truth was, I was no stranger to heavy machinery. I worked and lived in a factory. I was usually able to tell what machines did from their shape, size, and maybe even the awkward parts that stuck out. But here, I was totally mystified.

I had to hand it to Vadim. He'd made himself a functioning laboratory that kicked any high school chem lab's ass. Not only that, but it was paid for and housed by the kids least likely to think that science was cool. Somehow Vadim—*Vadim!*—had made himself into the kind of person that the kids who beat us up respected.

I fingered a fine powder that lay piled next to one particularly twisted plastic tube.

"You use all this stuff just to smash up Life Savers?"

"Well, no," said Vadim matter-of-factly. "The rest of it is for purifying the crystal meth."

"Oh my God!" I exclaimed. "Are you *making* drugs?"

Peter Piyotr cracked that crooked grin even wider. The final Life Savers were dropped into the pinball arrangement of machines. Vadim hit the switch. Peter Piyotr and Joe watched approvingly—feet parted wide like cowboys, mouths just short of drooling—as their candy was pulverized.

"You want a free sample?" He slipped his long, sinewy fingers in between curls of my hair, gripped hard, and gave my body a yank.

It wasn't just that I didn't do drugs. I didn't know what to *do* with drugs. When my nose bled, I couldn't even take drops because I couldn't figure out how to stop breathing long enough to use them.

Peter Piyotr lowered my face into the table. He got down on his knees and leaned closer. "We don't like the people who say, 'We are better than you,'" he snarled in my ear. "Only one thing we hate more than that. The people who come here and want free stuff. And we hate the giving stuff away, yes, Andrei?"

"Yes, this is right." One of the TV guys, who had switched from slowly passing out in the living room to passing out on this floor, gave a sadistic giggle.

"But you, you are special. You are friend of Vadim. You apparently like us here so much that you care to watch everything we do, yes?"

"No!" I cried out, feeling my hair pulled even harder. "I wasn't watching anything! I was barely looking at you!"

"I do not think so. Perhaps you are narc, sent to us from cops. Yes?"

"No!" He was bearing down on me, now, pushing me down to my knees. Seeing the table come desperately close to my face, I began to think fast. By which I mean, I didn't think at all. I began to hyperventilate. "You never made Vadim do this, did you?"

Peter Piyotr laughed. Flecks of spit shot in my ear. "Vadim must be kept straight. He must measure the stuff, you see." He stood the straw up vertically. It was almost in my nose. I tried to pull away. "You should say thank you for this, man."

I stopped breathing. I tried not to inadvertently inhale. If a few flecks up my nose, who knew what would happen?

On the floor, Andrei and the other guy peeled with wheezy laughter. Their eyes were half closed.

"Jesus," said Peter Piyotr in disgust. *Finally,* I thought, *he shows his true religion.* "You act like we torture you. You know how much this shit cost?"

He dipped his own head down, brought his nose to the tip of the candy-striped straw, and breathed deep. He paused before coughing, twice, from someplace deep in his lungs. His body keeled back.

I shook. I shook so hard I thought I'd lost control of my own body. His hand, which a moment ago had been on my collar, slumped down onto my back. The rest of his body lay in the inch-deep shag carpet. His eyes were closed, and his mouth was open. Drool was puddling. His chest rose and fell peacefully, reminding me oddly of a baby.

The other guys scrambled to their feet, instantly sober. They pulled themselves to their feet, jaws loose, limbs flailing. In seconds they were gone.

"Fucking slowpoke," Joe grumbled. He bent down over Peter Piyotr's body and started to fish through his jacket.

Vadim and I watched as he pillaged the rest of Peter Piyotr's pockets. He pulled out several plastic envelopes of powdery white stuff and a fat wad of cash, rolled up like I'd only ever seen in movies. I glanced at Vadim. Vadim was staring at Peter Piytor's body in horror.

Joe rose. In his jacket pocket, I spied the glint of a long silvery knife. He looked at us dead on. There were no questions about what we'd seen or hadn't seen. We'd seen it all.

"Is easy this time," he said, by way of explanation. "Did not even have to ask." His laugh made it clear that *ask* was a euphemism for something much, much less pleasant.

He moved to the door. "Is no problem. Peter he sniff-sniff too fast. Will . . . wake up, few hours maybe."

"You—you're not going to rob us, too?" Vadim said. His voice was so high it cracked.

Joe's laugh got bigger. "Why? You got any money?"

"I don't have anything. I—I was supposed to get paid," Vadim apologized, shaking his head.

Joe smirked, peeled a bill off the wad, and chucked it in

Vadim's direction. It landed on the floor between them.

"Here you go," said Joe. "No tip."

He ducked through the doorway, which was barely big enough to hold his massive body. When he was finally gone and we heard the door slam and looked at each other in utter disbelief.

"Come on." Vadim grabbed my hand and threaded his fingers in my own. If anyone saw us they'd laugh or chasing us, maybe both. But nobody did.

We waited just as long as it took for the roar of his engine to die out, then stepped onto the porch overlooking the streets of Russian Vodkas. The road was wet like it'd just rained, as if a flash flood had come through and we'd completely missed it. The sidewalks were completely empty. There was no one left in the world but the two of us.

Vadim pulled me off that porch. I pulled him out of that place. We ran. Together, we ran.

Inside the Inside

BY MAYRA LAZARA DOLE

SHE DIDN'T DO IT. I know she didn't do it.

I walk past The Last Bookstore in a daze and pluck my cell out of my jean pocket to read more of the news feed.

blyss gordon was last person seen w gustavo olivera . . .

gus's swollen, discolored body found floating under south beach pier . . .

cops hunting down blyss & likely accomplice, mik Donaldson . . .

My hands shake. I never thought I'd make the news this way. I've got to find Blyss, but she's not responding to my texts.

I pass Frugal Café and notice a boy in goggles, sipping blood-red pomegranate juice. He's got disheveled hair and looks like a sci-fi kid from a dystopian novel. His marble eyes—a swirling mix of violet, apricot, and lime—drill into me.

"She's over there," he juts his chin across the street toward Arte Gallery, "inside the inside. Just keep going up and up until you reach the apex."

"Who are you?"

"Whatever you do," he ignores me, "don't look back until you get there."

"What makes you think I'm looking for someone?"

"Don't waste time asking me questions. She's waiting for you." His stare pierces my marrow, and I speed up my pace. Maybe I'll find her safe, hiding somewhere, in a vault or crawl space. She must be terrified.

I used to be nothing before Blyss. Her electricity fired me up and melted me down, awakening me to a new world of feelings and temptations. She's my savior, and now it's my turn to rescue her. I won't let those crazy lies come between us.

I cross the street, remembering my first conversation with Blyss in French class. She had her head in a novel, and I plopped down on a chair next to hers.

"Whoa," my eyes widen, "you read entire novels in French?"

"It's no big deal." She shuts the book and her eyes meet mine. "I'm sure you have some secret talent too."

"I guess. My parents have forced me to play classical piano since I was four, but I hate it."

"Well, maybe I'll help you break a finger and you'll be all set."

Blyss has a crazy sense of humor that's misunderstood. She's caring, witty, and captivating. Sure, she might have hated Gus, but she wasn't capable of murdering him.

I enter the gallery and a pungent smell of raspberries explodes in my face. My feet feel leaden as I walk past rows of watercolors searching for my girlfriend. A massive painting taking up half a wall titled *Desert iLand: Inside the Inside* catches my attention. My eyes dart everywhere, seeking an entrance around it. I catch a glimpse of the slightly peach, almost translucent colored water that appears so real I can't veer my focus from it.

I press a finger into the canvas and dunk it in. When I pull it out, it's dripping wet.

"What the hell?" I say aloud as I stumble backward. My mind reels, trying to make sense of everything. This isn't possible. She can't be in there. I inch forward, taking in every detail of the painting. Tall, swaying palms line the left side of a long path. A vast ocean stretches along on its right, and a dense, chilling fog hovers over the open sea. Far in the distance, there's a dot of an island.

A flashing sign on top of the painting averts my attention: TAKE SIX STEPS FORWARD AND STEP INSIDE THE INSIDE.

I know I need to enter, but apprehension seeps into me when I hear crashing waves. This is insane. Just as I'm about to turn around and leave, I hear Blyss's voice filled with fear, calling to me through the canvas—at least I *think* that's where it's coming from:

"Come in and find me, Mik . . ."

"Blyss?" I peer into the artwork.

"Where are you?" she responds in a sharp tone.

I take one step. Two. Three. They get lighter and lighter as I float toward the painting. Gusting wind and sea spray batters against my body, flapping open my jacket and oversized shirt. A deep pull yanks me, spins me around and hurls me inside. I land on my feet, but just barely. I reach out to touch a palm and realize it's made of origami.

This can't be. My mind struggles to grasp reality, but there's no anchor.

Hissing noises, like creatures closing in, mock me from behind. I think of the guy in the café, his voice deep and steady, telling me: *keep going up and up . . . and don't look back.* So I do. I take off running with screeching, growling sounds chasing me, spurring me on.

I sprint on the trail, uphill, toward the summit. Every second that passes under the harsh, blinding sun takes an enormous effort. The footpath becomes steeper and my heart thumps harder in my chest. Stinging sweat drips into my eyes. I shake my long hair, spraying droplets everywhere. My feet ache and my lungs are about to burst as I pound up this endless, impossible hill. I stop to catch my breath, doubled over with eyes shut.

Keep going. For Blyss.

My leg muscles spasm as I battle to continue pushing forward. This damn jacket is dragging me down. I tear it off and throw it behind me, panting as I dash straight up to the apex. Out of breath, I look up at a cobalt blue sun, shooting vibrant rays into the ocean. I drop my head and scrutinize the waters. They're teeming with multicolored fish turning into white winged butterflies flattening into horizontal sheets. Twirling into whirlwinds, they spit out pink starfish-like creatures with antennas that whip back and forth.

That's some crazy shit.

I see a tiny dot of an island far in the distance. The man-darin scented water smells of Blyss's hair. She's close. I slide off my shirt, sneakers, and socks and dive into the peach sea. My cupped hands move through the warm, crystalline water, and I quickly catapult forward. With every stroke, the waters change colors like a revolving kaleidoscope, from peach to turquoise, to translucent with a light grape tinge.

I spy a raft in the middle of the sea and swim hard toward it.

"Blyss!?" I yell as loud as I can, desperate for it to be her. She's sitting on a raft, meringue white skin, black midnight hair cascading down to the middle of her back. I kick relentlessly as my arms move in a windmill motion. My hand smacks against the raft, and Blyss throws her arms around me.

"You found me!" Her shining blue eyes glow in a way that makes my chest swell.

"You look beautiful." My mind is blank. I can't think of anything but her. Even in the middle of the ocean, she looks svelte and graceful. Her small, sloped-up nose and delicate dimpled chin have always made me forget who and where I am. I scan her limbs and notice one of her hands is massively swollen and rolled up into a colossal fist the size of my head.

"What happened?"

She pinches it with her thumb and index finger. "It doesn't hurt. I might be allergic to something. . . ." I grip her gigantic fist to stay afloat in the middle of the vast sea. Her inflatable raft dips with my weight, and I'm careful not to pull her under. She flops on her belly and our noses touch.

"You're my hero, Mik. Now that you're here, I'm sure

we're meant to be together." She leans into me and presses her velvety lips against mine. I sink into a warm, melting feeling. She pulls away and points to a green dot in the distance.

"Let's swim over there. Doesn't it look like Paradise? We'll make it our home, where no one will find us." I hold on to her enormous fist and kick my feet hard as she lies on the raft. I paddle with one hand to propel us forward and remember the news reports.

"They think you killed Gus, but you didn't, though. Did you, Blyss?"

"Of course not. He threw himself off the pier and everyone wants to blame me. You believe me, don't you?" I nod. I trust every word she says and keep swimming.

Blyss and I met Gus at Riverview Academy, a private school for gifted students. He was homeschooled until he got there, and when he entered the school system he skipped two grades. Gus was only twelve, placed in our homeroom with kids older than him. He wore slinky dresses and strutted about in heels. Gus wanted to be referred to as a "she" and addressed as "Alyssa" but Blyss refused. Most of the class joined her in calling him "Gus," or "Pus."

Gus thought it would stop and we'd all get to like him once we understood his sense of humor, but that never happened. Blyss wouldn't let it. So when we were forced to watch *Everyone's Queer*—a play Gus had written, acted in, and directed—I knew Blyss would be upset. She didn't just tease him like the others. She loathed him.

Gus played his authentic self: Alyssa, a curvy "girl" with a soft voice, slinky dress, girly shoes, and glittery make-up that made his green eyes seem larger. His straight, naturally blondish hair hung down to his shoulders. The performance opened with Alyssa sitting next to Roly on the sofa—an Afro Cuban boy in conservative attire and buzzed hair—playing her straight stepbrother.

"Why do you have to be het?" Alyssa crosses one leg over the other and swings it. "How will a decent guy ever want to date you if you're hanging around those straights?"

"What's it to you if I'm into girls?" Roly toys with his tie. "It's not like I'm killing someone or shooting up."

When Alyssa and Roly's lesbian moms ambled onto the stage holding hands, I realized the play was a parody. "Mami" played a muscular butch in army attire—with boots, a mustache, and a husky voice. "Mima" was portrayed as a mega feminine mom, dressed fancy, draped in pearls and fake fur, like a glamorous Hollywood actress.

"Roly, when did you choose to become straight?" Mima twirls her long locks with her index finger. "No one is born hetero."

"It's true, baby. You're just mixed up." Mami pats her bulging stomach. "You need to date a few handsome, brilliant, interesting guys, and you'll turn homosexual fast. You hear me?"

Then Roly's older brother and his muscle-bound Chinese Cuban boyfriend strolled over wearing matching pink mini shorts without shirts. The audience started to crack up at the exaggeration, and at first, I thought it was funny too. But when

I felt Blyss squeeze my thigh and her body tensed up next to mine, I realized I should be furious.

"He's so damned disturbed," Blyss whispered into my ear. "What gives those assholes the privilege to inhabit this earth and spread diseases? People like him should kill themselves."

"Yeah," I agreed. Acid crept up my stomach and into my esophagus. I tried to swallow hard but it wouldn't go down.

As we continue on our way to Desert iLand, the day begins to fade but the sun is as relentless as ever. Blyss doesn't seem to notice though. She throws me a gleaming smile, and I realize she's a different girl from yesterday; the one sitting next to me during the play is gone. The stress engraved all over her face has dissolved, and she doesn't seem to notice her arms and back have turned a bright pink. They've started to peel and blister, just like my shoulders and top of my head.

Suddenly light bounces off the water, shooting an illusion of flashing daggers all around us. As we head toward our new home, I make out a dolphin leaping in and out of the water in front of us. He swims to us and nestles up against me. I pet the side of its slippery face.

"What a gift," I smile. I jut my nose to Desert iLand and ask, "will you take us there?" The dolphin moves its head, which I interpret for a nod.

"I don't trust him," Blyss squints. "He might pull us in the opposite direction, farther away from the island."

As if prompted, the dolphin slips under the water. I try to grab at him, to coax him back, but it resurfaces a few feet away from us, squirting red from its blowhole, staining the ocean with a shining crimson glow. He stares at Desert iLand while standing in the water, swimming backward, giving sideways head jerks with an open jaw and wide eyes.

I can't unfasten my gaze from the distressed dolphin emitting a series of loud, high-pitched whistles.

"He's telling us those waters are hazardous, Blyss."

"I *told* you. He's trying to lead us astray."

He nose-dives, resurfaces, and squirts a thick glob of red from his blowhole that splatters our bodies with blood. Ugh. I wipe off the viscous substance as I tread water. It seeps across the ocean with a dark red stain and the scent of iron as he leaps away.

"This is a bad sign." My throat ties up in knots and I gag. "Listen to me, Blyss. We need to turn around and head home."

"Are you nuts?!" She pushes herself forward on the raft and begins to paddle. "The dolphin is just hurt. We're almost at our paradise."

"We've got to get out of here, now!" I try to pull the raft around, but she kicks at my arms.

"We're heading to the island and that's *that*! Can't you see there's a perfect world awaiting us? It's the only place we'll be safe. We'll live there together, forever. No one will bother us again, or try to push their views on us. We can do as we please."

"If we don't turn back, we'll die."

"Why? Because a dolphin says so? Don't be spineless. We're wasting time."

I grab my phone from my pocket and press a few digits with shaky fingers but realize it's water-damaged. *Don't Panic. Keep your cool.* Damn. I'll never be able to call for help from the middle of nowhere.

The wind picks up and waves start to twirl and swirl around us at incredible speeds. Strong currents slam against me. A fierce wave breaks, pushing me deep underwater, holding me here. I spin around and can't tell which way is up.

I kick hard and finally hit the surface, gasping for air. Blyss is far away hollering for me, but I can barely catch my breath. Another wave crashes against me. I swallow water and cough. Shortness of breath turns into loud wheezes.

"You better not drown on me!" Blyss shouts as she makes her way closer. I gulp air but nothing seems to be filling my lungs. I wheeze and wheeze. Finally she reaches me and slips her arms around my neck. "Breathe slowly, deeply. The weather has calmed. You're going to be okay. . . ."

Her voice turns whisper-soft. The melody seeps into me, and I do as she says.

"If you drowned, I'd be left alone." She caresses my hair. "Let's think about the beautiful life we're about to have. We'll fish and feed each other berries and fruits. We'll drink rain and coconut water. We can survive perfectly happy, alone, just the two of us."

She presses her mouth against my closed eyes. The warmth of her breath runs slowly from my eyelids, down my entire body to my toes. She kisses my lips, and my mind is emptied of everything except Blyss's sweet taste.

Until I see flashes of Gus's contorted face.

I've got a dark feeling creeping inside me like a silent, deadly surf, rising and falling, bringing with it condemnation. I'm catapulted into reality. My voice is strong. "That island is much farther than it looks. We'd dehydrate and wouldn't survive without liquid in this heat." I let go of the raft and wave my hand toward the apex behind us. "Come on! In an hour we'll be back safe on shore."

Blyss slaps the water. "Stop pissing me off and let's go!"

"You don't want to be fresh bait for sharks, do you?" I keep a careful eye on the rapidly growing waves. The water begins to get colder. A shiver works up my spine.

She presses onward. "I would have never dated you if I'd known you were such a weakling." She pulls the raft in one direction while I pull in the other.

"Don't you ever want to see your family again? How about all your friends and Trigger, your dog?"

"Let go you stupid fucking son-of-a-bitch! You coward! I wish Knight were here instead of you." Veins pop out of her forehead as she thrashes about. "He's stronger and would have pulled me with him on his back all the way to the island."

"Calm down, Blyss. Please. Please. You're losing energy. We need to stay tranquil."

"Tranquil? Here's tranquil." She cocks her large fist and starts pounding the ocean. Waves hammer against my face, making me spit out water. "I wish I had never met you, Wimp!"

My eyes leap with surprise at the power in Blyss's punches and I let go of the raft. I stop a memory of Gus from flooding my brain. If she'd jabbed him with her inflamed fist, she'd have massacred him.

She stops and catapults all the power in her arms to help her paddle forward toward the island. I grab her foot but can't keep her from speeding ahead.

"Don't you get it?" she says without looking back. "I won't rot in juvie or get thrown in jail for a crime I didn't commit. That asshole's death isn't my fault." The clouds take on a dark, eerie hue as the sun sinks in front of us and the water becomes black as onyx.

"We won't make it out of here alive. We need food, supplies, and shelter. . . ." I start swimming in the other direction and momentarily look back. "Follow me!"

"No! Don't leave." She spins around on the raft and hurriedly gets to me. She holds on to my neck and won't let go. "I'm sorry for everything I said. I didn't mean it. . . ."

"I know," I try to assure her. "Let's go. Grab on and I'll swim you back to shore."

"I can't."

I slide out from under her grip and plunge into the sea, promising myself I'll come back for her. I swim as if a killer whale is chasing me, for what feels like hours until I hit a large rock. I haul myself up, gulping huge gasps of air as I look around. *Damn. That girl has guts. I can't believe she stayed, alone.* It's pitch black by now. I must be where I first started. I get up and move carefully, one foot in front of the other, making my way downhill. My eyes throb with so much pain. I reach up to rub them but my fingers penetrate the empty sockets. I shudder. My eyes have fallen out of my head.

This can't be. You're dreaming.

Carefully, I walk downhill without animals hooting, clawing, or hissing. I must be taking a different way out. I stumble upon a pliable surface. It feels like the taut canvas I came through. I step into it, listen to the material tearing and feel the cold ground under my feet. I hear city noises: barking dogs, car horns, and airplanes overhead. Truck exhaust, cigarette smoke, and perfume fill my nostrils. I'm definitely back in Miami.

Voices come at me from all directions, "Whoa, boy, watch where you're headed!" I shiver and hug myself. I'm back in frigid February temperatures and I'm fully dressed; I've got on my jacket, shirt, shoes, and socks. I'm not soaking wet like I was seconds ago. *How can this be?*

My hands feel frigid, unmovable. I'm sure they're turning purple. I blow warm breaths into them and clap them, but nothing helps the cold seeping my bones. I walk carefully, slowly, with trembling arms stretched forward so as not to stumble or crash into anything or anyone. A veil of hopelessness drapes over me. I no longer belong to the human race. I've lost myself, my girl, my eyes. The police are searching for me. My poor family is probably desperate to find me, and someone I know has died.

With every step I take, my head becomes crowded with flashes of Gus's play: Alyssa left the earlier scene and reappears as a totally different character: a drag queen named *Papayúa*, which according to our Cuban friends, translates to "immense vagina." It's something like having guts—except you know, huge balls—and it's supposed to be hilarious, but Blyss didn't find the humor in it, and so I didn't either.

When Papayúa batted long pink lashes, Blyss whispered to me, "The clickety-clacking of that sicko's stiletto heels makes me want to puke."

The crowd started getting rowdy. Some hooted and hollered while others tried to shush them. Mrs. Carrillo settled the hecklers by yelling, "Stop or you're all getting after-school detention!" It prompted everyone to shut up. Everybody except Blyss. She cupped her hands around her mouth and blasted, "Shut it down!"

Mrs. Carrillo stormed up to us and reminded Blyss in a brutal whisper, "If you start up again, you won't pass English, and I'll need to see your parents." She spun around and walked back to the front of the audience. Blyss threw the finger at her back, which made me chuckle.

"This is America," Blyss said as she shut her eyes. "I won't be forced to watch this piece of shit. If everyone can state their opinions, I should have the same freedom to express mine."

I agreed but had to keep my focus on the play. I didn't want to fail after how hard I'd worked all year to maintain As and Bs. Our parents took out loans and worked overtime to place us in such an expensive academy. I wouldn't think of flunking and doing Mom and Dad wrong.

Papayúa stormed into the stage wearing a tall orange wig, blowing wispy purple bangs out of her face, snapping fingers and saying things Blyss found morbidly distasteful, like, "Roly, if you've never dated another boy, how do you know you're straight?"

Roly turned on the TV to get away from listening to Papayúa, but the station was interrupted by an emergency news broadcast: "Don't let your daughters and sons befriend heterosexual counselors, teachers, or priests. Remember, child molesters and rapists in jail are ninety-nine percent heterosexuals. Sixty-five percent of heterosexuals are divorced. Ever since we granted straight people the right to marry and equal rights in some states, their divorce rate has been extremely high. . . ."

A handful of people in the audience belted out laughs. I could tell by the way Blyss grabbed my knee and squeezed it hard she was still furious. Instinctively, I cracked my knuckles, flexing with pent up anger that my girl could be so upset.

After the play, between periods, Blyss followed Gus. I trailed after her. "Pussy Boy thinks he's a glam girl, eh?" She kept teasing him. "Listen up, people. Gus has a tiny, squirmy little worm, not an orchid. I made him show me."

Peals of laughter filled the halls. Gus kept walking and called over his shoulder, "Please stop." That only made Blyss sing louder, "Fake Pussy Boy's feelings are hurt. Boo, hoo, hoo."

Blyss and I chased Gus home after the play. I didn't want to pursue him but needed to be with Blyss. We ran through an alley to cut Gus off, and Blyss stuck her foot out to knock him down. He fell face first and stayed put, probably hoping we'd leave if he didn't move a muscle. He seemed so helpless and pathetic I wasn't motivated to laugh along with Blyss, but I did. She pulled him over on his back and kept at it, with a singsong voice, "Gussy will never be a real girl like me / Wussy Gussy has no pussy. . . ."

Gus's eyes gathered tears. He begged, "Please quit. You've been at it every day, all year. . . ." His pleading inspired Blyss to continue singing even crueler things to him. When he wouldn't get up or stop sobbing, Blyss asked me to help carry him— which I did. I wanted to prove I was stronger than Knight, that guy who was into her, and she could count on me for anything.

I grasped his legs. She held on hard to his arms. We swung him back and forth, back and forth, until we gathered enough momentum to throw him in a Dumpster. He landed with a loud *bruunk*. The kid didn't even put up a fight. He was weaker and frailer than I had originally thought.

Blyss kicked the Dumpster and we began to walk away, back home I thought, until she pulled me to the side. We ducked in silence behind a cherry bush farther down, watching Gus climb out of the trash on his own. When he passed us, he was filthy, smelling of sewer, with rotted globs of slimy food clinging to his hair and dress. We trailed him. He sniffled as he wobbled home, wiping gunk that dripped down his body.

Gus lived in a wealthy, oceanfront Cuban community across the way from our school, which Blyss envied. Our neighborhood was always filled with dangerous police sirens and blasting music, but his had uppity classical compositions with lively cello and violin tunes seeping out of three-story waterfront villas.

The sky turned an ominous black as if it were about to storm any second. The scent of winter blooms and gardenias surrounded us. I wanted to get back home, but said nothing. Instead, I marched forward with my girl, proud to remain at her side, fighting against what she believed to be the evils of the world.

Before Gus turned the corner on a stop sign, Blyss boomed, "Listen, Pus Face. You're male and too hideous to be a girl!" Her bangs fell over her eyes and obscured her enraged, contorted face. "Cut the crap and stop trying to be like me. It looks retarded. Asshole!"

Gus turned around and faced Blyss, who walked up to him until she was inches from his face. He straightened his spine and stood tall, with his head held high, like he'd never done before. Gus's normally fearful jade eyes lit up. You could tell he was forcing himself to act brave.

His voice quivered and his chin trembled. "Why don't you and your boyfriend find another hobby, like bungee jumping back into the Mesozoic era. You know . . . the age of dinosaurs? I'm sure you'll feel quite at home there."

Something in me snapped. That kid had never, ever, talked

back to anyone, especially not Blyss. It hit me for the first time he was suffering. I knew by his twisted expression he could no longer withstand another second of the torturous, sickening lashings from Blyss.

I grabbed her arm and tried to pull her to me, but she thrashed out of my grip. "Leave me alone, Mik. If you can't deal, then run away to your mommy."

I crossed my arms over my chest.

She got right in front of his face and almost pressed her nose to his. She sniffed him. "You smell putrid, like you always do." She gagged and stepped back away from him. "Girls don't stink. We smell like lilies and daffodils. Not a single boy is ever going to love you or see you as a real girl, Dumb Ass. Being female means not having been born with a sausage and balls between your legs, imbecile. I'm a girl. You're not. Get it, sicko?"

He snapped his fingers in Blyss's face with a crooked, forced smile. "Ha, ha." His voice cracked like he might cry. "You're so comical."

Gus looked down at his feet with such a sad, devastated expression I knew Blyss had really sliced him up good. I wanted it all to end so I could be with Blyss. It just wasn't funny anymore.

"Come on. Let him go," I interrupted. "He's not worth our time."

She didn't even acknowledge me. Instead she pulled her arm back, and with hatred pulsating in her eyes, her fist delivered a sharp blow to Gus's jaw. I heard his bones crunch. She kept striking him with a left and then a right jab, with such force his neck snapped back. I watched as he wobbled around, then vomited chunks of undigested food and yellow bile. He kneeled and fell forward, right on the throw-up.

My stomach turned. I shifted my eyes away from Gus and listened to him moan.

"If you tell on us, I'll kill you." Blyss's voice was harsh. I grabbed her, and we took off. I should have stopped her, but I didn't. I liked that she could whip a guy's ass, but that had gone way too far. We ran home, holding hands. When I stood outside her house, Blyss kissed me, and I forgot all about the violence, as if it had never happened. We parted and I headed home in a love-sick daze.

Memories of last night dissipate, only to be replaced by haunting questions that won't leave my mind. *Did Gus die because of Blyss? Because of us? Are we to blame for the death of another human being?*

My chest feels as if it's caving in. I clutch at my stomach and imagine Gus's body, sinking deep into the ocean. Nobody helped him. Especially not me. No one heard him sob but us, and we ran away.

Horrified, I try hard to shake these thoughts and feelings. Recall something else. Anything. I twist and turn my brain around and think about my immediate reality: the horror my parents will feel when they see me without eyes. I see every-thing clearly now that I can't see at all. Is this my punishment?

Are these consequences I must live with forever? I want to run but I can't. A feeling of doom washes over me. My troubles loom huge.

I stop cold when I hear a loud siren whizzing by and remember that police are looking for me. I hear footsteps nearing me on what seems like a sidewalk. "Would someone please help me home?" I say aloud. I tell a willing lady I'm blind, that I forgot my cane, and give her my home address. I must confide in my parents about what's happened and find help for Blyss.

The woman grabs my arm and pulls me with her. "I know someone who lives on Oak Street, too. I'll get you to your house safely, young man."

The cold wind whips my hair across my eyes, and I thrust it back. I pit my eye sockets against the wind's assault, but the freezing breeze gnaws at my face as I put one foot in front of the other. The lady stops abruptly. "Oh my. We're in front of a *Santería* temple. A *Santera* in the community is having a preliminary ritual for her grandchild who died tragically."

Blasting conga-drums punch my eardrums from all corners. *¡Gun-bák-tak-prák!* "The funeral services will be held this weekend over at Gables by the Sea." She sighs. "Poor child. We live in a crazy world, my boy. Let's stand here for a moment of silence."

The *tumbadoras* keep blasting. A crowd is chanting in whisper-soft tones words I don't understand over and over again. A woman's crying voice raises above them. "Ochún, I invoke you to seep into me. Through your powers within me, I'll help my little granddaughter Alyssa's sweet, pure soul, the one I saw grow from a boy into a lovely girl, lift up into the sky."

My heart bangs in my chest.

The crowd chants, "Alyssa, Alyssa, Alyssa . . ."

Strong incense fills my nostrils. I let go of the lady's grip and wring my hands. I can't believe I'm here. What if someone in there recognizes me? *I never wanted to hurt you, Gus. You hear me? I was such a horrible person to have wounded you so much. . . .*

I visualize myself cemented to the floor in order to ground myself and keep this terrible urge to sprint under control. The chanting grows louder and louder. "Ochún, our goddess Orisha, send Alyssa into your arms. . . ."

The woman whispers, "The child's mother is a judge and his father, a brain surgeon; they're not *Santeros*. It's lovely they've allowed this type of ceremony and the whole community has been invited. But we should move on and get you home." She pulls me with her by my elbow.

I drag my weary feet on the pavement and groan. I'm so overwhelmed. I feel so damned conflicted and alone. The agony of it all is wearing me down. *Why did you have to die, Gus? Did you commit suicide or were you murdered?* The rancid air is filled with the pungent aroma of flowers mixed with the pain of death. It follows me and stings me with despair.

A realization hits me like a two-by-four: I helped murder Gus.

I shunned him the whole year and watched Blyss torture

him. And yesterday, for the first time, I took part in it. I threw him away like a piece of garbage. And now he's dead because of it, because of me. I shake my head to get rid of these devastating thoughts, but they won't leave. A tear drips into my mouth from inside my vacant eye socket. *Sorry Gus. I'm so deeply, severely sorry. I wish I could take it all back but I can't. It's too late. I helped kill you, Gus.*

I wipe my face with my forearm and ask the woman, "How much longer, ma'am?"

"We're at the park across the street from Arte Gallery. That's about two blocks west from your house."

Hell, where the hell was I before I found her? I'm back to where I started?

"I need to sit for a bit. Would you please take me to the bench next to the pond? I know how to get home from here." She walks me over, says good-bye and hurries off.

I plunk on the bench with slumped shoulders to think. A vision of Alyssa walks across my mind with her flowing dress. *I never even called you Alyssa. I kept calling you Gus and "he" even when you asked me so kindly not to do so. I didn't really hate you Gu . . . er, Alyssa. I swear. I should have called you Alyssa from the get-go and maybe none of this would have happened.*

My hands fall to the bench on either side of me. I feel something like two, sticky round balls. My eyes? I pluck them and plop them into my eye sockets. They fit perfectly. I can see again! My eyes swing quickly up and down, left and right. Everything looks outrageously beautiful. I do this over and over again. I'm under a Gumbo Limbo tree. There's a field of colorful flowers across the way. I want to run with arms spread out, yelling, "This is the most gorgeous park on Earth!" but I just sit here, taking in the beauty.

I'm ecstatic to have my eyes back but then I remember Gus. Nothing else matters right now. Gus is dead. I'm so utterly exhausted. I can barely lift a finger. I never want to move again, but I know I have somewhere to go. Something to do. *Get back to Blyss. Time is flying. The only solution is to bring her home.* I'll convince her to follow me here and face the truth: we killed Alyssa. I drag my aching feet back to Arte Gallery and walk past dozens of paintings searching for *Desert iLand*, but the piece is gone. I ask an attendant for help.

"That specific work of art you're looking for has been sold." He leaves to help a customer. I shake my head, wipe my sweaty hands on my pants and jam them into my pockets. I pass through dozens of similar paintings by the same artist, scrutinizing them slowly.

Movements don't catch my eye. I smooth my fingertips on each canvas as I go along but they're all solid and flat. The only thing I'm feeling is the thick texture of dried paint.

When no one is looking, I push my foot forward to try to enter a painting. My sneaker hits the canvas hard and almost tears it. Quickly, I go on to another painting but not a single one allows me to climb inside.

In the back of the gallery, I notice two sliding glass doors that lead to another room. I walk inside. The strong smell of salty seaweed attacks my nostrils. I turn my head here and there. It's empty except for two colossal, thickly textured watercolors that hang side by side on the wall.

I drag a stranded chair to the front of the room and sit directly across the works of art. I dissect the one on the left, where it's nighttime at a beach pier. As if a camera was panning out into the dock, the painting takes on a life of its own. Separate colors swirl around, come together and expand. They reposition themselves by shifting, shoving, and rearranging to form movable figures in what seems like a 3-D movie.

The lights suddenly dim and the "film" starts.

Blyss is there, wearing the exact same clothes she did last night after we threw Alyssa in the Dumpster. *You're so supremely gorgeous. And look at you, Alyssa. Woah. You're all cleaned up.*

"Why did you want to meet?" Alyssa asks.

Blyss leans into her. "Why do you think, idiot?" Alyssa shrugs. "I just beat the hell out of you two hours ago and you've come back for more? Can't you see how pathetic you are? I asked you to meet me here, and instead of sending me to the underworld ruled by Hades, you came? You're so weak. That's one of the many reasons everyone hates you, Gus."

"I don't want any trouble." Alyssa's voice trembles. "I thought maybe you wished to apologize. I would have accepted. That's why I came."

Poor kid. You were too good for this world. I hope Blyss didn't beat you again or push you off the pier.

"Tell *you*, a whiny bitchy fag, I'm sorry?" Blyss's laughter fills my ears. She sounds vicious. I wonder why I never realized that before.

"I'm not gay," Alyssa's drooping eyes make her look devastated. "I'm a girl who likes guys."

Blyss rolls her eyes and calls Alyssa dozens of awful names. "You're better off dead. You're an anomaly. No one wants you, and I'm sure your family is ashamed of you. Do humanity a favor. Kill yourself. Nobody will miss you or shed a tear." She spits on her face, and Alyssa doesn't even wipe it off.

I want to cover my ears and close my eyes, but I force myself to watch. I remember all the times Blyss abused her in the halls and I joined everyone in laughter. How could I have been so cruel? Why didn't I have the guts to stand up to Blyss and stop her? *I'm such a coward.*

Alyssa's face distorts in pain. She screams at the top of her lungs and lunges into the pier. Blyss leans over the railing and just watches Alyssa plunge into the sea, without any emotion whatsoever. Then, she takes off running.

I cover my face with my hands. I'm so sorry. *Will you ever forgive me, Alyssa? I don't think I can ever forgive myself.*

My eyes veer over toward the massive painting on the right that's beginning to have movement. I see Blyss in the middle of the ocean. Her hair is like an octopus on fire, flames spreading out all over the place. Dozens of sharks circle Blyss's tiny raft. She looks to me from inside the canvas with smiling eyes.

I whisper harshly to her, "Freeze, Blyss! Don't move a muscle. Sharks sense fear."

She sniggers. "Sharks won't harm me. They're my friends. I told you not to leave, but you wouldn't listen."

"Friends?"

"Yeah. Too bad you chickened out. So listen"—the edges of her mouth curl up—"you found out I didn't kill Gus, right?"

"Yes." I tell her about the "film" I've just seen.

"So, you see, it's not my fault. Gus killed himself."

Strength builds up inside me, and the blur of incoherence has vanished. "It's not 'Gus.'"

"Oh please, Mik. Not you too with this 'Alyssa' bullshit. . . ."

"Show some respect and call her Alyssa. We're responsible. We did her wrong and should pay for it."

"What's that supposed to mean?"

"I'm going to the cops, and I have to tell them."

Her eyes narrow. "If you do, I'll never, ever forgive you."

"Forgive me? You should be here with me. We should be asking Alyssa's parents for forgiveness."

"He did it himself." Her hair falls across one eye, obscuring it. "We're not guilty of anything. I'll be damned if I ask for anyone's forgiveness."

"We're definitely guilty. We took her to her grave." My voice fills with anger and agony. "We've got to tell them our side of the story."

"I'm not coming back, and no one will ever find me. It'll be just you. You'll be arrested, put on trial, jailed, and despised by everyone. Is that what you want?"

"That's what we deserve."

"*I* don't deserve that." She exhales and collapses on the raft. "I hate you! We still have a chance to live together in peace. Don't you dare involve the police. Get your ass back over here, now!"

"Never."

"Okay, then. Go to the cops and have a happy time in jail. But me? I've been given the opportunity of a lifetime. The waters are calling to me, and I've accepted." Her face takes on a strange appearance, wrinkled like hands and feet after too much time in water. The foam spray covering her hair turns it gray and then white. She looks one hundred years old now, and I shudder. "I'll never see you again, Mik."

Blyss's face and nose elongate and transform into a large grayish blue snout. Her body stretches twenty feet in length and turns into what looks like a sleek, gray torpedo. Eight fins pop out and gills appear on the side of her body.

I keep my eyes glued on hers.

Her underbelly turns white. A crescent shaped tail emerges where her feet used to be and a dorsal fin pops out on her back. She slides off the raft with an open mouth. I see hundreds of multiple rows of pointy, triangular, razor-sharp teeth embedded in her gums.

She starts to slow cruise around other sharks, propelled by her powerful tail. Her movement is like a flexible jet in flight. I follow Blyss with my eyes. She twists and turns in the water easily, as if she'd been doing it all her life. The shark that was once Blyss comes close to the canvas and throws darts at me with her stare. I feel the intense hatred in her eyes before she looks away and takes off on a sudden burst of speed. In an instant, she's gone.

I walk outside without looking back, tears dripping down my face. I stand under a massive downpour, shaking, rain kicking my body, wind punching my face. The night is pitch black and deserted. The lit moon swings eerily up and down. The world has an abandoned feel to it, as if it were a child left in a Dumpster searching for love.

And then Alyssa's silhouette appears, unexpectedly. I grab her hand, and it feels so soft and real. She smells like crushed strawberries.

"Will you walk with me?" I ask. "I need to do something important." We stroll hand in hand toward the police station.

"Look up." Alyssa blinks her long lashes. I'm taken by the serenity in her voice and melody of its tone. I search the sky to find a bright shooting star, its white light illuminating the dark sky for a brief moment. "That's me." Her smile gleams.

"I know." I gaze at the star as it evaporates and vanishes forever.

But Not Forgotten

BY JENNIFER BROWN

IT TOOK EXACTLY one week and three days of school for things to get right back to where they were freshman year. The girls weren't even original about it. It was, literally, the same so-called comedy routine they'd been performing every day since eighth grade.

"Anyone else smell a farm animal?" Sydney Weaver asked, loudly, as I tried to scoot past their lunch table unnoticed. She wrinkled her nose and sniffed the air. Holly joined her.

"Ew, gross. What *is* that smell? A pig?"

"Uh-uh," Sydney said, half-chewed carrot peeking from inside her mouth. "That's definitely a cow."

And then the mooing started, the whole table joining in. So clever. So original.

I could imagine Jenna, never able to just ignore them, turning and snapping, "Real mature!" just as she'd done a dozen times before while I stood by silently, hate filling me from top to bottom.

But this time Jenna wasn't there, and I couldn't bring myself to feel anger because my best friend had killed herself. I missed her so much I was numb inside. It all seemed so pointless to keep hating people who would never understand.

I don't know what I expected. A moment of silence, maybe? Some remorse? Holly and Monica and their pack of snots to be changed into better people? But there was none of that. Not one word of sorrow. Not an ounce of recognition that one of our students was missing this year.

That first week of school I waited for it—standing just outside of crowds, lingering in hallways, waiting for something. *Anything.* Someone to tell me they were sorry my best friend was dead. Someone to tell me they were sorry for what they'd done to her.

But mostly I'd stand there, unnoticed, remembering Jenna holding on to my sleeve that impossibly hot night in August. Her eyes gleaming, her face eager, hissing through her teeth about how sorry all those bitches would be when they found out what they'd done to her.

But none of the things she'd hoped for had happened—the big, remorseful crowds at the funeral, the media that would out Holly and Monica and Sydney, the bullies so utterly broken by what they'd caused.

None of it.

It was a funeral like every other funeral. The only reporter to show up at Jenna's house was some intern from the local paper that nobody reads, and Jenna's brother turned him away anyway. There was no tearful apology from Holly, her mother, or anyone else for that matter. It seemed like the only thing left behind was my sorrow, which was so big it felt like I was drowning in it. One thought repeated in my head: *Jenna is gone.*

So I let them moo and make their little comments as I edged around their table. I sat by myself next to the trash cans—staring at but not eating my mashed potatoes—wondering what to do next.

. . .

Once upon a time, we were best friends, Holly and me. We lived down the street from one another. We played together, had the same teachers, and took each other on family trips.

But when we moved up to middle school, everything changed. Holly was thin and cute and an only child who always had expensive toys and clothes. But more importantly, she had confidence to spare. I, on the other hand, was chubby and quiet. My grades were good, but my social scores were off the charts bad. I had zits and boring clothes and a habit of chewing on the ends of my hair, which clung in wet strands against the sides of my chin. Boyfriends were a distant hope for me, but I never actually imagined I'd ever have one. The thought of even *talking* to a boy scared me to death.

All of a sudden Holly was royalty, with an entourage of new friends who called me "Duff," or otherwise ignored me. Holly insisted that we were still BFFs and no new friends would ever change that, but she started hanging around the meanest two, Monica and Sydney. Sleepovers, skating parties, movies. Almost every Friday night I'd call her house to see what she was doing, and almost always she was gone.

But then I met Jenna in fourth period social studies. Mr. Yackie had us all pair up on a Civil War research assignment, and as always, everyone else was paired in a nanosecond. I sat by myself, turning seven shades of red and wishing teachers would understand: letting the class pair up on their own might *sound* like a good idea, but it was really just another way for outcasts like me to feel like crap about themselves. As if we needed that.

And the teachers always made it worse. They'd wait for the shuffling to die down and then yell, "If you don't have a partner, raise your hand!" As if Sydney or Monica or any of the other normal kids in the class were just idly sitting by without partners. Mr. Yackie might as well have shouted out, "Raise your hand if you're the fat loser in the class! Chloe, I mean YOU!"

But this time, I wasn't the only one raising my hand. So was the new girl, and we were paired.

Jenna was bigger than me. Her parents were divorced, and she lived with her mom and brother in a tiny basement apartment behind the grocery store. She'd been picked on at her old school for her weight, her red, frizzy hair and probably a multitude of other things that shouldn't have mattered, but somehow always did.

I shuffled to her desk and plopped my books on top of it. "Hey," I said. The kid in the desk next to her moved over by his partner, so I slid into his chair.

She looked up and smiled. "Hey."

We sat there for a few minutes while Mr. Yackie droned on

and on about our project. Jenna doodled on the front of her notebook, and I picked bits of paper out of the spiral of mine, sucking on a piece of my hair. When he finally finished, I turned my chair so I was facing her, but she was still doodling. I wasn't even sure she knew Mr. Yackie was done talking. I smoothed the hair I'd been chewing on between my forefinger and thumb, wiped my wet hand on my jeans, and took a breath.

"So, um, do you have any ideas?" I asked, feeling awkward and miserable.

She put down her pencil and shook her head. "I hate history."

I took a breath. "Great. I hate it, too. This should be interesting."

"We could just take our F's now and spend our time in the library reading *Cosmo*." She grinned, and something about her smile made me instantly like her. "I'm Jenna, by the way."

"I'm Chloe." I smiled back. "And it's a deal."

We didn't go to the library and read *Cosmo*, but that first day we met at Jenna's apartment where we talked about anything and everything other than the Civil War. Eventually we ended up doing our project on famous women of the Civil War, laying out our report magazine-style and surrounding it with photos and illustrations, sort of like our own 1800s-era *Cosmo*. And even after the project was over, we still hung out together whenever we got a chance.

Jenna and I had a lot in common, and neither of us was exactly rolling neck-deep in friends. I stopped caring so much about what Holly was doing on the weekends with Monica and Sydney, because I was busy with Jenna anyway.

Plus, there was the Fight.

It happened when I found out Holly lied to me about being grounded. It was my birthday, and we'd had the whole night planned for months. We were going to go to dinner with my parents, and even though I didn't even really like Japanese food, I'd talked them into the Japanese steakhouse that was Holly's favorite. After dinner, we were going to walk up to the mall, and she'd help me pick out new clothes with my birthday money. Afterward we'd planned to go home and spend the rest of the night trying on outfits, raiding the ice cream selection in her freezer, and watching movies together.

But the day of, she called and said she was grounded. She even sniffled like she was crying and griped about how unfair her parents were. But that night, while heading to dinner with my parents—at *her* favorite restaurant, mind you—I saw Holly as we drove by the movie theater, standing out front with Sydney Weaver and the others.

I slumped against the backseat, my mouth hanging open with disbelief. I turned and did a double take through the back window, sure that I'd made a mistake, sure that my best friend wasn't betraying me on my birthday. But there she was, head thrown back, laughing.

Suddenly I was not hungry at all anymore.

"Can we go back home instead?" I asked, crossing my arms over my stomach.

My mom turned around and looked at me curiously. "Why?"

I hoped Mom wouldn't see Holly out the back window, too. The last thing I needed was for her to pity me. I wasn't really up for the added humiliation. "I'm just not feeling well."

Understatement of the year. I felt I'd just lost my best friend in the world, and it hurt like hell.

"On your birthday? I'm sorry, honey. Are you sure?" and when I nodded she said, "Of course we'll go back."

Dad turned the car around and instead of raiding the ice cream and trying on clothes and watching movies, I spent the evening sprawled on my bed, crying and wiping my nose on my comforter.

But after I was done crying, I got pissed. So the next day I confronted Holly. I called her.

"I know you lied to me about being grounded."

"What are you talking about?" She sounded so chipper on the other end. It only made me angrier.

"I saw you, Holly. I know you went to the movies last night."

"Listen," she sighed. "I meant to tell you that something came up but—"

"How could you do that to me? It was my birthday!"

"You can't blame me for wanting to bug out on such a lame night."

"YOU planned the whole night!" I said into the phone, trying to keep my voice level. I didn't want to give her the satisfaction of hearing me cry. "I don't know what's happened to you. You're not even the same person you used to be."

"You're just jealous because I'm hanging out with the popular people now and you're with Jenna Roooundtree," she said, exaggerating her last name like Jenna herself was a joke. "You've been getting fatter ever since you met her, by the way."

I blinked, hardly able to believe that the person saying these things was my best friend. Correction: my *ex*-best friend. "God, you're such a snot now."

"I'm just trying to be honest with you. I'm trying to *help* you. Do you even know what 'Duff' means?"

"No, and I don't want to."

"But you should. It stands for *Designated Ugly Fat Friend*." She paused to let what she'd said sink in. "And hanging out with Jenna isn't helping you lose that nickname at all. Jenna's actually your Duff, Chlo. So maybe you should keep her."

I couldn't help the tears then. I tried to sound angry, but I was actually more hurt and embarrassed than anything. "I *will* keep her. Because she's a real friend. Not a bitch who thinks life is all about the way people look."

"Good. Then stay away from me. Like, forever."

"I'll never forgive you for this."

"Well, it's a good thing I never asked you to."

And that's when the mooing began.

* * *

After the lunchtime mooing incident, time crept by. It was a block day and every class seemed to last forever, especially psych class, which I had with Holly. Our teacher had us sit in alphabetical order, and Holly sat right next to me, constantly rolling her eyes and making little sighing noises every time I blinked.

This was Holly's sniper method. I knew it well. Act like it was a total tragedy to have to sit next to the grossest person on earth and be all martyr about it. She sighed loudly, and everyone around us kept looking at me with smirks on their faces.

I checked Holly's hands, nibbling on a strand of hair. Sure enough she was holding her phone under her desk, her thumb working the keypad. She was undoubtedly complaining to her crew about the misfortune of having to sit next to me once again, and they were probably all falling all over themselves consoling her. Poor Holly.

She caught me staring and narrowed her eyes at me. I knew this to be Holly's "vicious look," the one she gave when she wanted people to be scared of her. I remembered a time in fifth grade when she used it against my older brother's friend Jake after Jake called us "little girls." How she'd seethed after he'd done that—gone on and on about how we weren't little, we were almost in middle school, and how he'd be sorry one day when she was the hottest girl in high school and he wanted her.

"I mean you look like a little girl, but me? No way. I just look younger because I'm with you. No offense, Chlo," she'd said.

"None taken. You're totally right. You look a lot older," I'd replied. Her obedient little minion.

"Right," she'd said, pointing at me, "because you're taking so much longer to mature than I am. My mom says you're underdeveloped, and it's probably just because of the junk food you eat all day."

"Oh."

"Not that it's a bad thing." She'd laughed, but her eyes had still held that frightening narrowness to them. I came away from the conversation feeling like crap and wishing I didn't love junk food so much.

When I thought about those moments, it hit me that Holly had always been a jerk to me, even when we *were* friends. She was always doing that thing my mom called "backhanded complimenting." You know, like you tell someone you love their shirt but you couldn't pull it off because your boobs are so much bigger, and it just wouldn't look right on you? That kind of thing. She was forever saying, "No offense, Chlo," and I was always answering, "None taken." In truth, it hurt all the time, but I told myself I somehow deserved it. Back then, it didn't occur to me that my so-called best friend always made me feel like I wasn't good enough. Holly would constantly offer criticism and be sure to tell me her mom agreed with her, which stung even more, because in some ways her mom felt like my own mom. I figured if her mom thought these things, then they must have been true.

The bell rang, startling me, and I found the ends of my hair a wet, chewed-on mess. I realized I'd just totally spaced out the last twenty minutes of psych, two days before our first big test of the semester. Great. Already this year was starting out bad. I'd probably fail and my parents would blame it on my grief, when really, my grades hadn't been all that great since Holly and I stopped being friends. It was mostly because I was always scared to go to class—or too sad, nervous, and distracted to do my homework. And nobody would ever notice that the reason I couldn't concentrate in psych might have something to do with my ex-best friend giving me dirty looks and texting about me right in front of my face.

"God, stare much?" Holly said as she stood and shouldered her backpack. She spread her arms out and rolled her eyes dramatically, making sure as many people as possible could see and hear her. "Like what you see? I always thought you might be a lesbo."

"I wasn't—," I started, but she turned and walked away from me. Monica was waiting at the door, and I heard my name as Holly joined her. Then there was laughter as the two of them spilled out into the hallway, their long hair swishing against their backs in tandem.

I wanted to slink away. And honestly, I wanted Jenna. I wanted to storm to her locker and vent about everything. I wanted to call Holly names behind her back—Jenna was really great at coming up with hilarious ones, my personal favorite being Unshaven Mattressback Gorilla. I wanted my best friend there with me.

But Jenna was gone.

I thought it was a joke the first time Jenna brought up suicide. I even laughed. But then I saw the tears in her eyes—and Jenna like, never cried—and the way her hands were shaking. I pressed my lips together, my whole body growing cold. She was serious, and it felt really bad and scary.

"You shouldn't give Holly the satisfaction," I said, but Jenna only shook her head, letting a single tear drip down her cheek. "Don't let her get to you that much. She's irrelevant."

"It's not just her. My whole family is messed up, you know? I don't think anyone would even notice I was gone."

"I would notice."

"Not if you were with me."

My eyes got wide. Was she really saying what I thought she was saying? Not just that she was sad and wanted to die, but that we should both do it? Kill myself? Over Holly? I blinked a few times, unsure what to even say to that.

After a few minutes of me saying nothing, she waved her hand dismissively. "I wasn't serious," she said. "Just forget it." But something about the look in her eyes told me that maybe she was more serious than she was letting on.

I guess on some level I knew that it was wrong to not say something. Jenna's life was pretty shitty. Her parents were divorced, and her mom was one of those people my mom called a "Happy Hour Drunk." She had four drinks every night after work while she "made supper," but she'd always be too sloshed to finish it, and Jenna would end up preparing the whole thing herself.

Her dad remarried and was living about an hour away. Ever since he had a new baby with his new wife, he'd only come to visit Jenna and her little brother once. He always said he was "too busy with work," but we all knew he was really too busy being someone else's dad. It's why her mom drank so much; she never really got over the divorce.

So even though I knew you're supposed to report it when one of your friends threatens suicide, I didn't do it. Partly because I didn't think she'd actually go through with it, and partly because I didn't blame her. I knew how she felt: sometimes I was as sad and hopeless and pissed off as she was. And after she brought up the possibility of doing it together, I found it creeping into my thoughts on really down days.

"Think about it," Jenna said one night over a heaping plate of fries which sat between us on her bed. The grease spilled over onto the comforter, and she sucked some salt off of her finger. "They'll probably have to go through some special program. They'll have to admit what they did to us. The whole world will know what Holly and Monica and Sydney and all their precious prom queen populars are really like. They won't be able to charm their way out of it this time, because we'll be dead and people sit up and notice when kids end up dead."

I chewed and swallowed. "Couldn't we get the same thing done if we just turn them in or something? I mean, we won't get to see it all go down if we're dead."

Jenna shook her head, shoveled a fry into her mouth. "I've

tried it. I talked to my science teacher, Mr. Neeson, months ago after Monica purposely messed up my lab. Do you notice any changes?" She paused, chewed, then pointed at me with a fry. "Yeah, me neither. That's because there are no changes. Those bitches still run the school. They will always run the school."

I thought it over. I remembered a day, not long before, when Holly tripped me in the hallway as I was walking past her locker on my way to P.E.

"Ooops," she'd said in mock surprise. "Gosh, I didn't see you there, Chloe. Please don't tell on me." And she and her friends had all started giggling, and it hadn't really made sense to me then. But then, after Jenna's confession, it became clear.

And it was right then—with a mouthful of mushed-up french fry and my right leg falling asleep on Jenna's com-forter—that I realized it. There really was no way to beat Holly Abrams.

Maybe Jenna was right. Maybe suicide was the only way out.

...

Jenna was gone.

The thought was overwhelming from the moment I stepped into journalism class. Last year Jenna had been our editor, and this year it was Stuart Hampton. He was okay, nice in a quiet kind of way, and he seemed to have a really great rapport with Ms. Stepton, our new teacher. It was her first year out of college, and she was kind of all about, "Okay, friends, let's have some silent work time," and, "Friends? I'm hearing too much talking," and, "This is going to be the best issue ever, friends," like she was some sort of preschool teacher or something.

I squeezed into my chair next to Stuart and got to work writing out my interview questions for the drama coach. I had an article to do about tryouts for the fall play. I could almost hear Jenna chuckle over what a "fluff piece" it was going to be. "Spice it up, Chloe. Find a scandal in there somewhere," she would've said. She'd always wanted the paper to be more than it was, to out the people who'd wronged her, to open up the school's eyes to reality. And there was some reality definitely missing from our planned first issue.

I worked up my nerve and leaned across the aisle to tap Stuart's shoulder with my pencil.

He looked up, annoyed. "What?"

"I have an idea," I said, "for our first issue."

"We've got all our assignments," he said, turning back to whatever he was working on.

"I know," I said. "But I really want to write this. It can be an editorial. A short column."

He looked up again, screwed up his mouth to one side, and seemed to think it over before he sighed. "Have you talked to Ms. Stepton about it yet?"

No, of course I hadn't. I hadn't even thought of it until just then. "Yes," I lied. "She liked it. A lot."

"Okay," he said, pushing his glasses up on the bridge of his nose. "What is it?"

"I think we should write a piece about Jenna," I said. His eyes got big and hazy when I said her name, but he didn't say anything, so I went on, resisting the urge to gather a fistful of hair and twist it into my mouth. "She was the editor, you know, and she was signed up to be in this class again. I just think it's . . . wrong . . . that everybody's already forgotten about her. She didn't move away over the summer. She died."

He licked his lips, leaned in toward me, speaking conspiratorially. "She didn't die. She committed suicide. And Ms. Stepton already told me that the administration doesn't want anyone giving it a lot of attention," he said. "They're afraid it'll be, you know . . . contagious. They're putting some sort of special photo in the yearbook or something, but that's it. You're sure Ms. Stepton is okay with this?"

I nodded. "Totally. And Jenna wasn't contagious." I felt defensive over the administration's decision to let her suicide slip by unnoticed. "She was just trying to make the pain stop. It . . . it was a bad idea, but it was . . . it made sense when . . . I understood how she . . ." I realized my chin was quivering as I stammered, and I was dangerously close to tears. I took a deep breath, my hands shaking around my pencil. I tried to lean back nonchalantly, my desk chair creaking beneath my weight. My face instantly flushed with embarrassment, sure that he was going to say something about me being so fat I would break the chair. But Stuart didn't appear to even hear it. Holly would have held a freaking assembly over it. "I just think it would be a nice thing to do, to say good-bye to one of our own."

Stuart paused for a beat, looked down at his paper and tapped his pencil eraser on the desk top a few times. He swiveled back to look at me and said, "Okay. Sure. It's a good idea. You should write it. You guys were close, right?"

"The closest," I said.

I turned back to my reporter's notebook, but the questions I'd already written were swimming on the page. Was I really going to write about this? Admit I'd been in on Jenna's plan all along, and that I'd only backed out at the last minute? I could've been gone right now, too. My parents didn't even know. . . . Jenna's parents didn't know. Nobody knew the plan but me.

Maybe that needed to change.

I looked back down at my notebook and turned to a new page. Inside my head I was already writing, thinking of a way to say good-bye to my best friend.

About a thousand times since Jenna died, I'd wondered how I'd gone from one extreme to the other—of thinking no way would I ever kill myself over Holly—to planning a double suicide with my best friend. What was my tipping point? It had happened so suddenly, even I wasn't sure what had changed my mind.

But after hours and hours of lying on my bed, staring at the ceiling, tears pooling in my ears, I decided that my tipping point must have been the day we overheard Holly's mom at the pool.

It was early in the summer, on one of those days where the pool was pretty much the only option because even your house is oven-hot. Jenna and I went to the public pool down the street from my house, and even the pool water was lukewarm, but we didn't care. It was too hot to care.

Jenna had worn an old bikini from seventh grade because it was the only thing she had that fit, and I didn't have an extra one-piece. She pooched out over the top of it a little and her boobs kind of sagged, but she was covered up and we were going to be in water, so who cared?

And we were having fun. For once, Jenna wasn't complaining about Holly or talking about how depressing her life was. We were just goofing off in the deep end, and we felt like kids.

And then Holly's mom showed up with another neighbor and that lady's children.

My heart sank. The last person on earth I wanted to run into while in a swimsuit was Holly. It was hard enough going out in public practically naked as it was—but being practically naked in front of someone whose favorite hobby was to call you fat in front of the entire school—well that was something else entirely. But Holly wasn't with her mom, and I felt relieved. We went back to our fun and found a couple of rafts, racing each other across the length of the pool. We were laughing and being silly. We ended up on the shallow end, right where Holly's mom and her friend were laying out on a couple of poolside chaise lounges. Something about their hushed conversation got my attention.

"Someone needs to take those girls swimsuit shopping," the friend said in a low voice. "If I were their mother, I would never let them out of the house in those. They look like sausages."

"I know," Holly's mom had exclaimed, and then had added, "The one in the blue used to be Holly's best friend, and Holly was always embarrassed by her."

"Can you blame her?" her friend said. "Hanging out with a girl that looks . . . *and dresses* . . . like that would be so embarrassing."

"Exactly. Though Holly says the girl has made her out to be this big bully. She just wouldn't let go. It was very sad to watch. Holly thinks that she had"—and here's where she lowered her voice to an even smaller whisper, though what she said seemed to bounce off the pool walls and resonate like she'd said it through a megaphone—"a crush on her. You know."

"Oooh," the friend said in her normal voice. "I can see that."

"Me too."

Just like that, the laughter had dried up in my throat, and my face burned so hot I thought it might be blistering under the sun. I slipped off my raft and into the water, where I blew out bubbles and waved my arms and sat on the bottom as long as I possibly could until my lungs burned hotter than my face.

When I came back up, I saw Jenna, and I could tell by the look on her face that she'd heard everything too. And it occurred to me, really occurred to me, that Jenna wasn't really any worse off than I was. That I had as much of a big, fat nothing as she did, and that I would never get peace. I would forever be victim to the Hollys of the world, because even the adult version of Holly made me feel small, and all I'd been doing was swimming in my own neighborhood pool with my friend, minding my own business.

That night, I told Jenna that I was in. My tipping point.

The rest of newspaper class went by in a blur. I was so into my column and remembering the day at the pool that I barely even noticed when the bell rang. It wasn't until Ms. Stepton knocked on my desk and said, "We don't want to be tardy for our next class, friend," that I came back to reality, sort of like breaking back through the water that day. I blinked slowly, watching students from the next class (including Monica— God, I could not get away from these people!) file in around me. I slapped my notebook shut, shoved it into my backpack, and raced toward my last class of the day. The class I hated more than any other.

Team Sports.

There was no class more demeaning for someone like me than Team Sports. I was horrible at anything athletic, I hated everything that had to do with sports, and I was not exactly "team material" in pretty much anyone's eyes. Plus Holly and Sydney were in the class with me. It was nothing but humiliation and embarrassment. As if I needed more of that.

As soon as I walked into the locker room, it started. I tried my best to ignore it, the way my mom told me to when the shit first started hitting the fan with Holly, but it's hard to block out the cackles when they're bouncing off metal locker doors and are right behind you.

Ew, she wears granny panties.

Too bad they don't hide the cellulite on her thighs.

She's so fat her butt hangs over the bench.

Of course I knew they were talking about me. But I refused to turn around and look to see who was saying what. I just got dressed and trudged out to the gym floor, where I sat in my squad and chewed on my hair. We listened to Coach Lake explain the rules of our unit one sport—basketball.

Basketball. Great. Just what a short, fat nobody with no coordination loves to play against a bunch of tall skinny girls. If Jenna were here, she'd have faked a dizzy spell and would have asked Coach Lake to assign me to accompany her to the nurse's office.

But Jenna was gone.

Coach blew her whistle and we all stood up, two squads heading for the far half-court and my squad heading for the other one. We were playing against Holly's squad. Of course.

Let it be said that I really did try. My mom once told me that if I had fun despite them, if I showed the girls who were bothering me that what they said and did didn't even register, they would eventually go away. *Girls like that are just looking for attention, Chloe*, she'd said. *Refuse to give it to them and they'll leave you alone.* And even though I'd been following that advice forever and it had never once worked, I kept trying, because I wanted to believe that she was right. That there was a secret to making someone like Holly stop.

So the first time Holly tripped me and I fell face-first on the court, I laughed out loud, looking around for someone, anyone to join in and make it look like that was the best thing that had happened to me all day. Nobody did though. And then when Sydney elbowed me, hard, in the ribs, I gritted my teeth and just elbowed her back, but too softly, too timidly for her to get the point.

And then Holly threw the pass.

She dribbled down the court, swiveled on one foot like a freaking pro baller, and fired a chest pass right into my face. I heard a crunch and saw a flash of white light behind my eyelids as I stumbled back a few steps, my arms reeling to keep myself from falling backward. I stepped on Sydney's foot, and she let out a wail like I'd just crushed her. Instantly, I felt blood begin dripping down over my lips. I couldn't help myself; I started to cry, making gruff grunting noises while I cupped my hand under my chin to catch the blood.

"Ew!" Sydney yelled, pushing me forward. "Gross!"

Coach blew the whistle and Holly yelled out, "She dove right in front of it. It wasn't my fault. I was just passing to my teammate."

"Okay, okay, this happens in basketball. No big deal." Coach came over to me and put a hand on my shoulder. "You okay, Chloe?"

I simply nodded. I didn't say a word.

"Go clean up," Coach said, and then turned and yelled, "Tracy! Get a couple paper towels from the locker room so I can clean this up. Everybody take five, get a drink."

I turned and jogged toward the locker room, the rest of my squad rushing for the drinking fountain. I hated Holly. I hated her with everything I had. I hated her as much as Jenna hated her. Maybe even more. But I couldn't make myself stand up to her. Why not? Was she really that powerful?

No way, I heard Jenna say in my head, just as she had the night before she died. *She is totally powerless and she knows it. That's why she acts the way she does.*

But she always has the upper hand, I'd said. *Everyone else loves her.*

Uh-uh, Jenna had answered. *Everyone else is afraid of her. That's why, when we leave our note behind, telling everything she did, and all that mean shit her mom said, everyone will know her game.*

They won't care.

Yes, they will, she'd said. *Because this time we won't just be humiliated. We'll be dead. Everyone will see her for who she really is and will turn against her. We have to show everyone who she really is, Chloe.*

The blood was dripping through my fingers, and the tears really started to flow. I missed Jenna so much, and I was angry she went ahead and killed herself but didn't leave behind a note like we'd planned. And not only did Holly have just as much power as she did before, but Jenna had left me behind to deal with it by myself.

As if on cue, I heard Sydney's voice just behind me. "Probably wouldn't have hurt if it hit her in the gut."

"Yeah," Holly's voice responded, "but it probably would have hit all that fat and bounced right back at me and killed me."

And then the two giggled like they always did.

I turned through the locker room door and ran straight for the sinks, leaning over them to let the blood and the snot and the tears just fall right into the swirling water.

Jenna was wrong. Killing herself hadn't taken away Holly's power. A dead person couldn't take power away from anyone.

But a live one could.

...

I would never forget the night of August 21. It was steamy hot, and even the evenings felt like you were wrapped in a wet sweater. School was coming up, and the little kids were inside early, getting used to their bedtime schedules again. The streets were dark and quiet, except for the bugs, which practically owned the place in late summer.

I walked to Jenna's house with a backpack. Inside was a notebook, pen, bottle of cherry vodka (for nerves, Jenna had said) stolen from my parents' cabinet, and a yearbook with bright red circles around the photos of Holly, Monica, Sydney, and about a dozen other kids who'd made us miserable. I was all fear and doubt.

Jenna met me on the front stoop of her apartment complex, just like we'd planned. She stood when I approached, and the two of us walked to the basketball court at the bottom of the hill. We'd chosen the location weeks ago. The asphalt was cracked and the chains on the goals broken or missing. Nobody was ever there, but it was visible, and we knew eventually someone would find us. And we wanted to be found. Who wanted to rot in the woods with animals eating their face off for six months? Not us. Plus, her brother was home and so were my parents, and with only one gun and two shots to deliver, we wanted to make sure we weren't heard after the first shot and saved before the second.

Jenna walked right to the middle of the court and sat down. She shrugged out of her backpack and unzipped it, pulling out the one thing she was in charge of bringing—her dad's gun. I didn't know anything about guns; all I knew was this one was big and oily and ugly and it scared me to look at it. My fingers immediately went numb.

"Okay, so let's write it," she said, laying the gun on the ground between us.

I opened the notebook and put the tip of the pen to the first line, but my hands were shaking so bad there was no way I could write. I tried pressing harder.

"To Whom It May Concern," she said, and when my hand still didn't move, looked up at me. "Too formal?"

I shook my head and scratched out the words.

"Okay. To Whom It May Concern. If you're reading this note, we are dead." She paused so I could write what she'd just said. "You may think we're on drugs or something, but we're not," she continued, but my hand wouldn't move past "we are dead." My pen stayed on the tail of the last "d" as if magnetized, and my vision blurred on the words. "What's wrong?" she asked.

I swallowed, shook my head. All I could think of was my mom and dad reading the note. Reading those words—"we are dead"—and how they would be devastated. How they would cry. How it would ruin the rest of their lives. How shocked they'd be because they'd always been there for me to talk to, but I'd never taken them up on it.

"What about our parents?" I said, my voice sounding just as shaky as my fingers felt. "This is going to destroy them."

Jenna made a *pfft!* noise and laughed. "Maybe yours," she said. "Mine probably won't even notice. They'll probably be happy that they don't have to deal with me anymore."

My tongue snaked out and snagged a strand of hair. I sucked on it and stared at the paper. I felt like I was going to throw up.

"You said yourself that you're totally lonely, so obviously your relationship with your parents isn't all that great, right?" She ducked her head, looking up at me so our eyes could meet.

I nodded, still chewing. But was it true? I was no longer so sure.

"Listen, if you want out . . . ," she said, trailing off.

And it was the hardest thing I'd ever done in my whole life, but I nodded. Which is weird, when you think of it, that saying

I didn't want to die was the hardest thing I'd ever done. When had my life gotten so upside-down?

"I don't want you to do it, either," I said once I found my voice. "I think we should both wait. Do something else."

But Jenna had closed her eyes and shook her head, like a little kid refusing to listen to her parents. "I can't," she said, without opening her eyes. "I can't take it anymore, Chloe. They're making me miserable, and I want out."

"So we'll find another way out," I said. She finally opened her eyes.

"There is no other way."

"Please don't do it," I begged.

"I understand why you don't want to, Chloe. It's okay. Really. But I'm going to."

I felt tears rush down my cheeks. I wished I had a cell phone so I could call the police or my mom or someone, anyone who could help me change Jenna's mind. "I don't want you to die," I said. "I'll miss you." And as simple as that sounded, it was the truth.

"Then do it with me." Tears were streaming down her plump cheeks.

I shook my head. I reached out and held her hand. "I can't," I said.

She squeezed my hand, hard. "I have to," she said.

"Don't," I choked out, but she dropped my hand and picked up the gun, held it in her lap. And right then I knew that no matter what I said or did, she was going to do this. And I knew that no matter what she said or did, I wasn't going to.

"You should probably go," she finally said, and for a split second, I considered grabbing the gun and running. But I knew that it would do no good. Even if I got it away from her, she'd still find another way to do it. She'd made up her mind.

"I'm going to call the police," I said, a last-ditch effort.

She nodded. "It'll be over before you can get to a phone. But I understand."

I shoveled my things back into my backpack and stood up on noodly legs, unsure of how I was ever going to get home. My belly hurt from all the crying, but I couldn't stop as I ran back toward my house, the whole time listening for a gunshot I never heard.

But I knew it had happened just the same.

I knew, before my mom ever woke me up with the news: *Jenna was gone.*

...

With my nose all cleaned up, I left the locker room more sure than I had been in forever.

Jenna was gone and nobody seemed to care, but that didn't mean that I was gone, too. People would notice; all I had to do was make them notice.

I would set things right.

Class was still in session, but I didn't care. I wasn't going to go back out to let Holly and Sydney have another shot at humiliating me today. I scrubbed my face, changed back into my street clothes, and walked straight out of the gym toward Mr. Kinney's office.

Mr. Kinney was our guidance counselor. He was the one who was always talking about respect and tolerance, saying we could come to him with anything. For once, I was going to take him up on the offer. Because this was what Jenna and I should have done from the very beginning.

I stepped into the guidance office, and the secretary looked up in surprise.

"Yes?"

"I need to talk to Mr. Kinney. Like, right away."

She glanced at the clock. "Honey, final bell's going to ring in fifteen minutes."

"This is important," I said, and I dug my fingernails into my palms to give myself strength.

She leaned back and looked into his office, then slowly sat forward, frowned, and said, "Okay. He's in there."

I took a deep breath and walked toward his office, telling myself the whole way that *I was making things right I was making things right I was making things right*. . . .

"Hi," Mr. Kinney said when I stepped through his doorway. "Is it Chloe?"

I nodded, sat down in the chair facing his desk. My nails dug deeper into my palms. I felt like I was going to float away, out the window, over the parking lot, and into space. I wondered if this was how Jenna felt when she died.

"What can I help you with?" he said. The way he leaned

forward, his hands clasped in front of him and a concerned grin on his face, I knew everything was about to change.

"I'm being bullied," I blurted out. "By Holly Abrams and some other girls. Also Holly's mom. She said some really mean things about me and . . . my friend. It's been going on for two years, and I don't know what else to do about it. I need you to help me make it stop."

Mr. Kinney got up and walked around me to close the door. He made his way back to his chair behind his desk and leaned back, his palms on the desk in front of him. "Tell me what's going on," he said.

So I did. I told Mr. Kinney the rest of the story, all the way up until the basketball incident in Team Sports. He nodded, wrote some things down, and made disgusted faces. The bell rang, but neither of us moved as I told him about Jenna, and how I was supposed to kill myself too but chickened out. I told him everything. Then he called my mom, and she came to the office and I repeated the story. And while I talked, I felt myself growing heavy again, sinking, sinking, sinking from the stratosphere down to the parking lot, to the inside of the school, to the chair in Mr. Kinney's office. I could feel my nails still digging into my palms, the ripped chair vinyl against the backs of my legs, and a fan as it rotated every few seconds to blow air into my face.

I could feel it all.

Because Jenna was gone.

But I was not.

Because I'd bailed on her, Jenna never actually left a note, but I knew she had so much she wanted to say. So I wrote her suicide note for my column. It was everything we were going to say when we had planned to kill ourselves together.

Stuart refused to run it, and Ms. Stepton agreed with him, but I didn't really care because I just needed to write it out—and I'd already said everything it said to Mr. Kinney and my mom anyway.

Of course, this left a huge news hole on page three of our paper, and it was up to me to fill it.

So I filled it with this:

This edition dedicated to
Jenna Roundtree
Former Editor
Best Friend
1995–2011
Gone, but definitely not forgotten

It seemed like enough.

The Truest Story There Is

BY JAIME ADOFF

IT COMES AT me like a wave. Ready to wash me away into the depths of myself. Yeah, that's a deep thought, but it's true. This feeling that I'm skating on thin ice, no wait, thinner than that. It's cracked and broken, just barely frozen. I've got one foot soaked in cold water and the other one out—safe, on dry land—safe, at least for now.

"Shelly Stewart, you need to be gettin' your tired butt outta the house and to the store like I told you twenty times already. Are you deaf *and* lazy, boy?"

You should know. Ain't no one as lazy as you, Mumma. I said that in my head, 'cause in my head I won't get my ass beat. Or worse, get me put out of the house like she does sometimes when she says I'm unruly. *I ain't unruly I just don't respect you, Mumma, 'cause you fake. And you're a hypocrite. And you're a fool for marryin' Randy.* I try to block Mumma out with my thoughts, but it never works.

Mumma's about as ghetto as you can get. See, ghetto don't have nothin' to do with skin color. It has to do with how you act. Mumma's a big, white, tattooed, biker-lookin' woman who wouldn't know good sense if it knocked her in the head.

And that's a true story right there.

"Shelly, you hear me, boy?" I cringe automatically. I think I'll cringe until the end of time. Maybe three days after that. I mean—Shelly? Really, Mumma? Did you have to name me that? Why didn't you just tattoo a sign on my forehead when I was born that said, *Hey, everyone, kick this kid's butt when he gets older.* Hate that name. Mumma says it's from Daddy's side, but Daddy always said it was from Mumma's. Can't find out now, unless I want to go over to Hawthorne Cemetery and ask Daddy. But as far as I know he still ain't talkin'. The thought of Daddy in that cold cemetery underneath that cheap, chipped, stone makes me cringe even worse than hearin' my stupid name. Daddy was cool, at least what I remember of him. But that's been a long time gone now, a long time.

Nine years. The number appears in my head like a popup ad on one of those websites I'm not supposed to be on. I was six when he died. Natural causes. Cancer. Took him quick. Faster than that, even. I remember bits and pieces, but it's hazy and gray and full of whispering. Sometimes moans. Sometimes cries. But always foggy, never clear. Maybe it's better that way, maybe it's best. . . .

"I'm goin', Mumma," I answer out loud. The sound of my own voice lifting the fog off Daddy's death and busting me full force into *this life*, into this *right now*.

I always wait for her to catch it. But she never does. She never can tell that I don't call her mom, or *momma*. No, *Mumma* is as close as I come. It's as close as I *ever* want to come. It's my way of saying, *you may have birthed me, but you don't act anywhere near like a real mom. So you don't deserve to be called one.*

"Well, you best be gettin' on your way. I need what I need and I need it now." Mumma's famous line, no matter what it is she needs. Eggs, milk, cigarettes, and even beer. Don't matter a bit how old I am. It's all urgent. It's like the very spinning of this crazy planet depends on me gettin' what she needs. *What evs, Mumma, I'll get it when I get it.* I said that in my head too.

"Oh, *great*." It hits me like a brick to my head. It's Sunday, and that means I gotta go to Foodtown, or GhettoTown as I call it. It's only three blocks away, but it might as well be three hundred. I know I don't live in a good neighborhood, but where Foodtown is makes my neighborhood look like Park Avenue.

. . .

The walk to Foodtown is hot and slow. Hot, 'cause we're in a freak heat wave in the middle of September, and slow 'cause I ain't in no particular hurry to get Mumma what she needs. My mind fast-forwards to tomorrow and my walk gets even slower. Thinkin' about what I got to do to just get through one day at school. Just one day without ending up on the news 'cause some fools wanted to start some stuff with me. Just one day? Is that too much to ask?

I keep my head down as I pass two wannabes hangin' on the corner. You can tell they're not the real thing by how they act. Tryin' to look all hard. Starin' down old ladies on walkers.

See, a real gangbanger don't need to try, they just are—period. These kids look like they couldn't be more than thirteen, but that doesn't mean they ain't dangerous. I take a quick glance at them, and it's just like I figured. I don't know them. And I hope they don't know me either.

As I get closer to Foodtown, I make myself even smaller than I already am. Walkin' through the war zone. Ground zero for all kinds of "gang activity" or whatever they're callin' it these days on the news. This is not a good place to walk through if you're small and undeclared like me. Undeclared, not like in major, 'cause I ain't even close to college yet, but undeclared as in not gang affiliated. As in, I'm tryin' real hard not to get *got* by any number of folks who think I should be runnin' with their set. Since I'm not, they think I'm a danger and can't be trusted 'cause I might be an informant or somethin' ridiculous like that. But one thing you learn when you live where I live is that ridiculous happens every day. And ridiculous can get you hurt. Sometimes, like in the permanently stopped breathing kind of way, too.

What evs, they don't really want to mess with me. Don't they know I could be the biracial Bruce Lee? Hi-YA.

The Foodtown sign comes up quick, startling me for a second 'cause I wasn't paying attention. The store is between two boarded up houses that used to have families livin' in them. Back when there *were* families and lots of kids livin' in this neighborhood. Back when I was a kid. Back when Daddy was alive.

Oh no. If I could have screamed it, I would have.

"Hey, wuz up? What you doin' over here? Did ya get lost?"
I don't even turn around. I just keep walkin', pretendin' I
didn't hear. I should have been payin' better attention when
I was walkin' because them wannabes were followin' me. I
should have known they would.

"Hold up, what's your hurry?" Another voice, this time
connected to a body that's *now* right in front of me. A body
belonging to the other wannabe. He's got a half smile pasted
on his face, but the other half has me wantin' to pee my pants.

"Just goin' to the store for my mom." It sounds dumb as
soon as I say it. It sounds like I just made it up on the spot, even
though it's the truth. I hope all that church stuff is true. I really
hope *the truth will set me free*, 'cause if it don't . . .

"Yeah? The store? You think he's tellin' us the truth?" The
first kid says, turning to his friend. Both of them are young,
younger than me, just like I thought. But both of them have
some size to them too. Eighth grade muscles busting out of
too-tight T-shirts don't do much for my confidence. I feel
myself start to panic. I want to run, but I know I can't.

They've got me boxed in. Somehow in the last few seconds,
they corralled me like a piece of cattle, backing me up into an
alley. So if the worse happens, ain't nobody ever gonna know.

Both of them are losing patience—fast. I take a quick look
behind me, and what I see makes me wince. Just a brick wall, a
dead end. *There's nowhere to run.*

"I don't know if I believe him, T, I think he might be lyin'
to us." I hear the words and shut my eyes tight, trying to push

out of my mind all the bad ways this little encounter could end up.

"Hey, what are you doin'? Why you got your eyes closed?"

"We ain't got time to mess with you, so just give us what you got, if you don't want to get got. Got it?" I open my eyes and see the outline of a small handgun tucked into the first kid's waistband. I throw Mumma's money on the ground, and I can hear them move close, scooping up the bills and change. *I don't want to see that gun again. If you're gonna kill me, just get it over with quick, that's all I ask.*

"Come on, let's bounce." The sour smell of sweat lingers after they run away. I stand there, silent, and shut my eyes tight again. I want to open them, but I can't. Even though they're gone, I'm still their hostage. I am small. Smaller than small. I am frozen. Stuck in this spot. Stuck in this life.

. . .

Foodtown stinks of rotten fruit and bleach. It looks like some third-world grocery store that's had a bomb dropped a little too close to it. Shelves are half empty, and everything looks all old and run-down. Paint is faded and chipping, and some of the lights are burned out.

I scan the aisles for what Mumma needs. *Milk, OJ, and a loaf of bread.* Why I'm here I don't know. Ain't got no money, but I have to get what Mumma needs. *Gonna steal it, that's what I'm gonna do.* I try to get my nerve up, but I've got no real plan on how I'm gonna get a gallon of milk out of the store without anyone seeing me. I grab the milk and see if it will fit under my shirt. *Yeah, right.* It looks ridiculous. I *am* ridiculous for even thinking I could do this. I put the milk back and wander the aisles of the store, looking at all the things that I'd like to have at my house. All the things that Mumma never gets for me. *I see those wannabe kids' faces flash in my mind.* The ones who just jacked me. I hate those kids. I should've fought back. I should have said, *"Hell no, you ain't gettin' my money, whatcha gonna do about it, punk? You want some of me? Don't you know, I'm the biracial Bruce Lee?"* Yeah, right.

After Foodtown, I just started wandering, not really knowin' where I was goin' or what I was gonna do. I knew I wasn't gonna go home because, shoot, Mumma didn't care if you got jacked. If you didn't come home with what she wanted *and* you got her money stolen? That was just your ass, plain and simple. I was just gonna have to deal with all that later, and hope by the time *later* came, Mumma was gone or was too drunk to remember she'd sent me to the store in the first place.

Dixon's was usually a safe bet for me to escape all the drama. Yeah, if there was one thing my life had, it was drama, for sure.

• • •

"Dude, I tried to call you. I got a ride with one of my mom's friends, was gonna see if you wanted to go to church." Yeah, I was probably gettin' jacked when you called. Sorry I couldn't answer my phone.

"I don't think I had my phone on me, I was, uh out doin' some stuff." I throw out the first lie that pops into my head. Trying to say it as normal as I can. As normal as a person can after thinkin' they were gonna die. I don't look Dixon in the eyes; it's hard to look anyone in the eyes after you've just been jacked by a couple of eighth graders.

"You missed a great service, awesome message and the band was kickin'."

"That's good," I answer, my normal voice sounding pretty shaky to my own ears.

"Where you comin' from?" Dixon asked, reaching into a bag of chips but keeping his eyes glued to the TV. Both of us, plopped down on his couch. The cushions were worn-down so much their new color could just be called, "faded."

"I was out runnin' some errands for Mumma."

"Cool," Dixon says. Luckily he's paying more attention to what's on TV than to what I'm saying.

. . .

Dixon's apartment is quiet. Quiet, except for me and him and the low rumble of the TV. I look over at him, and he's out. Sound asleep on the couch next to me. His Coke bottle glasses half off his face, lookin' like a special-needs Harry Potter. *Dag, that's messed up.* I feel guilty even thinkin' it, but everyone knows Dixon's about as smart as they come. Knows the answer before the teacher asks the question. Dixon's "good people," as Daddy used to say. That one phrase that stuck to my mind like superglue. *Good* people. Too bad there's way more *bad* people than good ones.

I grab a pillow and make myself up a place on the floor next to the couch. Even though it's only around seven, I'm wiped out, and as soon as I stretch my legs out, I start to drift off too. I let my body relax and let go. Slowly, I start to come down from the high-alert stage that I'd been in since my "incident." I can feel the first twitches of almost-sleep begin to take me over. My left leg kicks out, then my right hand. Then, I'm gone.

. . .

We are walkin' down the hall, and all of a sudden she just starts kissin' me. I mean she's goin for it. And the cool thing is, nobody else notices. All the students and teachers just walk by like we're invisible. It's like we're on our own island of love and sloppy French kisses. Then one kiss takes the cake. A slow-motion kiss that seems like it's gonna last forever. It's like the longest kiss in the history of kisses. That is until Dixon's stale breath makes me cough, which then wakes me up so I'm face to face with his face and not Marketta Barrett's—numero uno—babe of all babes in the Junior class. Dag, that was a good dream.

"What?" I manage to say back, trying to stagger to my feet, pushing Dixon's face away from mine. I'm pissed off I'm with Dixon and not Marketta, and to add insult to injury, the blood rushing to my head makes me feel like I'm going to pass out and fall right back down on the floor.

"It's almost ten. Your mom's been blowin' up your phone. Now she's blowin' up mine. You gotta get home, dude."

• • •

My stomach feels like it's down to my knees as I start my death march from Dixon's apartment to mine. It's not like it's that far, but I'm walkin' so slow it might as well be twenty miles away. We both live on the same side of town: the messed-up side. Don't matter that Dixon's white. Race ain't got a thing to do with it. If you're poor this is where you live—period. Regardless of race, color, or creed, we got thugs that will jack you for whatever you got in your pockets. Equal opportunity gangsters, for sure.

It's not like I live in a major city. I don't even live in a *minor* city, just this little spit-drop of a place some *genius* decided to call *Helzburg*. Folks think because I'm in Ohio I'm supposed to be in the country, out in the cornfields somewhere, but they don't know. There's craziness everywhere and Helzburg is as bad as any *real* big city can get and that's a true story.

Luckily by the time I get home, my apartment is empty. No signs of Mumma or Randy at all. *Who knows where they are and who cares.* I caught a break this time. If they're not here, odds are they went to Mickey's Bar, and when they get home, Mumma won't even remember what day it is, let alone that she sent me to the store all those hours ago.

I settle into my bed and pull the covers up to my chin. Ready to pull them over my head if I hear someone coming.

Yeah, I know, a real punk way to live. *Real cool* for a fifteen-year-old sophomore in high school to act. Just like a little kid, still afraid of his *mommy*, still afraid.

Always afraid . . .

• • •

The alley, the wannabes. It all comes back fast. Shocking my brain into waking up, just like someone threw me into a cold pool.

Mumma. I sit bolt-upright in bed and glance over at the clock. "Six thirty-seven." I whisper to myself, straining to hear any stirring or movement on the other side of my bedroom door. *They have to be home.* But I don't hear a thing. Just the comforting sounds of silence. It would be the break of all breaks if they weren't here, if it was just me. It's happened before. They stay out all night, *drinking, or doing whatever they do* then crash at one of their friends' places. Right now it would be perfect timing.

I try to walk carefully out into the living room, but I almost trip over the coffee table. *I hate that stupid thing.* Peeking into their bedroom, I see the bed's still a mess, just like it always is, just like it was since yesterday morning. Nothing's changed. No sign of a return trip.

"Yes," I shout it out loud into Mumma's bedroom, almost dancing back out into the living room and into our tiny kitchen. "Thank you, God," I shout out loud again. *Today might not be a bad day after all.*

The bus screeches to a stop, and everyone goes flying forward. We're herded outside and up the stairs to the entrance of the building. I look for a cattle prod, but so far I haven't been able to find one. *There's still time.*

Helzburg High, is just that: Hell. At least it is for me. I'm small; I'm not white; I'm not black; and I'm not in a gang. Just like I said, *Hell*. Fifteen hundred kids, or delinquents, are more like it. Welcome to the Jungle, right here in the cornfields of Ohio.

The morning starts, and we're off. Uncontrolled chaos. The halls choked with kids who shouldn't even be here. They should be at Davis, that special school that takes all the kids that have messed up so badly even *this* school won't take them. Mumma's always sayin' I'm just one step away from Davis. But I know I ain't never done anything close to gettin' me sent there. Mumma probably wishes I would really mess up and get sent to Juvie. Then she'd be rid of me, at least for ninety days.

"Move." I feel a big hand push my chest as the strong smell of too-sweet body spray hits my nostrils. I get smashed against a locker, held there like a prisoner from the force of the kids rushing through the hall. The voice that belongs to one of the hands that pushed me doesn't have a face. It doesn't need one. It doesn't matter. They're all the same.

"Move shorty."

"Watch out."

"Move or get beat down." It's my morning welcome song, but I'm used to it.

· · ·

"Hey, Shell, what happened, I mean, with your moms?" Dixon whispers. Both of us sitting in our fourth-period history class. He sounds worried, kind of looking me up and down to see if I'm okay.

"Dude, she wasn't home. Neither was Randy."

"Where were they?"

"Who knows and who cares," I answer, my voice just slightly going above a whisper. I check to see if Ms. Lygant heard me, but she still has her back turned, writing something on the white board.

"What did she say this morning?" Dixon is really looking for all the 411. And I'm just not in the mood.

"I said they weren't home. Didn't come home all night. Maybe they'll never come back," I answer, this time even louder than before. I'm kinda shocked that I would say something like that, but also kinda excited about the possibility. I mean, I wouldn't want them to get hurt or anything, but maybe they could just leave the state. Or get arrested and sent to jail for a long time. That might not be bad. The thought makes me smile.

· · ·

Lunch is like a minefield. It's me and Dixon against, well everyone, or at least that's what it feels like. In this school, in my life—anything can happen.

"Dude, there she is," Dixon says, sounding like a little kid on Christmas Eve who just can't wait to open his presents.

"Who?"

"Your girl." Dixon nods his head to point to someone behind me. I turn around slow, trying to be slick. At first I don't see her, but then she comes in crystal clear like a high-definition channel on TV. Marketta Barrett, in all her sixteen-year-old glory, breathing the rarified air that only superbad, upper-class cuties breathe. *If I could get just one breath of that.*

Marketta is *all that*, and ain't nobody gonna argue with me on that one. She's biracial like me, except her mom's black and her dad's white. *Yeah, I do my research.* She's actually cool, which is unusual for a girl like her. She's the kind of girl if you sit next to in class, you better be wearin' a long shirt to cover up your growing—uh, *excitement* or you are *busted*, for sure.

"You need to go talk to her." Dixon is always tryin' to instigate something. He's good at instigating.

"You talk to her," I say back.

"Dude, she's *your* girl," he says all matter-of-factly. "I gotta girl, remember?" There he goes again. It's kind of a nerd thing that I guess we both do. Pretending some hottie is *our* girl. For Dixon, that would be Katie Walker, who's basically the white version of Marketta. Pretty face, slammin' body, but couldn't pick Dixon out of a lineup if her life depended on it. Now Marketta, she's different. At least she knows I'm alive. Shoot, we've even had a few conversations. I don't like to talk about it to Dixon though, no need to rub it in his face. What would

I say anyway? *My* pretend girlfriend is more real than *your* pretend girlfriend? *Shoot, we're both pathetic.*

"Dude, she's by herself. Now's your chance. Go over there." Dixon practically stands up.

"Chill, I'll get over there when I'm good and ready," I tell him. Both of us know I'm too scared to walk over and talk to her; both of us know I'm just stalling for time.

"Better hurry up, she ain't gonna be there forever."

"Dag, she's leaving," I say, trying to sound disappointed, even though I'm actually relieved. I watch her walk out of the cafeteria with a group of other superbad cuties. *Why do they always travel in packs?*

"Lucky for you, huh?" Dixon tries to give me a jab, but I let it go. I feel like my cheeks are flushed red. I take a swig of my fruit punch and feel the urge to pee. It's been building for the whole lunch period, the urge that I've been trying to ignore, but now. . .

"I gotta go to the bathroom." The words leave my mouth like a judge handing down a death sentence. Dixon looks at me like, *better you than me.*

"You want me to go with you?" Dixon asks softly.

"Dude, I ain't no girl. I can handle mines." I try to put on my fake, *I got this* gangster voice, but it ain't foolin' no one, most of all me.

I take my long dead-man-walking walk to the bathroom. I look around the hallway, trying to see if I can spy anyone who might want to mess with me. *So far so good.*

Oh no. I can feel him before I see him. I lift my head up from the sink and feel his breath in my ear. He starts whispering, taunting me in a singsongy voice.

"Hey, little girl with the red dress on, what you doin' in my bathroom?" It's Ben Reeves, but he goes by Benny. *Probably thinks it gives him more street cred.* I hate this dude. Always got to say I'm a girl 'cause of my name. He's only a junior, and he's already declared. Always trying to get me to run with his set. Gave me a good shiner last year. He don't play. . .

"What's wrong, you too good to answer my boy, here?" Another voice coming out of one of the stalls, another thug I didn't even know he was there. That's how they do. They're tricky like that. I should have known. I never should have gone to the bathroom.

"Look, I was just leaving. . . ." I can hear my voice crack and shake, breaking off in midsentence.

"We're not gonna hurt you. We just wanna talk." The thug from the stall says, moving past me and toward the door, blocking my only way to escape. I know they don't have much time before lunch is over, but I also know these dudes could do a lot of damage in a short period of time.

"I just wanna go back and finish my lunch is all." I try to sound calm. Try to get them to be calm, but the strange thing is, they already are.

"You can finish your lunch just as soon as we finish some bizness." Benny gets right up in my face for emphasis. He stinks somethin' awful, worse than that even. Like rotten fish and underarm funk. I take a quick glace at the door. The other thug's got a trash can wedged up against it. "We're gonna cut to the chase. We need you to do something for us." I hear the words and get an instant bad feeling in the pit of my stomach. *This is not gonna be good. . . .*

I lower my head and let Benny's words beat me up. You'd think it would be better to get hit by words than fists, but in this case, I would've taken the beat down of a lifetime than have to hear what Benny was tellin' me. Givin' me instructions was more like it. Tellin' me step by step what I had to do.

I shut my eyes, pretending that I'm listening real close like he told me. Really, I'm just pretending I'm someplace else. Pretending I'm anyplace but this hellhole of a bathroom and a school. Wishing I was any place but in this life.

Benny gives me a little push to my chest as I watch him and his *friend* leave the bathroom. I take a minute to collect myself, splashing some water on my face to try to wash away what I just heard. But there ain't no soap invented that will get rid of that mess.

. . .

My walk back to the cafeteria is even slower than my walk to the bathroom. Dixon has a look on his face like he just saw a ghost. Probably thought I was dead. In true Dixon fashion, he waited for me. Even though lunch is over and the bell is about to ring. He waited. *I gotta give him props for that. He is a true friend.*

Dixon stares at me like he wants to say something, but he doesn't. He doesn't even have to ask, and I don't even have to answer. My look says it all. I was in the shit, big time, and there wasn't a damn thing either of us could do about it.

. . .

Flipping through the pages of my American history book I try to concentrate, but it's no use. *History, that's what I'm gonna be, come tomorrow.*

"Whatcha gonna do?" Dixon's voice breaks into my thoughts. Both of us are *supposed* to be studying at the library. We always sit in the quiet section, away from the DVDs and computers.

The library is like no-man's-land, a safe haven in between gang territories. Nobody messes with you at the library. It's like an unwritten rule of the gangbangers.

"I don't know. Got till tomorrow night. That's when it's supposed to go down. That's when . . ." I can't even finish my sentence. I can't even think it.

"You think Benny was serious? I mean, if you don't—"

"What do you think?" I stare down at the floor, wishing I could stay in this library forever.

There's a long silence before either of us speak again. It's like I can feel the wheels turning in Dixon's brain, trying to figure out a way for me. But both of us know, no matter how fast those wheels move, there ain't no way out.

"I guess you gotta do what you gotta do," Dixon finally says.

"Closing time, boys. Did you find some more good books?" Ms. Anne asks, pushing a cart full of books that she probably still has to put away.

"Naw, not today," I answer her.

"Oh, that's too bad. How about you, Dixon?"

"No, we just came to study. We'll be back tomorrow, though; probably check some more out then." Dixon's always tryin' to get brownie points, even with a librarian.

"You two are my best customers, I have to keep this place stocked so you have new books to read. See you tomorrow," Ms. Anne says with her usual smile.

"Okay, see ya," Dixon says as we both head out of the library.

"Yeah, see you tomorrow," I say doubtfully, under my breath. *If I can make it through tomorrow.*

• • •

Sleep comes and goes, mostly goes. I know I must have fallen asleep at some point, but if I did, it wasn't for very long. I can see the sun coming up; trying to shine its way through my window. Just peaking the beginning of its rays into my room. Tryin' to tell me a new day has arrived. The day that could signal the end of my life.

"Go away, sun," I try to yell, but the words come out all scratchy and groggy sounding. "Go away." But the sun doesn't answer.

I walk out into the living room. I don't hear a thing. I check in to see if Mumma is home, but she's not. *They didn't come home last night either.* If I gave a two shits, I'd be worried, but since I don't, I'm not.

I throw my clothes on, brush my teeth, and head out the door to catch the bus. The school bus isn't the kind of bus I want to catch on this morning. I have a strong urge to walk to the Greyhound station and leave town. Out of the state, as far away as I can get from Helzburg. The feeling builds in me so strong that I actually start walking in the direction of the station. Just a few steps are all I take, and then I stop. *Where am I supposed to go without a dime in my pocket?* I realize. *I'm just gonna have to do what I gotta do.*

• • •

The day washes over me like dirty soap, and I can't get clean. I can't get clear of what I have to do. Lunchtime comes, and me and Dixon sit down in the caf. He is munchin' down on a sloppy joe, I'm just staring at my plate.

"How ya doin?" Dixon asks between bites. He's looking at me like it might be the last time he ever sees me. Which is not too far off.

"I'm doin'," I answer back. I hear my voice, but it doesn't seem like it's my own. Everything today is like from some sort of alternate reality.

"I'm feelin' kinda lightheaded," I blurt out, from nowhere.

"You know you don't have to do it. You could go to the cops."

His voice doesn't sound very convincing.

"Yeah, the cops, that's gonna go over real well. How long you think I'll last after I call them?" Dixon just nods, knowing that I'm right. Knowing that there's no way out.

. . .

I feel like I'm gonna puke as I walk out of my last class. It takes everything in my whole body and my mind not to just throw up all over myself.

"See ya later." Benny leans in and whispers in my ear as I leave school for what could be the very last time. He pushes past me with his "boys" laughing and pointing back at me. I keep my head down, like I'm invisible. *Damned if I do, dead if I don't.*

Me and Dixon get on the bus. I feel like a lamb being led to slaughter. I look over at Dixon, and he's got his nose stuck in a new zombie book. I just stare out the window, watching the school get smaller and smaller. Thinking, when I see it again, *if I see it again*, I won't be the same. I'll never be the same.

. . .

"So you know what you gotta do."

"I know," I say back, my voice even smaller than how I feel. Knowing that the next person who walks by is gonna get jumped, beat up, and possibly killed. And I'm the one who has to do it.

I know it's impossible, but I'm praying that no one walks by. It's not the most traveled area, but it's traveled enough. Just enough off of Rampart Ave. to be out of the way, but not far enough off so that no one walks past. Someone will come by. Most likely someone walking home from a crappy job, going back to their crappy life. They don't deserve what I'm about to do to them. No one does. But what can I do? It's either them or me. Benny made it crystal clear: if I didn't jump someone, rob them, and use the knife he gave me, then it would be used on me.

"Okay, get back here, behind this Dumpster like this. When you see someone, jump out, pull your knife out, and just stab 'em quick. Like this." Benny shows me with the knife. Stabbing at the air with a look of demented glee in his eyes. *He's really enjoying this. Psychopath.*

"Don't worry. We'll clean you up afterward," Benny says. A huge scary grin plastered to his face.

"What about . . . the . . . the person?" I ask. Feeling like I'm in a total out of body experience.

"Well, we'll call Nine-One-One, make sure they get taken to the hospital," Benny says, about as truthful sounding as a politician. I watch him takes a swig from a beer bottle he just pulled out of one of his jacket pockets. He takes another, then another.

The other thugs that came with Benny are drinkin' too. Just standin' around like they do this kind of thing every night. *Maybe they do.*

"Okay, Shelly girl, you're on." I can see someone coming, the outline getting closer, the shadow filling up the empty concrete squares of the sidewalk.

I get myself ready. I can't do this, I can't do this. I'll just scare them. Pretend to stab them and drop the knife, make it look like it slipped from my hands. The thoughts are racing in and out of my head so fast I can't keep up with them.

I can't do this I can't—I won't . . . Maybe it's a girl, a woman. Benny said no girls. Please let it be a girl. . . .

As the outline gets closer, I can tell it's no girl. It's like someone else is controlling my body, because before I can stop myself I am jumping out from behind the Dumpster screaming at a person I don't even know with a big-ass knife in my hand, praying to God that he just runs away, fast.

"Oh, you went and picked the wrong dude tonight." In almost one motion, the dude kicks the knife out of my hand, pushes me to the ground, and shoves a gun practically up my nostrils as he puts all of his weight onto my chest.

"I'm gonna do you right here," he whispers in my ear. "Don't you know who I am? Your momma ain't never gonna find you. They'll be parts of you all over town."

"No, don't, please, I—" I shut my eyes waiting for the bullet to explode into my brain. *At least it will be over quick.* The thought, the last thought I will ever have goes through my mind. This is it. I can feel the warm sensation of pee roll down my leg. Then after what seems like a lifetime I hear the dude speak.

"No. I ain't gonna kill you, why would I kill a homie?" I think I hear wrong and look up toward the dude. Somethin' about his voice makes him sound young. *He's a kid like me.* I didn't notice it before because he had a hat pulled over his face and a big jacket on. All of a sudden the dude gets up off of me, brushes himself off, and starts to laugh. I get up slowly, still confused, not sure if I'm really safe. Not sure if the dude is gonna change his mind and drop a couple rounds in me after all. I look up just in time to see Benny running toward me his hands outstretched.

"You had a choice to run with us, we got tired of waitin' so we decided for you. You were gonna go through with it. You were gonna do it." Benny is almost hopping up and down with joy. "This is Darrell, one of your homies now. Pretty convincin', huh?" Darrell comes in for a soul hug.

"What's up, Shell. Did I scare you?" Darrell looks down at the freshly formed pee spot on the front of my pants. Now everyone is laughing.

"But I—" I stop myself as the cold, horrible, reality of my situation becomes clear. *But I wasn't gonna do it. I'm not a killer—I'm not.*

"Now, Shell, next time is for real." Benny looks crazy, even crazier than he usually looks. But what's worse is the huge smile on his face. Like he just can't wait until I *do it* for real.

• • •

I hear the laughs and screams, like hyenas at a house party, as I fast-walk away from this nightmare. I stink of pee, and I'm soaked with sweat. But I'm alive, and I didn't kill anyone. I try to take solace in those facts. At least for now I'm safe. And I guess as long as I run with Benny's set I'll stay that way.

I take a long hard look in the direction of the Greyhound station. *It would be so easy to just disappear.* I start walking in that direction. No matter I ain't got no money in my pockets. No matter I ain't got no place to go. I stop dead in my tracks, frozen like I was stuck in a big block of ice. I do a three sixty and head back toward my apartment. Back to my life, the only one I know, the only one I have. At least I got Dixon, and maybe one day Marketta too. *Yeah, keep on dreamin', I know it.*

I pick up my pace, past all the fools hangin' on the block. Past all the liquor stores and check-cashing places. Past what people think the hood is like. *I can tell you, it's what it's like.*

I pass it all, knowing deep down there's gotta be more than all this madness. And somehow, someway, I gotta get to it, and I gotta get to it soon. . . .

I see a police car tear around the corner, lights flashing, sirens blaring. *They're gonna catch you.* . . . A homeless guy asks me for some change. I shrug my shoulders, shake my head, and keep on walkin'.

Still Not Dead

BY JAMES LECESNE

MONDAY

THE HOUSE IS DEAD quiet, which is kind of funny since I'm lying perfectly still and trying not to breathe. I can only do this for two minutes tops, but you get the idea. Practice makes perfect.

Most mornings my thoughts pinball round in my brain, making it impossible to get any shut-eye. If I happen to doze off, I wake with a start and remember my life sucks. Curious I'd even allow myself to forget, for even a second, that I've been miserable since school started up about a month ago. Kids call me "dyke" as they pass, and I have a daily appointment to get the crap beaten out of me by none other than Kyra Connors—a girl who is a foot and half taller than me. She and her friends roam the hall, smoke by the trash bins, talk back to teachers, and threaten anyone who dares to challenge their authority. My mom would call them roughnecks if they were boys, but since they're girls she just refers to them as *popular*.

I've been losing sleep about it. I guess you could say I'm

depressed. But the possibility of a world in which there is no hiding out in the girls' bathroom, no hits to my head or jabs to my ribs, no kids calling me names—no *nothing*—sounds amazing. So rather than lie wide awake on my bed, sick with dread for the coming day, I look forward to floating up near the ceiling of my room and gazing down on my dead body. I've read about this on the Internet; people who've died and come back to life always say how peaceful their lifeless bodies appeared as they watched. I want that kind of peace. In fact, I can't wait. Even now I'm imagining eternal rest, the ceiling, the floating, the end.

TUESDAY

I didn't kill myself. Obviously. But that doesn't mean I haven't been thinking about it. After yesterday, I'm pretty sure it's the best alternative.

After school, I was taking my usual shortcut through a tragic strip of parking behind the KFC. I do this everyday to avoid running into the likes of Kyra Connors. But there she was with her posse, all of them staring me down.

"Hey there, loser," Kyra drawled.

My tongue felt as large and dry as a loaf of bread. "Maybe we could talk about this and work something out?" I suggested, amazed I could even get the words out.

Kyra snorted. "The only way to work this out is to have a fistfight."

"Why?" I asked her. "Everybody here knows you can beat my ass. So why bother bruising your knuckles?"

Kyra squinted at me hard, making each one of her eyeballs look as mean as a buckshot. There was tittering from her badass girl-group, because for a split second it seemed as though I had the upper hand. But she responded by lunging forward and took a swing at me with her fist. She missed and I fell to the ground, grabbing my face like I'd been injured. Kyra walked over and kicked me hard in the shin to seal the deal.

"Bloody murder!" I screamed ridiculously, at which point her posse began pulling her away.

"She's already down," one of them argued.

"Yeah. Even dykes deserve some mercy," another said with a laugh. Had I known this unsaid rule, that it was unfair to beat up on someone who was already down, I would've hit the ground the moment I laid eyes on Kyra.

• • •

Back at home, I found Mom standing in my bedroom with her arms crossed and a black cloud over her head. She was pissed. While cleaning my room she just *happened* to read something that I'd been typing on my computer.

"What does this mean?" she asked, pointing to the glowing screen. "Explain it to me."

Apparently, it's not enough to get beaten up; I also have to endure the fact that my mother is a snoop who reads my e-mails. It was a confidential e-mail that I would have sent to my best friend—if I still had a best friend—but last month Fiona texted me that we were "getting a little too close for comfort" and that she "needed to step back a bit." Since then I haven't had anyone in whom I can confide. So there was my e-mail, just idling on the screen, my deepest and most intimate feelings that my mom feels like she can come along read whenever she wants to.

"My private life is none of your business," I told her. "And maybe I'm crazy but it seems to me that I ought to be able to have the freedom to express my own thoughts in my own room on my own *personal* computer."

"Really?" she said in a tone that indicated we did not share the same opinion. "Here's the deal: until further notice you are too young to have any kind of a life that doesn't concern me. Personal, private, or otherwise. Is that clear?"

I didn't answer right away because I was busy looking out the window.

"I'm your mother," she said louder than was absolutely necessary. "And in case you haven't noticed, I am in charge of your life." Then, because she knew what I was thinking, she added, "And your stepfather too."

I stormed out of my own room, which was a pathetic move leaving me nowhere else to go other than the garage. I sat out there for a good long while and thought about the injustice of being a teenager, deciding the only option left was to run away. I didn't leave a note or have a plan in mind. I simply packed a bag, snuck out of the house and headed toward the airport. I only got as far as the local carpet outlet known as the Rug-A-Rama before my legs began to feel as though they might give out. So I sat on the curb thinking until Mom's car pulled up. I couldn't tell whether I felt happy or hopeless, but either way I was glad when she got out of her car wearing only her nightgown and tattered pink slippers. She ran up and hugged me hard around the neck, nearly choking me, and I immediately burst into tears.

"Just get in the car," Mom said, holding back her own tears. And then when I didn't move she pleaded with me. "Emma. Please."

Even after I was belted into the passenger seat, Mom continued to sit there in silence gripping the steering wheel and staring at the Rug-a-Rama.

"I'm very, very, very worried about you. . . ." I couldn't believe she actually used three *very's*. "And I'm definitely going to have to tell Gary about this as soon as he comes home from St. Louis."

"Mom," I said in an effort to change the subject, "I've had a really terrible day. Could we talk about this some other time?"

"You know what we need to do?" she asked. "We really need to get down on our knees and pray. As a family."

I said a silent prayer that this would not ever happen. As we drove through town, I tried to explain to her that she was making a big deal out of nothing because what I wrote on my computer was completely normal.

"I was simply asking myself a question that we've been

pondering for weeks in English class, a question that Shakespeare was asking way back in a time when men wore tights: *To be or not to be, that is the question.*"

"Pondering?" Mom said as she raised her eyebrows at me. Mom totally missed my point: that posing such a question is part of the human condition, and to wonder about our existence when our lives have become unbearable is our right as thinking individuals. I explained all this to her.

"I am exploring the question as part of my report on Shakespeare."

"Are you telling me that your life is unbearable?" she wanted to know. When I didn't answer right away, she said, "Are you?"

She so doesn't get it.

"No," I barked as we pulled into the driveway. And then as I unbuckled my seat belt and jumped out of the car I explained. "I'm talking about *HAMLET!*"

In the play, Hamlet describes Man as the quintessence of dust—and okay, I wouldn't go so far as to describe myself in those terms, because surely I am more than that—but I still love the way it sounds. And I've thought a lot about the flip side of it too. I mean, aren't I also (as Shakespeare goes on to say) the beauty of the world? The paragon of animals? In form and movement how expressed and admirable? Aren't we all? Both man *and* woman?

Sometimes I look and look at myself in the mirror, but I never see much beauty, nothing like an angel, and forget being a paragon of anything. I'm not hideous. But maybe I'm over-looking some essential element that makes me a standout, makes people want to kick my ass. Is it my practically black hair cut short like a boy's? Could it be that my two blue eyes are set kind of close together? I wonder if my thick wrists and ankles, paired with shortish legs and arms, might add up to a message that only brutes can recognize and respond to. My clothes are standard issue—shirt, jeans, and Converse. Okay, so maybe I tend to go a bit too boyish, but is this a reason for someone to pick a fight with me? Why should Kyra care what I wear, what I look like, or how I act? And what made her decide that yesterday was the day to have it out with me?

Meanwhile there's no one around to point out my better qualities or to notice where there's been some slight improve-ment. And that's why lately I've been thinking—*not to be*.

No word from Fiona.

WEDNESDAY

This would be an ideal time for me to off myself, because Gary is away on one of his business trips. I'm not exactly sure what Gary does when he's gone, or what he does *at all* for that mat-ter, though I do know it has something to do with convincing people that they ought to give him their money before some-thing bad happens.

Sometimes Mom gets all dolled up and has to parade around for the benefit of Gary's boss. It's not an activity she's in favor of. Last time Gary proposed one of these outings and emphasized its overall importance to the continued well-being of his job, Mom announced that she was not going to be trotted out for a bunch of suits to gawk at. He countered with an offer to buy her a new outfit and a pair of fancy earrings. She then smiled, kissed him on the lips, and said, "In that case, I'd be willing to walk through Hell for you."

Married life.

Later Tyler took me aside and asked, "But wouldn't Mom's clothes get all burned up if she walked through Hell?"

Tyler is the youngest in our family, and he's at that stage in life when everything is understood literally. He'll probably take my death hard; but I'm not too worried. Tyler is always the last one to wake up in our house, and I'm confident that Mom and my older brother, Sam, will figure out how to break the news to him so that he won't be totally scarred for life. Besides, Tyler's still young enough so that he'll probably forget all about me by the time he reaches high school.

It's late. Mom is still up, and I can hear her; she's standing in the backyard calling for our cat to come in.

"MR. T. . . . YOO HOO. MR. T. . . . COME HOME, GIRL."

Mom named our cat after a TV personality from the 1970s before we knew she was a lady cat. Regardless, Mr. T. is a terrorist, but rather than target a mouse or a wren, she spreads her enmity all around to include everything and everyone.

I've read stories on the Internet about how cats are supposed to sense when a person is close to death. Apparently household cats have extrasensory powers or something that tells them to sleep outside the door of the soon-to-be-deceased. Possible? Sure. But no one's able to prove it. I think it's just an urban myth, the result of a weird aura that cats give off like swamp gas. In any case, Mr. T. would not be the right cat to prove this premise because on any given day of the week, she could care less whether I'm dead or alive. Like everybody else in this house, Mr. T. has no idea what I'm planning for myself. I imagine that if I actually go through with it, she'll hardly alter her daily routine. Life, as they say, will go on. But I will be spared the torture of having to face Kyra or another day at school. I'm counting on this whole charade being over and done with so I can settle into some kind of eternal silence. It'll descend on me like snow falling on Christmas morning.

Today on my way to second period Kyra stopped me in the corridor by standing in my way. She got in my face and said something about a fistfight, but I was distracted by her halitosis. I didn't want her to see me gag, so I looked down and focused on her shoes, which looked like they could use an upgrade.

"I will not be trifled with," she said. "And if you know what's good for you, you'll take my challenge serious."

I knew she wouldn't dare haul off and hit me right there in broad daylight. Mrs. Sweeney was standing not more than twenty feet away.

"So listen," I replied, trying to appeal to her sense of fairness. "If you're going to go around threatening people you ought to consider using the English language correctly. Maybe start with Shakespeare. Study his sonnets, which are possibly his greatest works. . . ."

Kyra stood there and looked at me as though I had just burned off all my hair. "What're you talking about?"

"If I know what's good for me I will take your challenge *seriously*," I replied, "not serious."

Judging from the expression on Kyra's face, she was pissed. Seriously. And to prove it she said: "If I ever catch you looking at me sideways, I will kick your lezzie ass. Got it?"

THURSDAY

I've been thinking—What if death isn't the end? And when I say *thinking* I actually mean *worrying*. A lot. I mean no one knows for sure what happens after we die, right? So what if I'm forced to hang around as a ghost or whatever and witness the whole unhappy course of events following my demise? What if I'm doomed to have some kind of fly-on-the-wall experience where I watch as Mom deals with my dead body, makes the funeral arrangements, buries me wearing a dress, and cries her eyes out. That would be awful. I went through it once with her when Dad died. I'm not sure she'd survive a second time.

And what if it doesn't work? Not much is said about the fact that death by suicide is not an easy way to go. It's not at all a sure thing. For weeks, I've been studying various means and the odds are not good. I've given each and every method plenty of consideration, trying to imagine if it's a good fit for me. Guns, for instance, are out of the question. I don't have the nerves for it. Everything I've read about guns mentions the difficulty of actually pulling the trigger, but that's all been written by people who chickened-out at the last minute. I can't take the risk of being one of them, a loser among losers. In addition to that, the notion that my mother or brothers would find my dead body in such a splattered state is almost too horrible to think about. How would they ever be able to walk into my room again? They'd never get over that bloody mess on the wall out of their minds. ("Out, damn spot!" as Shakespeare once wrote.) Neighbors would talk about what happened here for years, until finally my family would be forced to move out and start over. Besides, no one I know owns a gun, so . . .

Hanging is way too dramatic, and once again the idea of someone walking in and finding me in such a state is enough to dissuade me. Dangling from the rafters is not a pretty sight, and anyway I can't find a decent rafter. We live in a split-level, four-bedroom suburban dream house; it's nothing fancy, but rafters don't figure into it, not the kind that my Grampa Barlett had in his barn that are just right for hanging. I suppose a tree limb would do the trick, but I'm pretty sure that I'll want to be indoors at the moment of my death. I don't believe in dying outdoors unless you are an animal in the wild.

For a while I considered our garage because there is a kind of overhead crossbeam, but there's so much crap jammed into the every nook and cranny that it would require a major overhaul. Last week I started to remove some of the junk in order to make room. Mom took notice.

"And what d'you think you're doing?" she asked.

"Nothing," I replied. "Y'know, making some room in here."

"For what?"

End of story.

I considered jumping off a bridge, but there isn't a bridge within a hundred mile radius that's worth talking about, and getting to any one of those places without a car and on my own would be suspect. Plus I hear my Dad's voice in the back of my head, saying to Sam and me: "If everybody in the world decided to jump off a bridge would you do the same?" The answer was always *No*. What else can you say to a question like that? And if Heaven exists, I don't want my dad meeting me at the Pearly Gates and saying, "If everybody in the world decided to jump off a bridge . . ." You get the point.

I've seen old movies where people go and sit in a garage with their car motor running; it's the carbon monoxide from the exhaust that eventually kills them. But like I said earlier, our garage is crammed with stuff, and then there's the problem of finding a car that was manufactured back in the twentieth century when the levels of carbon monoxide fumes were lethal. Nowadays, if you choose that method to kill yourself, the best you can hope for is extreme drowsiness, nausea, and wasting a few precious gallons of gas.

Slitting my wrists or stabbing myself is definitely out of the question. I tried it once with a kitchen knife, but the thought of the pain kept me from making the decisive cut.

The point is no one realizes how difficult it is to do harm to yourself until you actually try.

For me, pills will have to do—even if it's the least effective way to go. I read something like 90 percent of the people who try to kill themselves with pills fail miserably, sometimes tragically. But it's a chance I'm willing to take, because considering the alternatives (see above) it's better than nothing. I have two pills so far, pain killers Sam never took after he broke his ankle last year. It's a start.

FRIDAY

Suicide is a tall order. You can't pussy foot around. You have to commit yourself—and not just to the *idea* of it, but also (and here's the hard part) the actual doing of it. Once the moment of truth arrives, there's no turning back. You can't choke, not now, not at the last minute or else it just won't happen. Few things are so final, so definite. And it's going to take more than just two pills.

Which is all to say—I'm still alive.

Earlier this morning, Sam forced the basement window and tried to get into the house without being noticed. Staying out all night seems to be Sam's new thing. Our old dog, Duke, barked at the sound of the screen popping out of its track, then he bolted through the house and gamboled down the basement stairs. He continued to bark his head off as Sam shimmied, head first, through the narrow window and eased himself into the house.

"Oh. Busted," said Sam when he turned around and caught sight of Mom standing at the bottom of the stairs. She had her hands on her hips, lips pressed tightly together.

I was standing behind Mom. No way was I going to miss this performance. Sam tossed his honey-colored hair out of his eyes so that he could give Mom the full-court press—smile, charm, and anything else he had in his bag of tricks and treats. His eyes literally twinkled as he brushed off his jeans and straightened his T-shirt.

Mom's eyes were doing the opposite of twinkling. Her jaw was set tight, and I could tell that she was calculating how many more seconds she could manage to hold the pose of disapproval. She doesn't really want to lose her temper, but she also doesn't want to lose Sam to the gang of heartthrobs and roughnecks that he's been hanging out with lately. So rather than unleash a pent-up scold, she looked up at the ceiling and forced a bitter smile.

"And what, Sam?" Mom said, clipping each word like a coupon. "What exactly did you think was going to happen here? Did you think that you could just stay out all night, break into your own house, and expect it to go unnoticed? Is that how it's supposed to work?"

"Kinda," said Sam. And the weird thing is he wasn't being a smart-ass; he actually thought that his strategy would work. "Don't tell Gary, okay? It'll only be drag for everybody."

I could see Mom weighing her options. "Right now, I expect you to get ready for school."

She then did an impressive about-face, which sent her crashing into me. She looked at me from head to toe and then said, "And would it kill you to wear a skirt every once in a while?"

Sam bent down and gave the dog's skull a knuckle rub. Duke is happy to receive whatever from Sam. Always has been. To Duke, Sam is a biscuit in human form.

"Don't look at me like that," Sam said.

"Like what?"

"Someday you're going to fall in love," he told me. "And you'll understand."

"I won't," I said. "Ever."

He looked at me like I was a lost cause, and I wondered if he'd heard any gossip at school about me and Fiona. Was he trying to tell me that I would eventually get over my massive crush on her?

"Yes, you will," he said. "Trust me. And when you do, you're going to do some stupid stuff."

He offered me a quick fist-bump and then sauntered off to the shower. I stood there thinking about what he said, realizing he had *no* idea what my life is like. Sam is a senior this year and he's got it made. With the undying love of the hottest cheerleader in the lineup, he can afford to do some stupid stuff. Not like me. I can't afford to take a breath without the threat of someone noticing.

• • •

I return to my room and lay the pills out on my pillow. One.

Two. Three. The third one is really just a fancy aspirin that was in Mom's medicine cabinet, but it's better than nothing. I smell the toast burning and the coffee brewing in the kitchen. Mom's cell phone rings in the kitchen. It's Gary. I can tell from the way she answers the phone that she's already decided not to tell him about how Sam stayed out all night. It's going to remain a mother-son secret. Another one.

"Hey, honey, can you hold a minute?" I hear her say before she yells up the stairs again, "TYLER? YOU AWAKE?"

"Yeah," Tyler says with his froggy morning voice. "'M up."

I hear Tyler as he shuffles toward my bedroom door. I quickly gather my pitiful stash of pills and flop onto my bed, reaching to open the drawer of the bedside so I can dump them all in. My heart is beating, and I'm praying, literally praying, *Dear God, please don't let Tyler see what I'm up to.* Funny moment to call on God, I think to myself.

The door swings wide and Tyler is suddenly standing there, all slouchy and sleepy-eyed. He blinks several times and cocks his head like Duke does when there's a high-pitched sound.

"Hey," Tyler says.

"Oh. Hey," I answer back. I must look crazy, splayed out on my bed. All my limbs frozen at awkward angles.

"Whata ya doin'?"

"Nothing. Go get dressed." But he doesn't move. "Don't look at me like that," I tell him as I slowly sit up.

"Like what?"

"Just go!"

He turns around like a robot that's programmed to respond to my commands and heads back toward his room; but before he's out of earshot, I call out to him: "Someday you're going to fall in love, and you're going to do some stupid stuff. Y'hear me?"

"Okay," he calls back.

SATURDAY

I counted the pills today. Again. This has become my daily ritual. I'm up to six. I'm not sure what my most recent finds are good for, but I found three of them rolling around in the corners of Mom's bedside table. There aren't nearly enough of them to do any real damage and certainly too few to do the deed, but at least I'm getting closer. I place them in the pottery vase that I made for Mom when I was six, back when Dad was still alive. It's the color of dust with a bumpy surface and my initials are carved clumsily into the bottom, making it an unsteady proposition. For this reason, it's never been used for flowers, and no one would ever think to look down its scrawny neck for anything worthwhile.

Got to find more pills.

SUNDAY

Instead of going to church this morning, I told Mom that I was feeling sick. Really sick. She rolled her eyes and then told me that I could stay home, but I was not to leave my room. I must have laid in bed for hours thinking about Ophelia. She was Hamlet's girlfriend. Mrs. Sweeney says that Ophelia actually lost her mind because Hamlet suddenly started acting weird to her. She couldn't take it and killed herself. Courageous or crazy? This is a question that her death seems to have answered once and for all. I'm hoping that my own death will do the same.

"Are you still alive up there?" Mom called up to me when she and my brothers got back from church.

I made a noise, just enough to indicate that I was living, but not enough to encourage an entire conversation.

"EMMA!" she calls out again. "Do you feel well enough to eat breakfast?"

As I lie here listening to breakfast bacon sizzling in a pan downstairs and its smell beginning to fill my bedroom, I'm thinking that I will force myself to eat a little something and pretend that it's my last meal.

MONDAY

Every morning before school, Mom harangues us with details, questions, and criticisms of the "*I thought you were going to wear a skirt today?*" and "*Did you finish your homework?*" variety. We rarely respond. We know that if we wait it out, she'll get tired and say something that actually requires a response, like: "Do you guys have your lunch bags?" Grunts and nods from us, and

then she moves onto the next thing which is usually her pumping us for information about some kid who's got a problem.

As a guidance counselor at the school, Mom needs to keep
up to date on all the local gossip, making sure that girls aren't
getting pregnant and boys aren't doing drugs. She's big on
abstinence and promotes it among my peers as though their
lives depend on it, though she's in denial about Sam's shenani-
gans. Mom doesn't realize that pretty much everybody is having some kind of sex all the time behind her back. Everyone
but me.

"Anything new with school?" she asks me while making
our sandwiches.

I consider telling her about what's going on between Kyra
and me, but before I can say anything Sam enters. He plops his
backpack on the counter and starts acting as though the
kitchen is his private kingdom.

"What's up?" he asks.

"I was just asking Emma if there was anything new going
on at school."

"Did you tell her about that Justin Guns kid?" Sam asks.
I'm assuming that he wants my opinion even though he doesn't
look at me directly. Mom stands at the counter, and by the way
the question hangs in the air, I can tell that her interest is
piqued.

"What about him?" she wants to know.

Justin Guns is a freshman starvling who was recently
diagnosed as anorexic. Usually, he goes around saying that

he requires less to eat than a typical American because he's naturally small-boned. But Justin Guns is far from a typical anything. He weighs like twelve pounds, tints his hair blue, and though he claims that his sartorial edits are unisex and "totally in fashion right now," he wears eye makeup and favors women's clothing.

"He's been out of school for over a week," Sam mumbles into his half-eaten toaster pastry. "I mean, besides being so obviously a gay."

"Not *a gay*," I remind him. "Just *gay* will do. And for the record, we don't know that Justin is gay. Not for sure."

"Please," Sam rolls his eyes.

Mom hands me an extra sandwich, and tells me to give it to Justin when I see him in the cafeteria.

"He doesn't eat," I say. But she doesn't understand and looks at me as though I'm joking.

"Everybody eats," she replies and to prove that she knows what she's taking about, she stuffs the sandwich into my back-pack.

"Even if I did see Justin in the cafeteria," I say with a bit of scold in my voice, "he would flat-out refuse a ham-and-cheese-whatever from me. To Justin, we are ALL the enemy, and food is poison."

"There's something seriously wrong with that kid," Sam announces. "I mean besides being a gay."

"I simply asked why the boy has been missing school," says Mom. "And I don't need a personality assessment from the peanut gallery, thank you very much."

Personally, I appreciate Justin's eccentricities. Ever since grade school when he moved here from Atlanta, I've been grateful that he's around in just the way he is. He's always been *so obviously gay* that any discussion about homosexuality naturally begins and ends with the mention of his name. "*Don't be such a Justin*," is a phrase we kids have used since middle school. Back then he was teased mercilessly and occasionally beaten up. He had walked around for three clueless days with the word *FAG* written in Sharpie on the back of his jacket. I've been witness to the kind of cruelty that kids my own age inflict on other kids who happen to be different. Only now, I'm the one who is different, and I wish I wasn't.

TUESDAY

Today I went to Mrs. Sweeney and told her that I wanted to discuss the final scene of *Hamlet*. She was sitting in her empty classroom eating her bagged lunch and reading a fat novel.

"It's crazy," I said to her, "By the end of the play the whole cast is lying dead on the floor. What's that about?"

She closed her novel and began to explain what Shakespeare had in mind when he wrote *Hamlet*, but to tell you the truth I wasn't listening. Instead I was examining the highlights in her hair and wondering about her apartment. I've never been there, but sometimes I imagine her standing in front of the bathroom mirror and preparing herself for the day. There was a tiny crumb from her bologna sandwich stuck to her cheek. *Do I tell her?* I wondered. And then the thought occurred to me that if I were dead I wouldn't be sitting there with her and then maybe no one would tell her about the crumb. I imagined her during the next period, standing in front of her students, becrumbed. The whole class would laugh behind her back.

That's when I started to cry.

"What's wrong," Ms. Sweeney said, putting down her novel and leaning toward me.

I told her the whole story. In between sobs I explained how Kyra had been terrorizing me and how I had felt my life just wasn't worth living. She placed her hand on my shoulder.

"Things will change," she said.

"But how do you know that?" I asked. I swooped big gulps of air into my lungs and then cried fresh tears. "How can you be so sure?"

"Because I'm going to help you," she replied.

"I'm sorry," I said. Then repeated it, over and over.

"You haven't done anything wrong, Emma. In fact, you did the right thing coming to me."

She handed me a napkin, and I blew my nose into it mightily.

"What warlike noise is this?" she said, which caused me to laugh out loud. It's a quote from Hamlet, something he says just moments before he takes his final breath. Then Ms. Sweeney leaned back in her chair, smiling, and I knew that she was right. It would get better, she would help me and unlike Hamlet, I would live through this ordeal.

"I hope you don't mind my saying this," I told her. "But there's a crumb on your cheek."

WEDNESDAY

The weirdest thing—Kyra was ignoring me at school today. Totally. It was as though I didn't exist. I couldn't tell if this was a blessing or if I should have been prepared for something really bad. I thought that maybe Ms. Sweeney said something to her, gave her a warning because as she passed by me in the hallway she didn't sneer or scoff or curse or push or shove or in any way take notice of me. But my heart breaks a little as I notice Fiona has joined her posse. She looks at me now as though we never knew each other's secrets, never slept over one another's house, never read each other sonnets or kissed on the mouth.

Then I opened my locker and found a note from Kyra. Though her penmanship is not the best, I was able to make out the message: YOU ARE SO DEAD. I faked being sick and was sent home early.

THURSDAY

Sam came home late last night, and this morning after breakfast, I overheard a conversation between him and Mom that went like this:

"You were with that girl last night," Mom said bitterly.

When Sam didn't answer, she pressed him, "You were. Weren't you?"

"Mom . . ."

"Don't Mom me," she said point blank. "I can smell her perfume from over here."

"Just for the record," he answered deadpan. "That's my deodorant you're smelling. And seriously, Mom, the thing is, she's not just some girl. I'm in love with Courtney. I mean, for real."

"Love?" Mom said, and I could almost hear her raising her eyebrows at him.

"Something like that," Sam replied. "I'm going to ask her to the prom anyway."

"Oh honey," I heard her sigh, "however you feel about her, wherever you take her, there will be *no more* sneaking out or staying out all night. *Especially* after prom. Got it?"

Mom is pretty cool for a Christian, but I think if I ever stayed out almost all night kissing some girl she hardly liked—and *then* announced the next morning that I was in love—she'd probably lose it. It's just a hunch on my part, but it's one I'm not looking forward to proving true or false. However much my mother loves me, she will never be able to come close to the world in which I intend to live my life. I exist in a parallel universe, one that is second-class and takes place mostly off stage, sotto voce.

Mom wheeled around the corner and found me standing there. I tried to look as though I hadn't been ear-hustling on her conversation, but pretending to tie my shoes gave me away, because in fact, I was standing there in my socks. Mom just shook her head and continued to breeze past me.

"Come on, everyone!" she called out. "Shoes on. Let's go. This train is pulling out the station in exactly two minutes. Anyone not on board has the privilege of walking to school."

I found my sneakers and quickly laced up. As always, I thought about my father at that moment. He's the one who taught me to tie my shoes in the first place. After he died, I made a promise to myself that every time I stopped to tie my laces I'd remember him. I gave up wearing slip-ons or flip-flops. It's my way of keeping my dad in my life on a daily basis, honoring him. Sometimes I use the time to speak to him, give him an update or ask him questions about whatever's troubling me. I've decided not to discuss the idea of suicide with him because the possibility that he and I might be reunited very soon would really piss him off.

FRIDAY

School is no picnic, but at least we're reading *Hamlet* in Mrs. Sweeney's class, and this guy seems as confused about life as I am. Thing is, English class takes up only a fraction of the time spent in that hive of adolescent angst known as Jefferson High. Whose idea was school anyway? A sadist, no doubt. My particular torture is being trapped in an environment in which everyone goes around saying that I am a muff-diver. That's fun.

In the hallway on my way to my locker I usually have time to scan the sea of faces looking for Kyra Connors to appear. I hadn't seen her for a whole day, and I knew this couldn't be good. Somehow her absence in the hallways loomed larger than her actual presence.

I imagine that years from now, the bully known as Kyra Connors will be living in a one-bedroom, high-rise apartment overlooking a parking lot. She'll be in an unremarkable third-tier American city that is in a state of steep decline. Lonely, fat, and with a skin condition which will discourage her from dating, she'll stay at home most nights waiting for the timer to announce her microwave dinner is fully nuked. Looking back, she'll try to figure out where she went wrong in life. How did she end up with nothing? She will conduct a not-so-instant playback of her life's story, which will go on for months. Then one evening while petting her cat, she will understand. "I see now! I should not have been so rough on that Emma Taylor girl back in high school." Before she has finished eating dinner, she will decide to make it up to me and look me up on the Internet or whatever. But she won't be able to find me, because by then I will be dead.

"Hey, you," I heard Kyra's voice call out in the hallway. I turned around and there she was, her hair and bobblehead cruising above the crowd, her face flashing mean in my direction.

My heart began to bang against my rib cage as though it was making a desperate attempt to escape. Suddenly my legs were making a run for it, my arms pushing open the side door as I moved quickly through the teacher's parking lot. I didn't know where I was headed—I wasn't going home and I wasn't going back to school—but I needed to get as far away from Kyra as possible. I wanted out. Of everything. I ran and ran up the hill behind the high school until my lungs burned and my sides ached. I started thinking I might die right there on the spotty grass beyond the football field.

There was a chain link fence at the far end of the school property, and I knew I wasn't allowed to go beyond this point. I've heard stories about seniors who smoke cigarettes and have sex there on a regular basis, and this seemed a much better option than anything I could think of on my own. I'd rather face whatever awaited me in the shady cool of the unknown than get beat up on school property. I hopped the fence and continued to make my way into the woods. Trees and bushes grew tall and wild there; they had never been pruned or clipped or shaped to be anything other than what they naturally were. *This was where I'll live*, I thought to myself. This is where I'll spend my school time until the whole Kyra thing blows over. Pretty soon she'll find some other target, and then I'll go back to being just another unremarkable face in the hallways of Jefferson High.

Up ahead I noticed a flash of color through, and as I came into a clearing, I saw a pattern that involved electric blue and lime green paisley. Not something you see every day in the wild. It looked as though someone had tied a sheet between two trees and pulled it taut to make a kind of tented area. As I approached, I heard a low, rhythmic humming and I caught sight of a foot sticking out from under the tented area. The toes were long and ladylike, the nails polished pink, and the ankle kept the beat of the hummed tune. Whoever this person was she hardly seemed a threat to my personal safety, so I decided to get closer and see what was up.

There was Justin Guns, sitting with legs outstretched and his earphones on, wearing an expression of pure delight. He wore enormous sunglasses and moved in time to a song playing on his iPod. I guess his eyes were closed because I stood in front of him for a full minute as he moved to the music, blissed-out and unaware of my presence.

I don't think I've ever said two words to Justin. He's not the type that people tend to talk to unless they have something rough to say, something mean, something to remind him that he's not normal. But seeing him working a deep personal groove, I realized that no one had ever really known Justin. He never had a friend. Even weird girls (like me) steer clear of his freakish fashion sense and outsider status. No one in their right mind would actually choose to go that far afield of the norm. No one other than Justin.

When he finally looked up and saw me he jumped to his feet. His earbuds went flying from his head and he backed away, like he was some kind of wild animal and I was the hunter.

"What?" he asked.

The earbuds were lying in the dirt, pumping out the once

glorious beat of his former bliss. When I took a step toward him, he quickly covered his face with his hands and leaned away from the punch, the insult, the assault that he figured was about to rain down on him.

"WHAT?" he said again, only louder this time.

My mouth opened, but nothing came out. I felt that anything I said would be heard through his ears, which had been tuned for too long to hear the worst. So I reached into my bag and pulled out my sandwich, the one mom made for me that morning. I held it out for him to take. He eyed it suspiciously, and then looked at me as if trying to figure out my connection to it. We stood there like that forever. Tears welled up in his eyes and his chin quivered.

"'S aright," I told him. "I've been sent to bring you back."

We Should Get Jerseys
'Cause We Make a Good Team

BY LISH MCBRIDE

"I'M SO BOOOOORED," Brooke's voice drew out the last part making it about a billion syllables. When I didn't look up from my book, she flopped around the dining room, knocking over stacks of books and singing the Muppets theme song at the top of her lungs. She was good at making a general nuisance of herself, so I just bent closer to the pages, holding the edges down so she couldn't muss them.

She popped her head up in the middle of the table, her blond ponytail swaying and her wholesome smile aimed right at me. She would look more at home in a dairy commercial or a Swiss Miss hot cocoa ad then an entity jutting out of a piece of furniture. But Brooke's a ghost, and she can do that sort of thing. It's kind of her schtick.

"C'mon, Fraaaaaaannnk." She drew my name out like she had with the word bored.

"I need to finish reading this. We have a lot to catch up on." We'd all only just found out that things like ghosts were real. Brooke becoming one had been a key component of that. My friend Sam learning he could raise the dead being another. I was the only part of the team who didn't have some cool power to add, so I'd thrown myself into research. Like most nerds, books were my only friends for a long time.

"That book isn't going anywhere, but I might die again if you don't help me. I'll croak from extreme ennui and it would *so* be your fault. I'd be so mad I'd haunt you twice as much as everyone else."

I sighed and carefully closed my book. Brooke had her mind set on something; therefore, complete surrender was really the only workable response. Besides, I couldn't say no to Brooke. When she was alive, I'd had something of a crush on her. And not just because she'd been *crawl-through-broken-glass-I'll-do-anything-for-you* hot. Well, that was part of it, but the real reason was because Brooke had actually talked to me.

Me.

No one talked to me. Not nicely at any rate. So though she'd become more friend than manic-crush, I still had a gooey-soft spot for her. When Brooke asked, I always said yes. There really was no other answer.

• • •

The bad side of being dead—besides what immediately pops to mind—is that it's kinda hard to get places. The floaty-misty thing gets old, and Brooke tells us it's exhausting to go great distances on her own. That's why so many ghosts stay put in one place. Especially if they spend all their energy appearing in front of people and saying, "Boo," which Brooke of course loves to do. Brooke says it's about endurance, which takes time to build—unless of course, you have someone like Sam around. If he were here, he could make Brooke corporeal and give her a body, because Sam's a necromancer and he can do suave things like that. But he was out on a date so Brooke was stuck with me, and I am not suave.

Sam figured out how to do enough mumbo-jumbo so that we could *see* Brooke, giving her a physical presence—which was fine in the house, but we were going into town, and that made things tricky. Brooke's death had been pretty publicized, and there's nothing like a dead girl walking the streets to get some attention. So no presence. Just me and my invisible friend. Which is probably for the best. I look like the kind of guy who'd have invisible friends.

Brooke picked a car from the garage, which was like a mini-museum for classic cars. The kinds that most guys don't get to touch until their mid-life crisis when they hock their retirement fund for one shiny, metal dream from their youth. And even then it's only one, but Sam had so many everyone in the house could play bumper cars and we'd still have some left over. Brooke climbed into her favorite, a 1957 baby blue Karmann Ghia. Never mind the fact that every time I drove it I spent the whole trip in a panic-sweat. You try driving around a classic car that you don't own and see if you have a different reaction.

Not that Sam would do anything to me. Even if I crashed it he'd probably just shrug. No, I was afraid of the butler, James, and if you'd ever met him, you'd understand why. As if summoned by my thoughts, a black and white cat leaped onto the hood of the car. He sat down, tail flicking in irritation, his silver eyes at half-mast. I don't speak cat, but I do speak James. Sort of. I'm learning. His manner said *and what do you think you're doing?*

"We're going to get Ramon a present," I said.

"Do you want to come with us?" Brooke asked, ever the peacemaker. James jumped off the hood, and before I heard his paws hit the cement, he started to shift. There was a billow of smoke. Not "poof" like with magicians and escaping villains, but like the slow twist of cigarette smoke. A few seconds later and the cat was gone. In his place stood . . . oh good, a dragon. In this form he was closer in size to a medium weight dog.

"You have three forms and you think that's the one to wear to the video store?" Brooke asked, her tone so dry it crackled. She could get mouthy with James. What would he do to her? But I kept my mouth shut. James was a little scary.

There was more smoke, and then he held his hand out for the keys. If he packs a lot of menace into his kitty form, he has even more as a human.

"No way," Brooke said, leaning against the dash. "If you wanna go, you better climb into the back." I expected him to argue, but he just stared at Brooke for a minute, then walked around to her side and got in. Cats are naturally fussy, and James carried that into human form. He brushed some lint off his shoulder, pushed back the lock of black hair that had tumbled forward while he was adjusting everything, and then sat up straight and elegant. He caught me watching him in the rearview mirror and his eyebrows raised in a *What?* type expression. I knew better than to say anything, so I adjusted the mirror and kept my mouth shut.

I buckled myself in, and Brooke did too, even though she didn't need it. Her blue eyes were bright and shiny and her blond ponytail bobbed as she bounced excitedly in her seat.

I couldn't help but grin at her. "So, where are we going?"

"Scarecrow Video. We need to get a proper present for Ramon when he gets home from the hospital. A welcome home gift." She was very firm about the when part—there was no possibility of "if" for her. Her friend was coming home safe and that was that.

I wish I had her faith.

. . .

Scarecrow Video is a local icon—two stories of movie geek wonderland. They had films so rare it took a five-hundred-dollar deposit just to take them out of the store. Everything was separated into sections. I'm not talking comedy, horror, and so on. What I mean is if you go in and ask for a Japanese zombie film, they will take you to that specific *section*. Sometimes they are organized by director, or country, or themes like awards or subjects. You practically need a degree in film just to find anything. Or the guts to approach one of the employees and expose your ignorance to the world.

Especially if you were me. And especially if the employee was Maren.

She was on shift when I walked in, and my pulse did that little fluttering skip I've come to associate with pretty girls. She was wearing boots today with a short tartan skirt held together with safety pins, her black tights the only nod to the outside temperatures. Her T-shirt was worn and faded, the words FLIGHT OF THE CONCHORDS almost unreadable. When I look at Maren, I sometimes think of the angry Japanese school-girls you see in Anime. She's petite, she's cute, and I'm pretty sure she could end me if she wanted too.

She pushed her jagged-cut bangs to the side, her face set in a grimace of concentration as she tried to explain something to her coworker, Andy. Maren had added pink to the two inches of blue tipping the black strands of her hair. It made her con-trast even more with Andy, who still dressed as he had in high school. Dapper, like someone out of a really expensive cologne commercial.

Brooke leaned in and whispered in my ear. "If you were a cartoon, there'd be little hearts above your head right now. Maybe even some sparrows." I don't know why she whispered it. No one could hear her but me. James, thankfully, had wan-dered off to look at a display. The last thing I wanted to do was give James even more ammunition for mockery. "You going to talk to her today?"

I sighed but didn't respond to her. Nothing quite like talk-ing to yourself to make an impression.

We ambled around the store, trying to decide what Ramon would want. I was staring at the cover of *Incubus*, a movie I thought he might appreciate because of its use of Esperanto and the inclusion of a very young William Shatner. At the very least it would be good for him to experience some classic film history. Or I could get him *Mega Piranha*. Black-and-white horror indie film or giant, poorly animated killer fish? I pondered the difficult choice until I felt someone bump me, hard, as they walked past. Out of reflex I looked up and saw the lean back of someone I knew well.

Tyler.

...

Back in school we only had those little half lockers. They said it was to accommodate all the students, but I think it was to make it impossible to stuff people into them. I had mine open, looking for my AP English binder, when I heard someone pound their fist into the locker next to mine.

I'd come to know that sound. Other kids like me, the rodents lurking at the bottom of the social food chain, all knew it for what it was: the death knell. Nature's way of announcing a predator in your midst, like the roar of a tiger or the scream of the hawk in the cloudless sky. It was the predator's way of getting you to run, to start the game.

You flinch when you hear it.

And then you bolt. You make for the bushes, the trees, the safety of the undergrowth. Or you freeze, hoping the call wasn't for you but another trembling mouse in the grass.

I could hear the other students as they scurried away. There was nothing I could do but reach my sweating palms for something else—anything else—that wasn't my AP folder. I actually needed that next period and I knew that whatever I grabbed might meet an unfortunate end. What didn't I need? Math . . . Science . . . my book report. Yes, my book report. I had that on a flash drive in my pocket. I could just print out another one; it wasn't due until tomorrow.

My hand wasn't trembling when I pulled out the slim folder. Not that it didn't feel like shaking like a clichéd leaf. It's just I had a lot of practice pretending I wasn't terrified. Tyler hadn't said anything yet. He was just unpleasantly looming. I'm pretty sure he rehearsed hovering ominously at home in front of a mirror right before he kicked puppies and chased baby ducks back into the water. He mastered the ability of being ominous.

Tyler was one of those depressingly average kids. He wasn't good at sports nor did he have a spectacular intellect. Tyler didn't hang with the popular kids and he wasn't a miserable freak. He wasn't ugly and he wasn't pretty, he just *was*.

His hair and eyes were a nondescript brown, and he had all the charisma of a ham sandwich on plain bread. He was the kind of quiet, normal kid who either ended up managing a chain store or became a serial killer.

I really think he could go either way.

Right then, as he stared me down, I was leaning toward

serial killer. He reached over and yanked my book report out of my hands.

"Thanks," he whispered. Then he held his hand out, patient. When I didn't move fast enough he reached into my pocket and yanked out my Thumbdrive. I closed my eyes, feeling a bead of sweat roll down my temple. I might be able to control the shaking but I'd yet managed to control my body's sweat response. Maybe someday. It was good to have goals.

He slid around me and mumbled the word, "*Freak,*" under his breath. I didn't open my eyes until the tardy bell rang. I knew I'd get in trouble, but I'd take the demerit in exchange for the safety of the empty hallway. My hand trembled as I reached for my AP binder. I guess I haven't totally mastered the not-quaking-in-fear thing. It took two tries to get my messenger bag open before I could push aside my backup Thumbdrive and slide my binder in. I had a third Thumbdrive on my desk at home too. It wasn't my first rodeo. Tyler took anything that wasn't nailed down; I was on my third cell phone, second backpack, and too many binders to even count.

Being a social rodent was expensive.

• • •

I stared at Tyler's back as he walked through Scarecrow, my fingers tightening on the plastic cover of *Incubus* until I felt the edges biting into my skin. Once you leave high school, it should be illegal to run into your former classmates. There should be support groups available for those that need it, like soldiers with PTSD. Or maybe some sort of program like Witness Protection where you're whisked away to somewhere else—new name, new identity, the works. A fresh start. That's all I wanted. To just walk away. Maybe it seems cowardly, but I'm not a fighter. I'd like to say I'm a lover, but I'm not that, either, which is both depressing and sad.

Brooke skipped up. "They have a whole section for that one guy—the one who made all those movies with the clay special effects creatures? You know, the one you made me watch a marathon of?"

"Ray Harryhausen," I answered absently.

"Yeah, that guy. Anyway, there's this one with cowboys AND dinosaurs. I don't think we can buy it here, but can we rent it? I think Ramon would be all over that."

I couldn't take my eyes off Tyler as he approached Maren, smiling at her, probably asking her the stupidest question ever uttered in the history of stupid questions. At least I hoped it was. I imagined Maren smiling at him as she pulled a katana blade from nowhere—slicing him neatly in two, from his skull to his big toe—before she turned and calmly finished restocking the shelf. In reality she set her stack down and walked him to a section. I wondered if Scarecrow had a bathroom so I could go vomit in it.

Noticing she didn't have my full attention, Brooke waved a spectral hand in front of my face until I blinked and looked at her. "I'd say you look like you've seen a ghost, but I've seen what that expression looks like. And this isn't it," she said, her head cocked speculatively. "In fact, your face looks like it did that time when we dared you to drink unmixed soda syrup straight from the tap."

I held my cell phone up to my ear and pretended I was talking to someone. It was the best way to talk to Brooke in public without getting stared at. "That's about how I feel." When I didn't continue, she rolled her hand in a "bring it" kind of gesture.

"Tyler." I didn't need to say anything else. Brooke already knew all about it.

. . .

The day I met Brooke was the happiest day of my life. It really was. Okay, so it didn't have much competition. The day before that my only social interaction consisted of the neighbor's cat hocking up a dead mouse on my shoe. Sure, it meant he liked me, but I could've done without it. My life wasn't bad. It just . . . was. If you picked up the *Life of Frank* movie case at Scarecrow Video, the best review on the back would just say, "Meh."

The day started out in a regular fashion: I got up early, ate breakfast in the company of a sticky note left by my parents, and went to school. Nothing exciting.

Most days I went to school early so I could park in the lower lot because it was the closest to the classrooms. It was the safest, most visible place since the school had a security guard patrolling the lower lot. He was supposed to patrol the upper lot too, but he had bad knees and tended to avoid the stairs.

Traffic was bad on the way to school, which made me later than usual. No cushy lower lot for me today. I assumed upper lot mode—messenger bag to the side in case I needed to run, key ring held in my fist so that the keys stuck between my clenched knuckles, and my headphones in but not turned on. I wanted to look like I wasn't paying attention but able to hear anyone approaching. I thought warmly of the day, somewhere in the near future, when I would be able to actually listen to my iPod.

I took the side stairs so I could cut across the field. Since I couldn't have safety in visibility, I figured I'd go for sneaky. The thing is, I'm terrible at being sneaky. I made my way down the steps, turned the corner, and ran straight into Tyler. He was maybe five feet away leaning against the cement wall at the base of the hill, smoking. He stared at me while he took a drag, eyes calculating. I stood frozen, staring as the smoke twined around his head.

"You see something you like, freak?" He ran a hand down his chest and laughed. I blushed and started walking, trying not to panic, struggling to keep a normal pace. I had to either walk past him or turn around and go back to my car, which really wasn't much of a choice. You needed to approach Tyler like you would an aggressive dog—running would only make him chase. He had longer legs and would catch me, no problem.

When I passed I felt the burning butt of his cigarette hit my neck. The sting was brief but painful, and for a second I stumbled, almost tripping over my own feet. Tyler came up beside me and I bowed my head, trying to avoid eye contact. That would only make it worse. I could see his sneaker by the fallen cigarette, feel his hot breath on the side of my face. Tyler never hit me—he was careful not to lay a hand on me on school grounds, and I was careful to never see him *off* of school grounds. But the threat of it was always there, imminent, like a shark fin circling a life raft. Would today be the day?

You can't go to a teacher and tell them that someone is menacing you. No one gets expelled for being ominous. I wasn't getting threatening notes left on my car or finding dead rats in my locker. If the security guard came upon us right now, the most he could do is walk between us to make Tyler back up. But if he never actually *did* anything, why were my palms sweaty? Why did my heart skitter like a gibbering thing every time he came near me? Because even though I'd never seen the shark, I knew what the fin looked like. I knew what followed.

There was a click and I saw the cap of the Sharpie fall next to the cigarette. Like the coward I was, I stood there and did nothing as he wrote on the back of my neck. His hand was almost gentle as he clasped my shoulder and leaned in so that the tip of the marker felt like it was biting into my skin. He took his time, and though it only took a handful of seconds, they stretched out until they were fat, bloated things.

I stood and I trembled even after he walked away, his shoeprints in the dew the only proof that he'd been there. It wasn't until I heard voices from other students approaching— laughing, happy, normal voices—that I started moving. I clapped a hand onto the back of my neck and bee lined for the bathroom.

There was a small restroom by the art building that I usually went too. It was totally out of my way but usually empty since it hadn't been remodeled like the others. The faint smell of mildew was always evident, the toilets were always broken, and it never had any TP. But since I never actually used it to go to the bathroom, none of that mattered.

Bent over the sink with my shirt off, I covered my neck in that abrasive powdered soap and started scrubbing. I was on my third handful of paper towels when I heard the door swing open. I'm sure I presented quite a scene.

There was no way to see who it was from the angle I was hunched; I could only make out a hint of black trouser leg, black leather dress shoes, and an honest to god black wool trench coat—complete with a bright purple scarf. I knew that a vest and a white shirt lay underneath it, because that was generally what Andy wore. I'd never seen him in T-shirt or flip-flops. No one else dressed like he did, like he was about to get into a limo and be whisked off to the opera. On some kids it would look affected, but on Andy it looked natural.

I stood up, keeping my fisted handful of paper towels to my neck as I turned off the water. Andy had an amused expression on his face, and he tapped his long fingers along his jaw as he watched me. "And to think I was going to go straight to class." He took of his scarf and folded it neatly. "Okay, out with it. This is a story I'd like to hear."

I didn't know Andy that well. We had a few AP classes together, but our paths didn't cross much. He was the only person I knew that read more than I did and his brown hair was neatly styled every day, his delicate features always composed. He belonged in the '40s, straight out of a New York City night-club. I think the only reason he didn't wear full suits to school was so he didn't get beat up all the time.

But he was kind and he was smart, and at this moment—as I sat hip-deep in humiliation—I was wishing we were friends. When I wasn't immediately forthcoming (I was staring at the small puddle by one of my shoes) Andy rolled his eyes. He put his scarf in his pocket and removed his jacket, pulling open a stall door so he could hang it up on a hook.

"All right, let me see." When I hesitated, he grabbed my wrist and gently pulled it away. "C'mon and show papa." He sighed when he saw it, and my face reddened.

"I didn't write it."

I didn't know you could raise an eyebrow sarcastically until I saw Andy do it. "Yeah, I figured you wouldn't be hiding out in this picturesque restroom, scouring off your skin to remove your own handiwork." He gave a matronly *tut-tut*. "I wish they would get more creative. I'd give all the bullies a thesaurus for Christmas, but I know they wouldn't read it. Still, slanders of the sexual orientation nature? Might as well take a time machine back to the eighties."

I didn't think my face could get any redder, but it had to be practically volcanic by now. "I'm not . . . not that I think there's anything wrong. . . . I—"

Andy laughed. "Don't blow a gasket there, my graffitied

friend. No one's accusing you of anything. Well, I'm not accusing you of anything at any rate." He reached for his leather messenger bag, the only thing he wore that looked old and worn, but in a loved vintage way. "Now rinse off so we can get you cleaned up and clothed, before someone finds us in here and we really confirm some rumors about you."

My face colored again as I went to rinse. "I don't mind, you know. There are worse things to be called."

He continued to search his bag. "You just don't want to walk down the halls with a homophobic slur on your person. I understand, Frank. Now shut up and rinse."

I did as I was told, and when I finally got all the soap off, I stood up straight and patted my neck dry. Andy stood behind me, holding a bottle of what looked like astringent and those cotton pads girls use take makeup off—which was kind of weird, since it didn't look like Andy wore makeup.

He must have seen the look on my face. "Let's just say this isn't the first time I've had to do this."

"This happen to you a lot?"

He put the pad to the top of the bottle and tipped it until the liquid seeped into it. "Not as much as it used to, but more often than I would wish. It's really hard on the skin." He leaned in to wipe my neck and hesitated. "This is going to sting since you've rubbed your neck pretty raw."

I grabbed onto the sink's edge and drew a deep breath. "Okay."

It did sting. A lot. But we got most of the marker off. All

that was left when Andy was finished was part of the *f* and a hazy *a* and *t*.

"Now it just looks like someone tried to write 'fat' on your neck while you were walking." Andy wiped a thin sheen of antibiotic ointment to help with the residual burning. He definitely came to school prepared.

"Andy?" I asked as I pulled on my shirt.

"Hm?"

"You're awesome."

"I know," he said.

The school day passed, as they tend to do. I caught a few people staring at my neck, but no one asked what was going on. If I'd had a friend they probably would have talked to me about it, but I didn't, so no one did.

At the end of the day, I walked back to my car, only to find that my tires had been slashed. All of them. I'd like to say I was surprised. Shocked. Angry. But really, I was just tired. I called the tow truck number I had saved in my phone and gave them my name and the location of the car. I didn't need to stay. They had my bank card on file. If this continued, I was going to have to get a full-time job. The money I'd saved from summer work just wasn't going to cut it. People often talk about the pain and degradation of being bullied. No one really talks about the cost. Not that money is more important than those other things, but having to pay the expenses of your own humiliation just rubbed rock salt into the wound.

I didn't feel like going home to an empty house. After

today I needed noise. I needed to hear people and sit in the middle of their mindless chatter and pretend—just for a second—that it was directed toward me. That I was in the middle of something, even if it was imaginary.

I put my headphones on and started to walk. The school had mostly emptied and in a moment of recklessness, I actually turned my iPod on. It felt decadent. The gray of the morning had burned off leaving the sky blue and the day warm. Sunlight filtered in through the trees, and I felt the weight lifting off the farther I got from school.

It was a mistake, really. As close to hubris as I got. I'd made it all the way down by the skate park when I tripped on something and hit the ground hard. My iPod went skittering along the ground. When it landed face up I could see that the screen was fractured into a hundred tiny pieces. I lay there listening to the sounds of wheels on concrete, the clack as the tips of boards kissed the smooth edges of the bowl.

I caught sight of a girl sitting on the top of a bench, her back to me, her face turned in profile. She was wearing a black uniformed polo shirt with the word PLUMPY'S scrawled in red cursive over a cartoon chicken, its wing holding a hamburger. The chicken looked pretty happy about the meal, even though I wasn't sure if a chicken would even eat a hamburger. The girl's blond hair was pulled back into a ponytail, her eyes bright even from this distance. It was the first time I saw Brooke. She had a water bottle held loosely in her grip and was frowning at me.

An arm grabbed me by the back of my shirt and yanked me roughly to my feet. Tyler. Of course it was. He'd probably been following me for ages and I hadn't heard him because I'd had my stupid headphones in.

He started roughly brushing me off, smacking a little too hard to knock the bits of leaves and twigs off my arms. "I thought you guys were supposed to be graceful. Didn't you take ballet with the rest of the fruits?"

Nothing quite like a little ignorant stereotyping to really round out my day. Andy had to deal with this crap all the time and he managed to do it with style; I knew that because that's how I'd seen him handle everything. I wasn't as quick-witted as Andy, but the least I could do was not break down in tears of frustration. I gritted my teeth and just stood there as Tyler continued to "dust me off." Abuse masquerading as kindness. My eyes were shut and I trembled, but I didn't cry. I didn't shout.

"I think he's clean enough." A girl's voice said. Tyler stopped smacking my legs, and I finally cracked my eyes open. Brooke stood there, her arms crossed.

"Mind your own business," Tyler said.

She gave a tight-lipped grin as she looked between us— Tyler doing his best bad boy routine, me a pathetic wreck of a human being. "Yeah. Okay. This is my business."

Tyler turned toward her. He did his best loom, making himself look as big as he could, like some animals do when they face another predator. (I don't have a social life to speak of, okay? So I watch a lot of Animal Planet.) It failed to make an impression on Brooke. He raised his finger to poke her in the chest, but she grabbed it and twisted, turning his whole body around and pulling Tyler's arm behind his back. Before he could even get out a full shout, she'd bent his arm up at an odd angle and I heard him grunt in pain.

Brooke wasn't grinning now. Her lips were firmly set and her eyes had lost their playful twinkle as she leaned in and whispered. "Look, buddy, I may not know what your deal is— maybe you weren't hugged enough growing up, maybe you were just born a jerk—but I do know that I don't really care. And I know that it ends. Now." She pulled his arm up a fraction and he whimpered. "This kid here? The one you just tripped? He's my friend. You got that? Mine. Which means you leave him alone. Understand?"

He looked like an angry hunchback and started to call her names I won't even repeat. Brooke laughed and let go him go with a light push, causing Tyler to stumble before he spun around to glare at us. I took a half step behind Brooke. Not hiding exactly. More like cowering. Two guys—one dirty blond and blue eyed, one brown-haired and with a quick, easy smile—came up to stand beside Brooke. They were both sweaty from skateboarding and wore the same PLUMPY'S shirts on as Brooke. My introduction to Sam and Ramon.

"Is there a problem, *chica*?" Ramon asked. He was spinning his skateboard slowly in his hands, his eyes lit up in a rather maniacal fashion. His friend Sam just laughed, wiping sweat off his forehead with one hand and leaning on his board with the other. He was smiling too. Perfectly pleasant. Sam didn't loom or menace or anything like that; he had no need for one of Tyler's parlor tricks. Yet there was something about him, something unmovable and steady that while good-natured and not fear inspiring, clearly said *hands off*. How did he do that? How could *I* do that?

"Nope," Brooke said. "We were just leaving, weren't we?" I felt my stomach bottom out. My saviors were abandoning me. Tyler grinned, something more fitting for a shark then a person.

Brooke put her arm through mine. "Coming?" I nodded dumbly, too surprised to speak. Tyler's vicious smile began to crumble into a look of confusion. All he could do was stare as I was escorted out of his reach. "C'mon," Brooke said gently. "I'll buy you a milk shake. You like milk shakes?" Again I nodded. Ramon hopped onto his board and skated down the sidewalk in front of us.

Sam stayed walking, apparently content as he was. He glanced at me from the corner of his eye. "Sucks about your iPod," he said.

I jammed my hands into my pockets trying hard not to think about what Tyler had cost me today. Patches on four tires, if they were able to be patched, the iPod, and a whole lot of self-worth . . . and I was already in the red in that department.

"Can you get a new one?" Brooke asked.

I shook my head, my eyes suddenly growing blurry. Just

what I needed to do to impress these people—cry over a damn iPod. Looking away, I swiped at my eyes with the back of my wrist and hoped no one noticed. "I can't afford it." And lying to my parents by saying I'd dropped it would just earn me a lecture on responsibility, so I couldn't do that.

Sam lazily spun one of the wheels on his board with his finger. "We're hiring, you know. Plumpy's sucks, but the people aren't bad."

A sudden constriction in my chest made it so I had to clear my throat to answer him. "Well, I could use the money."

. . .

Brooke stared at Tyler as he talked to Maren. Her eyes were in a squint and her mouth was slightly downturned. "Well, he hasn't changed, has he?"

"No," I whispered. "He hasn't." And I felt the old fear coming back, the tightness, the panic sweat.

"His kind never really does." Brooke slipped a spectral arm through mine. "But you have."

I shook my head. I didn't feel any different.

"Are you kidding me? You're chatting with a ghost like it's no big deal. You're driving a classic car, and you live in a house with a necromancer. You regularly talk to werewolves, and this morning I saw you give one of the attack gnomes a dressing down."

"He set my pants on fire. I felt like some sort of discussion was in order."

"Exactly," she said. "And what about the time you talked to my severed head, huh? I bet ol' Tyler would've wet his pants."

"Brooke, if I remember correctly, I screamed and threw shampoo bottles at you. Not really one of my finer moments."

Andy slipped up next to me, his arms full of DVD cases. "If ever a man was a waste of resources, it would be Tyler." He tipped his chin toward James, a wistful cast to his expression. "Now him . . ." And he gave a low, appreciative whistle.

I shook my head. "He's not into . . . well, actually, I'm not sure what he's into. He's just scary." James came over then, a box set of DVDs in his hand.

Brooke peered at the cover. "What's *Murder, She Wrote*?"

"The blood has left your face," he said, ignoring Brooke as he examined me coolly. "And your heart rate is up." He did a quick scan of the room, catching sight of Tyler halfway. "Ah. A friend, I see." Though he was smiling faintly his look reminded me of the expression some cats get when they see a moth. Kind of a *oh good, a new toy* sort of thing.

"I should haunt his ass," Brooke said. "Think Sam can teach me how to haunt people?"

"Tyler," I explained to James.

Andy jumped forward, his hand extended despite having to juggle DVD cases to do so. "And I'm Andy." James shook it absently.

"Frank and I were just discussing how much carbon and water were squandered when Tyler was created."

"I suppose we should be the bigger people." I shuffled my

feet on the carpet, trying to channel their instinctive need to run. "You know, forgive and so forth. Let the existence he's carved out be his punishment or something."

Brooke continued to size Tyler up. "No way—we totally did that before. That was stupid. Maturity is for amateurs."

Andy turned to me, his eyes wide and his eyebrows up, as if really seeing me for the first time. "Are you serious? I mean really? This isn't some PSA afterschool special pile of crap. We don't have to be better men—for crying out loud, man, we don't even have to learn anything." He jerked his chin at Tyler. "That pile of poly-cotton blend and testosterone certainly doesn't deserve our consideration. You think he's learned anything? He still calls me pansy and hits on Maren because he thinks, and I quote, that it's 'all sexy when she speaks Chinese.'"

"I thought she was Japanese."

Andy rolled his eyes and started roughly shelving the cases. "She is. And before you ask, no, she doesn't speak Chinese. She just repeats quotes from Sun Tzu her dad had her memorize. She only speaks Japanese because her adoptive parents wanted her to 'know her heritage' or something."

"She sounds awesome," Brooke said. "You go talk to her while I figure out how to possess Tyler. . . ."

"You should do something. Attack before your enemy knows you're coming," James said as he handed the box set to Andy. "I wish to purchase these."

Andy's face burned red. He mumbled something that sounded vaguely like it might be English before cradling the

DVD set to his chest. I'd never seen Andy be anything but one hundred percent suave. It was almost reassuring to see him falter.

"I'm gonna try to make his head do a three sixty!" Brooke added.

"Shush," I said. When James scowled at me, I assured him, "Not you. And not you either, Andy."

"Ah, I see," Andy said and nodded sagely. "The inner monologue is a harsh mistress."

Film students take so much in stride, and of course, that's what Andy was majoring in. We had never really become friend-friends. He was—is—a little too cool for me. I'm still a flyweight when it comes to popularity.

But he had a point. I was so used to rolling over and making things easy on everyone else. Avoiding confrontation. Trying to be *good*. And for what? For who? Was I really trying to make life easier for Tyler of all people? What about Andy? Maren? And for the first time I thought, *What about* me?

It was like an angry volcano had been lying dormant in my chest and only now was it waking up. Steam and heat escaped from its seams while beneath it red-hot lava boiled and churned. I didn't want Tyler to change me. Brooke was right; I'd come a long way and I didn't want to lose who I was now. I'm generally happy keeping the peace.

Just, you know, not today.

"Andy, do you have a Sharpie? The biggest, fattest, permanent marker you can scrounge."

Andy shelved the last of the cases, juggling James's box set while he did, and nodded. "Yes, and based purely on the look on your face, I'm not even going to ask what you need it for, because I feel like the less I know, the better." He came back and handed over the marker without making eye contact, then went to ring James up. I could see him trying to make small talk with James as they walked away. James wasn't saying anything back, because he doesn't understand the point of chatting to begin with.

I held up my cell phone again so I could talk to Brooke without looking crazy. I explained my idea to her, and she grinned wickedly. "I was just going to pants him, but this sounds way better."

"So you can do it?" I asked.

She crossed her arms and snorted. "Ninja, please. I can move objects, for a short time at least. You think I've been wasting my free afternoons? I've been learning things." She took the marker and was gone.

I went up to the counter where Tyler was still monopolizing Maren's time. James had inexplicably vanished, so I chatted with Andy, asking him different questions about movies, partly to make sure I was getting a good present for Ramon, but mostly so I could have an alibi. Sensing salvation, Maren joined in our discussion.

"I agree with Andy," she said. "*Black Sheep* is amazing. WETA did the creature effects and man, those killer sheep look spectacular. Totally gory." She shook her head. "I love that movie."

"Well, I don't see how I can argue with both of you. I'll bow to your knowledge. Follow-up question—I was thinking of getting him another film. *Incubus* or *Mega Piranha*?"

Andy rested his elbows on the counter. "That depends. Do you actually like this person?"

Maren tapped his head with a movie case. "What a crap answer." She turned toward me. "You get him *Incubus* now. Then, the next time he deserves a present, you get him *Mega Piranha*, *Mega Shark vs. Giant Octopus*, and of course *Mega Python vs. Gatoroid*. That way you can have a marathon that not only covers giant mutant creatures but also features washed-up pop singers who can't act."

I pulled out my wallet to pay for the movies, noticing out of the corner of my eye that James had rejoined us at some point. "That's a little harsh, don't you think? I mean, clearly the directors were going for camp. Poor acting and camp go hand in hand."

"That's not entirely true," Andy said.

Maren shrugged and started checking in movies with the scanner. "Look, all I know is the entire time I was watching those movies, I wanted to feed Debbie Gibson a sandwich. She's too skinny."

"I think you mean Deborah Gibson," Andy said. "She goes by her grown-up name now."

I laughed. Tyler looked between us, clearly confused by our conversation and Maren's choice in joining it. Finally he gave up and left. Well, for a minute. Then he came back in spitting and fuming, his face apoplectic and red.

"Car . . . words . . . I . . . not cool" were really all I could make out as Tyler sputtered. The rest sounded like he was trying to say several words at the same time. Tyler turned on me and pointed a shaking finger. "You——I know it was you, freak."

I didn't even have to argue with him. Maren beat me to it. "I don't know what you're accusing him of, but he's been inside the store this whole time."

He jabbed a finger into my chest. "And how would I know what car was yours?" I asked calmly, serenely, downright Zen-like. I've become much better at lying over the last year.

"Let's just go see what this is all about, shall we?" Andy asked, but he was nudging us out the door as he did. Well, he nudged most of us. Instead of herding James, he opened the door with a little bow and a hand flourish. James of course acted like all doors were opened for him in this manner. Andy didn't touch Tyler, either. He followed behind us like an angry satellite, moving out the door with a sort of slouching gait, his hands shoved into his jeans' pocket.

Tyler drove a junker about as nondescript as he was——or it had been. Now it was covered in marker. From where I was standing I could make out just a few of the slogans: *I <3 High School Musical. To Wang Fu-Tastic! Somewhere over the rainbow . . .* the last was surrounded by musical notes. And rainbows. There were hearts and stars. And what looked like a dancing pony. Brooke had really gone to town.

Andy examined the front of the car. "Huh, I didn't know

you were Team Jacob. I would have pegged you for Team Edward for sure."

Tyler swore and rushed at Andy. I stepped in between them and Tyler was surprised into an awkward stop. Unbalanced, he stumbled backward. I stuck my hands into the pockets of my hoodie.

"I understand you're upset—really I do. It's terrible to be labeled and vandalized." I pretended to think about it. "I mean, I'm assuming that you've been vandalized. I can only guess at the feelings of humiliation you're feeling right now." I waved at the pristine Karmann Ghia off to my right. "I know if anything happened to my car, well." Tyler's face went from red to white as he stared at my car. Now I'm not a car dude and I don't think of myself as a petty guy, but I have to admit I felt pretty good rubbing my ride in his face. Too bad he couldn't see Brooke sitting on its hood grinning like a goon.

Some color returned to Tyler's face. "If it wasn't your little *boyfriend*," he said, giving Andy a little shove. "Then what about this guy?" He didn't touch James. I think he knew instinctively that it wasn't a good idea.

James cocked his head to the side, his arms tucked neatly behind his back. "If I had wished harm upon your car, there would be nothing left." And something about the way he said it, so matter-of-factly, made you instantly believe it to be true.

"He played lookout!" Brooke shouted happily and I had to suppress a grin.

I patted Tyler's shoulder sympathetically. "Assaulting Andy

is just going to land you in legal trouble, and you don't want that, do you? I didn't think so," I said without letting him finish.

James gave him a tight-lipped grin and held out his phone. "Do you wish to call the police? Your insurance company? Perhaps a solicitor? If you don't have one, I'm sure mine can suggest a few names who would take you on. . . ." He scrunched his nose at Tyler's rust-heap. "Pro bono."

Tyler stared at his phone like it was diseased. I bet that getting the cops involved was the last thing he wanted to do. As for insurance, he probably either didn't have it or his parents were still paying for it.

He mumbled something. It sounded like, "Whatever." Then he got into his car and took off with a squeal, almost hitting the parked car behind him.

"I don't know how you did it," Andy said. "But I'm more impressed by you now than I've ever been."

"How did you even know which car was his?" Maren asked James.

"I don't know what you're talking about," he said. "I didn't go near his . . . *vehicle*."

"He should clean his car more often," Brooke chirped. "He had mail and stuff all over his seat. His name was *everywhere*." She pushed herself off the hood. "I still think I should have pantsed the jerk. Maybe I could follow him," she mused.

"I admit to nothing but to the fact that I have the best friends on the planet," I said.

We went to go back into the store. Andy couldn't stop

smiling. "We need to hang out more, man. I like your style." I blushed from the praise.

Maren punched me in the arm, which just made me turn a darker shade of red. I thought I was going to self-combust. "All I know is you get my discount for *life*."

Behind me I could hear Brooke going, "Ooooh, you're going to have ten million baaaabies. Frank and Maren sitting in a tree, K-I-S-S-I-N-G." She even had a little dance to go with it. It involved a lot of booty shaking. James walked behind her and sighed. I think he felt we were bringing down his level of classiness.

"They're really immature, like ridiculously so, but my friends rock." Friends. Plural. Brooke was right. I had changed. My grin was so big I thought my face might crack. I let Brooke continue her booty dance. She'd earned it.

Author Biographies

JAIME ADOFF is the author of *The Song Shoots Out of My Mouth*, *Names Will Never Hurt Me*, *Jimi & Me*, *The Death of Jayson Porter*, and *Small Fry*. He has won numerous awards, including the Coretta Scott King/John Steptoe New Talent Author Award for *Jimi & Me* and the Lee Bennett Hopkins Poetry Award (Honor Book) for *The Song Shoots Out of My Mouth*. Jaime's latest novel *The Death of Jayson Porter* won the 2010 Teen Buckeye Book Award, and received starred reviews in *Booklist* and *VOYA Magazine*. Jaime is a highly sought-after speaker, presenting across the country on teen issues, diversity, and YA literature and poetry. Jaime is the son of the late Newbery Award-winning author Virginia Hamilton and renowned poet Arnold Adoff. He lives in his hometown of Yellow Springs, Ohio, with his family. Visit jaimeadoff.com.

RHODA BELLEZA is a freelance writer and editor based out of Brooklyn, New York.

JOSH BERK is the author of *The Dark Days of Hamburger Halpin*, named a best book for teens of 2010 by *Kirkus Reviews* and Amazon.com. It was also awarded a Parent's Choice Silver medal, a starred review from *School Library Journal*, and a "Perfect Ten" from *VOYA*. His second comedy/mystery teen novel is *Guy Langman: Crime Scene Proscrastinator*. He has previously been a journalist, a poet, a playwright, and a guitarist (mostly in bands known for things other than fine guitar-playing). He is a librarian and lives in Bethlehem, Pennsylvania, with his family. Visit him on the web at www.joshberkbooks.com.

JENNIFER BROWN is a two-time winner of the Erma Bombeck Global Humor Award. She wrote a weekly humor column for the *Kansas City Star* for over four years, until she gave it up to be a full-time young adult novelist. Jennifer's debut novel, *Hate List*, received three starred reviews and was selected as an ALA Best Book for Young Adults, a *VOYA* "Perfect Ten," and a *School Library Journal* Best Book of the Year. Jennifer's second novel, *Bitter End*, received a starred review from *Publishers Weekly*. Jennifer writes and lives in the Kansas City, Missouri area, with her husband and three children.

CHRIS CRUTCHER is the author of such books as *Deadline*, *Whale Talk*, and *Staying Fat for Sarah Bynes* and has been awarded the NCTE National Intellectual Freedom Award, the ALAN Award, the ALA Margaret A. Edwards Lifetime Achievement Award, the CLA St. Katharine Drexel Award, and *Writer* magazine's Writers Who Make a Difference Award. His work as a teacher and alternative school director coupled with twenty-five years as a child and family therapist specializing in abuse and neglect has infused his literary work with realism and emotional heft. Crutcher makes his home in Spokane, Washington, and you can visit him online at www.chriscrutcher.com.

MAYRA LAZARA DOLE was born in Havana and raised in Miami. Her Americas Award Commended Title, *Down to the Bone*, received a starred ALA *Booklist* review and was nominated for the National Book Awards and ALA Best Books for YA. It made the following lists: *Booklist*'s Top Ten Novels, ALA Rainbow List, and CCBC Top Choices. Dole's next YA novel is *Spinning*

Off the Edge. Her essays, articles, Cuban dialect poems, and short stories have been published by *Hunger Mountain*: Vermont College Fine Arts Journal of the Arts, *Cipher Journal*: A Journal of Literary Translation, *Palabra*: A Magazine of Chicano and Latino Literary Art, and other paper and online magazines. Her bilingual picture books, *Drum, Chavi, Drum! / ¡Toca, Chavi, Toca!* and *Birthday in the Barrio / Cumpleaños en el Barrio*, were critically acclaimed.

ZETTA ELLIOTT was born in Canada and moved to Brooklyn in 1994 to pursue her PhD in American Studies at New York University. Her poetry has been published in several anthologies, and her plays have been staged in New York, Chicago, and Cleveland. Her essays have appeared in *Horn Book Magazine*, *School Library Journal*, and *Hunger Mountain*. Her first picture book, *Bird*, won the Honor Award in Lee & Low Books' New Voices Contest; it was named Best of 2008 by *Kirkus Reviews*, a 2009 ALA Notable Children's Book, and won the Paterson Prize for Books for Young Readers. Elliott is the author of the young adult novels *A Wish After Midnight* and *Ship of Souls*. She is Assistant Professor of Ethnic Studies at Borough of Manhattan Community College and currently lives in Brooklyn, New York.

KATE ELLISON grew up in Baltimore, Maryland, where she took a lot of heat at school for wearing weird-o outfits and for just being, well, generally weird. She has a degree in acting from The Theatre School at DePaul University, has made a pilgrimage on foot across Spain, makes Shrinky-Dink jewelry, and can play two songs now, albeit poorly, on her three-quarter-sized guitar. She hopes to travel often and everywhere and to someday own a large dog. Her first novel is *The Butterfly Clues*.

BRENDAN HALPIN is a teacher and a writer. He is the author of several YA novels, both by himself and with co-authors Emily Franklin and Trish Cook, including *Forever Changes*, *Tessa Masterson Will Go to Prom*, and *Notes From the Blender*. He lives in Boston with his wife Suzanne and their three children.

SHEBA KARIM was born and raised in Catskill, New York, where she never saw Rip Van Winkle but frequently crossed the bridge that bore his name. She is a graduate of New York University School of Law and the Iowa Writers' Workshop. Her fiction has appeared in *580 Split*, *Asia Literary Review*, *Barn Owl Review*, *Kartika Review*, *Shenandoah*, *South Asian Review*, and *Time Out Delhi*, among others. Two of her stories have been nominated for a Pushcart Prize. Her young adult novel, *Skunk Girl*, was published in the United States, Denmark, India, Italy, and Sweden. She was a 2009–2010 Fulbright-Nehru Scholar and is currently working on a historical fiction novel set in thirteenth-century India. Visit www.shebakarim.com.

JAMES LECESNE is an actor, writer, and activist. His Academy Award-winning short film, *TREVOR*, inspired the founding of *The Trevor Project*, the only nationwide twenty-four-hour crisis intervention and suicide prevention lifeline for GLBT and, Questioning teens (www.thetrevorproject.org). He has published two YA novels, *Absolute Brightness* and *Virgin Territory*, and written for TV and theater including his own one-man show, *Word of Mouth*, which was awarded both a NY Drama Desk Award and an Outer Critics Circle Award.

LISH MCBRIDE is the author of *Hold Me Closer, Necromancer*, which was a top ten BBYA pick, nominated for the Morris Award, and winner of the Washington State Book Award. This makes her feel fancy. It also makes her a little obnoxious at times. Her follow-up book is *Necromancing the Stone*. You can find her on the Internet at LishMcBride.com. You can find her in real life in Seattle, possibly under a rock.

ELIZABETH MILES is a journalist and the debut author of *Fury*. She lives in Portland, Maine, with her boyfriend and two cats, and she just may have a magical defense mechanism of her own. Learn more at www.elizabethmilesbooks.com or www.thefuryseries.com.

KIRSTEN MILLER grew up in the mountains of North Carolina. At seventeen, she hit the road and moved to New York City, where she lives to this day. Kirsten is the author of the *Eternal Ones* series, as well as the acclaimed *Kiki Strike* books, which tell the tale of the delinquent girl geniuses who keep Manhattan safe.

MATTHUE ROTH is the author of the Orthodox Jewish punk-rock novel *Never Mind the Goldbergs* and the screenplay *1/20*, currently in production as a feature film. His newest book, *Automatic*, is a Kindle single about falling in love and falling into a coma. He keeps a secret diary at www.matthue.com.

DAVID YOO is the author of the YA novels *Stop Me If You've Heard This One Before* and *Girls for Breakfast*, along with a middle grade novel, *The Detention Club*. His first collection of essays for adults is *The Choke Artist: Confessions of a Chronic Underachiever*. He teaches in the creative writing program at Pine Manor College and at the Gotham Writers' Workshop. David lives in Massachusetts with his wife and son, where he still plays soccer. Visit www.daveyoo.com.

Dedications

JAIME ADOFF: This one's for the kids that live this every day.

RHODA BELLEZA: To Jasy, for being a braver, better person than I could ever hope to be.

JOSH BERK: This story is dedicated to all the crazies I've made music with over the years and every kid in every garage who picks up a guitar and finds a way to turn their suffering into art. Rock on.

JENNIFER BROWN: For the mooed-at, the punched, the teased, the humiliated. For the ones sitting by the trash cans at lunch and hoping for invisibility in the hallways. For those who endure bullying with grit and determination. Because you're worth it.

MAYRA LAZARA DOLE: Ricky, they killed you but not your spirit. You'll always be my shooting star. To LGBT's being bullied. Millions are fighting for you. We love you. Don't give up. Reach out: 866-488-7386.

ZETTA ELLIOTT: "Sweet Sixteen" originated as a play that I developed in the New Perspectives Theater's Women's Work Lab. I dedicate this story to all the women and girls who dare to speak their truth from dim margins and shadowy corners.

KATE ELLISON: To the real Jean-Carlos, whom I do not know, and who left a stack of classmate-apology cards in the snow outside of his elementary school one winter day out of which this story was born. I hope, wherever you are, you are surrounded by people who are kind, and, if still they are not, I hope you are strong, and I hope you are loved.

BRENDAN HALPIN: To Suzanne, my favorite troublemaker.

SHEBA KARIM: To my Albany Academy for Girls crew, Annsunee, Jane, and Katie, who eased the pain of high school with their cooking, humor, and generosity, and reminded me I was never alone.

JAMES LECESNE: For my girls.

LISH MCBRIDE: To my brothers, Darin, Jeremy, and Alex. You kept bullies at bay, gave me a safe place and continued support. Thanks for letting me grow up weird.

ELIZABETH MILES: To Laura, Laura, and Jackie, who all have superpowers.

KIRSTEN MILLER: To the person who made freshman year hell. You're lucky we grew up before YouTube came along.

MATTHUE ROTH: For my favorite Russian gangster.

DAVID YOO: Just about everyone gets bullied at some point in their lives, and just about everyone at some point bullies someone else. The only way to stop the cycle is to start with yourself. Fact is, there's nothing good to gain from bullying someone. Remember the words of Abraham Lincoln, "When I *do good*, I *feel good*; when I *do* bad, I feel bad, and that is my religion."

Do you dare to speak the truth?

FEW THINGS ARE MORE FRIGHTENING than facing the truth about yourself. Fitting in can be as difficult as understanding why you stand out, and the heart wrenching excitement of it is all a part of coming into one's own. *Truth & Dare: 20 Tales of Heartbreak and Happiness* features stories from such unapologetic and honest authors as Cecil Castellucci, Emma Donoghue, A. M. Homes, Gary Soto, and Ellen Wittlinger.

TRUTH & DARE:
20 Tales of Heartbreak and Happiness
978-0-7624-4104-4

• • •

Check out our other Running Press YA anthologies:

BRAVE NEW LOVE	**CORSETS & CLOCKWORK**	**THE ETERNAL KISS**	**KISS ME DEADLY**
978-0-7624-4220-1	978-0-7624-4092-4	978-0-7624-3717-7	978-0-7624-3949-2